HIGH-ALTITU

THE NOVELS OF

TAR

"Truly excellent . . . the best white-knuckle ride I've taken in a long time!"

—Lee Child, *New York Times* bestselling author of *Without Fail*

HARD LANDING

"Dead-on . . . expose[s] how both a major airline and major airport really work."

—Jeremiah Healy, author of *Spiral* and *The Only Good Lawyer*

"An edge-of-your-seat thriller that sweeps you up and carries you along for the ride."

—Lisa Gardner

"[Heitman] gives us an insider's view of how airlines deal with routine (and not so routine) problems in customer relations, labor, and management. . . . Heitman leads Alex on a lively dance while avoiding the obvious clichés. This is a debut novel, but I like it because it is also a good novel."

—*The Boston Globe*

"*Hard Landing* goes down easy, and will keep you guessing—and flipping pages—till three A.M."

—John J. Nance, author of *Blackout*

"Fasten your seat belt—this story, written by an industry insider, is exciting from start to finish."

—*American Way*

LYNNE HEITMAN

FIRST CLASS KILLING

POCKET BOOKS
New York London Toronto Sydney

An *Original* Publication of POCKET BOOKS

POCKET BOOKS, a division of Simon & Schuster, Inc.
1230 Avenue of the Americas, New York, NY 10020

For information address Pocket Books, 1230 Avenue of the Americas, New York, NY 10020

ISBN: 0-7434-5615-7

First Pocket Books printing April 2004

10 9 8 7 6 5 4 3 2 1

POCKET and colophon are registered trademarks of Simon & Schuster, Inc.

Cover design by Jae Song
Interior design by Melissa Isriprashad

Manufactured in the United States of America

For information regarding special discounts for bulk purchases, please contact Simon & Schuster Special Sales at 1-800-456-6798 or business@simonandschuster.com.

FIRST CLASS KILLING

prologue

HE DIDN'T LIKE TOUCHING HER, BUT SOMEtimes he couldn't help himself. He would start out with both hands clamped to the bottom of his seat. He would keep them there as long as he could, until both arms shook with the effort of his resistance. When he could fight it no more, one hand would slide over and entangle itself in her long, silky hair. Then the other, and, before he knew it, he was guiding her with both hands through the rough rhythm his body craved. Not that she needed much guidance. For someone so young, she was preternaturally gifted at reading a man's desires and anticipating his needs.

After he finished, he would leave the chair and turn his back on her.

"Go wait for me out front," he would say. "I'll be right there."

He would listen for the door to close before buckling his belt and zipping his fly. He would stand in front of the small mirror on the wall, smooth the hair on both sides, and wait until his breathing had slowed and his face had returned to its normal pinkish tint.

When he was ready, he would walk through the door and down the aisle, use his key to open the door, and take his place in the small, cramped booth. He would slide back the screen that separated the two of them and wait for her to begin.

"Bless me, Father, for I have sinned . . ."

Sometimes the sound of her voice would excite him again and distract him as he tried to listen to her recite her transgressions. She would talk about how she had cheated at school or said a mean thing about a friend behind her back. Sometimes she lied to her parents. Inevitably, there would be the pause. He would have to urge her gently to continue. She would tell him that she had been unclean. He would listen, he would assign her penance, he would say the prayers of absolution, and, with God working through him, he would bless her and forgive her her sins.

He would always leave her with the same thought. If she ever told anyone what he had made her do, she would go straight to hell.

chapter 1

SHE LOOKED RIGHT AT ME. I WAS SURE OF IT. First her head whipped around. Her hair, blond and loose and foamy as the head on a latte, swept across her bare back. I was freezing and miserable in my rental car. Had been for almost two hours. How could she be standing on the sidewalk looking so comfortable and so damned elegant in a strapless silk cocktail dress? But then, that's how hookers are paid to look. Her shoulders turned next. They were battleship-wide, which they had to be to support the extravagant forward weight of what she carried out front. Her hips swung around, and finally the Jimmy Choo cha-cha heels upon which the whole package balanced. Perfect.

Smile, Angel.

I hit the button and let the camera run. It clicked and whirred for four or five exposures as I studied her face through the zoom lens. It was disconcerting, the way she stared in my direction, the way she bore down with an intensity so ferocious I was sure her eyes could see through the night, through the wrong end of the lens, and into mine.

But she couldn't see me. I had chosen my parking space carefully—across the street, half a block down, parallel parked in a line of cars away from any streetlights.

As Angel stood and glared, the limo driver loitered respectfully to the side, holding the back door open for her. Eventually, the second subject, Sally, came swiveling out the door of the hotel and down the driveway. She put a hand on Angel's shoulder, and they exchanged words. Sally apparently did not have her friend's wary nature. She slipped right into the back of the limo, pausing long enough to extract a cigarette from her bag, which the diffident driver lit for her.

Without ever looking completely satisfied, Angel folded herself into the backseat, and I pulled the camera back inside the car, careful not to bump the horn. I wasn't accustomed to the heavy weight and wide turning radius of the long lens. But I had to use it because, so far, I'd never been able to get close enough to capture anything useful without it.

I waited until the limo was off the hotel drive and on the street in front of me before clicking off a few shots of the license plate. The driver accommodated me nicely by slowing almost to a crawl. When his brake lights engaged, the camera was still in position in front of my face, which was why it took me longer than it should have to realize he was moving backward. *Roaring* backward. Motor-gunning, rubber-burning backward up the quiet street and toward me.

Oh, shit.

I dumped the camera on the seat and fumbled for the keys in the ignition. But the second I touched them, I knew, even if the driver didn't block me in with his limo boat, there was no way I was getting that car out of that space in time to get away.

I grabbed my gear bag from the floor and threw it

over the camera. I hooked my finger into the door latch and was about to pop it open when I remembered. Dome light. It would flash on when I opened the door, lighting me up like a beacon. I prayed for the switch to be in the vicinity of the light itself. I reached up. Prayer answered, but with a nasty twist. The switch had *three* settings. One would turn the light off completely. The other would turn it on. Which one? *Which* position?

No time left.

I braced myself and flicked the switch all the way over. Still dark. No light, either, when I opened the door and slithered through. I went out headfirst, activating the power locks on my way by. I landed on the curb just as the limo screeched up. I leaned against my door, barely able to hear anything over the sound of my heart whomping in my ears. I waited for the driver to step out and slam his door shut. When he did, I pushed on mine until it latched and locked.

Who knew a Lincoln would be built so low to the ground? The space between the curb and the car's undercarriage was almost too narrow for me, and I thanked my lucky stars that I wasn't built like Angel. I flattened out on my back and wriggled through. Barely. The driver was rounding the back of the car when I pulled the last appendage under the chassis.

The lower half of his legs and his shoes were all I could see, but that was plenty. From across the street, he had looked like an usher at a mob funeral. He paused on each side of the car, probably to peer through the windows. I lay there, sniffing the vehicle's greasy underbelly and inhaling the limo's carbon monoxide. My head was swimming from the toxic mix as he loitered on the side where I'd hidden the camera.

When he finally moved on, it wasn't to the limo. He

went to the car parked in front of mine and did the same casual, half-assed inspection, and I got the distinct feeling the impromptu search had been Angel's idea and not his. Lucky me. If the driver had been slightly more invested, or perhaps a tad more limber, I might have found myself staring into his big, fleshy face instead of his muscular calves.

I stayed in my grimy pit until I heard the limo pulling out. I waited until I was sure it was gone. Then I had to stay down another few moments, long enough to fire up my circulatory system. I crawled out on the street side, which had more clearance. Smelling like oil and smeared with a thick layer of grit, I staggered to my feet and leaned against the car.

With my hands on my knees, I enjoyed a few deep breaths of nontoxic air and thought about Angel. I kept seeing her face, and her eyes, and the way she had fixed on my position and stared for no reason I could think of, except that she had a sixth sense, the one coyotes use to survive a hard life on the high plains. Or the one a leopard uses to stalk, attack, and tear the hide from its prey before the unlucky victim ever senses mortal danger. Angel was a pro. From everything I'd heard, she'd been at this game a long time. If I wanted to catch her, I'd have to quit acting as if this were my first case.

Even though it was.

chapter 2

IRENE SURVEYED THE SIGHT IN FRONT OF US and shook her head.

"Being a flight attendant used to be so much fun." She sighed.

It was the kind of bittersweet lament reserved for things that were loved and lost to the past. Like the first days of a new romance or the last days of blissful childhood, the airline business as we knew it had vanished. It was never coming back.

The two of us stood at the head of the concourse, staring at the OrangeAir security checkpoint. It was morning rush hour in Pittsburgh, so the operation had the frantic quality of an earthquake response. Everyone talked at once, trying to be heard over the whine of the machinery. The X-ray belts cycled constantly. The magnetometers went off regularly, each alarm adding to the number of bored/angry/confused passengers that waited like an army of scarecrows for an individual wand search.

"Thank God we're in uniform," was all I could say as we cut to the front of the line and flashed our airline IDs. I waited for Irene to pick her queue and then jumped into one that was guaranteed to take longer.

As expected, she triggered the alarm as she passed

through the metal detector. Airports all over the country had dialed up the sensitivity on the magnetometers, and we never failed to trip them. It was the multitude of buttons on our uniforms, which meant every OrangeAir employee all over the United States made them go off every time he or she passed through. It seemed needlessly inefficient to me, but then, I was no longer in charge of an airport operation. I was no longer in charge of much of anything.

To my relief, Irene slipped through with only a quick pass of the wand. She was cleared before I had even begun digging out my laptop and my cell phone. When it appeared she was intent on waiting for me, I dropped my phone and kicked it under the X-ray machine. Down on my hands and knees to retrieve it, I motioned to Irene across the great divide. "You should go on. I'll be here a while."

"Okay. I'll see you onboard."

When she was well out of sight, I pulled the camera equipment from my bag and sent it through on the belt. The agent monitoring the X ray called over a supervisor, who took one look at the gear in my bucket and let out a weary sigh.

"What is this for, ma'am?"

"I'm a photography buff."

He hoisted the long lens and studied it. Then he studied me. "What do you need this for?"

"Close-ups. I'm a bird watcher."

"Uh-huh." He tipped his head back and looked down at me through narrowed eyes, and I knew I was one more irritation on a shift that didn't need any more. "Step over here if you will, please."

It would have been so much easier if I could have just checked the equipment through, but that would have been a guaranteed way to blow my cover. Real flight attendants never checked baggage when they worked. Any flight attendant would tell you a good one can circle the globe twice on the items that could fit into the space of a single carry-on bag, and still have room for souvenirs. But then, as I was demonstrating almost daily, I wasn't a very good flight attendant.

I was through the gauntlet and headed down the concourse when I heard the sound of my name.

"Alex*aaaan*dra."

Tristan's voice rang out over the communal airport mumble. I turned to find him. He was easy to spot since he was traveling, as he often did, at the center of a rolling circus. Today, as always, he was the ringmaster, the obvious instigator, and the lone male, leading a posse of women who were many sizes, shapes, and colors but had one thing in common: they liked to laugh. Riotously.

I waved and stepped outside the swiftly moving current of travelers to wait for him. There were half hugs and air kisses all around as he parted from the group. The women headed down a separate concourse. Tristan trundled my way, dragging his bag behind him. Tristan was so elegant he even trundled gracefully.

"Where were you last night?" He greeted me with my very own smooch on the lips, and we rejoined the march toward the departure gates. We were working the same trip home. "Reenie and I looked all over for you. We were worried."

His concern was genuine. During my assignment, I'd flown with an overwhelming majority of women, but it turned out that Tristan McNabb, a gay man, was the person with whom I had bonded most quickly. That also made him the person I had to lie to most often.

"I unplugged the phone and went to bed early."

"Then why do you look so tired?" He turned to look at me more closely, doing a quick inspection of my face as we moved. "Getting overtired is not good for your skin. I've told you that. You need a facial."

"I can't afford facials. I've told you that."

"That's like saying you can't afford food. Where's Reenie? Have you seen her yet this morning?"

"She's already onboard."

"Not likely." Just as he did, I caught sight of the steady stream of passengers coming off our aircraft, which had obviously arrived late. Irene had to be in the departure lounge somewhere. I spotted the back of her head. "Over there." We threaded our way through the arriving and departing passengers to join her at a far grouping of seats by the window.

"Hello, Reenie, dear." Tristan had to lean over to give Irene her good morning kiss. She had settled into one of the seats in the lounge to work on a knitting project. Tristan reached down to get a closer look. "Please don't tell me this is more dog attire. Knitting is so terribly banal to begin with, but knitting for a dog—"

"Do not make fun of my babies. They require a lot of attention. Even more than you." Her tone conveyed just what an incredible concept that was.

Irene was a rescuer of basset hounds, someone who took in lost and battered pooches. She also ate brown rice, wore leather sandals as big as snowshoes, and wouldn't buy self-adhering stamps because it was bad for the environment. When she wasn't working, she favored baggy shorts and T-shirts with meaningful logos, an amusing contrast to her work self, where she was one of the more proper wearers of the uniform. It reminded me of how little we know of each other just from what we can see.

"Reenie, what is the name of that Indonesian restaurant we always go to on Saint Martin? I was trying to recommend it the other day, and I could *not* think of the name."

"I never remember stuff like that," she said. "I just go where you take me."

"Yes, you do remember. I know you do." Tristan settled into the seat next to his friend.

While they chatted, I stood back against the window and scanned the terminal, a habit I had acquired when I had managed my own operation. Back then, I had been looking for anything out of the ordinary, any problem about to emerge that could disrupt the day's smooth exchange of aircraft in and aircraft out. I had a different purpose now. I was looking for any of the targets of my investigation, but most especially the tall blonde with the fulsome physique and the predator's eyes. I knew she would be here somewhere. She was on a layover, just as we had been.

"Reenie, it's the place where we sit outside on the screened-in porch. They serve the dinner in courses on those little plates that look like soap dishes."

"I know the one you're talking about, T. I just don't remember the name."

She was four gates down. I spotted her with two other women: Sally, the blonde she had been with in the limo the night before, and Sylvie Nguyet, a French-Vietnamese woman—girl, really—whose picture I also had in my hooker files at home. Taller by a head, Angel stood next to them like a great marble statue, a Venus de Milo with arms and a bombshell silhouette that made her two pals look downright wispy.

"Tristan, come here."

"What?"

"I want to ask you something." He was my absolute best source for what I needed to know. The prostitution ring was an open secret among flight attendants, but still a secret. Most would talk about it only in private, and none would talk about it with someone as new as I was. Tristan was the exception. He shared freely with me, partly because we were friends, partly because he liked to show off what he knew, and partly because he was an incorrigible gossip.

"Is that Sylvie over there with those other two women?"

He peered down the concourse. "Oh, Lord, it is, Reenie. And she's standing with the Dairy Queen herself."

"Be nice, Trissy." Irene, on the other hand, had no use for gossip. She wanted to set an example, she always said, for her thirteen-year-old daughter.

"Dairy Queen?" I was confused. "Do you mean Angel?"

"Angela." Tristan lounged back against the window with me. "No matter what she calls herself, her name is Angela."

"Is Dairy Queen a mammary reference?"

He laughed. "That works, too, but no. She's trailer trash from the side of a one-lane West Texas dirt highway, out where they have Dairy Queens at every other mile marker. She should be working at one of them serving up chocolate-dipped soft-serve ice cream in Styrofoam cones instead of trying to be one of us."

"That is such a mean thing to say." Irene finished a row, turned her needles, and started on the next.

"You know it's true."

Angel, Sally, and Sylvie gathered their gear and rolled through their boarding door and out of sight. According to the monitor, they were bound for La Guardia and then probably home to Boston, like us.

I shifted my attention to Tristan. "That's an interesting perspective for someone who hails from the great state of Wyoming. At least Texas has Neiman-Marcus."

"I beg your pardon." He raised his chin in mock indignation. "Angela is trash because of what she is, not because of where she came from."

"She should get involved in Toastmasters." Irene looked up to find us both staring at her. "I think it would help her. It would certainly help build her self-confidence. Have you ever heard her try to give a PA? It would make her a better flight attendant."

"Honey, Angelina might need to learn how to read, but she does not need any more confidence, and she certainly does not need to be a better flight attendant. She makes her money on her back."

Irene sniffed. "Those are just rumors, Trissy. You shouldn't spread them."

He shook his head. "Go back to your knitting and purling, sweetie pie. We'll let you know when the conversation turns to beagles or Birkenstocks."

"Bassets," she corrected. "Basset hounds."

"What-*ever.*"

I checked the area. The only people near enough to hear were a man on a cell phone and a young woman reading a paperback. Still, I lowered my voice. "Are you saying she's one of the hookers?"

"Angela is not one of them; she's the queen bee. The madam. The übertramp."

"I thought they were all just freelancers."

"They were, until Angela came along and turned a ragtag bunch of disorganized whores into a lean, mean fucking machine. Sounds like the story line for a

Broadway play, doesn't it? *Send in the Whores? Don't Cry for Me, I'm a Hooker?*"

"Tristan." Irene did her own check around the lounge. "All you're doing is encouraging a nasty and unfair stereotype. It's like saying all Italians are mobsters, or all Muslims are terrorists."

"If the Manolo Blahnik fits . . ."

"You have no proof."

"That's the nice thing about gossip, Reenie. The standard of proof is so very low."

"For all you know, you *are* the source of all these rumors."

"Tell me this. If you're a flight attendant making forty thousand dollars a year, how do you afford a condo at the Ritz?"

"The Ritz?" He was teasing Irene and clearly delighting in it, but I was the one hanging on every word. Oh, for a microcassette, or at least a pad and pencil. "The new Ritz-Carlton?"

"Angela has a two-bedroom. Not even a one-bedroom or a studio, although I doubt they even have studios in those buildings. Do you know what she paid? Just under two million. That's more than twelve hundred per square foot."

"How do you—"

"Barry."

"Oh, right." I had forgotten his partner was a real estate agent in the city. "Is that a lot for that area?"

"No, but that's beside the point. It's a lot for a flight attendant, especially one who already owns a cottage on the Cape, where she keeps her second car, her Hummer."

"Maybe," Irene said, "she has another source of income."

"She does, dear, and I just told you what it is."

"Another source besides . . . what you're saying."

"No one seems to be able to locate any other source of income. Ditto for her slut posse. Sally and Sylvie and Claudia and Ava and the rest. You can often find them at the spa or working out at the LA Sports Club. Or having lunch in Paris."

We all heard the boarding door at our gate close, which meant the aircraft was ready for us. It was time to pack up and go.

"You're jealous." Irene wrapped her doggie sweater around the needles and put the whole thing into her World Wildlife Fund tote bag.

Tristan stood up straight, shook out his slacks, and smoothed his jacket. "I'm quite happy with my life, at long last. Have you heard the latest rumors?"

He asked it in a way that was irresistible. I couldn't wait to hear the answer. In spite of herself, neither could Irene. We shuffled a little closer together. "What," she asked, "is the latest rumor?"

"Angela is trying to start up a West Coast shop. My sources tell me there are at least ten dirty girls on the transfer list to LA."

This was news to me. "Is Angel herself on the transfer list?"

"Not that I've heard. She must be sending some minion of hers out there. Can you believe it? The woman has no shame."

We were now at the point in our ongoing conversation on the subject where I was better off keeping my mouth shut. And yet . . .

"I still don't understand why you don't turn these women in."

They both turned to blink at me. "Alexandra, you are so management. We'll have to work on you."

"You should talk. You were a flight services supervisor once."

"That was temporary insanity, and it was only two years." He squinted at me. "You spent, what . . . fourteen . . . sixteen years?"

"Fourteen."

"I'm a union officer, Alexandra. My job is to protect union members, not help management fire them. They tried to terminate a bunch of them last year, but we got them all back."

Irene found that amusing. "You're full of baloney. They came back because the company couldn't prove anything. They never can. That's why they go on and on."

"Would you defend these women," I asked, "even if the company could prove their case?"

"Of course I would." Tristan put a fatherly arm around my shoulders. "You're union now. When you're union, you stick together, no matter what. They might be hookers, but they're our hookers."

He glanced at Irene, who was already on her way. I glanced at Tristan, my friend, who had just declared himself my sworn enemy. I filed it with all the other bridges to be crossed when I got there. Right now, I had to serve cold muffins to eighty-five passengers who would want more from us than we could give them.

Tristan grabbed his bag and turned to me. "Ready for another day in the friendly skies?"

"I'm ready."

chapter 3

THE FLIGHT PASSED WITHOUT INCIDENT . . . without major incident. Tristan did spill a carton of orange juice on a man wearing a business suit. He made him happy with the promise of a free upgrade. That in spite of his suspicions that the savvy passenger had knocked the carton out of his hand on purpose, expecting exactly that result.

"That's not a suit," he fumed. "It's a polyester sponge from off the rack at the Men's Wearhouse. It's probably his designated spill suit. His real suit is up in that Tumi bag he stashed overhead."

Eventually we made it to Boston, flying hard, low, and late into an early-autumn rainstorm. With the wings rocking and the tail hammering, the cabin was quiet, filled with the brittle tension that hardens inside an airborne machine that seems to be rattling too much. But if there were silent prayers and last-minute promises to God, they all evaporated when the wheels touched the runway and we landed safely in the steady, soaking rain.

It was still raining an hour later when I emerged from the T station at Copley Square in the Back Bay. My standard flight attendant's umbrella, which was the size of a salt shaker when folded up, kept me dry from the waist up, but it was too small to protect my lower half. By the time I had walked the two blocks to the restaurant, my stockings were damp, and my dark blue leather flats, the best pair of working shoes I owned, had turned black. I was bitter about it. I couldn't afford a new pair.

Inside the restaurant, it smelled like rain and felt like the onset of winter. Maybe it was the dim lighting. Maybe it was the rack full of raincoats inside the door. Maybe it was the lack of progress on a case that had begun back when it was summer and the Red Sox were still in first place.

"Hello, Miss Shanahan." The hostess took my coat and umbrella. "Mr. Harvey is in the back."

"Thanks, Yumiko."

Harvey would be in his favorite booth in the back. I couldn't see him, which was the point, but Harvey Baltimore was always where he said he would be and always at least twenty minutes early.

The first time I'd heard the name Harvey Baltimore, I had assumed it was a nickname, a street moniker bestowed upon a swaggering private investigator who happened to hail from Maryland. In fact, Harvey was a person as mild of manner as I had ever met and Baltimore was his real name. His great grandfather had emigrated from Poland in 1898. When asked at Ellis Island for his destination, he'd told them. According to Harvey, in later years, the old man would pronounce that he was glad he hadn't been going to Schenectady. His name, he would always add, had not been too dear a price to pay for his new life in America.

I knew enough by now to get myself settled before walking into Harvey's line of sight and unsettling him. I slipped off my raincoat, shook out the little umbrella, stomped the water out of my soggy shoes, and stowed my bag behind the bar. Only then did I make my way back, where Harvey sat, hunched prayerfully over his cup of tea. As I approached, his head popped up. He blinked at me, and didn't even wait for me to sit down.

"What is happening? Is something wrong? Why did we have to meet today?"

"Hello, Harvey." I slipped into my side of the booth. "I'm fine and it's nice to see you, too."

He was dressed in his gray suit with the windowpane plaid—one of the two suits he always wore when he left his big house in Brookline—and the expression of deepest gloom, which he wore at all times.

"Sorry. So sorry, but your phone call had me worried. What is happening?"

"I didn't mean to worry you and I'm sorry to drag you out in this weather." I picked up the menu and signaled for the waiter. "Let me just order some dinner and I'll tell you what's happening."

"Dinner? It's not even four o'clock." Harvey didn't like the natural order of things to be disturbed.

"I'm starving and I didn't have time to eat on the flight. Are you having something?"

"Soup. I will have soup."

"That's it?"

"Yes."

When the waiter came, I gave him my order for two bowls of miso soup, a California roll and . . . and . . .

"A plate of mixed tempura, please."

I put the menu aside with a twinge of regret. What I really wanted was the sushi special—seven different varieties of raw fish on cubes of rice that I could drench in soy sauce, ginger, and wasabe. But every once in a while, I succumbed to the screeching warnings about the health hazards of eating uncooked fish. It must have been the proximity to Harvey and the influence of his chronically jangled nerves.

Harvey spent the majority of his time in a high state of agitation, convinced that if a meteor fell from the heavens tomorrow, it would fall on him. But he had good reason. He had been diagnosed five years ago with multiple sclerosis. It was a devastating blow that had peeled away the last defenses of a chronically nervous, fifty-one-year-old man and left him feeling vulnerable and scared. Working with Harvey was by turns murderously frustrating and heartbreakingly sad.

He reached up with his napkin and dabbed at the dew on his forehead.

"What did your doctor say?"

"I am still, unfortunately, as diseased as ever. Perhaps a little more."

"I'm sorry, Harvey. I know you were expecting better news."

"No matter." He said it with that offhand nonchalance that left no doubt about how much it did matter. "What did you do?" he asked me. "Did you get fired? Is that what you are keeping from me?"

That was the other thing about Harvey. He was highly perceptive.

"I'm not keeping anything from you, which is why we're here."

"Then you did get fired."

"No, I did not." I slumped back in the booth. "I got a stern letter of warning."

"I knew it." He launched immediately into his quietly hysterical mode. "This thing is falling apart. I knew it would. Did I tell you? Did I not tell you this?"

"It's not falling apart."

"How can they fire you after only six weeks? What did you do?"

"I am not fired. I am warned, and all I did was melt a couple of ice buckets, which were not supposed to be stored in the ovens in the first place. I've had a few customers gripe, and a couple of trips ago—" I glanced up at him. There was no point in unsettling him further.

"How will you conduct an undercover investigation if you cannot hold on to your cover? You have to be a working stewardess to do this job."

"Flight attendant."

"What?"

"I'm working as a flight attendant, not a stewardess. I'm also working for you as an investigator, which means I am working virtually around the clock. I spend more than half my time on the road. When I'm not flying, I'm on surveillance. When I'm not on surveillance, I'm writing reports. It's hard to smile all day and be nice when you've had no sleep for three nights running. All things considered, I think I'm keeping up pretty well. Did you get the pictures I sent from last night?"

"I never should have let you talk me into this. This is not what I do. Insurance fraud, background checks, forensic accounting. That's what I do. What do I know from hookers and pimps? Nothing. That's what."

"Harvey, I thought you should know what's going on, but if this is the way you react, you will discourage any further impulse I might have to keep you in the loop."

"I do not wish to be in the loop. I would rather not know. Dear God."

"Is that true?"

"No. But I am no longer convinced this case is worth it for me anymore."

"Look, maybe I am—" The waiter appeared with our soup. I waited for him to set the lacquered bowls in front of us and retreat. "Maybe I do cause you undue aggravation, but you have to be fair. This case has been worth a lot of money to you. Shall we review the billings we've generated from this job over the past few months?" It wasn't enough to buy new shoes, but it certainly was enough to pay the rent.

He stared into his cup of miso. He tugged on the sleeves of his worn suit coat. He tried to pull the collar of his pressed white shirt into the next larger size. With his fortunes as a private investigator deteriorating along with his health, he had agreed to take me on because he needed cash fast and I brought a presold job with me. I had agreed to be taken on because I needed to work for a licensed investigator for three years before I could qualify on my own. I thought we were the perfect match. He had the contacts, the license, and a lot of things I wanted to learn from him. I had the mobility and the enthusiasm for the work that had been sapped by his condition, although I had to wonder if he'd ever had much enthusiasm to begin with.

"Do you know how the client will react if you are terminated from this job after they have invested twelve weeks in you?"

"Eleven weeks, half of that in training, which doesn't really count."

"The point is the client is dismayed that this case is taking as long as it is and disappointed in our lack of progress."

"We have progress. If you get the photos out, I'll show you."

He pulled a manila file out and slipped it across the table. He must have had it tucked under his thigh, because it was still warm. I opened it and quickly reviewed the report that was on top, reminding myself of what I'd written in the middle of last night. I thumbed through the stack of photos. Not bad images, considering the distance from which I'd had to shoot and the bad lighting and the fact that I'd almost been busted by the target. I pulled out the best image of Angel.

"That's Angela Velesco. She calls herself Angel, of all things, and she runs the hooker ring."

"Alex, as we have yet to establish the validity of your ring theory, I would prefer that we not refer to it as such until we have firmly—"

"There are constants in every transaction. The women involved almost exclusively work the first-class cabin. They only turn tricks when they're on the road. They never do business in Boston. They do not solicit onboard, and they never flash the cash in the open, which means there is some sort of scheduling and payment system behind the scenes, and I'll bet any amount of money it's on the Internet." I had to stop and take a breath. "This is a prostitution ring, Harvey. It's all very smooth and organized and sophisticated, and she"—I pointed to the picture of Angel—"is the one who made it that way."

"Can you prove that?"

"Proof, no, but I know it's going on. I heard something interesting today, that Angel is trying to expand her operation to the West Coast."

He cleared his throat, straightened his napkin, and cleared his throat again. "We are supposed to be winding down, not expanding the scope."

"Harvey, the case is what it is. I'm not expanding it. I'm trying to keep up, and I'm trying to do it given the severe limitation imposed by the airline."

"Limitation?"

"You know the one I mean. We're conducting this investigation as if were after the men. We're after the women, which means we have to prove that money is being exchanged for sex. If I can't ask the men, how am I supposed to do that? Photos aren't enough, but they would be enough to leverage statements from the johns. We have the names. I could approach—"

"No." He sat back in his booth and shook his head hard enough to make his cheeks ripple. "Absolutely out of the question."

I sat back in my booth. "Option two would be me hiding under the bed while they have sex."

"I know I do not need to remind you that the client has asked us, I dare say demanded, that we leave their passengers out of the investigation."

"Can we refer to the client by his name? Can we please call him Carl? I prefer to think of our client as a person, a human being who can be influenced by other reasonable human beings."

"Very well. As the director of corporate security, Mr. Wolff has made it clear on behalf of the airline that we are not to approach their passengers under any circumstances. We abide by his wishes. It is part of being a good investigator."

"Oh, and me thinking the goal was to solve the case."

"Your goal is the client's goal, and might I remind you that we sold this case on the idea that you could infiltrate the group, that there would be no need to approach the passengers? Metaphorically speaking, you promised them you would be able to get under the bed to get the evidence we need. I am loath to say this because I know how hard you are trying, but we are three months in, and you are not any closer today to becoming an insider than when we started."

There was that perceptive Harvey again. I had collected lots of information and taken lots of pictures but had yet to make the right contacts to get really inside, mainly because I had overestimated my ability to fit in with a cadre of gorgeous women at least ten years younger than I who had sex for a living and aggressively rejected anyone who didn't. I stared at the delicate rice paper partitions that separated our booth from the next one.

"Is there some reason you bring this up?"

"The client—Mr. Wolff—is scheduled for his budget review in two weeks. He plans to present one of two scenarios. Either we brought the case in and he is a hero, or we failed to bring the case in and he has fired us."

"How can they fire us when they're under pressure to deal with this problem?"

"Apparently, the wife who complained and threatened to go public has been mollified with the promise of several free tickets to destinations of her choice."

"So they fixed the immediate problem. This ring is not going away. In fact, it's getting bigger. More wives will find out about it. At some point, one of them will decide not to be bought off and she'll go public. An airline that is aware of illegal activity going on in the operation and doing nothing to stop it would make a great investigative report, don't you think? If they're allowing prostitution, what else are they turning a blind eye to? Smuggling? Maintenance problems?"

"The client is aware of what is at stake. Do not forget that he has the option to hire someone else to take our place."

My tempura had materialized in front of me sometime during the debate. It looked heavy and smelled greasy compared with the clean and simple sushi I should have ordered. Another opportunity missed.

"What do you want to do?" I already knew the response, but every once in a while, I held out a hope that Harvey might surprise me.

"We should put what we have in a final report and turn it in with our last invoice. They are not going to court. All they want is for the suspects to resign quietly. For that, they need reasonable evidence, which we have given them."

"It won't work. I'm getting to know these women, or at least about them." I picked up a photo. "If you put these in front of one of them, she will not dissolve in tears. She will not implicate her friends. She will say, 'So what? I went out on a date with a passenger in Pittsburgh. That's not against the law, and let me introduce you to my union rep.' The union is solidly behind these women. If we confront them now, we will drive them further underground, which is exactly what happened the last time they tried to get them without the proper evidence."

"What is your suggestion?"

"Give Carl a plan that gives me until the end of the month, when I have to go back to flying reserve. That's the two weeks up to his budget review."

"What will you do in two weeks that you have not already done?"

"Find a way to get under the bed."

chapter 4

THE VESTIBULE OF MY APARTMENT BUILDING looked shabbier than usual when I rolled in. The tiles were mud streaked and the grout a few shades smudgier than when I'd left. The mailbox area looked like a flea market, littered as it was with free newspapers, delivery notices, and piles of take-out menus from Wong Fu's Wok and Gianella's Pizzeria. Both rows of boxes were festooned with yellow sticky notes and scraps of taped paper, temporary tags meant to identify permanent residents.

My mailbox wore a clean, computer-generated label I had slotted neatly into the cutout provided for that purpose. My life felt like a mess in so many ways, I figured I'd try for neat and tidy wherever I could find it. The inside of my box was another story. When I keyed it open, it looked like a cross-section view of a trash compactor. As near as I could tell, the postman loaded the narrow boxes from the top, making the envelopes fit by jamming them down with a pile driver. Anything that didn't fit—magazines, catalogues, tax returns, divorce decrees—went into the communal pile on the floor and ultimately into the trash if not promptly claimed.

I dug out the slug of mail and locked the box. I pulled two magazines from the pile that were mine. With arms full, I maneuvered my key into the front door, made my way to the elevator, and punched the button with my elbow. It wheezed into action, sounding much the way I felt. After three days on the road, including two nights of surveillance, I was anxious to get off my feet.

Inside the elevator, I rejiggered my cargo so I could sort through the mail. One of the magazines was from the Wolfborough Gun and Hunt Club. I couldn't get used to seeing my name on anything with the word *gun* in the title. Stranger still was the presence in my mailbox of the *Wings Report,* the official publication of the Union of Professional Flight Attendants. Labor relations in the airline business are on a par with those of coal mining, and I had spent fourteen years on the other side of the table as a manager. If anyone had told me I would be a member of the UPFA, or any labor union, I would have thought that person clinically insane. It just wasn't in my background.

My apartment when I opened the door was dark and cool, which meant I had left town once again with the window open. The damp air from outside had pooled in my one-bedroom unit, but it wasn't cold enough for the radiators to kick in, and I was glad to be wearing long sleeves. I flipped the switch in the entryway and immediately felt warmer for the light.

I dropped the mail on the kitchen counter and went to close the window. The old wooden frame was warped and stuck. When I finally banged it loose, it slammed shut. The thick old leaded glass shuddered but held firm. I turned on a lamp in the front room and searched around for the remote for the stereo. It was never where it was supposed to be, which was a strange problem for someone who lived alone. The search took me into the kitchen and past my answering machine, where not a single message had come in during my absence.

I needed a dog.

The remote was not in the kitchen, so I manually started the CD player, going with whatever disc was already in there. It was the Blind Boys of Alabama. I loved the Blind Boys, the way their gritty and imperfect voices blended perfectly in songs about sin and salvation, eternal damnation, and the promise of redemption. I cranked it up so I could hear them in the bedroom, where I went to peel off my uniform. I found a soft gray sweatsuit in the pile of wearable play clothes, the ones I didn't use for running. In what was becoming my favorite part of every workday, I went into the bathroom, ran the warm water, and washed the makeup from my face. During my long hiatus from work, I'd gotten used to the way I looked without powders and pastes. Wearing them now made me feel like a rodeo clown.

Marginally rejuvenated, I went out to the couch and dug out my laptop to do some work. Harvey had e-mailed a new batch of surveillance photos from one of our contractors in Florida and he wanted me to review them. I had little energy for the task. I was tired of looking at the same faces on the same women, strutting, primping, and going about their business as if I had not spent the past two months trying to get each and every one of them fired.

While waiting for the computer to do the mysterious things it did when called upon to wake up and be useful, I went through my daily ritual of self-flagellation. What had possessed me to give up a good corporate career with a very agreeable income to become a private investigator? On what evidence had I concluded that I could successfully perform a job for which I had no training, no background, and no support, except from Harvey, who leaned on me almost more than I did on him? How did I expect to support myself, who did I expect to hire me, and would I ever have made this decision had I known the cost of health benefits for a self-employed individual? In summary, what the hell did I think I was doing?

The photos were up on my screen. Here was Sylvie Nguyet, the French-Vietnamese exotic flower, wearing a liquid blue silk dress that hung on her delicate shoulders from wispy spaghetti straps. She was caught in the embrace of her client, laughing like a child, her face more animated than her usual serene demeanor ever allowed. When Sylvie was on a date, she seemed to have a need to convince herself she was having a good time.

Not so with Ava Ashby. Ava, cool and lithe, had the boneless quality of a boa constrictor and the personality to match. She looked as if she could squeeze herself in or out of any situation. Her silver lamé dress—sleeveless with a choker neckline—clung to her like a second skin as she uncoiled from the limo.

I plowed through the batch, clicking faster as I went, putting names with faces and generally ignoring the photos of the men nuzzling the women's necks or glancing out furtively from inside the limos. When I got to the end, I closed the file, but then I clicked it open again almost instantly. Without knowing why, I went straight to the shot at the end, the last one I'd seen. I had given it no more weight than all the others, perhaps less. When I pulled it up and studied it more closely, I understood what had drawn me back, and what I saw there made me smile because I knew we had finally caught a break. I knew I had something to work with, and that feeling, all by itself, was enough to get me through tonight and all the way to tomorrow, when it would be time to ask again what the hell I thought I was doing.

chapter 5

THE RAIN HAD PASSED THROUGH DURING THE night, leaving in its wake one of those high-resolution fall days, the kind that make living in New England worth the endless, bone-cracking winters. The Commonwealth Avenue mall, which would spend much of the next several months in monochromatic stasis under a blanket of snow, was vibrant with fall colors. The venerable old elms that lined both sides of the wide promenade were thick with broad leaves at the vivid end of their life. They looked spectacular, but what I loved most was the sound they made. When the wind blew against them, the large, stiffening leaves shook into a sound that had the soaring resonance of applause, as if the trees were rewarding your walk among them.

I was in search of my car, certain of the general vicinity of where I had parked it last but fuzzy on exact longitude and latitude. It had been a while since I'd had the old Durango out, but I knew it was on Commonwealth somewhere west of Exeter.

The car did not reveal itself in the Exeter-to-Fairfield block, so I headed for the next block, pulled out my cell phone, and turbo-dialed. I was certain I would get voice mail, but a real, live human picked up.

"Dan Fallacaro."

"Hey." I was pleasantly surprised. "What are you doing?"

"I'm working, Shanahan. Hold on." I could hear the familiar sounds of the Majestic Airlines ticket counter behind Dan, and then his voice. "What flight are you on, sir?" The response was too far away to be clear, and I knew he had stuck the cell phone under his arm to take the man's ticket and scan it. Dan's voice was, as always, loud and clear. "Do you have any bags to check today? No? You need to go over to that line. You see the one that says first class?"

The response was muffled but probably something like, "I'm not flying first class."

"Tell them I sent you. I'm the boss. Tell them Fallacaro sent you."

Dan was doing his favorite thing, monitoring the lines in front of the Majestic ticket counter, making sure no one missed a flight. He was one general manager who spent less time in his office than in the operation, and I was always secretly envious that having taken over my job, he did it better than I ever had.

"What do you want, Shanahan?"

"I want to stop by and see you. I can be there in twenty minutes. You're right on my way."

"Only if you want to come over and help me lift tickets. They're hanging from the rafters out here."

"I like to get paid when I work. We can meet in front of your ticket counter at what? Eight-fifteen? Better make it eight-thirty in case the tunnel is backed up."

"Shanahan—"

"Come on, Dan. Take a break. I haven't seen you in . . . too long."

"You're full of shit. You want something from me."

"That, too. I need your help."

"I'll give you fifteen minutes," he said. "Don't be late." *Click.*

Dan approached the way he always did—walking fast and talking faster. When he spotted me, he vectored over, barely clearing the slow movers as he sliced through the crowd.

"Hey, Shanahan, get me a pillow from the overhead bin, and top off my rum and coke. Just kidding. C'mon, let's get a doughnut or something."

He took off again and I caught up with him at Dunkin' Donuts, leaning over the counter, having a speed-talking contest with the woman pouring his coffee.

"What do you want to drink, Shanahan?"

"Tea." I pulled out my folding money, ready to slip him a couple of bills.

"Fucking tea from a coffee stand." He shook his head. "Put your money away."

"I invited you."

"I'd hate for my cup of coffee to tip you over into bankruptcy." He reached for his own cash, digging deep into the pants pocket of his very sharp charcoal suit, which, I noticed, was suspiciously well tailored to his wiry frame. His tie was silk instead of a polyester blend, and it matched his precision-pressed cotton shirt.

"Is that a custom-tailored suit, Dan?"

"Don't talk about the suit." He reached up and dragged the knot of his tie off center, as if to make it less perfect. He was trying hard to be insulted, because true operations guys never cared how they looked. He certainly hadn't the first time I'd ever seen him. On my first day on the job at Logan, I looked out the window to see him sprinting across the ramp in a heavy rain with a kidney in his hands. Not his. A transplant kidney in a cooler. It had arrived on a late inbound flight from Chicago and was overdue at the hospital. He was soaking wet. Just another day at the office for Dan.

"Awfully spiffy, Mr. Fallacaro. *Very* corporate."

"I'm warning you, Shanahan. Don't start."

But now, despite himself, he had become a mucky-muck, and he had people to run out into the rain for him. He liked his job, had been surprised to find out how good he was at it, and I would have bet any amount of money I didn't have that he loved that suit and the way he looked in it. God forbid he should let anyone know.

He handed me my tea and took his jumbo steaming brew, and we walked to a couple of chairs that faced the ticketing lobby. "What do you want from me now, Shanahan? I already got you a job, for Chrissakes."

"You didn't get me a job."

"I gave you the contact at GrapefruitAir, didn't I? I hooked you up with Harvey. How's he doing, by the way?"

"He's okay. Physically up and down, but mostly down about the case."

"The hooker case? Are you still on that? Jesus Christ, how long has it been? Months, right?"

"Please, don't you start."

"What'd I say? What's so hard about chasing hookers around?"

I looked around to make sure no one was listening. Dan had, indeed, been our first contact on the case with OrangeAir, for which I was eternally grateful. I just wished he didn't talk so loud. "It's not hard to find them. It's hard to find them doing anything actionable. Right now, all I have are a bunch of shots of women in killer evening gowns and Prada shoes coming and going from expensive hotels, climbing in and out of limos, and leaving parties and restaurants with passengers. It's not enough."

"What more do you need?"

"Proof that money is changing hands. I need statements from the men in the photos saying they paid for sex. But since the hookers' customers are also the airline's best customers—"

"Don't tell me, the airline doesn't want you fucking with their revenue base."

"Exactly right. They think it would be a bad idea to accuse their full-fare first-class business travelers and heavy-duty frequent fliers of patronizing a prostitution ring. Go figure."

He pulled the stirrer out of his coffee, stared at the ceiling as he sucked on it, and put it back. "Okay. Here's what you do. You sit down and draft up a proposal for the airline. Call it a new business opportunity. Outline a revenue-sharing arrangement. Get the hookers to cut the airline in on their action. In return, they can continue to operate with no hassles."

"That's your idea?"

"Think about it. They've got the same target market. They can do joint marketing. 'Use your frequent flier miles to get laid.' It's a win-win."

His delivery was so perfectly deadpan it made me laugh. "I don't believe this is the kind of advice the airline called on us to provide."

He leaned back and shrugged. "It's a new day, Shanahan. You have to think outside the box."

"Well," I said, hopping out of the box, "it is an intriguing idea. The airlines are always looking for ways to burn off that frequent flier liability. Ten thousand for a lap dance. Think of all the liability you could burn off on a single New York–LA transcon."

He stared at the ceiling. "Seventy-five for a threesome. In Bermuda."

"You're such a guy, Dan."

"Threesomes and girls doing each other. Are you kidding me? They'd put the rest of us out of business in a week. I'll let you have that idea. You should think about it."

"I think I'll stick with the client's fundamental premise that prostitution is a bad thing."

"Suit yourself. I'm just saying, don't fuck with market forces. These guys love to play the frequent flier game. This is just another way to do it."

"I have a different idea. I want to get someone from the inside, a client, to give me information about what's going on."

"What kind of an asshole in his right mind would do that?"

I unzipped my backpack and pulled out the envelope I'd brought. I slipped out the photo I'd printed, the one that had caught my attention last night, and passed it over to Dan. "This kind. Look at the man behind the brunette. He has his hand on her butt."

"Holy shit. Is that—"

"It is, isn't it?" I was delighted to see the flash of recognition in his eyes. "It's that guy from Florida who used to fly in and out of here about once a week. You used to meet and greet him."

"Still do. He's one of my best customers. Filthy rich. Lives down in West Palm, but his mother is still out in Weymouth. Every time he comes through here, I take care of him. Every time he goes out, he offers me a job with his company. His old company. I don't even know what he does. He had a bunch of businesses and sold them."

"That's a prostitute he's fondling, Dan, one of the ones I'm chasing."

"Good for him."

"So, here's what I was thinking. I really need information on this group. Your buddy from Florida is obviously on the inside. I was wondering if you could talk to him for me."

"Talk to him about having his hand on a hooker's ass? I don't think so. I just told you he's one of our Very Important Travelers."

"You could talk to him as someone interested in becoming one of their clients."

"You mean a trick."

"Well . . . yeah. That way, you could ask him questions about how it works, is it secure, how does he schedule dates, does he know many of the women. I can give you a list of questions if you want."

"Shanahan . . ." We were perfectly isolated in the hollow center of an airport din. There was no more private place to talk, yet he still checked around and leaned closer. "The reason I had to hire Harvey in the first place was because my ex accused me of hiding assets. Can you believe that shit? That's all I need is for her to get wind that I'm out blowing the child support on hookers."

"I'm not asking you to take a survey. I'm asking you to talk to one guy in private, man to man, and see what he will share with you. If he tells you to mind your own business, so be it."

He shook his head, a distant smile on his lips. This wasn't the first favor I'd asked of him. He always bitched and moaned, and he always came through for me.

"I'm desperate here, Dan. If I can't make this work, I don't know what I'll do. I might have to go back into the airline business for real and for good."

"The way this business is going, you wouldn't want back in, anyway. It sucks. Besides, I don't think anyone would hire you."

"Why do you say that?"

He handed the photo back. "I'm just saying you've got a lot of baggage. With what happened when you were here and the way the rumors fly about you—"

"What happened here is fully documented by the police, the airline, Massport, and everyone else who was involved for what it was—self-defense."

"You don't have to tell me. I was here. But lots of people don't read the fine print. They hear that an employee died on your ramp, and they move on to the next résumé."

I stared down at the picture in my lap and felt a wobble in my heartbeat. He wasn't saying anything I hadn't already thought myself, but it felt different hearing it from someone else. It was as if I'd looked down from the high wire, only to discover someone had made off with the safety net. That was all I needed. More pressure to perform.

"Will you talk to him?"

"I'll look and see when he's due to come through. If he's not scheduled in, maybe I'll give him a call."

"Thanks."

"Cheer up, Shanahan." He looked over and nudged me with his elbow. "What's the matter?"

"If this doesn't work, I'm not sure what I'll do. I can't get in tight with a single one of these hookers."

He laughed. "That's because you don't exactly look the part."

"What do you mean?"

"Not for nothing, but if I was a hooker, I wouldn't be spilling all my secrets to you."

"Why not?"

"Because you look like . . . like what you are."

"Which is?"

"A . . . a manager. A . . ." He started talking with his hands, which is what he did when he couldn't find the words, which was almost never. "A businesswoman. Someone who wears . . . suits. I don't know. What I'm saying is I don't look at you and think blow job."

"You think I can't give a blow job?"

"Did I say that? What I said was that you don't look like a hooker, and if I was a hooker, you wouldn't be the first person I would tell all my secrets to."

"Well, what . . ." I uncrossed and recrossed my legs. I clasped my hands together in my lap. "In your opinion, what would I have to change to be more like one?"

"Everything."

"Start small."

He scanned the terminal. The good thing about airports is you can always find a type, an example of whatever you're looking for.

"There. See that girl? The blonde?"

"Looking at magazines?"

"Her. Yeah. What do you see when you look at her?"

"Nice figure. Spiky heels, black roots, a skirt that's too short. Attractive face, but more makeup than an anchorwoman wears. It looks kind of pancakey."

"Here's what I see." He sat up straight and trained his attention on her. "Big tits. Blond hair. Big tits. Short skirt. Big tits—"

"There is not a chance in hell I'm getting a boob job to work this case."

"She's dressed like she wouldn't mind me coming up and asking her what her sign is. You know what I mean?"

He looked at me looking at myself in my smart linen pants and my silk shirt and my leather flats. "Now, you, for instance—"

"That's enough. I get the picture." I couldn't help but think about what a strange twist my life had taken when I was accused of not looking like a hooker and resented it.

"Anyway," he said, one hand smoothing his hair in back, "I don't know if that helps you."

"No, it helps. You know what it's like? It's like being back in high school. Did you like high school?"

"Nobody likes high school, Shanahan."

"These women, these hookers, they're like the cheerleaders. Revered or despised by all who are not they. They're completely unapproachable . . . a world unto themselves. You don't get into their little clique—their tiny, exclusive clique—without being invited. And they don't invite anyone."

"You didn't hang out with cheerleaders in high school?"

"I didn't hang out. I was either taking care of my little brother or working."

"That's a sad story. But we're grown-ups now. We get over that shit, right?"

I stared across the terminal at the blonde buying the magazine. She had probably been a cheerleader in high school. Or at least one of those girls who always knew what to say to boys. Regardless of who she was then, she was now a woman at whom men like to stare, and I wondered what that felt like. I also wondered if changing my clothes would be change enough.

"Shanahan, your fifteen minutes have been up for fifteen minutes." He stood up and stretched his back, then leaned over and used his most discreet voice. "All I'm saying, you're working undercover, right? That means you have to be undercover. Maybe if you looked the part more, you'd feel it more. God knows you've got the body to pull it off."

"Yeah?"

"The real question is, do you have the balls?"

chapter 6

THE WOLFBOROUGH SHOOTING RANGE WASN'T much more than an opening in the trees at the end of a long dirt road. It was easy to spot Tristan leaning against a Porsche—a *Porsche*?—in the lot down at the open field that served as the pistol range. As far as I could tell, he was the only living organism there at ten-thirty on a Friday morning. I pulled into the space next to his and climbed out.

"You're late," he said.

"Sorry. Since when do you drive a Carrera?"

"It's Barry's, and you're changing the subject. Don't even think about screeching up at the very last second when you go to Moon Island to take your range test. They don't like that, and you'll get all flustered, and you won't shoot straight, and you won't pass the test, and you won't get your license, and I'll feel like a failure. I have a personal stake in this. In fact, when are you scheduled?"

"The week after next."

"I'm going with you. I'll pick you up. We'll get out there in plenty of time. That's what we'll do."

Tristan had switched into his shooting instructor role, one he obviously took seriously. I had been amazed when he'd told me he could teach me to shoot. Tristan didn't exactly exude machismo. But he had grown up in Wyoming and when he'd told his parents he was gay, his father decided he needed to know how to defend himself and taught him all about guns. It turned out he needed less protection from the rednecks than from his own mother. She disowned him and tossed him out.

When my old instructor had left town, Tristan had happily volunteered to take over my firearms instruction and help me prepare for the test. Not only was he an excellent teacher, he had lots of guns. He also had accepted without question my vague explanation that I just wanted to learn how to shoot. Most important of all, he refused to charge me for his services.

"What's today's lesson?"

"Large-caliber weapons." We walked out to the shooting range and the setup area, which looked like a long, covered picnic table, on which Tristan had displayed his usual array of small arms, ammunition, targets, and headgear. He picked up a big revolver with a long barrel, something Billy the Kid might have worn strapped to his thigh. "You've got the twenty-two under control. Let's see how you do with this baby."

He offered it to me, and I wrapped my hand around it. Thanks mostly to Tristan's impressive array of handguns, I was beginning to know the weights of the various calibers. In the month we'd been shooting together, this was the heaviest I'd held.

"It's a Forty-four Special," he said. "It will be even heavier with these." He handed me a box of shells. "Load it. Get ready to fire."

I opened the box and emptied out a few rounds. The shells were large, about as big around as my little finger, which made them much easier to work with than those slender .22-calibers. I slipped one into each of the six chambers.

"On the range!" Tristan yelled out from behind me. We were the only ones around, but he was a stickler for safety and doing everything according to the rules, a fact that I found reassuring. He waited for me to put the gun down and step back before walking out and slapping a couple of standard paper bull's-eye targets onto the holders.

I still had the first target I'd ever hit, the flimsy documentation of my faltering early steps to learn to shoot. I kept it in a place where no one could see it, which was the perfect metaphor for my complicated relationship with firearms. The instructor I'd been working with had told me the tight cluster of small holes I'd made on my first attempt, though not in the bull's-eye, was evidence of a steady hand. He'd called me a natural, which meant I had an innate ability for something to which I had traditionally claimed an aversion. Not a "repeal the Second Amendment" passion. I hadn't grown up around guns and had no use for them. But learning to shoot was part of my training, a necessary arrow in my quiver of professional skills, and I had decided if I was going to do it, I was going to do it right. I just hadn't been prepared for how much I would like it.

Tristan positioned the targets where he wanted them. When he came back, I was ready. I picked up the loaded weapon and donned my headphones. I waited until he put his on, then assumed my stance—feet shoulder-width apart, both hands on the pistol, arms straight in front.

"Single action first." Tristan's voice was clear, held close to my ear by the headphones, which were intriguingly designed to filter in all sound except explosive gunfire.

I pulled back the hammer until it caught and placed

my finger gently on the trigger. *"Firing on the range!"* I yelled, waited a beat or two, and then squeezed.

The sound was muffled. The kick was not. The explosion drove my shoulder back and the barrel of the gun straight up. I peered through the lingering smoke and saw that I had missed the target completely. Judging from where the gun had ended up, the round had probably gone over the stand and lodged in the dirt and grass berm that formed the back perimeter of the range.

"Wow."

"Keep firing," he said. "You have to compensate for the extra kick. Aim lower this time than you would normally, and remember it's all in the way you pull the trigger. Squeeze gently. Single action again."

I cocked the hammer, moved my feet two inches farther apart, and settled in, trying to lower my center of gravity. I used the sight to aim below the target and squeezed off a round.

"There you go, love. That's much better."

I lowered the gun and felt a warm satisfaction rising. A large, round hole had appeared in the outermost ring of the target. I couldn't wait to take my range test. There was nothing subjective about it. It was finite and measurable. There was a clear demarcation between passing and failing, and if I accomplished nothing else in this, my first official case, at least I could do that.

"Fire all the rounds," he said. "Reload, and try it double action."

The last four shots all hit the target, one actually close to where I'd aimed. I felt more comfortable with each shot, but knew I'd have to build up more arm and chest strength ever to feel truly comfortable with a large gun like a .44. Tristan had been encouraging exactly such a workout program all along, but I barely had enough time and energy to get my running in.

When the gun was empty, I found the release, opened the cylinder, emptied the spent casings, and reloaded. As I was doing that, Tristan was firing an automatic at a target that was twice the distance of mine. When the smoke had cleared, I could see he had fired six shots straight into the heart of his target.

We worked for another twenty minutes, or until I could no longer hold up the heavy weapon. Afterward, we sat at the table, and he showed me how to clean it. The sun, higher in the sky, had baked off the moisture from the day before and warmed the air to a pleasant temperature.

I wanted more information on Angel, but I was afraid of pushing too hard with Tristan. It was just so tempting. He was one great source of information. I decided to test the waters.

"I'm supposed to fly with Angel next week." I used my most offhand tone.

"That's too bad. Maybe you can swap off." He was watching my hands as I worked with the gun. "No, here." He took if from me and demonstrated. "It's easier if you do it this way."

"Do you think the management of this base is aware that there is a prostitution ring flourishing under their noses?"

"Most certainly. But our current management team is of the let-sleeping-dogs-lie tribe."

"That seems like a dangerous position to take. What if they get caught? Management will look pretty clueless."

"They won't get caught."

"Why not?"

"No one wants to catch them. Can you imagine the

headline? 'OrangeAir Shuts Down Flight Attendant Hooker Ring.' Besides, they're careful. It's like I said yesterday, Miss DQ has made them much more discreet and low-key than they used to be."

"I still don't think that just because Angel has a condo at the Ritz, that means she's a prostitute."

"It's not just her. It's a pattern. These women all live lives they cannot possibly afford. They disappear on layovers, and they show up in the schedule where they have no business being. What else can they be doing?"

"Sightseeing?"

"In Wisconsin? Why would anyone swap onto a trip to Milwaukee three weeks running? It's one thing to get stuck with that trip, but to go out of your way to get it when you have the seniority to avoid it? They end up in odd places at odd times. It's because they need to be there to meet their dates. But that's just my theory."

"So, they must do a lot of swaps."

"Tons, and those are all well organized, too." He peered across the table at me. "Why are you so interested?"

"Curious. You've got to admit; it's pretty fascinating. I've never met a hooker."

"Are we going to have to do an intervention on you? Throw a blanket over you and whisk you off to Bermuda for deprogramming?"

"An intervention?"

"I don't want you slipping over to the dark side. There's so much money in being a hooker, and you're so poor."

"Do you think I want to be a hooker, Tristan?"

"I think you might have some sort of fascination with the whole bad girl thing. You being such a good girl and all."

"Sometimes being good is boring." I finished cleaning the .44 and put it in front of him for inspection.

"I've been bad," he said, squinting down to check my handiwork, "and I've been good. Good is better."

"You've been bad? I want to hear."

"I'm not kidding about this."

Something in his voice made me look up at him. His face, usually so mobile and animated, had turned in profile to all right angles and sharp corners—his nose, his chin, even his jaw line, which made a sharp turn where it hinged to his skull.

"You're not serious. Do you think she's going to convert me?"

"How do you think she got them all organized? Do you think they all just fell into line and happily started handing over a cut? Did you ever hear the name Robin Sevitch?"

"No."

"She was a spitfire like DQ. One of the first girls to start hooking on the job. She made a lot of money, and when the new regime came in, she didn't like it much. She said she'd rather turn everyone in than have to pay part of her fee to Angela. Guess what happened to her?"

I swallowed hard and felt a faint stirring in the pit of my stomach. "What?"

"She went to Omaha and never came back."

"What happened?"

"Supposedly, she went out for a walk by herself along a deserted canal. They found her body with her head bashed in."

"You think Angel did that?"

"Let me put it this way. She never had another single complaint from the rank and file." He unzipped the case for the .44 and set the gun inside. "Stay away from Angela Velesco, Alexandra. She is one twisted sister."

chapter 7

THE SUN WAS HIGHER IN THE SKY AS I DROVE back to the city, and I couldn't find my sunglasses. The last time I'd had them was on a turnaround to Phoenix sometime last week, which meant they were buried in my suitcase, which was still sitting unpacked in the middle of my living room. That left me approaching the tollbooth for the Sumner Tunnel, fighting with my balky sun visor, digging for money, and juggling my cell phone all at once.

"Hold on, Harvey."

"Wait, you cannot—"

"Hold on."

I rolled down the window to greet the toll collector. "Good morning." I got no response in exchange for my three bucks, but I did get passage back through to the city.

"Harvey, are you there?" He was. "Did you talk to Carl? Did we get the extra time?"

"I spoke to him yesterday afternoon. He will give us until a week from Monday." His voice was in and out, but I was surprised we were connected at all, since I was in the tunnel under the harbor.

"Harvey, that's only ten days."

"He also gave me a warning. If he pays for the extra time, he wants to see results."

"I don't blame him. Listen, I just spent time with Tristan, and he gave me an idea for an analysis we can do that might help us identify the players." I hit the brake and slowed to a stop behind the car stopped in front of me. "Dammit."

"What is it?"

"One of the lanes in the tunnel is blocked." I started inching the Durango into the other lane, hoping for a chance to shoot over. When I caught sight of a Miata in my rearview, I made my move. I almost didn't hear its little horn bleating. Sometimes size was all that mattered.

"I am asking what is your idea?"

"Oh. Top swappers."

"What does that mean?"

"Swaps, Harvey. Swapping. Trading trips among ourselves. Being able to manage your work schedule is part of the beauty of being a flight attendant. If the hookers are using their ability to swap to get on the trips with their dates or to get to the cities where their dates will meet them, then a high level of swapping might be a way to spot the hookers."

"How would we identify the swaps?"

"We get a copy of the base schedule as it was bid and then a copy of the schedule that was actually flown over the past several months. We compare them and use the results to identify the top swappers."

"Where am I to get the schedules?"

"Carl should be able to get you electronic versions of the as-bid and as-flown schedules. That would make it easier to work with the data. While you're at it, ask him for a list of earnings for everyone at the base. I'd get last year's and this year's earnings to date."

"Income versus lifestyle analysis," he said, anticipating where I was going. "I can match salaries to asset purchases, estimate a cost of living, and see if they can afford what they have on their reported salaries."

"Exactly what I was thinking. It should be easy, too. These women are not shy about spending money. They wear expensive jewelry, have second homes down on the Cape or on the Vineyard, and there is a lot of plastic surgery going on, which is not cheap."

"Nor," he said, like the accountant he was, "is it covered by health benefits."

"Right." I came up out of the tunnel and into the chaos of the Big Dig, the massive roadway rearrangement project designed to rationalize Boston's interstate highway system and sink most of it underground. It was already years in the making and years from completion, which made it one of the world's largest semipermanent construction sites. From a practical standpoint, they changed the detours almost every night, so you had to pay close attention if you didn't want to end up in New Hampshire. I made the crossing successfully and headed toward my neighborhood.

"So, what do you think, Harvey?"

"It could work. It would be fast."

"Your enthusiasm is killing me. I thought it was brilliant."

"Alex, even if we do come up with a list of names, none of this necessarily proves anything."

"You said it yourself. We're not trying to convict them. We're trying to scare them, which won't be easy. The more we know about them, the better chance we have. There's something else I think we should do."

"What?"

"Look into an unsolved murder in Omaha. An

OrangeAir flight attendant named Robin Sevitch got her head bashed in there. Tristan says Angel arranged it."

"Dear Lord."

"I know. It could be urban legend, but he implied she did it to send a message about who was in charge."

"I will see what I can dig up."

"Good." I spotted a space on the street almost too late and had to throw it into reverse and barrel backward for half a block, a maneuver that required my full attention.

"Harvey, I have to go. I'm at the pharmacy."

"The pharmacy? What is the matter? Are you sick?"

"Not sick," I said, looking down at my smart linen pants and silk blouse. "Just dull and flat-chested. I'll call you later."

I heard my phone ringing through my closed door as I stepped off the elevator. The answering machine picked up as I fumbled my keys out and unlocked the dead bolt. I tried to hook the dry cleaning on the bedroom doorknob as I hurried past but missed and ended up with piles of OrangeAir uniforms and plastic sheathing on the floor.

"Hey, Shanahan, where the fuck are you? Too bad, because you're gonna want to hear this. Anyway, call me when—"

It was Dan, and I had a matter of seconds before he hung up. I lunged toward the phone. "I'm here. I'm here, Dan. Don't hang up."

"What the fuck? Are you screening your calls?"

"I just walked in." I dumped my bags on the counter and my backpack on the floor. One of the shopping bags fell over, spilling out my do-it-at-home hair color kit and a new bottle of fingernail polish. "What's going on?"

"Ask and you shall receive."

"You talked to our guy?"

"I had to hunt him down. He's in Dubai on business. I got him on his cell phone." That was one of the great things about Dan. Once he committed, you knew he wouldn't stop until he came through for you. "He thought I was calling asking him for a job, but then I had to tell him no, I was calling about getting laid."

"How did it go?"

"I sweated through my shirt and my suit jacket and had to take an hour after I hung up to go walk around on the ramp. I don't know how I'll ever be able to look this guy in the eye again."

"I know this wasn't easy, but did he give you anything?"

"He told me he would sponsor me, if I was interested."

"Sponsor you?"

"It's like a club. You don't just call up and hire a hooker. It's members only, and according to him, it's harder to get into than the CIA. You have to fill out an application, and on this application you have to put the names and phone numbers of three active members who are willing to sponsor you."

"Do they actually call them for references?"

"Sure as shit do. They pretend to be someone else, but they do a background check. A better one than we do, it sounds like."

"What exactly are they checking for?"

"To make sure the guy is who he says he is and not a cop. If he checks out, he gets a temporary ID and password, which he uses until the first time he bangs one of them, the idea being a cop wouldn't go that far. Once they do that, they get a permanent ID."

"Impressive. This is some operation she's running. How do they hook up?"

"What do you mean?"

"Did he talk about scheduling and meeting and—"

"Web site. It's all done online."

"I knew it. Payment, too?"

"Shanahan, for Christ's sake. He was in fucking Dubai, and I was sweating through all my clothes. It wasn't a lengthy and detailed conversation."

"Okay, okay. Sorry." I waited a beat for him to calm down. Otherwise, he would talk so fast I couldn't understand him. "Just tell me what you did get."

"I asked him for the name of the Web site. He said it wouldn't do me any good without a password. He also said there's nothing to see there. It's just a sign-in screen. So I asked him, how do you see the girls, how do you know who to ask for, and he says they have these introduction parties where you can meet them. There's one scheduled for tomorrow night. Supposedly, lots of hookers will be there. He's not going, obviously, but he told me where it was in case I wanted to."

"Great. Let me get something to write with." I slid the magazines and unopened mail around on the counter until the pen I was searching for rolled off the edge. It probably made sense for an investigator to have writing tools at the ready. I made a mental note as I plucked the pen from the hardwood and found a napkin to write on. "Where is it?"

"LA."

"LA? Los *Angeles?*"

"Little town on the West Coast? Palm trees . . . movie stars . . . big international airport?"

Turning around and going right back out on the road again was the last thing I wanted to do. I wasn't even sure I had any clean underwear. But Tristan did say that Angel was expanding her wings to LA. Maybe this was the kickoff, in which case, clean underwear or not, I should be there.

Dan was waiting. "Do you want it or not?"

"Give it to me."

He read me the address, and I wrote it down. I knew virtually nothing about LA, but he said it was at some producer's house in the Hollywood Hills. Nothing intimidating about that. "Okay, here's the most important part. You have to have this password to get in. Are you ready?"

chapter 8

"ALEXANDRA!"

Tristan screeched down the jetbridge and onto the quiet aircraft. I jumped and clanged the coffee pot against the coffeemaker. Fortunately, onboard coffee urns are nearly indestructible.

"You startled me."

"Is that you? Oh, my God, dear, you are a *blonde!* But when did you do this?"

I stuck the pot on the burner, reached up, and plowed my fingers through my new do. It was a familiar habit through unfamiliar territory. I wasn't used to wearing products on my hair.

"Last night, and I'm not a blonde, I'm merely highlighted."

"Look at you, all poofed and moussed. You look fabulous."

"Do you really think so?" If I had been unsure before, now I was totally convinced—I had made a terrible mistake. It was too much. "Is it too much?" I knew I shouldn't have done it myself. What was I thinking taking fashion advice from Dan? "Do you like it? Is it a good color? Is it okay?"

"Better than okay. Is that new makeup, too? *Look* at those nails. Girl, what got into you?"

He turned me around, and I had to admit, it was nice to be noticed. "It's your influence," I said. "I knew I couldn't show up with you at a Hollywood party without looking anything less than fully buffed."

I'd had no luck arranging my own swap to LA—apparently, it was the place to be for flight attendants this evening—so I'd had to enlist Tristan, with his seniority and his pull and his vast number of sources around the base. He got the job done, but the price was that he insisted on coming with me. In my heart of hearts, I was relieved. I hated parties. The sound of ice tinkling in glasses or the smell of a Sterno can burning under a fondue pot was enough to trigger the party vapors, the inability to function in large gatherings of schmoozing people, all of whom knew each other, none of whom knew me. This particular confab, put on by a Hollywood producer, had the potential of being the most intimidating party I'd ever attended.

"I can't believe I let you talk me into this." He stowed his bag in the first-class coat closet. "My days of jetting out to LA for a party are long over. But this might be fun. Did you turn on the ovens?" He reached past me to check. "Still gun-shy, I see." After opening the doors to make sure no ice buckets were hidden inside, he turned them on. "Tell me again why going to this party is so important to you."

"I told you last night."

"I know you did, but I want to hear it again. I am so excited for you."

"There's someone there I want to see." Not exactly a lie . . .

"A passenger, right?"

"He is, yes." Still not really a lie. There would be passengers there.

"Oooh, a handsome prince. Did he invite you? Tell me everything about him. Did you meet him on a flight? You must have. Does he live in LA? You have to be careful of handsome princes from LA. Mostly, they're starving gay actors. I can help you scope that out. Introduce me, and I'll tell you within thirty seconds if he's gay. Unfortunately, it's the toads that have all the money, and if you kiss them, they will still be toads, albeit wealthy ones. You don't have to worry about them, anyway. Most of them are only interested in jailbait. Boys and girls. Oh—" He checked quickly to see if he had offended me. "I did *not* mean you were old. Thirty-four is not old except by the standards of Tinsel Town." He put his arm around me. "Don't worry, Cinderella. I'll take care of you."

That was one of the nice things about Tristan. I often didn't have to fill in the details for him, because he did it himself.

Work began with the sound of the first-class passengers stampeding down the jetbridge, racing each other for overhead bin space. Boarding went smoothly, and after a slow but steady procession, Tristan worked with the gate agent to close out the flight while I checked in with the cockpit for beverage orders. Behind me, I heard the telltale signs of runners, passengers huffing and puffing as they leaped aboard after an all-out sprint down the concourse. Eventually, the door closed, the jet-bridge retracted, and we were set, sealed in for the long flight west.

As we pushed back and started our taxi, I did a pass through the cabin to prepare for takeoff. My focus was on empty cups and seat belts, so mostly what I saw were elbows and laptop keyboards and wristwatches and cufflinks, and then I got to the guy in 4B, who must have been one of the runners, because 4B had been empty last I'd seen, and for some reason I looked at his face and not his elbow, and I saw who it was, and everything stopped, and I started to say something from the shock alone but caught myself because he didn't see me, and my next thought in a flood of them was that I didn't want to be seen.

Not like this. Not by him.

I spun around and lurched back to the galley, where Tristan was organizing the catering cart. "We don't have enough beer," he said. "They never give us enough beer. We'll be lucky if we make it to the Mississippi on what they gave us."

When I didn't respond, he looked up at my face. "What? What's the matter?"

I could barely get the words out. My feet felt heavy, because all my blood had drained down and collected there. "I can't work up front on this leg. I have to go to the back."

"Why? What's going on?"

"The passenger who just boarded, the one in 4B, I know him. I can't work the cabin with him there."

" 'Him'?" He turned instantly puckish. "Let me see, who could that be? Ex-husband?"

"You know I don't have one of those."

"Old boyfriend who came home to find you in the shower with your neighbor's husband? That could be fun. Or maybe *you* came home and found *him* in the shower with your neighbor's husband. Even more fun, for me at least, although probably not for you—"

"Tristan, please stop." I was unhinged enough that he knew I wasn't joking. My heart was up inside my skull, pounding against my eardrums. "I can't believe this.

Where's the . . ." I reached for the manifest, but he grabbed it first and scanned it. With the start of a big grin, he stepped outside the galley and checked out 4B. "Oh, my God. I can't believe it. Dear, he looks just like you."

I pulled him back in. He looked at me with eyebrows raised. "James P. Shanahan?"

"Jamie. He's my brother." Maybe I could sit in the lav for four hours. "Where did he come from? He wasn't there earlier."

"He was a runner." He clipped the manifest back to the wall. "And an upgrade. He showed up at the last minute."

"Figures. He never could be on time for anything. What is he doing here? He lives in New York."

"How would I know? He's your brother. Wait, you didn't know he was in Boston?"

"No."

"Oh." He wasn't sure what to make of that, and I didn't feel like expounding. "Well, what are you doing here? Go out and say hello."

"I can't."

"Why not? Don't you want to see him?"

"It's more the other way around." I folded my arms across my chest and backed as far as I could into the galley. "He doesn't know I'm a flight attendant. The last he heard, I had left my job at Majestic and was looking for another management assignment."

"You've been flying for almost two months, in training for almost as long. Don't you two talk?"

I reached down and straightened my name tag. "Not lately."

"I see." He started setting up his clipboard to take breakfast orders. "How long?"

"Eight months. Since the day before Christmas."

"Christmas was ten months ago. Hello? What's going on with you two?"

"It's a long, boring story." Which I didn't want to discuss. I was busy thinking ahead, trying to figure out how to work the entire flight without ever leaving the forward galley. Maybe the captain would let me sit in the cockpit for the duration of the flight. "Tristan, would you do the safety demonstration?"

"Under one condition."

"Anything." The thought of standing in front of my estranged brother demonstrating how to buckle a seat belt made my skin vibrate.

"You have to promise to tell me that long, boring story the second we get the chance."

"Fine. Done."

"You also have to do color commentary for the briefing. I can't do both."

I was mildly concerned that Jamie would recognize my voice if I read the safety briefing, but there was only so much work I could weasel out of. Besides, no one ever listened, and he was no exception. As I recited the instructions, he kept his head down, working on his laptop.

When the demonstration ended, Tristan made a last sweep through the cabin to take drink orders, which I was supposed to have done. I peeked around the corner to look again. Jamie's hair was shorter than I remembered. We hadn't spoken for eight—ten months, but the last time I'd seen him had been six months before that. Could it have been that long? I stole another peek. When he lifted his eyes, I pulled back.

Seeing him after so much time, seeing that he had changed while I wasn't looking, even if it was just a haircut, caused a sharp pain in my heart. It made me wonder what else had happened without me. Not much had ever happened in his life that I hadn't known about.

The captain came on with his prelaunch announcement. Tristan arrived, bounced into the jumpseat next to mine, and strapped in.

"He's adorable, Alexandra. Just like you. Polite. Considerate—"

"You talked to him?"

"Yes, I did. I said, 'I love your suit. Is that Joseph Abboud, and did you know your sister is cowering up in the forward galley?' "

"You're such a comedian."

"His eyes are a really cool shade of dark blue. Yours are blue, aren't they?" He turned to me, leaning forward and away so he could check.

"Gray. Jamie looks more like my mom. I look like my father."

"He has that smoldering boy-next-door thing going on. How does one do that, I wonder? The boy-next-door thing I get, being from Wyoming. It's the smoldering I can't seem to master." Tristan reached up and adjusted the knot of his tie. "Does he work out?"

"I thought you were in a relationship."

"That doesn't mean I can't look." He smoothed his hair behind his ear. "Is he straight?"

"Happily married with two kids."

"To a woman?"

"Tristan—"

"What does he do?"

"He's an investment banker. Very successful for his age. Last I heard, he was up for partner at his firm."

"The plot thickens. Let me see if I can get this right." He tipped his head back and did the Freud chin stroke.

"He thinks you're still a master of the universe. Mistress of the universe? In the meantime, little brother has turned into a Wall Street whiz kid. He's never seen you in your cute little uniform, and now you have to serve him his first-class orange juice." He looked at me with unabashed delight. He had nailed it, and he knew it.

"Tomato juice," I said. "He likes tomato juice."

"If it wasn't you, dear, I would say this is all rather delicious."

"I don't know what to say to him."

"'Hello. Nice to see you. Oh, by the way, I'm a flight attendant now. Can I freshen that drink for you?'"

I brushed my hand across my skirt. A single wayward thread poked up to mar the smooth cotton expanse. What would I say to him? That I had become a flight attendant without telling him would be obvious. Not so that I was an investigator pretending to be a flight attendant, which, of course, I hadn't told him, either. Could I even tell him that? He was not one step behind but two, which is what happens when you don't speak to each other.

"Or we can cut two holes in one of the trash bags, and you can wear it over your head while you do the service. What are you so ashamed of?"

What a complicated question that was, made more so given who was asking. There was just enough arch in Tristan's tone to remind me he had an investment in my answer.

"I'm not ashamed to be a flight attendant. Great people do this job and love this job, including you, and so many people do it so much better than I do. It's not that. It's the going backward part. I used to run a big airport operation with hundreds of people reporting to me. I had responsibility and authority that I worked hard to get.

Now I don't. He'll think I gave up, that I got scared and threw in the towel, because . . . because that's how he thinks. Jamie is very driven. You gave up a management job. You know what that's like. Some people don't get it."

"I always preferred to think of it as making a better choice for myself."

Okay, here was the further complication. Jamie would think I had lost my mind if I told him the real choice I had made. It might be hard to convince him otherwise, since I spent the first five minutes of every day trying to convince myself that I hadn't.

"I don't know if Jamie would accept my choice."

"Does it matter?"

"What?"

"He's your brother, not your husband. It would be a shame if he didn't support you, but he's got his life, and you've got yours, right? At some point, even families end up going their separate ways."

"I guess so." We were in a lineup on the taxiway, so every once in a while, we would inch forward and stop. Mostly we were idling in one spot. "It's just . . . he's my only real family now."

"Yet you're not speaking. Isn't that interesting? What's it about, anyway?"

There was no point in trying to resist him. He would be relentless until he pried it out of me. "Jamie and his wife invited me to come down for Christmas dinner last year, and I didn't make it, and he got angry, and I got angry, and we never really made up."

"That's it?"

"It seemed big at the time." I stared down at the worn rubber floor covering, where a thousand flight attendants before me had rested their feet. "It has to do with my father."

"Doesn't it always? Go on."

"We hadn't had anything close to a family holiday gathering in ages. I've worked in airports forever. You know what that's like. Christmas at the airport."

"Or at thirty-five thousand feet."

"Right. But I didn't have a job last year, so I was excited. I bought gifts for the kids and for Jamie and Gina. I got them this really neat . . . anyway, I ended up sending the gifts."

"Why didn't you go? This doesn't sound like you at all."

"Because after I accepted their invitation, he invited my father."

"You said it was a family dinner. What am I missing?"

"I can't stand my father." The sharp pain in my heart was now a stabbing pain in my gut. "I can't remember the last time I was in the same room with him."

"My goodness, you have a lot of estrangement in your life. Are you sure you're not gay? Who in your family *are* you speaking with? Your mother?"

"My mother is dead."

"She is? Oh, dear. I'm sorry." He reached for my hand in my lap, gave it a quick squeeze, and let go. He always seemed to know just the right grace note to hit.

"It was a long time ago."

"How old were you?"

"Fourteen."

"And that made Jamie how old?"

I always had to think about it. For some reason, instead of just subtracting five from my own age, I always did it by taking the year she died and subtracting the year he was born. "Nine. He was nine."

"So you're his mom-sister. Complicated. Did he beat you?"

"Jamie?"

"Your father, ninny. Is that why you hate him? Or maybe he molested you."

"No. Nothing like that. My dad's a bully. He's intellectually abusive. He loves to club you in the head with his massive intellect. He convinced Jamie he was stupid."

"How stupid can he be if he's a big cheese in a Wall Street firm?"

"He's not at all stupid. He has a learning disability, and before it was diagnosed, he had a hard time in school. Really hard. My father used to make fun of him, of how hard he tried. Called him lazy, stuff like that."

"Sounds as if Daddy is the one who was fucked up."

"Once Jamie was diagnosed, he learned how to compensate. He might even overcompensate."

"Thus the whiz kid stuff."

"Yeah. But back then, he was just this little kid with no friends and no mother and a miserable, self-loathing prick for a father who got his kicks by picking on him. My stomach is seething right now just talking about it." Which was exactly why I hated rehashing the stuff.

"Why would Jamie invite his prick of a father over for Christmas?"

"I have no idea. Honestly, I don't know why he invited him."

"You didn't ask?"

"I got pissed off, and then he got pissed that I was pissed, and we had a big fight and hung up and never called each other back. This is the first time I've seen him since."

I felt the aircraft turn. We were in the pause between taxiing and blasting down the runway. The captain hit the gas, the aircraft surged, and the g-forces pushed us forward against our harnesses. I didn't much like flying backward. The two of us sat quietly as the aircraft lifted off and settled into a steady climb.

"I have the solution," he said finally.

"What?"

"Apologize."

"No way. I didn't do anything. I mean, I did, but . . ." That all came out much too fast, and I started feeling how I probably sounded—like a ten-year-old. "I know I need to, but I can't right now. It will turn into a big thing. Everything is a big deal between us these past few years. It takes so much time and energy and—"

"And he's not worth it."

"I didn't say that. What I'm saying is I can't deal with it right now."

"Then when?"

"It's on my list." I said it quietly. Maybe I really didn't want him to hear it.

He shook his head. "You're an idiot. Truthfully, Alexandra, I'm not trying to be mean, but who else do you have in your life? I know I'm wonderful, and Reenie is, too, and we love you, but shouldn't you have some connection to some member of your family? It's cold out there without them. Take it from someone who knows."

The aircraft was banking left, making a grand, sweeping turn west. It would be time to go to work soon.

"What," he asked, "did you end up doing for Christmas, anyway?"

"I ate a frozen pizza and half a pint of ice cream and went to the movies by myself."

"I rest my case."

chapter 9

TRISTAN WAS IN THE GALLEY, WORKING FROM the seating chart to prepare the drinks. I stared over his shoulder, bounced on the balls of my feet until my calves ached, and did nothing useful. "Do you have any celery? Jamie likes celery in his tomato juice."

"He didn't ask for it, but I'll check." He found a stalk, dropped it in, and placed the glass in the last empty spot on the tray. I stared at the drinks for half a second, then picked up Jamie's and left the rest. "I'll be back for those. Let me do this first."

I tried a couple of smiles, all of which felt forced and painful. I picked the one that felt the least cheesy. When I pulled up next to Jamie's seat wearing my forced and frozen smile, he didn't even raise his head.

"Jamie."

He glanced up and didn't quite register who it was leaning over him to deliver his drink. He reached for it with a polite smile that turned to stunned surprise.

He blinked at me, then looked up toward the galley, as if it would help his understanding to see precisely where I had just come from.

"What are you doing here? What are you wearing?"

Then I watched his eyes as they made the slow and

deliberate sweep from my face to my uniform to my name tag and back. The look that crossed his face in the moment of comprehension was pure reaction, a translation, stark and true, of the thoughts running through his brain. He recovered, but not in time. I hadn't seen my brother in ten months. The first thought he had when he saw me in my uniform was disappointment.

"Hi, Jamie." I crossed my arms as though I could hide my entire body behind the two bare lengths of skin and bone. Awkward was not even close to what I was feeling. He was strapped to his seat, bound by FAA rules to stay that way, so we couldn't greet each other as we might have before the great estrangement—with a hug. I didn't feel comfortable leaning down to kiss him, and shaking hands would have been beyond weird. So we did nothing, and the space between us might as well have been the space between Mercury and Pluto.

My smile was gone, but he offered an uncertain one that grew bigger when an idea came to him. "Wait. Is this one of those management walk-a-mile-in-my-shoes programs?"

"No. I'm your flight attendant, and I'll be serving you today."

"Oh." Now his smile was frozen.

"How are you, Jamie? How have you been?"

"Good. I've been good. When did you start—"

"A couple of months ago. How's Gina?"

"Good."

"The kids?"

"Great."

My next question would have been about what he was doing in Boston, but if I asked it, he might feel obligated to offer a lame excuse about why he didn't call while he was there, something he didn't want to say and

I didn't want to hear. But with that question in the way, I couldn't see past it to another. I smiled and nodded. He smiled and nodded and moved his juice a centimeter to the right.

"You changed your hair," he said, looking and then not looking at me.

"I did. Yeah." I reached up and pulled at the ends in the back. It hadn't occurred to me that I might look different to him, too. "Do you like it?"

"It's really different. I'm not sure I would have recognized you." He looked at me steadily for the first time, not at my uniform or my waistband or the tray table. I was the one who flinched.

"We should talk, Jamie, but I have to serve the other passengers first. I'll come back."

"Wait, are you . . . will you be in LA tonight?"

"I'll come back when I have a minute."

"Okay. I'm not going anywhere." He managed a real smile for the first time, one that helped me recognize that he was really in there. It was good to see, but I didn't have one for him, and I wasn't sure why.

Not being the best flight attendant ever to travel the skies, I'd had difficult trips, most of which were memorialized in my personnel file. But I'd never had one as tense and nerve-racking as this one. I mixed up meal choices twice. I had to be asked three times to bring creamer out to a coffee drinker. I actually dropped a sticky almond pastry onto a man's sleeve when the tongs slipped. Eventually, Tristan took pity on me and swapped positions, leaving me to hide out in the galley, where I hoped Jamie wouldn't come and find me, and I hoped that he would.

"Alex."

I turned, and he was standing there with his hands in

his pockets, his expression a little hopeful and a little nervous, and now what I thought about when I looked at him was last Christmas Day and my celebration of pizza, butter pecan, and self-pity. It made me feel vulnerable, and I couldn't have that, so I went with angry, which was why I couldn't make myself hug him. I knew he was waiting for a sign. That's the one he got. I felt crummy about it, but it was how I felt.

He tried to find a comfortable place to lean against and couldn't seem to. "I . . . uh, so I got promoted." He pulled his hand out of his pocket and offered his business card. I took it.

"You switched firms." I ran my thumb across the raised letters and the phone number I had never called. I wasn't the only one who had made changes.

"They offered me a partnership."

"A partnership. Wow, Jamie, that's . . . great. I know that's what you've been working for. Congratulations." I reached down to slide the card into my pocket and saw something on the back. A phone number he'd written in. "What's this?"

"Our new home number. I bought a new house."

"You did?"

"About six weeks ago. We just moved in."

Hearing that was like a blow to the chest. He had changed practically his whole life, and I had missed it. I couldn't tell if I was angry or sad or . . . I couldn't be angry. I had done the same thing. We had done it to each other.

Tristan slipped around behind Jamie and joined me in the galley. I introduced them, and they shook hands. "Alexandra told me you were onboard. I'm so delighted to meet you, Jamie."

"Alexandra." Jamie grinned at me. "I thought Mom was the only one who ever called you that."

"It's a wonderful name," Tristan said, managing to do a lot of bustling in a very confined area. "I see no reason not to use all of the syllables."

Jamie kept shifting from one side of the doorway to the other. "Am I in your way? I feel like I'm in the way. I'll go back to my seat."

"Not at all. I'm leaving now. Please, you two. As you were." He vanished and left us alone again, but not without a quick wink that only I could see.

Jamie reached up and scratched the back of his head, which changed his view just enough that he wasn't looking at me when he asked, "Do you want to get together tonight? I have meetings all day, but I could . . . I'd like to take you to dinner."

Instead of raising his head, he stared at his shoes, waiting for me to accept or reject his offer, and I remembered how after Mom died, he wouldn't let me buy him new shoes. He only wanted to wear the ones she'd bought him, so he walked around for months in sneakers that hurt, but he wouldn't let them go. It was completely unreasonable to be in such pain, and it made perfect sense, and for a second, as I stood watching him stare at his shoes, I wanted nothing more than to go sit with him and talk and try to put things back together, to make them the way they used to be. But I couldn't. I might be able to talk, but I didn't know how to make us the way we used to be, and I was afraid I would make it worse, because any relationship I had with him could not include my father, and I was afraid to ask about that.

I looked down at my own feet. We were both standing there in shoes that hurt because they didn't fit anymore, but we had no new shoes to put on.

"Jamie, I don't . . . I can't make it tonight. I'm sorry."

"Don't you think it would be good for us to talk?"

Now he was looking at me. I noticed as I turned away.

"Yes. I do want to talk." My hands were moving, and things were happening on the galley surface in front of me. I just wasn't sure what. "I can't do it tonight."

"Fine." He said it with bite, the verbal equivalent of a door slamming.

"I have to work."

"Doing what?" He may not have meant to put that sneer in his voice, but it was there and I heard it. It was all I heard.

I turned to him, one hand on my hip. "This is a job, Jamie. I do real work. I earn real money. It might not be something you can feel proud of, but I'm proud of the choices I've made."

"You chose this?"

"Jamie—"

"Come on, Alex. The last I knew, you were on a VP track at a major airline. Then you lose your job, and you show up serving me breakfast. I'm trying to understand what's going on with you. Not that you would ever tell me, anyway."

"I didn't lose my job."

"What?"

"I resigned my position at Majestic. It makes a difference."

"What makes a difference?"

"The way you say it. I didn't get fired, Jamie. It makes a difference to me."

"It makes a difference to you what I think? Since when?"

That was a dig that could not go undefended. "Maybe we can get together for dinner next time you're in Boston."

He looked at me, and he was angry and hurt, and he

seemed to feel betrayed with an intensity that went beyond this little encounter we were having. I was feeling all those things, too. He walked back up the aisle to his seat, buckled in, and spent the rest of the flight staring out the window. I spent the rest of the flight in the galley.

As he walked off in LA, he was polite and distant, and I knew it would be a cold day in hell before he ever called me from any city, and I wasn't even sure how it had happened.

chapter 10

THE GRASS WAS BROWN AND BRITTLE IN THE Hollywood Hills, and the trees looked exhausted.

"Must be a drought out here," I said, to no one in particular. No one in particular answered. Our cabbie, a man with only consonants in his name, spoke a weirdly paced version of English with the accents on the wrong syllables. He and Tristan were busy trying to locate the party. It seemed the number we had was not marked on the street where it was purported to be. Maybe it was one of those "if you have to ask, you don't belong here" deals.

I could have been still back at my hotel for how connected I felt to what was going on. After checking in, I had gone straight to the workout room, where my only company had been the droning television mounted in the corner. By the time I was finished pumping and running and lifting and generally trying to make myself stronger and better, I'd gone through six gym towels, three bottles of water, two and a half episodes of the *Knots Landing* marathon on TV, and I hadn't thought about Jamie once.

I'd left barely enough time to get back to my room and dressed for the party. I almost cried when I looked at myself in my party clothes. Like my hair, they were new. After buying hair color at the pharmacy, I had stopped in at the mall for some speed shopping. The store had been too hip and the saleswoman too young, which had resulted in a skirt that now felt too hip, too young, and way too tight. The stilettos exacerbated what seemed to me a serious proportion problem—my legs looked as if they took up a full two-thirds of my height. The top was a spaghetti-strap knit thing that had the coverage of a cobweb. A very short cobweb, which raised another objection. I rarely went out in public with my belly button showing. Thank goodness I had thrown in a long-sleeved sweater at the last minute. As I sat in the cab, I kept pulling at the sleeves until they fit over my hands like mittens.

"Pull all the way up the hill," Tristan told the cabbie. They had found a hidden driveway that looked promising. "Let's see if there's a house up there."

There was. As Tristan settled the fare, I dragged myself out of the cab and peered up into the purple dusk at the house. All I could see was a solid face of unvarnished concrete. Admittedly, my vantage point was not ideal, but it looked like a World War II bunker without the turrets, also without an entry mechanism, at least not one that I could see.

"This way, Alexandra." Tristan had located a trail. We dove through a hole in the trees and started up a series of terraced steps and stone walkways that wound in an ever-rising attitude through a landscaped garden with rocks and waterfalls.

"Whose party is this, anyway?" he asked.

"A producer of TV commercials," was what Dan had said.

"You look fantastic, by the way. I love that little skirt.

Truthfully, I'm surprised you have something like that in your closet."

"Is it too—"

"It's perfect. Relax. You look great."

"Thanks." I tried to believe him. Tristan could walk out of the Goodwill store looking like a German fashion designer. He had style to burn. He also had longer legs than I did and a fluid grace that seemed to have him gliding up the hill. I had to work hard to keep up and was glad when the front door, which was really a side door, came into view.

The guy posted there seemed to function as a maître d' but was shaped and dressed more in the style of a bouncer.

"Names?"

We gave them. The bouncer checked his laptop, which sat atop an official-looking podium. Temporary fixture or permanent installation of the house?

"You're not on the list."

"No," I said. "We wouldn't be, but I have the code word. Tuna casserole."

"Tuna casserole?" Tristan hooted. I hadn't previously shared that secret with him. "That's a bit prosaic, isn't it, for a Hollywood bash?"

Mr. Bouncer ignored the critique and tapped at the keys with heavy fingers. "Give me your names and e-mail addresses. Business address preferred."

"Why?" I asked.

"It's for the mailing list. For future events." Mailing list of business addresses. That was a heck of an idea on Angel's part. A way to stay in touch with her target market without the wives and other significants getting a clue. We both gave our OrangeAir addresses, and we were in.

We moved through the entryway, turned a corner into the main house, and both stopped at once to behold the breathtaking view. The façade of the house might have been dull and blank, but that just made for a more spectacular contrast. Beyond the concrete windowless wall was an airy and open cloudlike dwelling, an ethereal pod hovering above the dry hills. The entire back wall of the house was windows and doors, thrown open both in design and in fact to the deep blue amazement that was the Pacific Ocean at sunset.

"Wow." That was the only word I could come up with.

Tristan was even less original. "Ditto."

When I brought my focus inside the house, all I could determine was that the lights were low, the music was loud, and every woman who wasn't me looked like someone you'd see on a TV commercial. With their Botox faces and silicone breasts and augmented hair, they were the human equivalent of artificial plants. It was creepy.

"What would you like, love?" Tristan had guided me by the elbow to the bar.

"Club soda."

"Club soda and what?"

"Nothing." He placed the order, addressing the bartender as one service provider to another—politely. Would I prefer Perrier? That would be fine.

"I suppose not drinking is the wise choice." He offered the cold glass to me. "Whatever is going on between you and your brother, it's obviously knocked you for a loop. Trying to drown your sorrows will just make matters worse. That's something I would have done in my younger, wilder days."

"This has nothing to do with my brother."

"Of course it doesn't. And maybe someday I'll grow out of this gay thing." Something or someone behind me caught his eye.

"Come," he said, sipping his cocktail. "There are people you must meet."

We strolled out to the pool, a bright bar of turquoise that was languid and desultory in the evening air. In what seemed to me an engineering impossibility, the pool and the wide redwood deck were cantilevered straight out from the side of the hill.

"Tristan, oh, *my God!* I can't believe this." As usual, Tristan was swarmed by a group of women—flight attendants, no doubt—and I wondered if there was anyone who flew in the OrangeAir system anywhere whom he didn't know.

"I didn't know you were coming out," one of them burbled.

"Dear, I've been out for years."

They all laughed, and the typical cheek-to-cheek embraces ensued. Care was taken not to splash alcohol or flick cigarette ashes on the attire, which ranged from cocktail chic to funky tequila casual. The only thing they all had in common was a lot of skin showing, even though the setting sun was taking much of the warmth with it. I was glad I had my long-sleeved cover-up with me.

"Alexandra, these are some of your colleagues from LA." Tristan turned to present me. "*Girls,* this is my friend Alexandra. Everyone be nice to her. She's from the Boston base, and she's with me."

For a brief second, I was center stage, and I had exactly what I wanted. This was my chance to meet and get to know some of the LA crowd. This was my chance to hang around and listen to gossip, to be the eager

DustBuster when the dirt on Angel started flying. What I had in front of me was an opportunity.

"Um . . . hello."

I got an array of tepid greetings and casual nods. I couldn't think of what to say, and before I knew it, they had turned their attention back to Tristan. After a few minutes of floating and bobbing around outside the circle, I realized the window had closed. There was also no way to siphon energy away from the Tristan vortex. He enjoyed his place in the center too much.

I was looking around for a less-intimidating situation, when I was very nearly run over by a stout, balding guy with one too many buttons open on his black silk shirt and what looked like a large, yellowing mammal's tooth dangling from a leather thong around his throat. He introduced himself as Tony Something, the actor—not *an* actor. He was vaguely familiar. What does one say to actors? I couldn't remember ever meeting one.

"So, Tony, where do I recognize you from?"

He reeled off a few titles, one or two of which I'd heard of, then launched into a few questions of his own. "I heard your friend say you were a flight attendant from Boston."

"I am."

"For OrangeAir?"

"Yes."

"Thank you, Jesus." He pushed his palms together and let loose with a long sigh that appeared to relieve some serious pent-up tension. Then he took me by the wrist and guided me rather insistently to a more secluded spot. I pulled my arm away and stopped before we were too secluded.

"Is there something I can do for you, Tony?"

"I need help. I lost my password." He had this curious

lockjawed way of speaking. His mouth didn't open much when he talked.

"What password?"

"I know you gals have rules, but I didn't give it to someone. I didn't sell it. I lost it. I think I wrote it on the back of one of my scripts and it got thrown out. I've got so many goddamned sign-in names and passwords. Who can remember all that stuff? You know what I mean?"

I was beginning to. Flight attendants . . . Boston . . . secret passwords. He thought I was one of Angel's "gals." Cool.

"Anyway, how can I get it? Or get another one. Or whatever it is you gals do in a situation like this. I'll pay the charge. I just really need it soon, you know what I mean? If I can't sign in, I can't get laid, and if I can't get laid, you gals don't get paid."

That was almost too much information to deal with in one blast. I had to break it down. "I can get that process started for you, Tony, but I have to ask some questions first. This isn't how we usually do things."

"Absolutely. Anything. Can't be too careful, right?"

He took a step back and inhaled deeply while staring at a spot on the ground. Some kind of acting exercise, no doubt. While he did that, I worked on my Perrier and tried to plot a course that would get me the most information for the least amount of suspicion. The key would be to get him talking. So far, that hadn't been much of a challenge.

He looked up at me with a quick nod. "Go ahead."

"How long have you been a client?"

He peered up into a palm tree. "About . . . five months. First part of the summer. I was doing a location shoot."

"In Boston?"

"Yeah. I was flying every week, back and forth. LA–Boston. Boston–LA. I gotta tell you, it was killing me. But I had to be back here for some redubbing. Meanwhile, back in Boston, they keep cutting my lines. My agent is all the time telling me, 'Tony, stop kvetching. At least you got work.' It was a bad time for me. A lot of pressure. You girls saved my life."

"How did you hear about us?"

"From a friend of mine in New Hampshire who knows one of the girls. She got him started, and he told me about it."

"What's her name?"

"I don't know her name. She was one of the pool girls."

Pool girls?

"Why would you want to know that?"

Uh . . . "Because we give bonuses to women who recruit new clients. It sounds as if she deserves one. Besides, she obviously has a pitch that works. I'd like to hear it."

"Listen, you don't need much of a pitch to sell this thing. I wish I had a piece of it. You must be raking it in."

"We do all right."

"I'll bet you do. I can't wait to get back in the saddle, if you know what I'm saying. This password thing has got me crazy. In fact"—he stepped back and looked me up and down, as if it had just occurred to him to see who he was talking to—"are you available tonight, hon? Are you on the clock?"

He reached out and covered my left breast with his right hand. My belly button snapped back against my spine, and I was sure he would notice my eyes nearly bugging out of my head. He'd grabbed me with the hand that had been holding his drink. It was cold and clammy, and it was disgusting to have him touch me that way and beyond offensive that he would presume to do it—and I was working undercover trying to be exactly the person he thought I was.

"You're not my usual type," he said, moving his body up against mine. "But for something quick to take the edge off, I'd take a free taste from you."

Now, this was getting tricky. How to continue to extract information without kicking him in the balls? I smiled, calmly took him by the wrist, and gently removed his hand. "Sweetie, I'm fully booked tonight, and why in the world would I give you anything for free?"

"To keep me from switching. Aren't you here for the countermeasures?"

Countermeasures. He must have played a soldier in his last role.

"I just thought you girls from Boston might want to throw a counteroffer on the table. Like the airlines do it. Instead of triple miles, I get triple pussy. You know what I'm saying? Or those phone companies. Each one offering better and better deals, trying to get my business. I love being the prize."

He was a prize, all right, and what was he talking about? "I need to know what I'm competing against. What kind of deal are they offering?"

"Two freebies with any girl of my choice in any city I choose, even in LA. They don't have that rule about not doing it at home. I get more if I can get my friends to switch."

Doing it at home . . . even in LA . . . which must have meant . . . *ahhhh* . . .

"Switch from Boston to LA?"

"Didn't I just say that?"

Tristan had been right about a new group starting in LA, only it wasn't Angel. It was a competing group and they were going after her business.

"Do you want to make me an offer, hon? I've got a few minutes."

"In Boston, Tony, we believe the quality of our service should be enough to keep you in the fold. With us, you know what you're getting. Besides . . ." This time, I made the move. I took his drink to free his hands, then pressed my body against his, making sure to touch all the right spots. "If you leave now, you'll never know what sort of countermeasures we came up with."

He put his hands on my back. I felt his chest—and other parts—expand as he breathed through his nose, which was mashed against my throat. Then I squeezed my hand up between us, stepped back, and handed him his drink. "But if you want to switch, I understand completely, and I'll hold off on getting that password."

"No." He wiped the moisture from his forehead. "Don't hold off. I haven't signed up with them yet. I'll take the password. What do I need to do?"

"Just answer a few more questions for me."

chapter 11

My first stop after Tony was the bar, where I knocked back not one but two postfondling margaritas on the rocks. No salt. It was just something, as Tony had suggested, to "take the edge off." I could still feel his cold, grubby fingers grasping at me. I felt like dousing the area with alcohol to disinfect. Gin would have done nicely for that purpose.

So, Angel had some competition. That certainly thickened the stew. According to Tony, there was a group at the party from Boston, sent out to protect the business interests of Angel's East Coast operation. He'd also said the LA women had controlled the guest list and stacked it with clients of the Boston ring, mostly using names brought in by defectors from Angel's group. This wasn't an introduction party; it was a mass conversion effort. I wondered briefly how the Boston crew had gotten in, then realized how easy it had been for me to get the password.

I took my third margarita with me and started wandering, being invisible and eavesdropping on conversations. At one point, I walked past the front entrance and the massive foyer where the bouncer-greeter remained steadfastly at his post, even though the incoming crowd had dwindled to nothing. He looked bored. In fact, was that . . . I circled around to get a better look at his computer monitor. Yes, he was playing solitaire. As I watched him, an idea formed somewhere in my fast-pickling brain. I had to wait a few moments for it to float to the surface so I could pull it out and check it over and see if it made sense. It seemed to.

I should steal the guest list.

If the attendees at this party were, indeed, members of the high-roller, Hollywood target market with bulging frequent flier accounts, money to burn, and an enduring interest in extracurricular activity on the road, then a list of their names and addresses was a list Angel would want, especially if they were clients being targeted for conversion away from her group. The names of hooker recruiters and potential recruitees from either coast certainly would be of interest.

I watched for a few moments from the doorway and tried to formulate a plan. Perhaps I could distract the big guy with one hand while downloading, copying, and swiping the file with the other. That might have worked if the guy had been Tony, and it assumed there was even a disk available.

I sipped my drink and tried to discern if I was in any condition to pull it off. I was a little thick by then, but I had all my senses. I could still taste; it was just that all I could taste was tequila. I could still hear, mostly the beat of the music, and I could still walk straight if I really, really concentrated hard. I thought I could pull it off, but I wasn't positive. What if I got caught? How would I explain? What would I tell Tristan? I should never have started drinking. I knew that, and I had done it anyway. I drained the glass and started back to the bar to think it over some more.

"*Excuse* me. *Walk* much? God, watch where you're going."

I had bumped into someone. The bumpee twisted in my direction and flipped her hair across my drink. It was Sally, the woman I had photographed with Angel in Pittsburgh. She was standing with Ava and Sylvie and Charlotte and Claudia. Angel's crew was here, after all, looking scathingly gorgeous in skirts that were micro, boots that were tall, and bell-bottoms lashed low on slithery, tattooed hips.

Having already brushed me off once, Sally had turned away, which meant I was staring at the back of her head. It seemed she hadn't been quite so impressed with my new look as Dan might have suggested and I would have liked. I was trying to figure out an approach, when Sylvie, who couldn't have been a day over twenty, gave me a genuine, if fleeting, smile. It wasn't much, but it was all I needed.

"Excuse me, you're Sylvie, aren't you?"

"Yes. What's your name?"

"I'm Alex Shanahan. We work together. I mean, we've never actually flown . . . I'm based in Boston. You are, too, aren't you? I'm new. I've only been flying about six weeks. I don't know anyone at this party. I thought I recognized some familiar faces over here. May I join you?"

Now all in the tight nest were staring, with expressions that ranged from completely blank to insulted by my presence. They seemed none too happy with Sylvie, either, who somehow got shuffled to the back of the group.

"We know who you are." That was Sally again, addressing me as if I were a wad of wax she'd just pulled from her ear. "No, you cannot join us. This is a private thing." She started to turn away but didn't. "By the way, did you do that yourself?"

"What?"

"That." She pointed at my head. "You colored your own hair, didn't you?"

My hand started automatically toward my head, an instinctive flinch of self-defense.

"Nice outfit," she said. "It's so . . . young. Is this a second career for you?" Her Greek chorus snickered and twittered. She leaned down and whispered, "You shouldn't try so hard. It's unbecoming."

I wanted to make my skirt longer and my heels lower. I wanted to stretch my sweater down to my knees. But what I wanted more than anything was to come up with a bitingly clever, equally demeaning remark that would cut her down to size, or at least keep me from sinking into the hole that was opening in the floor beneath me.

"Here you are, dear." I heard Tristan's voice just as I was about to disappear completely. "What are you doing over here with these toxic bitches?" He draped a protective arm across my shoulders. "I see the dirty girls are here. What is this, a call girl confab? A hooker hoedown? A prostitute parlay? Where's your Queen of Dairy?"

Sally seemed to have lost her flair for slashing insults, because all she could come up with was, "Fuck off, Tristan."

He laughed. "So, so clever, Sally, dear. Come, Alexandra. Did she touch you? Maybe we can find some moist towelettes."

We turned and made our retreat, winding through the crowd. "Oh, my God. What were you doing with them? Didn't I tell you never to go near that crowd?

They are evil, wicked women, and I take it your friend didn't show up?"

"My friend?"

"The passenger you came here to meet."

"Oh, him." That fictitious fellow. Just one of my lies. "No. I haven't seen him."

"Poor dear." He smiled. "I'm sorry. Come out and be with us, the only fun, interesting, and interest*ed* people at the party, although most of them are wasted by now. But that shouldn't be a problem. So are you."

We walked outside past a large, raised platform that was crowded with dancers. Off to the side was a grouping of lawn chairs. Lounging among the chairs and on the grass like a pride of inebriated lions were beautiful young men, all talking at once—to each other, to cell phones, to people on the dance floor. Surrounding them were empty bottles and used glasses and ashtrays piled high. They were, as Tristan introduced them, his gay LA friends.

They adopted me immediately, and for the first time all night, I started having a good time. They wanted to know about me—if I liked living in Boston, if I was straight or lesbian, if I had seen much of LA, if I liked flying, and whether I wanted to dance. At first I didn't. Too depressed. But they kept shuttling over drinks from the bar and stroking my ego, and I started feeling better, and eventually that writhing mass on the dance floor started to look like fun, and the next time one of them grabbed my hand to pull me up there, I went.

I climbed up on the platform, where the temperature must have been fifteen degrees hotter than on the ground. I pulled my sweater over my head and tossed it . . . somewhere.

They all took turns dancing with me, but when my

last partner left, I didn't want to go. I stayed in the middle of the floor and felt the crowd throb around me. It was like a human heart, pushing its raw, sweaty, sexual energy—the party's lifeblood—out into the night. People danced in pairs, in threesomes, in groups, and in every permutation of man/men and woman/women. Bodies rubbed, hands roamed, boundaries evaporated.

I was far from home dancing under the stars. I was among people I didn't know, doing things I wouldn't normally do. When someone came up from behind and put his hands on my hips, I let him because it made me feel connected in all that disconnectedness. I felt anonymous and intimate at the same time, which was exactly right for me at that moment, so I put my hands over his, closed my eyes, and let the music come inside. Soon my body was twisting and shimmying and slithering in ways it should never have been able to. I took his hands from my hips, raised them over my head, and turned, and when I opened my eyes, the music came to a crashing halt, at least in my head, because it wasn't someone I didn't know smiling back at me.

It was Angel.

I let go of her hands and stepped back, and all the places where she had touched me started to burn.

She tossed her head like a stallion and laughed. "What's the matter, sugar? You look so surprised."

In a cacophony of sounds and sights and smells and tastes, she was the most vivid of all, mainly because there was so much of her. Up close, she was several inches taller than I had expected and bountiful in every sense. Handfuls of platinum blond hair framed her face and cascaded glossily down past her shoulders. Her breasts, full and meaty and freckled, overflowed the low-cut top that tried to hold them back. Her waist was small, her hips generous, and all the features of her face boldly outlined—eyes in black liner and mascara and lips in bright red.

It was hard to break through the blur of tequila except to know that she was there, right in front of me, and she'd caught me at exactly the wrong moment.

"Sweetie . . ." She reached out and took my hands in hers, then curled to the left and winked back at me over her shoulder. "Are you following me?"

I started to move again to the beat, mostly because she did but also because if I didn't, my nerve endings, already crackling and hot, might overheat and melt me into a puddle.

"I saw you in Pittsburgh, you know." My stomach clenched, thinking about her staring in the dark through that camera lens. She couldn't have seen me. She couldn't have. "I saw you at the airport with your little friends, Tristan and Irene."

"I was working a trip," I said. It was hard to talk in the crowd. I kept getting bumped and shoved, and we had to lean into each other to hear. "Why would you notice who I'm with?"

"I notice everything. What I don't see, people tell me. What they're telling me about you is that you're asking a lot of questions, trying to get close to me." She put one hand back on my hip and started an upward slide to forbidden territory. Unlike Tony the Actor, she knew how to keep her eyes where it counted—on mine. "Do you want to get close to me, Alex Shanahan?"

I did a quick spin, pivoting away from her. When we were facing each other again, I moved in closer but took both her hands in mine before she could put them where she wanted.

With no hands for grabbing, she began to use the rest

of her body, rubbing her hips against mine. "You don't like to be touched, do you?"

"Not without permission."

"I don't ask permission." She snapped her hands away and, before I had a chance to react, clamped long fingers around my wrists, holding them with just enough pressure to make me aware of the bones underneath. She paused for a few hip swivels, long enough to let the new dynamic sink in. Then she pulled me close enough to put her lips to my ear. Her breath against my skin was so hot it felt cold. The smell of her perfume, sweet and heavy, floated around us. "Do you want to get close to me?"

The music was so distant that all I could hear was my breathing overlapping with hers, and then all I could feel was the tip of her tongue, wet and warm, tracing the edge of my ear. I tried to turn my head away, to fight her off, but she was strong. She held me where I didn't want to be, which seemed to excite her. I stopped straining, because I could tell it was what she wanted. I also knew I couldn't win.

"This is close enough," I said.

She backed a step away, and we were facing each other again. "No one gets close unless they're invited, sugar, and someone like you with your tight-assed, don't-touch-me-I'm-so-much-better-than-you attitude will never be welcome in my company. So, fuck off."

When she finally released my hands, my fingers were numb.

Of the several thousand things that bothered me about the encounter—hell, about the whole evening—I realized as I stood and watched that what bothered me most was what Angel was doing now. She was dancing with her eyes closed, so certain was she that she could put her tongue in my ear and I wouldn't come after her.

Just before she was about to disappear into the crowd, I stepped forward, reached in, and pulled her out by her very solid upper arm. I pulled her close enough to whisper in her ear, which I could do if I stood on my toes. I left out the licking part.

"I know why you're here tonight, Angel. I know all about what these girls in LA are doing. They want to put you out of business, and it would be my pleasure to help them, unless—"

She tried to pull away, but I squeezed tighter, ignoring for a moment the pain in my fingers as the blood rushed back in. The two of us stood perfectly still, a calm center in the middle of that surging dance floor.

"I know you've checked me out," I said. "I'm not a hooker, and I don't want to be a hooker. I'm a tight-assed, keep-your-fucking-hands-off-me management type with homemade hair and enough skill and experience to fix your little business problem here in LA without breaking a sweat. Or I could do the same for the women out here. You decide. But don't take too long, because, like you, my services go to the highest bidder."

I let go of her arm. She said nothing, just drifted back into the crowd wearing an enigmatic smile that said either *I'm going to kill you* or *I'll give you a call.*

"What are you doing here by yourself? What's with all the hand wringing?" Tristan had come up behind me. Both my wrists were adorned with flame-red bracelets. Holding them as if they were eggs, he inspected the damage. "What is this? What happened?"

"Nothing." I tried to pull away, but he wouldn't let go.

"If you don't want to tell me, Alexandra, say so. Don't treat me as if I were your mother."

I looked at him and lied again. "I'm fine. Nothing happened."

He pulled his hands, with mine in them, almost imperceptibly toward his body, as if to recover from a blow to his midsection. "You should put something on them."

I turned him, looped my arm through his, and walked him off the dance floor. "I'm going back to the hotel."

"I'll go with you. We'll get a cab."

"I'd rather go by myself, if you don't mind. You look as if you're having a good time here. Is that all right? I'll get the bouncer guy to call me a cab."

"If that's what you really want. Just be careful. Do you have money?"

"I'm okay. Thanks."

He gave me a hug. "I'm sorry you didn't have a better time. Don't forget, we have an early call tomorrow morning. I'll see you then."

I made my way back through the house, past the bar, and to the doorway that led to the foyer. Bouncer Guy was alone, still absorbed in his game of solitaire.

I puffed myself up, wet my lips, straightened my teeny-weeny skirt, and strutted over to see him.

"Excuse me."

He straightened up and clicked the game off the screen. Behind it was what looked like an Excel worksheet, one filled with names and addresses. I could see the disk inserted in the A drive as I leaned closer to him. I took that as a sign that I was supposed to have a copy of that guest list.

"I wonder if you would call me a cab. I don't want to be here when the police show up."

His brow furrowed deeply. "Police?"

"There's a young woman in one of the bathrooms upstairs. It looks like an overdose. Someone is calling the police."

"Which bathroom?"

"I don't know. I'm telling you what I—"

He nearly knocked me flat as he bolted out of the entryway, pulling a cell phone from his pocket as he went. I swept around to the working side of the podium. The list was indeed in an Excel worksheet, saved in a file with the day's date. I steadied my hands, put my fingers on the keys, and went to work.

chapter 12

I HAD BEEN UP ONCE ALREADY WHEN THE ALARM went off, so the banging on the door confused me. If I had already gotten up, what was I doing still in bed?

"Alexandra, are you in there?"

It was Tristan. That much I knew. I lay on my back in total darkness, which confused me even more because my eyes were open. The one thing I was completely sure of was how much my head hurt. I reached up to touch it to see how it could be the size of a basketball and found a damp washcloth on my face. It had probably started out cold but was now tepid, cooked by the sick heat radiating from my skin.

More banging from the vicinity of the door, each loud blast registering in my entire body like a seismic event. "Wake *up*, girl."

I peeled the washcloth off and took a couple of daggers to the deep cortex as the light hit my eyes. *Make the pounding stop* was the only thought that emerged—the pounding on the door and in my head. Everything felt wrong. My heartbeat was too fast. My breathing was too shallow. I was cold, and I was hot.

"Alexandra, do I have to—"

I cleared the rubble from my throat. "I'm coming. Hold on."

"Thank God. If you're not completely dressed and ready to walk out this door, you are *so* in trouble."

It took all the focus I could gather to sit up and push myself to the edge of the bed, where I had to pause to see if I could stand up without throwing up. Tristan was yammering about being late, and I knew I was, and about people waiting, and I was sure that was true, but all I could think about was whether my legs would support me if I tried to stand up and walk across the room.

They did. I even managed the strength to turn the knob and open the door. The dead bolt was not engaged, and I had a fleeting thought about how stupid that was and how drunk I must have been to forget to lock it. Or not to worry enough to lock it.

The door flew open, and Tristan bolted into the room. He was in uniform, looking marvelously groomed for . . .

"What time is it?"

"It's five twenty-five A.M., and you're due to leave on the five-thirty shuttle to the airport. Seven thirty-five departure. Hello? Is any of this ringing any bells?"

He disappeared into the bathroom. When he came back, he had two of those squatty hotel room glasses filled to the brim with water. He balanced them both in one hand and carried my toiletry bag in the other.

"Sit down before you pass out again, and drink both of these. Every drop. Then go into the bathroom and throw some cold water on your face." He checked his watch. "We have exactly four minutes before the courtesy van leaves. Everyone is downstairs waiting, and they will leave without us and never look back."

I did what he commanded and watched as he shifted

into emergency mode, flying around the room, gathering my things. I was wearing my uniform except for my shoes, which was the good news. The bad news was it looked as if I'd slept in it, and I had a dim recollection of coming in last night, which had actually been this morning, and putting it on so I wouldn't have to worry about it later.

Tristan plucked my jeans from the floor. "You should have listened to me." He smoothed them on the bed and did a nice trifold. "I never should have let you come home by yourself." He fit the jeans into my crew kit and looked around the room. "Once you're past the point of no return, which you most definitely were, it's better to stay up all night." He spotted one of my shoes peeking out from under the bedspread and snatched it out. "We should have gone somewhere for eggs."

Drinking the water helped. Listening to him talk about eggs did not. I found my way to the bathroom, but when I looked in the mirror, more confusion. It wasn't me. It was my face with someone else's hair. No . . . wait. It *was* my hair. I had changed the color. Gone blond, sort of, in that color-out-of-a-box way, something Sally had been nice enough to point out.

"Fix your face at the airport, dear. We have to go. Chop-chop."

I took a last look in the mirror, trying to see myself objectively, as, say, a passenger might see me. I looked the way I always did when I'd had too much to drink. Bloodshot eyes floating on puffy dark pillows underneath. In fact, my entire face was puffy except for where it flattened into a network of tiny lines at the corner of each eye. The lines were more pronounced today than I had ever seen them. *"Nice outfit. It's so . . . young for you."*

"What about this computer?" Tristan called in from the other room. "Is it one of those where I can close the lid and go? Did you leave it on like this all night?"

Computer? My computer was on? Why was it—

"No. Don't touch it." I flew out of the bathroom. From across the room, he turned and looked at me, then at the computer on the desk.

"I'm surprised you can move that fast. What have you been doing that you don't want me to see?"

There was no telling, but if I'd had it out and turned it on, chances were good I'd at least tried to record what—if anything—I had learned at the party. I powered down, folded the laptop, stuck it in my backpack, and then pulled it out again because I remembered something. Something important. I found my A drive, pressed the release, and the disk popped out.

"Well," Tristan said, "it's good to finally see a smile."

It was good to feel a smile again. The disk I had swiped from Bouncer Guy popped right out. I had the list from the party.

"Dear, did you know Angel would be at this shindig last night?"

"No. Why would you think that?"

"What did she say to you when she whispered in your ear?"

"I can't remember."

"I told you once, and I'll tell you again. Stay away from her. She's dangerous."

"Is she a lesbian?"

He laughed as he picked up my case, dropped it to the floor, and telescoped the handle. "No, dear. She's just always hungry, and she doesn't care who she eats. Are you ready? We are going to be so late."

✱ ✱ ✱

We weren't late. In fact, for all the pounding and worrying and racing around, we arrived early for the departure. While the rest of our crew went down to the lounge, Tristan insisted that we board the aircraft early. The only other person onboard was the captain, and the second he disappeared into the lav, Tristan grabbed me and pulled me into the empty cockpit.

"Here." He offered me the captain's oxygen mask. "Take this. Oxygen is great for a hangover."

"You've got to be kidding." I stared at the mask in his hand, the one they use for emergencies, like . . . when the plane is on fire. "I can't do that."

"You are *so* management." He peeked past me to check the cabin—empty—and lowered his voice anyway. "You need to be perfect today, Alexandra, and so far you're not off to a good start."

The urgency in his tone seemed to convey far more concern than was warranted by my headache. "Why perfect? What's going on?"

Again with a quick look over my shoulder. Nothing back there but a long, empty tube. "There's a ghost rider on this trip."

"What's a ghost—is that a check rider?"

"Undercover check rider is what that is. We don't know if she's in first or coach or what she looks like, and they might have put her on to watch you, so—" He pushed the mask toward my face. "It's up to you. Break a rule or lose your job."

This time, I checked for the captain myself, but he had taken a newspaper in with him. I grabbed the mask. This day was getting worse by the minute. "How do you know about this?"

"Oxygen? It's an old trick. Everybody knows—"

"How do you know about the check rider?"

"I told you. I still have connections from my management days. Hurry up before he comes back. Put it over your nose and mouth and breathe, just like the PA says."

I held the mask to my face and filled my lungs with pure oxygen. It made me dizzy.

"Again." Tristan had moved outside the cockpit door and closer to the lavatory so he could listen for the captain's progress. "Keep going. Take as much as you can."

I got in at least six good draws before we heard the toilet whoosh. Tristan shook his hand at me, motioning me to put the mask back. When I dropped it on the floor, he shifted, waited, and timed his move so that he was directly in front of the lav, hips forward. When the captain swung the door open, there was contact.

"Owww." Tristan grabbed his crotch and doubled over, providing enough of a distraction for me to get organized. "Oh, *shit,* that hurt."

"Didn't see you there, guy. Sorry." The captain shuffled around in the aisle, trying to get by, trying not to look closely at the injury he had inflicted. "You should put some ice on that, buddy."

I slipped out of the cockpit and met Tristan in the galley, where he was crumpled over with his hand over his mouth.

"Tristan, oh, my God. Are you all right?" I straightened him up, expecting his face to be purple. But when I saw his eyes, I reached back and closed the curtain behind me. His hand was over his mouth to cover the sound of his laughter.

"You scared me to death." I took a deep breath and longed for more pure oxygen. He looked at my face and tried to hold back the merriment that was clearly present in his eyes.

"What? What is so funny? Because I have to tell you,

I'm not finding much comical about this day so far."

The dam gave way, and peals of hysterical laughter burst forth. "You should . . . you should . . . have seen yourself. You looked like a crack fiend inhaling your first hit of the day. When that toilet flushed, your eyes got *huge.*"

I tried to keep from laughing. I didn't want to encourage him. He was, after all, laughing at me. But then he made his hand into a surrogate mask, clapped it over his nose and mouth, and showed me a look of wide-eyed alarm, all the while snorting ravenously and loudly sucking down the make-believe oxygen. He looked insane, and I felt ridiculous, and then I realized how absurd the whole situation was and felt a smile sneak up, then a laugh bubble over. I made the mistake of making eye contact with him, and pretty soon it was a full-blown, rolling giggle fest—as soon as one wave stopped, we'd look at each other and the next would begin. We leaned over and bumped shoulders and held our sides and tried to calm down and couldn't. I was out of control, and somewhere in the back of my swollen, hungover, throbbing brain, I thought it wasn't such a bad place to be.

I found a cocktail napkin, wiped my face, and counted it as a stroke of good luck that I hadn't had time to apply makeup. I tried to breathe deeply and make sure not to look at Tristan, who was also coming back to earth.

"Feeling better now?" he asked.

My back creaked, and my joints needed oiling, and my head would probably explode once we reached cruising altitude. But I had to get through this day. The oxygen helped a lot. Laughing helped more.

"Thank you," I said, "for everything."

Tristan put his arm around me and gave my shoulders a squeeze. "Go comb your hair. You look like shit."

chapter 13

BY THE TIME I CROSSED THE THRESHOLD AND slouched into my apartment in Boston that evening, I had been in constant motion for nearly twelve hours straight, much of that on an airplane doing six hundred knots from one end of the country to the other.

I dropped my bags in the middle of my living room, collapsed onto the couch, and let my head loll back onto the soft cushions. My apartment building was alive and noisy at that time of the evening. The heavy door downstairs swung open and slammed shut with dependable frequency as my neighbors came home from work. Next door, the baby cried, and I could smell the onions cooking in someone's dinner. I sat with my eyes closed, luxuriated in the deeply tranquil state of being still.

I had managed to get through the flight by maintaining a single-minded focus on not dropping, burning, melting, or breaking anything. But the brain at rest is fertile ground, and as I sat there, memories from the day and night before began to bubble up and come back in a flood of odd details. A palm beside the pool with one brown frond. A white napkin with a dark wet ring soaked into it from where the glass had been. My glass? The taste of tequila still on my tongue like a thick paste. Margaritas first, then shots while I was dancing. I couldn't remember going to bed.

But I remembered Angel.

I remembered the way she had looked at me and touched me and made clear that she took what she wanted. *Do you want to be close to me?* Those words whispered in my ear felt as if they were still there and would always be there, tattooed across my consciousness.

Then there was Jamie. The look on his face when he had seen my uniform, or at least recognized it for what it meant. Watching him as he walked away from me and never looked back. Most of all, the dull ache in my heart that I managed, like the pain in my chronically sore hamstring, simply to ignore. Or live with. Tristan was right. I needed my brother in my life. I needed to call him.

But first I needed to talk to Harvey, and before I talked to Harvey, I wanted to check out my prize. I booted up the computer and shuffled straight over to the A drive, where the disk containing the purloined data was still seated. When I pulled up the directory, it appeared that I had two files on the disk. I clicked on the one with last night's guest list.

When it popped up, I smiled. All the names were there. They weren't encoded or garbled or self-erasing, which I decided to count as a big plus. Included on the invitation list were not only names and addresses, almost all from the West Coast, but in many cases e-mail addresses as well. Mr. Bouncer did not seem to have been as meticulous in getting the women's information as the men's. The gender was predominantly male, and places of business were frequently included. The list included two hundred names, which didn't seem like so much in the harsh light of day. I tried the next file.

I didn't know if I had copied it from the laptop or if

it had already been on the disk, but it was large and helpfully labeled "Master List." The data in the master list were set up like the invitation list, with all the same information, but there were a couple of additional dimensions to the way these data were organized. I read the column headings, and as I began to appreciate what I had stumbled upon and what I could do with it, my brain function stirred awake.

I scrolled down, getting more excited with each page. By the time I reached the end, I was downright gleeful, primarily because it took so long to get there. There were more than thirteen hundred names in this file.

I picked up the phone and dialed Harvey.

"It's me," I said when he picked up. "I'm back, and I know how we're going to get her."

"Excuse me?"

"I've been going about this all wrong, Harvey. I know how we're going to get Angel."

"How?"

"Angel has a big problem, and I'm going to be her solution."

chapter 14

HARVEY'S HOUSE IN BROOKLINE WAS LIKE THE suits he wore—formal for the rest of the world but comfortable for him. Also like his suits, if you looked closely, you could see the seams coming apart or the creases fraying from too much wear.

We were in his office, which was the only room in which I ever felt comfortable. That wasn't because it was so cozy. Harvey's office was like an elegant reading room in a venerable old library—darkly paneled, highly burnished, and plush with an overstuffed wingback chair, a thickly upholstered couch, and a deep burgundy and blue rug. I always had the urge to whisper there. But I liked it better than his kitchen or his bath or bedroom, because that's where he kept all the trappings of his illness—pill bottles, heating pads, and walking aids—that he didn't want anyone to see.

The only personal item he seemed to want anyone to see was the lovingly framed picture in his office of the dark-eyed woman with the luxurious auburn hair. She sat on his desk with a sweet smile, looking like the loving wife who would come through the door any minute to fix his favorite dinner and tend to him in his illness.

She wouldn't.

It was a picture of his ex-wife, Rachel, and though he might have thought of her often, he talked about her rarely. It took him a long time before he would tell me their story.

He'd met her years before when he traveled to Boston on an insurance fraud case. Rachel was his contact at the insurance company. He fell in love, they married, and she dumped him seven years later, because, he insisted, he snored and enjoyed *Diagnosis Murder.* She had moved out, leaving him in the duplex in Brookline they had shared. When I asked why he didn't go home to his people, especially since he was bound to need more help at some point, he said he couldn't bear to leave the city, the neighborhood, the very house where he'd passed his happiest years. But I knew the real reason he stayed. Rachel lived nearby, and on a good day, he caught a glimpse of her. On a very good day, he saw her without her new husband.

"This list is extraordinary." He leaned back in his executive swivel chair. I had printed out a hard copy of the master list from LA and laid it out for him on his big desk. Even with a small font, it made for a thick stack of pages. "All of these men are patrons of prostitutes? Is that what you believe?"

"Patrons or potentials. According to the column headings, they're either clients of Angel's or clients and potential clients of the LA crew. Look, there are even notes showing which of Angel's clients have already been converted."

"Where did you get this?"

"The party was put on by the LA women. They were taking names at the door on a computer. It must have been one of theirs, because the lists were in it."

"It is fascinating, but what value to us and the case? I

know I need not remind you that these clients are no doubt passengers and therefore—"

"Off limits. No, you need not. I have a different idea. I want to use Angel's adversity to our advantage." I was pacing around Harvey's furniture, trying to burn off the nervous energy that comes from the birth of a bright new idea.

"How?"

"Angel was not at that party last night to expand her horizons. She was there protecting her interests. She wasn't there to recruit. She was there to scope out the competition."

"Please do not suggest to me that you want to open a new front on this investigation."

"No, I want to finish this one. What I learned last night was that Angel has a business problem."

"It would seem so."

"People with business problems need business strategies to solve them."

"Ideally."

"Where do you get a strategy if you can't think one up yourself?"

"Consultants."

"Exactly." I stopped and presented myself for inspection. "You're looking at Angel's new management consultant."

"Oh." He leaned all the way back in his chair. "Oh, my."

I never seemed to get the reactions I expected from Harvey. This idea had rejuvenated my confidence about the case, but he seemed intent on being ambivalent. I came around the couch and sat in the chair in front of his desk. "That's how I'll get close to her. I'll pitch myself as someone who can help save her business, and

I'll use these names as a teaser. She'll want those names, Harvey."

"Dare I ask, what do you know about her business?"

"All businesses are the same when it comes down to it. She's losing market share to a start-up that is offering promotional rates and discount services to undercut her pricing structure. A problem," it occurred to me, "not unlike one of the many currently roiling the airlines. That's how I thought of my strategy."

"You have a strategy?"

"A frequent fucker program."

"Excuse me?"

"A frequent fucker program. That's the solution to Angel's problems and to ours. It will revolutionize her business."

"I thought our goal was to destroy her business."

"Yeah . . . well, it is. But I have to make her think I'm helping her. I'm a consultant. I have to come up with a strategy, which I have. I just need your help in fleshing out some of the details. I was hoping we could brainstorm. Also, we need to put it in a PowerPoint package so I can present it to her."

"Oh, my word, you must be joking."

"Let me explain it to you before you reject it outright. Angel needs a way to retain her women, especially the top earners, and a way to keep her clients loyal to her. The frequent fucker program solves both problems at once."

"Could we perhaps refer to it as something else?"

"Okay, the FFP. We create a loyalty program with tiers, just like the airlines. Clients will earn points in the program by buying services. The more they buy, the more points they earn. The more points they earn, the more hooked in they are to the provider of those services. It's like crack. Once you start, you're in."

"What are the points for?"

"Free stuff. Prizes. Same as any other program."

"What sorts of prizes did you have in mind?"

"What do you think? Providers of air service offer free trips. Providers of sexual services offer free f—"

"What would keep the women in LA from just copying it?"

"That's the genius of this plan, if I do say so myself. Angel has something they don't have: history."

"History?"

"She has records of all her clients' activity to date. She can award points and status retroactively based on prior transactions. She'll lock in the current customers so they won't leave, and she might get back some who have left her. She can throw up a limited-time offer. Come back within the week, and get credit for all your prior activity. I love this plan."

"The LA group could create history, could they not?"

"It's not the same. Harvey, you have no idea how much people like the concept of a loyalty program. It's like Dan said: don't fuck with market forces. Use them."

"This was Dan's idea?"

"Sort of. He started me thinking about it."

He offered one of his stingy smiles. "Why does that not surprise me?"

"The best part is, it works not only for Angel but for us, too."

"How?"

"I'll insist on meeting her Web master to develop the specs for the program. I think the Web master is the key to getting Angel."

"Web master? She has one of those?"

"She has a Web site. That means someone built it and

maintains it. I suppose it's possible she does it herself, but Irene and Tristan seem to think she's borderline illiterate. My guess is she has someone who does it for her. If the scheduling is done through the Web site, then probably payments are as well, which is the jackpot for us. That's how we prove that there is payment for sex. All that information would reside right there with the Web master."

He shoved out his lower lip and tapped on the temple of his glasses. "Do you really think she will hire you?"

"We'll see. I planted the seed with her last night. The fact that she was out there with her crew tells me she knows she has a problem."

"I am hesitant to implement a change like this so close to the end of the case."

"Harvey, we are nowhere near the end of this case, and I have already wasted a lot of time trying to fit in with a group of women who will never accept me. I don't have the goods to be a hooker. I don't look like them, I don't think like them, I don't dress like them, and I'm too old. But this—" I reached over and drilled the stack of pages with my index finger. "This is the kind of stuff I'm good at. I have years of business experience, and so do you. This we can do on our terms."

"Very well. If you think you can do it."

"I know I can do it. I got some stuff at the party, new intelligence." I pulled my backpack up off the floor, unzipped it, and started digging for my notes. "Have you been able to do the top swapper analysis?"

"I am still waiting for the schedules. Apparently, they are quite large."

"What about the Robin Sevitch murder?"

"I have done a bit of research, which I can give you. Her death was quite violent. She was beaten to death by a homeless man. One of the detectives who worked on the case is supposed to call me."

"Here they are." I pulled out my notes—four pages from my small notebook and two cocktail napkins, all wrinkled and some stained. My notebook hadn't fit into my little skirt, so I'd ripped out some pages and stuck them in my waistband. When I ran out, I had apparently switched to cocktail napkins. I spread everything across the desk and smoothed them flat. It was the first time I had looked at them since I'd written them, and it was deeply disconcerting to see words and phrases written in my hand to which I felt not even the barest cognitive connection.

"What are those?"

"I did an interview at the party."

What was even more disturbing was to follow the change in my handwriting, the slow loss of function, the slow *surrendering* of function from early to late in the evening. I stared at the completely illegible scratches on the last napkin. How had I become the person who had written that?

"Tony" was written on the first loose page. I saw his name, and I remembered his seedy smell. I shivered all over again at the feel of his cold, fumbling hands through the thin knit tank top. But I felt something else, too, as I looked over the notes—a stirring of anticipation, because Tony, a client of the ring, had given me the name of the Web site he accessed to schedule dates, along with his sign-in name.

"Harvey, type this Web address into your computer."

He swiveled around to face the typewriter stand on which he had replaced his IBM Selectric with an old and slow desktop PC. He used his index fingers to tap himself into his browser. I read the address, and he typed that in. I walked around to see just as the error message popped up on the screen.

"It does not work."

"Try it with 'dot org' and 'dot net.'"

He did. "Nothing."

I went back to the source documents and studied them again. Tony the Actor's information had come earlier in the evening, so it was perfectly legible. The Web address was there, but so was something else that caught my eye.

"He said something about pool girls."

"Who?"

"This guy I was talking to. He thought I was a hooker. He mentioned pool girls."

"Pool girls? Such as cabana girls?"

"I don't know. I wonder if it was something about the pool at the party?" I tried to think back to my conversation with Tony. There was so much about it I didn't want to remember; it was hard to pick out the wheat from the chaff.

"Do you have the Web site?"

I found the address and read it off again, this time assuming the *i* was an *l*.

"That one works," he said, leaning in to study the results.

I went over and insinuated myself in front of his keyboard. "Scoot over."

The two of us stared, Harvey sitting and me crouching next to him, at a screen that was blank except for a sign-in box and a password box, just as Dan's contact had said it would be.

"I have the sign-in name." I found it on one of my wrinkled pages. "It's TonyThesp001. But that doesn't help us much without the password, and this guy had no password. That's why he was talking to me."

We stared for a few more seconds. I knew very little when it came to what was behind the slick surface of the Internet. Harvey knew less. But I knew someone who could help.

"Harvey, would you be averse to me bringing someone in who might be able to help us on this Web stuff?"

"Help how?"

"He's a hacker. We worked on that case down in Miami earlier this year. He's phenomenal. He helped me break it."

"What can he do for us?"

"First of all, he can get us past this screen. That would be a snap. Maybe he can track it all back to the Web master. If he can, he might be able to suck everything we need right out of there without anyone ever knowing."

"Can we afford him? Our margins at this point are razor-thin."

"He worked for free last time. I don't want to ask him to do that again. I'll pay him out of my end."

"If you think he can help, call him, by all means. You do not have to pay from your share, but keep in mind that we are time-constrained."

"I know. That's one reason we need him. He's fast." I checked my watch. It was after eleven, which must have been the reason Harvey was in a robe and slippers. My internal clock was wacky from traversing time zones. All I knew was this one day had already seemed two days long. I had to go home to bed. "I'll call him tomorrow."

chapter 15

FELIX MELENDEZ, JR., PICKED UP IN THE MIDdle of the first ring.

"Majestic-Airlines-Passenger-Services-this-is-Felix-how-can-I-help-you?"

He sounded the same, his voice as bright and sparkling as the morning sun streaming through my window. I wondered if he looked the same, tall and lanky, all joints and hinges, like the kid he still was. I also wondered if Majestic had let him keep his spiky hair with the frosted tips.

"Hello, Felix."

After the slightest pause, there came a gusher of excitement that flowed over the phone lines and practically lifted me off my stool, where I sat enjoying breakfast at home and not in some hotel coffee shop on the road.

"Miss *Sha*nahan? Is that you? Wow. This is so cool to hear from you. How did you find me . . . I mean . . . of course, you could find me. How are you? How have you been? I can't believe it. Are you in Miami?"

"I'm in Boston. How is life at the airport? Do you love it?"

"Way cool, Miss S. Way, *way* cool. I love it so much

here. The people are so nice to me. It's exactly what I wanted."

Same old Felix. He lived in a world without skepticism, irony, or sarcasm. He was delighted by life, all parts of it, even something as dispiriting as the airline business. I loved talking to him.

"Listen, Felix. Do you have time to do some work for me? I'll pay you this time."

"Really? Are you *serious*? That would be, like, so awesome to work for you again. But you can't pay me."

"Why not?" I finished my last spoonful of oatmeal, went to the refrigerator for an orange, swung by the sink for a paper towel, and sat back down to start peeling. "I don't want you working for free."

"It's a rule. I'm employed full-time for Majestic Airlines, which means no way I can have any other jobs."

"It wouldn't be a job. It's more like a . . . a . . ."

"I read the regs, Miss S. It says it in there."

"You read the regs?" A staggering thought. The rules and regulations of Majestic Airlines were collected in three thick volumes written in the driest prose this side of the phone book.

"Yes, ma'am. All three volumes."

I hadn't even considered the conflict of interest. But I needed his help, and I did not want to take advantage of him. "I won't tell if you won't."

He batted the suggestion aside, which, having said it, I realized he would. Felix was an honest fellow. "I'll do it as a favor to you, for getting me this job. I love this job."

"No, Felix. Remember, I got you this job to repay you for the last bit of work you did for me for free."

"Miss Shanahan, please. It would be my pleasure. I insist."

It was too tempting an offer to turn down. Felix was

masterful with a computer and was just plain fun to have in my life. I would figure out some other way to pay him. "I don't want to interfere with your work schedule there."

"Whoa, cool . . . I mean, that's not a problem. I make my own schedule."

"You make your own schedule?" There was no making of your own work schedule at an airport that operated around a real schedule—departures and arrivals.

"They made up a new job for me. I'm in charge of all the computer equipment. Do you know how often the baggage system goes down?"

I finished peeling my orange and pulled apart the sections as he rattled on. It was good and sweet and sticky, and the juice got all over my fingers. "Are you having fun?"

"This is so much better than working at the hotel. I'm going to owe you for the rest of my life. What do you need? Do you need me to come up there? Because I can be on an airplane tomorrow—"

"No, Felix. I think you can do this from the comfort of your own home. I need you to track down the origination of a Web site." I gave him the Web site address from Tony the Actor and his sign-in name. "I have no password."

"I don't need a password."

"Right. Sorry." I'd forgotten that offering a password to Felix was like offering a key to a locksmith. "What I need you to do is try to find a way into this site so I can see the screens and the customer interfaces. Also, if you can track back and get any information on who pays for the domain and/or who maintains it, that would all be useful. Best-case scenario is we can find the person who runs it, track back to his computer, and suck out all the data it collects."

"Do I need to know what to look for?"

"Good point. I'm investigating a prostitution ring run by flight attendants. This is supposed to be the scheduling site, but don't be alarmed if any skin shows up."

"Skin? Oh. *Ohhhhhh.* Ohmygosh. Wow. Okay, then. Like I said, I'll get going on it. And Miss Shanahan?"

"I wish you would call me Alex."

"I'm really, really glad you called me. Thank you so much for letting me do this for you."

It was the same as last time. I had Felix thanking me for letting him do me a huge favor.

"Call me if you get anything."

"I will."

I hung up with the sure knowledge that no matter what Felix ended up doing with his life, he would always be underemployed.

I took my bowl, now filled with orange peel, to the sink to dump down the disposal. While it was grinding and the water was running, the phone rang again. The message in the spy window announced a private number. Not helpful. I turned everything off and answered.

"Hello."

"How are you doing this morning, doll?" The sound of Angel's voice was like a rocket booster kicking in to redirect the planned trajectory of my day.

"I'm doing well. Are you ready to listen to a proposal? I can offer you something I know you will find interesting."

"We'll see. Meet me at the Saffron Spa at ten-thirty. Do you know where that is?"

"On Arlington?"

"They'll be expecting you."

chapter 16

IT WAS AMAZINGLY BUSY AT THE SPA FOR A workday. I never knew things like this went on while I was working a real job. The two women staffing the reception desk both had the same hairstyle. It looked as if it had been cut with a meat cleaver yet was still strangely trendy.

The one who wasn't on the phone greeted me when I walked in. "May I help you?"

"I'm Alex Shanahan."

"Oh, yes. You're the guest of Miss Velesco. Go right on up the stairs, and Siobhan will help you." She pointed to a spiral staircase.

Siobhan guarded the checkpoint at the top of the stairs. She was slightly older, but no less hip, than her colleagues downstairs. Like all of the spa's employees, she wore a pink lab coat and a flowery fragrance.

"Follow me," she said, after she'd checked me in. "I'll show you to the locker room."

She took me to the changing area, where the only thing locker room–like about it was the neat row of lockers. Otherwise, it looked like the master bathroom at Versailles. I stashed my street clothes, pulled on my robe, and managed to walk in my paper slippers to the waiting room, where the air was filled with Enya and the scent of heavily spiced candles. I poured a glass of lemon water and looked around for where to sit.

Something odd caught my eye, something so completely out of place it took me a second to register what it was. My long-sleeved sweater, the one I had last seen flying over the dance floor in LA, was lying like a throw blanket across the back of the velvet love seat. About then, I felt a growing sense of unease that turned into an inkling that turned into the certainty that I was not alone.

The chaise longue in the far corner was draped with cranberry-colored mosquito netting that hung from the ceiling. It was just sheer enough that I could see someone lounging behind it, and I realized where the sweater had come from.

The drape billowed, and a voice emerged. "Y'all naked under there, sweetheart?"

"Naked as the day I was born. Spa rules." I went over to the love seat, pulled off the sweater, folded it, and sat down with it in my lap. "Thanks for returning my sweater."

The curtains parted, and Angel came out. Her size made the terry-cloth robe seem skimpy on her. Her hair was piled and pinned on top of her head, and she wore little or no makeup. Women as young as Angel tended to look even younger without makeup. Angel looked harder, and I flashed on Tristan's warning that she was someone to stay away from.

She walked in her paper slippers over to the armoire, where the liquid refreshments were arranged. She twisted the end of her towel and dipped it into the pitcher of cucumber drinking water, then unrolled it and used it to dab at her face.

"You have my attention," she said with her lazy scrub brush drawl. "Now, tell me what it is you think I need from you."

"Is it safe to talk in here?"

"No one in here but us chickens."

I had no idea what kind of attention span she had, so I figured it would be best to get to the point. "I know what you do, I've heard you do it well, and I'm here to offer my services in dealing with the LA problem."

"The LA problem?" She dropped her head back and laid the damp towel against her throat. "I don't have a problem, and if I did, I wouldn't need anyone's help to fix it."

I sat back on the love seat, trying to look confident. It didn't help that my terry-cloth robe kept getting bunched up against the velvet seat cushions. "If I were starting a rival group to challenge you," I said, "the first thing I would do is go after your top earners, the ones who probably generate the bulk of your revenue. I'm in LA, so I already have the advantage of sun, surf, and palm trees. I'd get them to transfer to my base. Then I would start paying them for their clients. I'd give them bonuses for every client they brought. Then I would run a promotion to reward clients for bringing their friends over. I would deprive you of that income and at the same time use it to get myself established quickly in LA. I would copy your strengths, avoid your weaknesses, move into your territory, and keep the pressure on until I wiped you out."

She drifted around the small waiting room, touching things as she went—the armoire, the back of a chair, a tall potted fern, a picture on the wall. I assumed she was listening, because she hadn't drifted out.

"I don't have any weaknesses."

"Every business has weaknesses. The more women I

hired away, the more I would know about the ones you have."

She stopped moving and took up a position next to a side table filled with crystals of all sizes and shapes. She found one she liked, a purple obelisk, and picked it up to study it. As she turned it this way and that, she pulled up one leg and braced it against the wall behind her. Her robe came open all the way up to her hip.

"What would keep me from sending someone out to break both your legs before you could get all that done?"

I shifted around on the couch. There was something about the brazen way she exposed herself that made a physical threat seem very realistic. Maybe it was her willingness to use her body in any way that was necessary. "As pimping strategies go," I said, "breaking legs is not a bad one. A little unoriginal, perhaps."

She dropped the crystal into her pocket and fixed me with a cold stare. "I'm not a pimp. Don't you ever call me one."

"Here's the problem with that strategy," I said, staring right back. "First of all, if you come at me, I come at you. A catfight like that would find its way into the papers and scare off the clients, not to mention put both our jobs at risk."

As I talked, she moved toward my love seat.

"Second, I'm not some scared hooker who will pack up and quit at the first sign of push back. I'll keep coming. Intimidation doesn't work with me. If you want to beat me, you have to be smarter than I am."

Now she was standing next to me. With great effort, I kept myself from leaning away as she lowered herself into the compact space next to me. It was a love seat, after all, not a full couch. Being that close was like sitting in the front row at the movies.

Leaving her slippers on the floor, she folded her legs up and tucked them underneath her. Her robe loosened across her thighs. Angel apparently didn't know any unprovocative poses. She put one hand on her bare leg and used the other to play with a strand of hair that had come loose. "Let's say you were me, doll. What would you do if you were me?"

"Mobilize an immediate response."

"What would this response look like?" She edged a little closer. All I could figure was this was her effort to get the upper hand by distracting me. I focused on her eyes.

"I'd find out why my women were so willing to walk, and I would give them more reason to stay than to leave. That would be my first step. Next, I would find out which clients are leaving or thinking of leaving."

I pulled the diskette from the pocket of my robe and held it up between us. "That's why you need this."

She didn't even look at it. She kept her eyes on me. "I hate computers."

"This disk contains the guest list from the recruiting party the other night in LA. There are two hundred names with contact numbers, mostly men."

The left corner of her mouth tweaked up. "How did you happen to come by this list?"

"I stole it."

She let out a little whoop and nudged my shoulder with hers. "Aren't you the little spitfire?" Without the slightest hesitation, she snapped up the disk, and it disappeared into her own pocket, the one without the crystal she'd already swiped. "I can put that to good use."

"That's not all there is," I said. "I have a master list from the same computer with another thirteen hundred names. It shows which of your clients are being targeted and which have already left you. It also includes the client list and the target list for your LA rivals."

"Names with contacts?"

"Business e-mail addresses."

She pushed her robe open a little more, leaned back, and brushed the towel across the swell of her breasts. "That is interesting."

"I also have a strategy that will help you crush LA before they ever get off the ground. It's a program that will help you keep your women from leaving and retain your clients. I think we can get all your clients back with this program."

"What's the program?"

"That's what I'm selling. That and the rest of the names. Hire me, and you get the whole package."

"Hire you as what?"

"Your management consultant."

Another whooping cry. "You must have heard all the talk about me, about how I'm nothing but poor, dumb white trash from the wrong side of the trailer park. Is that it? Miss Dairy Queen?"

"If I thought you were dumb, I wouldn't have approached you first."

"What do you mean by first?"

"I just told you how I would put you out of business. Hire me, and I'll tell you how to do it to them."

She grabbed her lower lip with a couple of front teeth and considered that. "You were right about something, what you said the other night. I have checked you out. You were one straight arrow at Majestic. A big superstar flying up the corporate ladder, working your ass off, always spouting the party line. A company gal, that's what you were. How the mighty have fallen."

"I was a company gal . . . right up until the day they

fired me. Now I can't get work anywhere else, my income is a fraction of what it used to be, I'm schlepping drinks at thirty-five thousand feet and hawking stolen names of married men to you to make a living. I'm through doing the right thing."

"Now you're broke and bitter, and you want to run with the bad girls to prove what a bad-ass you are."

"Right. I'm a real bad-ass."

She sat back against the armrest and checked me out. She seemed to be taking my physical inventory. "You say you won't do the nasty, right? Isn't that what you told me? You're not in the trade, and you don't want to be."

"That's what I said."

"Why not?"

"It's not for me."

"Yet you figure on making money off all the girls who are, including me. You want to have your cake and eat it, too. Or have my cake without letting anybody eat yours. That just ain't gonna fly, sweetie. Not in my world."

"Why not?" Here was the stickiest wicket of all, one I wasn't sure I could get past. "You must have business arrangements with people who are not prostitutes. Accountants and programmers. Other support types."

"I chose them. Not the other way around."

"If you don't trust me, trust my motive."

"Which is?"

"Money. Don't have enough. Need more."

"That's not good enough, sweet pea. I never work with anyone who won't get her hands as dirty as me, and here's a little secret." She leaned toward me, probably to whisper, but I didn't want her tongue in my ear again, so this time I pulled away. That seemed to amuse her. "I'm not dumb. I know, for instance, that you being my business consultant would mean me showing you my business. The who, what, where, why, and therefore of things."

"The more I know, the more I can help you."

"The more you know, the more you can hurt me. But I tell you what. I will buy those lists from you. Name your price, we'll haggle a bit, then we'll come to an arrangement, and we can go on about our separate business."

"It's a package deal, Angel. If you want the lists of names, you take me with them."

She retreated to the armrest again to think that over. "How about this? How about you spend the next couple of months getting to know and understand up close and personal the kinds of services we offer? Then maybe we can talk turkey."

"You don't have a couple of months, and I'm not interested."

The door opened, and one of the pink coats stepped in. "Good morning, Miss Velesco. We're ready for you in massage room three."

"I'll be right there, darlin'."

"Of course. Take your time. You know the way back. Miss Shanahan, someone will be out for you shortly."

After the pink coat left, Angel dropped her legs down and found her slippers on the floor. "I do give you credit, doll. You can play the game."

I felt her slipping away. I felt my chance slipping away. "So can you," I said. "You've built something of value, Angel. I don't know if you fully appreciate how difficult that is. I can help you keep it. You don't need me to turn tricks to prove it."

"If I've learned one thing about the world of business, it's this," she said. "You can't get ahead without being willing to spread your legs every now and then for the right person or the right reasons. In my business, it just happens to be for real."

"Thirteen hundred client names, Angel. Going once . . . going twice . . ." She watched me closely. It was a standoff, and I knew one thing about negotiating. You had to be willing to lose. "Gone." I drank down the rest of my lemon water and got up. "Keep the disk with my compliments. Thank you for your time."

"I plan to keep it." I was halfway out the door when she called me back. "You know what you need, sugar? You need some lessons from me. Life lessons."

This was interesting. I came back in and leaned against the back of a chair. "I don't want life lessons. I want cash."

"You can have that, too."

"I don't want to be a hooker."

"Could you say that one more time? I don't think I got it yet. I'm talking about life lessons, sweetie. I want to teach you how the world works."

"What do you care what I know about the world?"

She raised her arms to stretch and folded them over her head, a move that pulled her robe open and thrust her chest out, revealing almost everything she had to see from the waist up. "For every lesson you give me, I'll give you one in return. I like the sound of that. It has a certain . . . what do you call that when it's all balanced out perfectly?"

"Symmetry."

"Right. That's a good word, and that's my counteroffer. What do you think of that?"

I didn't like the fact that she was always coming up with the last word, the one final thing I had to do to get what I wanted. But she actually seemed vulnerable in her own brittle, cocky, self-serving way, as if she really, really wanted the chance to strut her stuff. Her *other* stuff. That was probably a good position to have her in—showing off.

"I'll do it."

"Good. There's one more thing." She stood and wrapped herself back together, then casually tossed one more condition on the table. "You have to go on a date."

"No. I told you—"

"You could be a cop. You could be a spy from LA, for all I know. One date is all I'm asking. I'll set it up. It's a deal breaker, too, so think carefully before you make up your mind. If you want to tell me after your massage, that's okay, too."

"I'll pass on the massage."

"Suit yourself." She winked. "But I usually do my best thinking with someone else's hands all over me."

She moved toward the door. Once she was through it, I knew it was all over. I thought about what little time we had left for the case. I tried not to, but I also thought about the way Jamie had looked at me in my flight attendant uniform. I thought about Harvey . . . well, best not to do that. I chewed the inside of my cheek. I stuffed my hands into my pockets.

"One date will make the difference to you?"

"There's a world of difference, darlin', between one date and no dates."

I swallowed hard and handed my soul over to the devil. "Deal."

chapter 17

"YOU TOLD HER *WHAT*? HOW COULD YOU? What were you thinking?"

Harvey was beside himself. The numbness in his legs made it hard for him to pace, but he made an exception in this case, pushing himself from one end of his office to the other, even once around the couch. It seemed I was always driving him to new heights of consternation.

"It's a test, Harvey." I sat in one of the more worn chairs, plucking at a flaw in the upholstery where two mismatched seams had been forced together. It was a weird role reversal for me to be sitting while he was moving. "Angel has to have a reason to trust me. I have to prove that I'm willing to get as dirty as she is. That means I have to go on a date."

"If you go through with this ridiculous plan, you will be alone in a hotel room with a strange man who will be expecting you to have sex with him. Do you not find that the least bit intimidating?" His voice was on the rise, becoming more and more high-pitched.

"I've handled worse than a horny businessman trying to get some on the side." I hated sounding so cavalier, but his tendency to leap directly to Defcon One always forced me to the opposite end of the reaction spectrum: cool nonchalance. I never knew if it was sheer contrarian stubbornness that made me do that or a genuine quest for balance. "Again, I won't have sex with him. The plan is to make Angel believe that I did."

"By blackmailing him." Now he was barely getting the words out. His voice had a strangled quality, as if he had a tourniquet around his throat.

"Harvey, all I need . . ." I sat back and tried hard not to get pulled into his hysteria. "All I need him to do is call whoever he's supposed to call and tell them I did the deed. What I need you to do is find me some leverage so I can convince him that would be a good idea."

"Like what?"

"The names of his wife and kids." I stared down at my hands on my knees, then looked up in time to see the withering look before he turned his back. "Harvey, the man will be in a hotel room expecting to have sex with a hooker. He will not be entirely blameless."

"My objection has less to do with his integrity than mine. And yours. I find this tactic despicable."

"Me, too. But this is the business we're in. We deal with despicable people, Angel Velesco chief among them. Besides, what else do we have? Do we have top swappers?"

"Not as of yet."

I tried to think of the other avenues we'd been pursuing. "I just gave Felix the information yesterday. It's too soon for anything there. What about that detective from Omaha? That woman's murder. Did he ever call you?"

"Yes."

"You didn't tell me?"

"He said nothing, only that the case was solved, there were no loose ends, and he had no real interest in resurrecting a murder that was difficult enough the first time around."

"Difficult how?"

"To have a young flight attendant beaten to death on a layover in Omaha was quite the civic black eye, as you can well imagine."

"Is it worth pursuing?"

"Doubtful."

"Then what do we have if I don't find a way to get close to Angel?"

He continued to move around, albeit more slowly and in a more confined area. "I do not like this. Not one bit. Why did you keep me in the dark about going to meet her?"

"Did you check your messages? Because I left one on your home phone."

"I must have been on the computer."

"And your cell phone wasn't on, as usual. I am reporting to you now, minutes after having left the woman. She's still on the massage table."

He fumed around a little more. I checked my watch. I was due to meet Tristan at the range within the hour. He had not appreciated my last late arrival. "Do you want to quit now when we're so close?"

He did an abrupt change in course and ended up in front of my chair. "That is the same argument you have been using on me for the past week. It is a specious argument at best."

"What is specious about it?"

"Every time we get close, the line moves. You keep moving it."

"Harvey, the case is not finished. I don't want to quit when there is still work to be done and we have the time."

"If we use the time Mr. Wolff gave us and we come back with nothing, it could be disastrous."

"On the other hand, imagine walking into the briefing on Monday with a full list of all the hookers, a detailed description of how the scheduling works, and proof that these women are being paid for sex. We'd blow them away. That's what we get if we get the Web master. If I pass this test, it puts me one step closer."

"You are sure she has one of those?"

"A Web master? Positive. She told me she hates computers. They make her eyes glaze over. Machines aren't her thing. People are her thing."

He made his way over to his bookcase, where he began touching each book on one of the shelves, running his index finger along the spine, top to bottom. Checking for dust? He held his free arm awkwardly at his side.

"I can't do this without you, Harvey."

"How will we know which flight you will be on?"

"The call comes in advance." I considered it a positive that he was beginning to think specifically about the plan.

"How far in advance?"

"A day. They'll arrange the date and set up the swaps to put me on the right flight. Then they'll call me with the flight number and the code names for the client and me."

"Code names." That elicited a humorless chuckle. "Like spies."

"Once I know the flight, we can pretty much narrow the options to men booked in first class. The date will be one of them."

He continued doggedly swiping spines until he had finished one row and begun the next. "I do not like it."

"You said that. What else, specifically?"

"We are not prepared for an operation of this nature. It is too dangerous."

"I can appreciate your concern, but supposedly these clients are well vetted. I'll be fine."

"You cannot know that."

"I also don't know if the next plane I board will crash, but I get on it anyway."

"That is not a valid comparison." He turned toward me and was suddenly fully engaged. "There is an infinitesimal risk that your airplane will crash, a conclusion based on millions upon millions of hours of data analyzed over—"

"All right, then." He did have the ability to drive me crazy. "Let's make a decision based on the data. Depending on what you find out, we can decide at the time whether I go in or back off. That's the ultimate out, right? I can be a no-show."

"It won't work."

"Why not?"

"Because no matter what I find, you won't back off."

I twisted my watch around my wrist but managed not to look at it. "If you get me good information about this man that suggests I shouldn't proceed, then I won't. But you have to promise you'll do the best you can to find the dirt, that you won't rig the outcome. I have to be able to trust you."

"We will have to trust each other."

chapter 18

"WHAT IS *WRONG* WITH YOU?" TRISTAN HELD up the paper target so I could see. Except for a crescent-shaped nick on the right side of the upper border of the page, it was completely intact. I had taken fourteen shots at it. "Are you still hung over from the party?"

"That party was two days ago."

"You were pretty wasted."

I wasn't hung over. I was frazzled by the high-speed dash in late-afternoon traffic to get out to the range, and I was distracted by the details of the case. It might have been a mistake to turn down that massage. I could have used an hour of deep-tissue relaxation.

"Not my day, Tristan. I'm sorry. I can't concentrate."

"That excuse will not fly when you take your test. What if that day is a bad day, too? You have to learn to push through it. I'll help you. Come on."

"Can we take a break, please?" I didn't leave him much choice. I set the weapon down and went to the picnic table to grab a seat. Eventually, he came and slipped onto the bench across from me.

He gave me his stern face, which could be comical. But then he lightened up, pulled a piece of paper out of his pocket, and unfolded it. "Maybe this will cheer you up." He began to quote from the page.

" 'Subject was alert and observant and treated each passenger as if he or she were the only one onboard. Highest rating.' "

"What is that?"

"This, my dear, is your sparkling report from yesterday's ghost rider."

"Alert and observant?" I had to smile at that. "Imagine what I could have done if I hadn't still been half in the bag. How do you have access to a report like that? I thought results were top secret."

"It pays not to burn your bridges. Here's something else I know. If you had missed that trip, you'd be on the street right now."

"Did I tell you how much I appreciated all your help yesterday?"

"Yes, you did, but it's always good to hear it again. You need to pace yourself. Take it from me; the lifestyle gets really old really fast, and it's not good for your skin."

Again with the skin.

"Drinking too much and going on two hours of sleep. And then getting on a six-hour flight with all that recycled cabin air. Although I give you special dispensation because of what happened with your brother. I suppose that could drive anyone into a tequila embrace. Speaking of which, what have you done about him?"

"Nothing."

"Why not?"

"I lost his number." He gave me the look that lame excuse deserved. "I did. I had it in the pocket of my uniform out in LA. I was moving it from pocket to pocket, and then it was just gone. I don't know what happened to it."

"You need to straighten this out, dear. I know it's why you're so spacey."

"No. Jamie and I have been fighting for a long time."

"But you saw him. That had to do something."

"We've had fights before, and we've always made up. If this were about anything but my father . . . this feels different."

"Because it is. It's big. I'm sure the idea of Jamie reaching out to him like that really hurts."

"I'm not hurt. I'm angry."

"You're lying, sweetie. I'm sorry, but you just are."

He looked one way. I looked the other.

"You know what?" He turned sideways on the bench, pulled one of his long legs up, and folded it like a coat hanger. "I don't usually talk about nine-eleven, but I'll make an exception for you." He inhaled deeply and, as he let go of the breath, seemed to age ten years in front of my eyes.

"On the morning of September 11, 2001, I was in Fort Myers at the airport getting ready to work a flight home. We heard something had happened, something bad. We all went up and crowded into this bar to watch TV. It was one of those rare moments in life when you feel completely accepted, totally on equal footing with everyone around you. There were passengers there, first class and coach. Pilots. Ramp rats. CEOs. Janitors. We all had our arms around each other, and anyone who wasn't completely struck dumb by what we were seeing was crying or trying to get through to someone on a cell phone. I was one of the ones crying.

"The next day, I picked up the phone and called Barry, and I told him yes, I would move in with him. He'd been asking me for months. Then I rented a car with a couple of the gals from the crew, and we drove back to Boston, and two weeks later, Barry and I were cohabitating like an old married couple, and now here I am participating in a 'committed relationship,' something I said I would never do because even the term itself makes me retch, and I've never been happier. Next thing you know, we'll be having babies, God help us, and in case my point is not obvious enough for you—"

"It is."

"I'll say it anyway, because I love hearing myself give sage advice. You could get up to go to work tomorrow, Alexandra, board your flight, and never come back."

"I'm aware of that."

"One minute, you're serving up orange juice and seltzer on a tray, and the next, you've become part of some dreadful historical event, and you disappear from the face of the earth. Poof! You're gone. I mean *gone* gone. Vanished. Not even so much as a molar left—"

"Tristan, I get it."

He tipped his head and looked at me. "Think about it this way. If you had to make that last call on your cell phone, who would you call? If it's your brother, don't you think you should know his phone number?"

chapter 19

ON MY WAY BACK INTO THE CITY, I CALLED information on my cell phone and asked for the number of Jamie's firm in Manhattan. Then I paid the outrageous fee to have them connect me, because I was afraid if I did it myself, I would crash my car.

After one ring, a woman with a soft voice and a prim tone answered.

"Mr. Shanahan's office. Can I help you?"

Mr. Shanahan. How could that kid who used to leave his coat on the floor be Mr. Shanahan? I wondered if he still did that, if he waltzed into his office, walked out of his cashmere overcoat, and left it lying in a heap where it fell. Did his assistant come in behind him and hang it up for him?

"Is he in, please?"

"May I say who's calling?"

"I'm his sister."

I saw him through the window, and it stopped me. Jamie sat on a stool at the street-facing counter, bathed in that mellow, hip-and-happening-but-not-adequate-for-reading Starbucks lighting. It was dark out, so he couldn't see me. Somewhere in the back of my mind, I had made room for the possibility that he wouldn't show, that he would leave me waiting for him, watching the clock with a sick feeling in my stomach. But here he was, and he was waiting for me.

I walked through the door behind a large man who took up a lot of space. Jamie didn't see me, so I surprised him when I put my hand on his shoulder.

"Hi, Jamie."

He did a pirouette on the stool and stood up, all in one graceful motion. "How did you . . . I didn't see you come in."

Unlike when we'd met on the plane, I felt like hugging him, so I did. He was only a little taller, so neither one of us had to bend down. It felt comfortable, the way it used to, but when he started to pull away, so did I, making the parting seem as mutual as the embrace.

I started but not well. "Um, I wanted to apologize for—"

"Watch out." He took my arm and guided me away from the door. It kept opening and closing with each new latte-starved customer. He reached up and scratched the back of his head. "Can I get you something? Do you want tea?"

"I'll get it. Do you need a refill?"

"No, thanks. I'll just . . ." He reached around for his wallet. "But let me get this."

"Don't be silly. Tea costs all of a dollar here. I'll be right back."

I didn't have to go far to join an ordering line that snaked almost to the back of the store, and it didn't take long to figure out that waiting for a cup of hot tea behind the venti caramel soy macchiattos and grande decaf nonfat with whip white chocolate mochas was a bad idea. Given the sound level, it also occurred to me that I had not picked the best place for a reconciliation discussion, not if we actually wanted to hear each other.

I bailed out of the line and walked back. "Do you want to get out of here? Maybe go for a walk?"

"Let's go." He was off his stool before I had even finished the question, which reminded me of how much Jamie liked being in motion. Not in the hypercompulsive way Dan did but because he had always thought he was better at doing than thinking.

We stepped out onto the sidewalk, which was crowded with workers who had fled the surrounding office towers when the white-collar whistle had blown. I directed us toward the Common and, as we walked, practiced in my head all the things I had thought of to say. *Jamie, I'm sorry about what happened on the flight to LA, and I'm really sorry about last Christmas. If what I did hurt you or Gina—*

Wait. *If* I hurt you? I sounded like every rap star, movie star, sports star, or ex-president who ever offered a conditional apology, one designed to shift responsibility to the victim for having the audacity to feel hurt. What I mean is . . . what I meant was . . . damn, this was hard.

"Jamie."

"What?"

"On the flight to LA the other day, I wasn't nice to you. I was surprised, and I didn't handle it well, and I'm sorry I hurt your feelings."

"I was sorry not to spend the time together."

"Yeah, well . . . of course. That, too. Me, too."

We walked for a ways without saying much and ended up at the traffic light in front of the State House. I looked up at the dome. It was beautiful, especially at night when it was all lit up. It looked as if it had been covered in gold tin foil.

"That's nice," he said.

I turned to see that he was looking also, gazing at it the way he used to peer into the sky at the fireworks on the Fourth of July. He was always trying to see them before they exploded.

"Jamie, I want to talk about last Christmas. I've been thinking about things . . . everything . . . and I'm sorry about the way I reacted."

The light changed, and I followed him across the street, over the sidewalk, and down the steps into the Common, trying to talk the whole way. "I was wrong. What I did was wrong, and . . . I was . . . I think I was angry about being out of work for so long and not having any money and . . . none of which matters, because the end result was I took it out on you, I guess, and I shouldn't have, and I'm sorry." It was getting harder to keep up with him, and not because I was slowing down. "Do you mind if we stop?"

We did, but I should have asked for us to stop *and* look at each other, because all he did was stare over my right shoulder at one of the dozens of memorial statues scattered about the park.

"I'm sorry I backed out on you. I should have explained myself better or maybe come after Walter had left. I missed seeing you. I missed being with you guys. I screwed up, and I'm sorry."

I felt myself saying the word *sorry* a lot, and I wanted him to look at me, to give me some sense of how this was going, but he seemed to be enduring me, which really pissed me off, since I was the one who had broken radio silence and called this meeting. And then he took off again. I didn't.

"Jamie."

He turned and doubled back. "You're sorry. I got that. What else do you need to hear?"

"It's generally good to acknowledge an apology when one is offered. That way, I know that I wasn't talking to myself."

"What good is an apology if you don't mean it?"

That was totally out of the blue. "Why would you say that?"

"If we had the same set of circumstances today, would you make a different decision?"

I had to stop and consider that, and when I did, for about two seconds, the answer was no. "I still wouldn't come, but I would try to see your side of things, and I wouldn't get so angry and bitter and emotional and reactionary and . . ." I needed to stop, because I was getting angry and bitter and emotional and reactionary.

"I knew it."

"You knew what? That I didn't want to sit across the Christmas turkey from Walter? You knew that before you ever invited him, and yet you did it anyway. Just because you've decided to go all buddy-buddy with him doesn't mean I have to. Things don't change just because you want them to, Jamie. People don't change."

"So you would."

"Would *what*?"

"You would do the exact same thing again. You would bail on me, because that's what you do, Alex. If the situation is not perfect for you, you bail."

"I have never bailed on you, Jamie. Never. You bailed on me when you invited him. Did you think for one second about how I might feel? I hope you two had a great time together and I hope—"

I could feel myself getting pulled back onto the grooved tracks of attack and defend and attack and defend, and all I had wanted to do, goddammit, was apologize, and now I couldn't even keep my voice steady. I stared at the ground, at a cluster of rocks alongside the walking path, and I tried to will the conversation in a different direction. "I called you because I miss you, Jamie. I miss you, and I thought there should be a way for us to get through this. Someone had to make the first move, and—"

"And since it was you, I should be thankful? That makes you the bigger person?"

"Jesus *Christ.*" I looked at him. He stared back with so much darkness in his eyes that I had the terrible thought he wanted to hit me. "Why are you so angry with me?"

He jammed both hands deep into the pockets of his coat, turned away, and began a slow, aimless meander toward the Frog Pond. Feeling suddenly exhausted, I found a bench and sat on it. The walking paths were busy with walkers this time of the evening. Some had the brisk heading-home-from-work pace. Others strolled leisurely, taking their wool sweaters and anoraks out for the first spin of the season. Soon they found the widening path between my brother and me.

I sat on the bench and watched Jamie and wondered how it was that we could get to this place so quickly. Maybe fighting was better than dead silence, but in that moment, it didn't feel that way. I wondered if he would care or even notice if I got up and walked away. I wondered how I would feel if I did that.

Before I had a chance to wonder long, he came back. He sat beside me, but only on the edge of the bench, hunched forward with his elbows on his knees.

"When you didn't come for Christmas, I felt like . . . you just should have been there."

"Why? To fulfill some fantasy you have of a happy family? We don't have one of those. We never have."

"Because I . . . wanted you there."

I started to barrel in with another defense but stopped. His voice had cracked. He had tried to raise it in anger and swat me down, much as our father used to do, probably still would if given the chance. But Jamie didn't have it in him. He hadn't figured out how to turn his fear into bluster and insults. He wasn't quite able to hide his human frailty and I loved him for that. I also realized for the first time that maybe he had wanted me there because he was still scared of Walter. Maybe he still did need me. That felt different from being judged a failure of a daughter and a sister for not wanting to be there.

I dropped my head back and stared up into the trees. "Why did you invite him in the first place?"

"He's our father."

"Since when does that make any difference?"

"Since I had kids of my own. Gina and I have talked about it. He's their only living grandparent. I wanted you to be with us and I knew you wouldn't come if I told you he was invited. I was just trying to give you a little push."

"I don't like to be pushed."

"No shit."

"And it's my choice whether I want to see him or not."

"Mine, too."

"I know, but why would you—" He was right. He was right, and I was right. We were both entitled to our choices, and we had to respect each other's. It was just that I wanted his choice to be the same as mine. "Just make sure you want him around for the right reasons."

"What does that mean?"

"I think you're still trying to prove yourself to him and what better way to do it than to show him all your stuff?"

"My stuff?"

"Your cars and your big house and your big job."

He stared across to the Frog Pond. It was still too early, but within months, it would be frozen over and used for a public skating rink. I didn't skate, but I still thought that was one of the nicer things about winter in Boston.

"Sometimes," he said, "I think the reason I have all those things is that he made me want to work harder."

"Oh, please. Don't tell me that's what you think. What he did to you was—" I put my hands on my knees and waited until I didn't feel as if my face were on fire. "Parents are supposed to make life easier for their children. You know that. You have your own now. All he ever did was make yours harder."

"Yours, too, Za."

I looked at him, and he was grinning. Za was my family name, and Jamie was the only one who ever used it anymore. He had given it to me when he was learning to talk, because he could never get all the way to the end of Alexandra, which was what he heard my mother call me. In that strange and magical alchemy that exists only in the minds of toddlers, Alexandra begat Zandra, which became Za. He could be pretty damned disarming when he wanted to.

"Jamie, you are a good person, and you are what you are in spite of him. I can't stand for you to give him credit for all of your hard work."

He leaned forward again and stared into the ground. "It doesn't mean I give you any less."

"I'm not . . . it's not about . . ." But it was. He was right. He'd gotten me again. I put my hand on his back and let it settle there, and that felt about right. "Jamie, I've got my own issues with Walter, and someday when

I grow up, I'll deal with them. If you want him around, then you have to deal with him on your own. But I give you a lot of credit for trying. It's more than I'm willing to do."

He nodded. We sat for a few minutes in silence. It was nice to be able to sit quietly together. I had so much I wanted to tell him, but not tonight. I wanted to stay in the space we were in right then. He might have felt the same way, because I knew he had questions, but he didn't ask any.

"Where do you live?" Not the hard ones, anyway.

"Down Beacon." I pointed west. "A few blocks that way. Not far. Where are you staying?"

"In a corporate apartment downtown." Which meant we were walking in opposite directions. Speaking of home and directions seemed to be the cue to stand. He reached into the inside pocket of his suit jacket and pulled out a snazzy business card holder and a pen and started jotting. "These are all my numbers. Call me when you're free. Gina and the kids want to see you. You can come down and spend the night with us. We have plenty of space in the new house."

"So . . ." I took the card and looked it over. "How was it, anyway?"

"How was what?"

"With Walter at Christmas. How did it go?"

He looked toward a streetlight, and his shoulders dipped just enough to make me angry at my father all over again. "It was . . . complicated. That's a longer conversation."

"Jamie . . ."

"What?"

"Please don't make me have to forgive him, or be with him to be with you."

It seemed like a long time before he answered. "I'm glad you called," he said, and hugged me tight.

As I walked home, the evening felt fresh and promising, like a shiny new CD that hadn't been played yet. On my way there, I saw things—a beautiful bay window with Irish lace curtains, a building's delicately sculpted façade that featured a pineapple theme, a lavishly landscaped yard. I had noticed none of these things in the year I had lived there. It was as if I were seeing my own neighborhood through new eyes.

Inside my apartment, the red message light on my answering machine blinked. I punched it up and listened.

It was a woman's voice but not Angel's. I didn't know who it was, but I knew what it was. Flight 1807. Chicago. Tomorrow afternoon. Code words *Saturn* and *Mercury*. The swap had been arranged for both outbound and inbound flights. I played it again and saved it; then I called Harvey.

"Hello?" He sounded sleepy.

"Harvey, the date is on."

"For when?"

"Tomorrow."

"*Tomorrow?* I am not ready. I have had no time to prepare. You said it would not be for a day at least." Now he was awake.

"Yes, you are ready, and this is good for us. The sooner, the better, right? The flight is not until three in the afternoon. I should get in around five-thirty, and I'm sure the date wouldn't be until quite a bit later than that. That gives us all night tonight and most of tomorrow. I'll help you. I'm heading out to the airport right now to pull the reservation records. I'll bring them over to you, and we'll get started. Don't worry. You're ready."

He might have been ready, but he was not happy when we hung up.

I put the phone aside and went in to change my clothes. This thing was happening. It was really happening, and I couldn't help but feel that I was about to pass a point of no return.

chapter 20

FORTUNATELY, THE EQUIPMENT OPERATING AS flight 1807 to Chicago was an older narrow-body, which meant there were only twelve first-class seats. I stood in the galley, watching the face of every man who boarded, wondering which ones went with the four names Harvey had researched so thoroughly for me.

It had been a tour de force performance on his part last night as he'd orchestrated data from multiple sources, both legal and illegal, to research the backgrounds of all the men booked on the flight in first class. We worked on the assumption that one of them would be my date, so doing all of them was the safest bet. Nine seats had been booked in advance. After eliminating the women and the other half of a Mr. and Mrs. duo, six men were left. We crossed off two of those on the basis of age. One was eighty-two. The other was in high school. Granted, age in itself didn't eliminate either one, but it was hard to dig up dirt on a kid too young to have any or a man too old to care if he did.

That left the four potentials, all of which Harvey had researched with skill, confidence, and even a bit of cunning at times. It had been fun to watch him do something he liked for a change.

As everyone settled in for the flight, I took my clipboard and went out to meet the candidates. It was an odd-numbered day of the month, which meant snack orders were to be taken from the back forward. That put 5E up first.

Aaron Sayer was twenty-eight years old. In his starched white shirt and suspenders, he looked like a baby titan of industry. He was single, had graduated from Columbia Law School, owned a condo in the Back Bay not far from my place, and was a member of the University Club, where he liked to play squash and swim. If he was my date, I was in trouble. So far, the only threat we could make would be to call and tell the partners at his law firm that he had hired a prostitute. They would probably promote him.

He was doing this thing with his cell phone, flipping it open and shut with one hand as he squinted through the porthole window.

"Good afternoon. I'm Alex, and I'll be serving you today. Welcome ab—"

"Gin and tonic. Light on the tonic, and toss in a lime. Not a twist. A slice." He did the whole thing without breaking rhythm on the phone flipping and without looking at me.

"Certainly. Would you care for—"

"Nothing to eat." At some point, he hit upon the idea of using his cell phone as a communication device. He covered one of the buttons with his thumb and pressed. "Just keep the GTs coming."

He put the phone to his ear, and I was thinking what an annoying little prick he was, when he turned his head and I saw something curious. The eyelashes at the corner of his left eye were damp and clumped together, the way they get when a teardrop has rolled by. His face was drawn and pale, and he looked like a man, a boy, really, who had lost something important. Girlfriend . . . best friend . . . the firm's biggest client. When I looked more closely, his eyes hinted at a deeper reservoir of feeling than I would have given him credit for. He reminded me of my brother, which gave me a great big reason to hope he wasn't my guy.

"Is there anything I can get for you? Would you like an aspirin? A glass of water before we take off?"

"No." He closed the phone quietly and turned toward the window. Whoever he had called had not answered. "No, thank you."

The second of my mystery men was seated in 4B. His name was Malcolm Bryce, and when I pulled up next to him to take his order, he actually looked up from his paper and acknowledged my presence.

"How are you?" he asked, and I could have sworn by the intense way he looked at me that he really wanted to know.

"I'm good, thank you, and welcome aboard. Would you like a snack after we take off, Mr. Bryce?"

"I'll pass, but thank you. Are you new on this flight? I haven't seen you before."

"It's my first time working this flight."

He was in his early to mid-forties. He had a widow's peak and wore his almost-black hair pushed off his face as if the sheer abundance of it were a nuisance. His eyes were a pale, elusive shade of green set off nicely by the deep jade color of his shirt. He was excitingly handsome and, at least on paper, my top pick for the man who had purchased my services for the evening.

He was a sports agent, which put him in the company of severely wealthy, high-profile athletes who lived the life of the rich, famous, and indulged. It also made him easy to Google. He had his own profile on the Internet. He was good at his job, which made him respected and loathed in equal measure, depending on who was asked. Wealthy in his own right, he was also a super-duper frequent flier. Malcolm Bryce fit the profile of Angel's clients perfectly, and the longer I looked into those intelligent green eyes, the more I hoped he wasn't the guy, because all I could think about was how that richly woven shirt lay across his chest and what it might be like to slip a hand underneath. I thought I might be getting some vibes from him, too, but I had to shake it off. I was working.

"How about something to drink after we take off, Mr. Bryce?"

"Call me Malcolm, and I'll have whatever you recommend in the way of a nice red wine."

"I'll check the wine cellar and see what I can come up with."

His easy grin revealed a row of perfectly charming, slightly imperfect teeth. I checked for a wedding band—none—and reserved the right to come back and hit on him later if he wasn't the guy.

My interactions with the two men in the bulkhead row, Dr. Dal Pressman in the window seat and Curt Guransky on the aisle, were dull by comparison. They ordered beers to drink and pasta salad to eat and otherwise seemed to have absolutely nothing in common. Dr. Pressman was thin and wispy and typed his computer keys very quickly with smooth, manicured nails. According to Harvey, he was a reasonably prominent business ethics professor at a reasonably prestigious university in town. Harvey had been most impressed by some of his articles. He was also married. If it turned out that he was my date, I looked forward to the philosophical discussion that would ensue.

Mr. Guransky was chubby and abrupt and bored-looking. He was a thirty-eight-year-old divorced chiropractor with his own practice and not much else. The split with his wife had cleaned him out and left him living in a rented apartment in Waltham. So far, Harvey had been frustrated in his search for dirt on this guy. He was easily the least-attractive candidate and the one who got me thinking about what it would be like to do this thing for real.

When I got to the galley to prepare for takeoff, I looked back at my four potentials. I pictured their bodies under their clothes and all the different ways they could feel—soft, bony, hairy, taut, smooth, sweaty, dry, and oily. I looked at their faces and their hands and thought about what it would be like to have one of them touch me in the most intimate way. The idea brought forth so many disruptive images and feelings I barely noticed the two passengers hustling onboard as I closed the door. But when I did my final walk-through, it was impossible not to notice that both of them had settled into first-class seats, one next to the baby titan and the other next to the eighty-two-year-old man.

I went back to the galley, tossed the cups I'd collected in the vicinity of the trash, and missed. This was exactly what I didn't need, and one of the things Harvey had worried about. Last-minute upgrades. Wild cards about which we knew absolutely nothing.

With the door shut and taxiing under way, I couldn't call him. I would have to try him on the Airfone once we were at altitude, always a dicey proposition. Half the time, I couldn't make the damn thing work. I didn't like this. Nope, I didn't like it at all, and if Harvey knew about it, he would hate it.

I strapped myself into the jumpseat and stared out at the only two passengers I could see from where I was: Dr. Pressman and the chiropractor. The doctor was reading a journal. The chiropractor was tossing goldfish crackers into his mouth. I was partway to a good sulk when the answer came to me. The only reason we had researched all of them was that we didn't know which guy it was. If I could get my date to raise his hand and identify himself, problem solved. If it turned out to be one of the wild cards, I would call Harvey and give him the name. If it was one of the original four, we were already set.

By the time we were airborne and I was released to the galley, I had a plan.

I fixed the kid's "double GTs" with an extra slice of lime and put a couple of Advils on the side. I poured Malcolm's red wine, opened the two beers, and got a scotch and water, orange juice, and club soda for the other passengers. While the almonds were heating, I found a pen in the pocket of my apron, smoothed out six cocktail napkins, and wrote the password on each: *Saturn.*

When they were ready, I gathered the nuts, picked up the tray, and emerged into the den of possibilities. I served the passengers in the sequence I'd taken the orders. The baby titan was asleep. One of the wild cards, a guy named Leland Cole, was in the window seat next to him. He was reasonably young but seemed determined to discourage anyone from thinking so. His lightweight short-sleeved shirt was buttoned one button too high and was made of the same lightweight suburban madras plaid my father used to wear to barbecue in the backyard. When I put the marked napkin in front of him, he handed it right back.

"May I have one that's not been used?"

"Of course." Cross him off the list.

Malcolm didn't even notice the napkin I placed on his tray. He was busy looking at me. I set his drink down and served the woman next to him her orange juice.

I dropped the other two marked napkins in front of the bulkhead boys. Dr. Ethics didn't even look up from his screen. The chiropractor saw that his napkin had something written on it and flipped it over, apparently eager to get his pudgy fingers around his beer.

No sooner had I returned to the galley then I turned to find Malcolm, hands in his pockets, relaxed against the coat closet. I was disappointed but not surprised. I stacked some cups that didn't need stacking. "The seat belt sign is still on," I said. "You're in violation of about twelve different FAA regulations."

"You wouldn't turn me in, would you?"

"I'd be taking a risk not to. There could be an inspector onboard."

He gave me a look that made me believe the risk might have been worth it. He was clearly the kind of man who didn't have much use for rules.

"Would you be available to join me for a drink this evening in Chicago?"

I stared at him. He was disarmingly flushed and a little nervous. He was obviously flirting, yet he offered no password. What was I to make of this?

"Well . . . that depends."

"On what?"

"It's possible I will be otherwise engaged this evening."

"Is that true, or are you giving me the brush-off?"

I lowered my voice. "I'm not brushing you off. I'm waiting for verification."

"Verification?"

When he said it back to me, I realized what an odd choice of words that must have seemed if he wasn't the guy. Maybe he wasn't. That would be nice. "I'm waiting to hear back from a friend. We're supposed to get together tonight. Otherwise, I would love to get a drink with you."

He grinned. "Do you mind if I check back with you later, then?"

"Please do. I expect to hear something soon."

After he'd gone back to his seat, the cockpit called to say they were hungry. I was setting up their trays when I heard the curtains rattle behind me and felt a hand on my butt.

"Hey—"

I whipped around, expecting that Malcolm had finally made his move. Instead, I found myself eye to eye with the pudgy chiropractor. He didn't look bored anymore. He held his empty beer glass in the hand he wasn't using to grope me.

"Just sampling the merchandise. So far, I like what I see."

He set the glass down and started to reach for me again. I grabbed his wrist. "I'm not exactly on the clock right now. Not yours, anyway."

His blue eyes danced in his raspberry soufflé face as he leaned in close enough for me to smell his deodorant. "You like it rough, right?" He let out a low groan that might have been aiming for sexy but sounded as if he had sciatica. "That's what I asked for."

I squeezed his wrist, roughly, and moved close enough that my knee brushed the inside of his thigh.

Not a lot of tone going on there. "You can't get rough enough for me, baby. What's the code word?"

"Mercury."

The correct response sent my heart pinging around in my chest like a copper BB in a tin can. I had successfully connected, a realization that both excited and terrified me. I couldn't wait to get him out of my space.

"Go back to your seat. I'll bring you another beer."

"Nine o'clock," he said. "Seven Oaks Hotel. Call before you come up."

After he disappeared behind the curtain, I picked up the Airfone and dialed up Harvey. I crossed my fingers that the call would go through. When it did, he picked up quickly.

"It's the chiropractor."

"Oh, dear. I still have not heard back from my contacts. I believe we are short of the critical facts we need for him."

"We have several hours yet. I'm not meeting him until nine o'clock. I'm sure you can come up with something by then."

"Is everything all right?" he asked. "You sound—"

"I'm fine."

"Are you sure? We can call this off."

I took a deep breath and tried to let my heartbeats space out. "Thanks for worrying, but I'm okay. I'll call you after we land." As I was hanging up, the toilet flushed, and my date for the evening emerged, gut first, tugging at his pants. About then is when what he said really started to sink in. He wanted rough sex.

Please, Harvey, please, come up with something good.

Malcolm took my rejection cheerfully. I wished he'd been a little less cheerful. Once I knew he hadn't tried to buy me for the evening, I had spent time talking to him—maybe flirting was more like it—throughout the service and after, mostly to keep from having to look at the chiropractor in 3E. Every time I looked his way, he seemed to be leering back at me.

We landed routinely, and as the passengers filed out, I stood at the door to bid them adieu and ask them to fly us again sometime. Malcolm slipped me his business card as he deplaned, which I tucked into a safe place. The baby titan dragged himself off, still looking distraught and listless. He did thank me for the Advil. My date went by with a wink that might not have seemed lewd to a casual observer.

I was gathering my own things, getting ready to leave, when my colleagues from coach started to filter up from the back. One of them, Monica, tapped me on the shoulder as she went by.

"I need to talk to you," she said. "Meet me out front."

Monica's name was as much as I knew about her. Besides one point late in the flight, when she'd come forward foraging for snacks, we hadn't spoken except to introduce ourselves. She didn't look happy when I approached, and I wondered if I had screwed something up again without even knowing it.

"We're switching," she said.

"Switching what?"

"We're swapping dates."

For about five seconds, I had the luxury of not completely absorbing the meaning of what she'd said. But then confusion gave way to understanding, which turned immediately to the highest state of alarm, and as she stared back at me and it all started clicking into place, I wondered why I had never come across her name or her face in my investigation.

"No. No way." I worked hard to keep my voice from turning shrill. "I'm not swapping dates with you."

"I know the chiropractor," she said, smiling a smile that could have been carved with a razor blade. "He's a big tipper, and I have seniority, so I'm taking him."

A big tipper? The guy cleaned out in his divorce? It had never occurred to me to look for another hooker onboard. Even if I had, what were the odds she'd recognize my date and decide to swipe him? I was so screwed.

"I'm not telling you where he's staying." I said it with more than a little desperate belligerence.

"Sweetheart, it's done. I've already talked to him. I'll be at the Seven Oaks tonight." She held up her very own cocktail napkin. It had notes scribbled on it in big, loopy, cheerleader handwriting. "You'll be here."

When I didn't take it from her right away, she let it go, and it fluttered to the floor. "Your code word is *Dallas*, and his response is *Alice*. He's expecting me."

"You didn't tell him you switched?"

"He's a first-timer. You'll do. And by the way, Curt prefers me to you, anyway. See ya."

Picking up the napkin seemed like a gesture of surrender that I didn't want her to see, so I waited until she was on her way before reaching down for it. Apparently, I was going to the Days Inn, which was bad enough. Worse than that was the time we were supposed to meet—eight o'clock. I checked my watch. I had two and a half hours to turn this thing around. I had to get to Harvey. I looked again at the napkin. No name. I checked the front and the back. There was no *name*.

Monica was almost out of sight. I felt like a cartoon with my rolling bag flying and sweat popping off my forehead as I maneuvered through the concourse to catch up with her.

"I told you it's done," she said, when I finally caught her, panting and gasping. "Don't bother me, or I'll give you a bad report, and you'll never get in. I know this is your test run."

"There's no room number here."

"Duh. He hasn't checked in yet."

I could barely talk, and not because I had exerted myself to catch her.

"Go to the hotel, and ask for him by name. He said he would leave word with the front desk that he had a guest coming."

"I don't *have* his name."

"You served him all through the flight."

"I did?" Oh, no. "Who—"

"I don't remember his name, but he was in 5F. Have fun, sweetie."

Monica pulled ahead quickly as I slowed to a stop and tried to think. 5F . . . 5F . . . 5F . . . was the *madras plaid shirt,* the man I had eliminated and proceeded to ignore for the rest of the flight. Leland Cole drank club soda with no ice, dressed older than he was, and that was the extent of what I knew about him. I couldn't even remember what he looked like.

I was so screwed.

chapter 21

THIS WAS A CHALLENGE. I KEPT REPEATING THAT to myself as I rolled down the concourse. The situation was not impossible. If I concentrated hard, I could find the way out. I could recognize the thread of an idea that, if followed to the logical conclusion, would spin itself into a workable plan, and where the hell was my cell phone? Miniaturization run amok. Electronic devices so small you can't find them in a space the size of a grocery bag.

By the time I'd reached the escalator, I had my phone in hand and Harvey's number ringing.

"Hello?"

"Harvey, it's Alex."

"Good. I have what you need. I could have used a few more hours, but I think I have managed to come up with something that will be useful to you."

"Harvey—"

"You already know that your chiropractor is thirty-eight years old and divorced, so nothing there. But listen to this. He coaches his thirteen-year-old daughter's soccer team. This all seems so unseemly to me, but—"

"Harvey."

"Yes? What is it?"

"Forget the chiropractor."

"I beg your pardon?"

"We have a new target."

"We have a—I do not understand. How could the target change?"

I hated even to go into it with him. I was barely staying afloat in my own whitewater rapids of anxiety. "There was another hooker onboard, and she decided to take that guy."

"Take him?"

"Yes. I have a new one, and I need you to do it again. I need you to check him out."

For the longest time, he didn't talk, but his breathing was perfectly audible, a faint whistle through his perennially blocked nasal passages. It grew shallower and quicker until he finally exploded. "This is absolutely preposterous. What in the world have you gotten yourself into?"

"Harvey, I know how ridiculous this seems . . . is, but I need your help. I can't do what you do. Give it a shot, please. If we can't do it, we can't, but let's at least try. Maybe there is something obvious we can use. If not, I'll have to bail."

"How much time?"

"I'm meeting him at eight o'clock my time."

I stepped outside to the curb. It wasn't until the cool breeze coming off Lake Michigan hit me that I realized how much I had been sweating. A shower would definitely be in order if I were going to pretend to have sex with a man I didn't know.

"This is absurd. You are putting yourself at unnecessary risk. I cannot support this. I will not. It is not worth it."

"Think about this, Harvey. The risk is no more or less

than it was half an hour ago. It's the same scam. Angel might also be doing this on purpose. We know this is a test. Maybe the switch is part of it, and if I bail, they'll know I'm a plant. I think we have to go through with it."

I checked up and down the curb, looking for the crew van, hoping they hadn't left without me. I wondered if I was in the right spot. I hadn't flown into O'Hare that much for OrangeAir.

"Do you understand that you will be in a room by yourself with a complete stranger?"

"Yes, Harvey."

"Have you considered the possibility that if you threaten him, he will not take it lightly? Have you considered the possibility that he could rape you? Or injure you? Or kill you? Please do not do this."

He could have been right. Maybe he was right. But I also knew Harvey was inclined to give up, whereas my bias was toward never, ever giving up. I knew that I was capable of holding out beyond the point of all reason, trying to salvage what was clearly already lost. I just didn't think this cause was lost yet. I closed my eyes and pressed the heel of my hand against my forehead. I had probably missed the damn shuttle.

"Harvey, I appreciate the fact that you are worried about me, and I am really annoyed that this thing went off the tracks, but I don't think it's too late to get it back on. I believe we have to try, and if you won't help me, I'll do it myself. It would be nicer to have the information, but if I don't, I'll play the trump card."

"Which is?"

"No matter who he is, he will not want the world to know he hired a hooker for his layover in Chicago. I'll threaten to look him up and tell his wife. Or his kids. Or his boss. Or the good citizens of the PTA. Whatever makes him vulnerable. It might work." I was talking to myself more than to Harvey. I hadn't really given this option much thought until now. "I'm not asking him to do that much."

"I knew from the beginning you would do it your way no matter what."

"You were right. Will you help me or not?"

He hung up.

Even for a Days Inn, the hotel struck me as shabby, more so because it was supposed to appeal to families and may have at one time. Just off the lobby was a dingy game room with tired pinball machines and electronic games about one generation too old. It had an indoor swimming pool behind a greasy wall of windows. I knew because I had been walking the halls procrastinating and trying to get in touch with Harvey.

He hadn't answered his phone for more than an hour, so it was no surprise when he didn't answer again. He hadn't categorically stated that he wouldn't help, although that could have been one interpretation of his hanging up in my ear. I chose to believe that his line was tied up because he was working on his computer. That wouldn't explain why his cell phone was off, but his cell phone was usually off.

His voice-mail tone sounded.

"Harvey, I don't know if you're checking your voice mail, but I hope so, because I want you to know that I'm sorry. I had no right to pressure you, but I'm so wound up over this case. I feel somehow that if I don't . . . if we don't solve it, then everything I want to do will be out of my reach. That doesn't leave much room for you and your point of view, and for that I'm sorry. If by any chance you have managed to find something on this

Leland Cole, please call me on my cell phone. I'm going up there right now."

I slapped the phone shut. A searing pain shot across the webbing that held my thumb to my hand. I had pinched it at the phone's hinge. *Dammit,* that hurt. I jammed the throbbing wound into my mouth and paced around the lobby again. It was already four minutes after eight. If I waited much longer, my date would call hooker central and report me as a no-show. I could make up an excuse. Traffic. Illness. The dog ate the address. Monica ate the address.

I went to the elevator and pressed the call button. After waiting at least two seconds, I decided to take the stairs. With no other delay tactics available, I found myself at his room in front of his door. I raised my hand to knock and didn't. I stood there, frozen in front of the last barrier between my client and me. If I was going to do this, I had to do it.

I knocked once, then three more times quickly.

Mr. 5F opened the door, and I realized how little attention I had paid him throughout the flight. Seeing him in this entirely new context, as a patron of hookers, was like seeing him for the first time. He was probably five-nine or five-ten—only slightly taller than I was—prissy, flat-chested, and fragile. His head was small compared with his squared-off ironing-board shoulders, and he had the posture of a man married to a woman who wore sleeveless shifts and tailored shorts and kept him on an allowance. If it came down to a fight, I could take him.

He looked at me with an expression of stunned surprise fluttering his almost-invisible eyelashes.

"I'm Alex. We have an appointment for this evening. You got my message, didn't you?"

"Yes, but . . ." He poked his head out into the hallway

and checked left and right; then he spoke to me with tight-jawed urgency. "You changed clothes."

I looked down at my ensemble, a simple little black jersey dress and the obligatory high heels, a pair of strappy sandals. The outfit was more age-appropriate than the one I'd worn to the party in LA, and I thought it was perfectly acceptable for a faux date with a real john, and why did everyone feel obligated to comment on my clothing choices?

"Yes, I changed clothes. I also showered."

"You weren't supposed to change. That was my arrangement."

Arrangement? "I wasn't told of any special arrangements, but if you let me in, I'm sure we can work something out."

"Like what? You're wearing the wrong thing."

Another door opened and closed a few rooms away. A woman with her two small children headed for the elevator. They were excited, going swimming in that chlorinated scum pond downstairs.

"Let's talk about it inside, shall we?" I swept in, giving him no time to object. At least, if I was in the room, I had a chance of getting what I needed. Outside, I had none.

It was a standard hotel layout. The bathroom was a few feet inside the front door, which could be handy if a hasty escape was called for. The rest of the room was dominated by a bed that seemed gigantic, although I was pretty sure that was in my head, since it also resembled a large vat of quicksand.

When I turned back to find him, I saw that he was doing an inventory of his own, staring at my body in much the same way Tony the Actor had in LA. I was beginning to understand this cold and dispassionate precoital inspection was included in the purchase price.

Still, I took his heavy sigh of disappointment personally. Couldn't help it.

"You were supposed to come in uniform," he whined. "You were supposed to come in the one you wore on the trip out. The one that smells like you." He gestured with his hand, as if he could wipe me away. "This is not what I paid for."

Great. A fetishist, and me here without the object of his fetish. Monica had not shared this crucial piece of information with me. "Look, I can't give you the uniform, but I can give you anything else you might like." I pulled the straps of my dress off my shoulders and tried to show a little cleavage as I posed for him. That's exactly what I had—little cleavage. But I squeezed together and made the best of what was there. "After all, I wasn't going to have the uniform on that long, anyway, was I?"

He stared for a long time. His thin lips parted enough that I could see the tip of his tongue playing across the edge of his straight white teeth. His eyes shone with a quavering anticipation, and when his weight shifted from one foot to the other, I knew I had him. Now, what to do with him?

I turned to drop my bag in the nearest chair. "So, you have a thing for flight attendants." Before I could turn back, he was on me. He had slipped in and clamped his arms around me from behind, one arm pressed against my throat.

"Whoa—"

My first thought was that he wanted to hurt me. His arms were rigid and inflexible. But then I felt him awkwardly but persistently grinding his hips against me.

"I wanted to do it onboard the airplane," he whispered. "I wanted to be in the Mile-High Club, but they said they didn't sell those. They said I could get the uniform instead. They promised me that."

He was much stronger than I would have guessed, and though he might not have wanted to hurt me, the faster he pumped, the tighter he squeezed my throat. I could feel his excitement mounting. I could feel his control slipping away and my head getting lighter. I reached up to pull on his arm, then thought of a more vulnerable target. I worked my arm around behind me, grabbed a handful of his most excited appendage, and squeezed through his pants. Hard.

"Owww!" When he released me, I released him. I spun out of his grasp and backed away, where I could observe from a safe distance.

He looked up, genuinely perplexed. "What was that?"

I rubbed my throat where his wristwatch had dug in. "I thought we were playing rough," I said. My voice was squeaky from the pressure on my larynx. "Isn't that what you were doing?"

"No. That hurt."

"That's the point, sweetie. Now, if you'll excuse me, I have to go and powder my nose."

As I headed for the bathroom, I spied the Spectravision tent card on top of the TV. Dirty movies. Perfect. "Hey . . ." I took the card and tossed it onto the bed. "Do you like to watch? Pick something to set the mood. I'll be right back."

I left him still holding his crotch and reaching for the remote.

There was no lock on the bathroom door, so I sat on the floor with my back against it and tried to calm down. My face felt hot, and the tiles were cold, and I closed my eyes and tried to split off, to make myself into two different people. That must have been what these women did, anyway, split off and disconnect from their bodies. How else could they do this night after night? One puny, horny guy had grabbed me from behind, and I was reeling.

I pulled my phone out of my bag and held it against my chest as though it could absorb the shuddering of my heart. I listened for the sound of the movie to begin on the other side of the door. For the first time, I began to really consider what Harvey had said about being in over my head.

The moment the cheap porno sound track kicked in, I flipped open the phone and called Harvey's number. This time, he picked up right away.

"Alex?"

"Harvey, you were right. I shouldn't have come here, but I did, and if you don't give me something in the next thirty seconds that I can use, I'm in trouble. Please tell me you've been working on this. Please tell me you found something."

"I was sitting down to call you. I think I have what you need."

As I listened, I felt all the tension in my shoulders drain out. My core temperature came down from triple digits. After I hung up, I stood in front of the mirror and reorganized myself. I straightened my hair and smoothed my skirt. When I came out of the bathroom, my date was lying on the bed, staring at the small TV screen. Judging from the bulge under the sheet, he had started without me.

"I've been thinking about you," he said.

"I can see that. I've been thinking about you, too . . . Reverend Cole."

chapter 22

I WAS OUT OF THE GOOD REVEREND'S HOTEL room in half an hour, which was not soon enough for him. He had readily agreed to vouch for me with the powers that be and insisted on making the required contact right in front of me so I would have no reason to doubt him. I insisted he do it with his pants on.

I tried to pry more information out of him, but he was a basket case. He had only the Web site we already knew about. His ID and password were temporary since he was new. My guess was, it had expired after he'd booked. Since this was his first time, that was all he had to offer. Judging by his horrified reaction, it would be his last.

Feeling good about the successful operation, I called Harvey on my way back to the crew hotel. He managed to act as excited as Harvey can, only once referring to the dangerous circumstances. He never mentioned our disagreement, but something had shifted in our relationship. I could feel it. He knew he could no longer trust me. I had meant what I said when I told him I wouldn't go in unless we were both comfortable. In the end, I had done what I always did—exactly what I wanted. It had worked, but at what cost? I hadn't meant for it to happen, which only proved something else. When it came down to it, maybe I couldn't trust myself.

Yawning and creaking from the long, tense day, I unlocked the door to my own hotel room, pushed through, and dropped my key on the dresser. I wasn't listening for the door to close behind me. I wasn't thinking about it at all until it didn't close. When I turned, it was already too late. A big man in a yellow sport coat had followed me in. With one large hand on the door and one foot already in, there was no way he could be pushed back out, but I tried anyway, throwing all my weight against the formidable metal and wood door. It was no contest.

He reached his other oaken arm up and pushed back so hard the door slammed into my head, and I was on the floor. When I looked up, he was inside my room. With a calm manner that I found chilling, he closed and locked the door. The snap of the dead bolt as it slipped into place was like a rib cracking in my chest.

Oh, God.

Phone. They were usually . . . it was across the room on the far nightstand. I crabwalked backward to the bed. I was on it, across it, and down the other side in seconds. The base of the phone went flying when I grabbed the receiver. I crouched low and peeked at him across the top of the bed. He lingered at the door with his back turned.

Where the hell was the *O*? I couldn't think. There was a sea of information plastered across the front of the phone. Housekeeping . . . messages . . . bell stand . . . the *O*. It was there. I punched it, punched it, punched it. The line began to ring. It kept ringing, the sound teasing me into thinking someone would pick up. Answer. *Someone, please answer.*

He was moving toward me now, buttoning his jacket on the way, a jacket that was the color of lemon chiffon pie. I looked around for anything that wasn't nailed down. Lightweight floor lamp. Heavy chair. Clock radio. Fight or run? Notepad. Magazine. Pencil. Run or fight? Pillows. Run *where?*

He cleared the corner of the bed. Since his hands were at my eye level, that's where I focused. They were big. His nails were smooth and square. His only adornment was a ring large enough to fit around a bratwurst. Gold with a red stone, gaudy like the rest of his attire. I was halfway to my feet with the receiver pressed to my ear. I reached down around my thigh, found the cord that led from the base of the phone to the wall, and started to wrap it around my hand.

"Hang up the phone." His voice was heavy with a choppy accent that sounded eastern European.

"What do you want?"

"I want you to hang up the phone."

"Um . . ." I needed a few more twists of the cord. It was slow work because of the way my hand was flopping and jerking. "Who are you?"

"If you do not hang up now, I will be forced to take the telephone away from you."

I tried to look as if I were thinking it over. Hard to do when I was actually checking for ways to get around him. I could slip over the bed. If I waited for exactly the right moment, I could beat him to the door. I was quicker, more agile. Probably.

"Do not try to run from me. You will not make it, and it will go worse for you."

What would go worse for me? "All right, I won't."

I jerked the phone cord from the wall and used it as a whip to sling the base at his head. He batted it away. I dove across the bed and landed hard enough to crush the air from my lungs. His hand closed around my ankle. I kicked at him with my other foot. Hit nothing. Kept my legs churning and my arms swimming toward the side of the bed. Tried to scream but couldn't draw enough breath to get anything out.

He yanked my leg, but I held tight to the far side of the mattress. He yanked again, this time snapping my hipbone in its socket. The sharp pain of bone jammed on bone pissed me off. I kicked harder. When he yanked for the last time, I shot backward and over the side and back to the floor. The heavy bedspread with sheets, still bunched in my fists, came with me. I pulled it over my head. He tried to grab me, and I scrambled under the bed. He found my wrist and used it to fish me out. With my free hand, I reached up and felt the top of the bedside table for anything I could grab to fend him off, drive him away, stop or at least delay whatever it was he was about to do to me.

Then I was on my feet, back flat against the wall, with his face close to mine and my right wrist caught in his left paw. It felt odd to be suddenly still. Breathing was hard, because I was so scared and choked with panic and because his other hand was clamped around my throat.

His respirations, on the other hand, were quite normal, his shoulders relaxed, and both grips steady. The only physical response my frantic fleeing had caused in him was a slightly ruddier complexion and a glistening of the deep gouges that lined his forehead.

"Please, I asked you not to run. You said you wouldn't." His voice held more than a little disappointment.

"Sorry." My voice was a dry croak. "It's in my nature."

He stared down at me for a few seconds, and I thought I saw a hint of a smile ghost across his chiseled lips.

"I am here to deliver a message. It stops now. Do you understand?"

"Okay. What stops now? I don't—"

"Stay away from Arthur Margolies," he said. "You will not call. You will not send e-mails. You will not see him. If that video ever sees the light of day, I will find you, and I will kill you. If you contact the police, I will kill you. Do you understand?"

"I don't . . . I didn't—" I didn't know what he was talking about, but I couldn't talk. It didn't matter. He wasn't listening.

In one seamless motion, he gripped my throat, lifted me nearly off my feet, and slammed me so hard my head bounced off the wall. The pictures rattled. My hands flew up to claw at his.

"Don't try to fight it." His voice had a soothing, almost-comforting quality. "It makes it worse."

I couldn't *not* fight. It wasn't a decision my brain made. Tears streamed from my eyes like blood from a fresh wound. I felt them on his hands as I tried to pry his fingers loose. My mouth stretched open. My stomach wanted to squeeze up the back of my throat. I gagged against the feeling of his hand on my windpipe. My chest heaved, trying to pull in oxygen. Every time I thought I would pass out, he'd ease up just enough to let air in so I wouldn't.

"You get one chance, and this is it. Do you understand? Stop what you are doing. Destroy the videos."

I tried to dig my fingernails in, but he only squeezed harder. I felt the tips of his thumb and his fingers almost meeting at the nape of my neck. I felt his palm, dry as sandpaper, against the concavity of my throat. He eased off again.

"This is the end of the message."

The pressure resumed, and I felt myself drifting. I closed my eyes and concentrated on breathing, and everything turned black.

I woke up in the dark, the side of my face mashed against a pillow. I rolled onto my back, reached for my throat, and stared up at the ceiling. For the longest time, the only messages that got through to my congealed brain were those telling me how many parts of my body were in pain. My hip and my side just below my armpit. My wrists and my ankle and the back of my head. I reached back and touched it, felt the scar from another time, another mishap. Everything in my throat felt improperly arranged for swallowing, so that hurt, too.

Eventually, other stuff started to seep in. I was on a bed. I pushed up against the headboard until I was sitting. I squeezed my eyes shut and held still, both hands cradling my head. In time and with great effort, I remembered that I was in a hotel room and had been attacked. What I couldn't remember was climbing onto the bed. I didn't like having whole swaths of memory deleted from my consciousness.

I moved to the side and dropped my legs over. The floor seemed like a long way away, so I sat with my legs dangling, thinking about standing up. A glass of water sat on the nightstand. Everything else that had been on either nightstand was scattered on the floor, knocked there during the fracas. But there sat a glass of water, and why was my bed made? I vividly remembered dragging the linens onto the floor.

I tried to stand, but the room slanted and slid across the surface of the earth, so I went down on my hands and knees and crawled into the bathroom. After a short rest leaning against the bathtub, I stood up and checked the mirror. Lint from the carpet had collected on my face in streams made damp by my tears. My eyes were bloodshot. My pale face made the pools of bright red around my throat burn that much hotter. I leaned in to take a closer look at the violated area. The splotches were red fingerprints in the configuration of his hand on my throat. Remembering the pressure and what it had done to my body almost made me vomit.

The water when I turned it on was cold. I leaned over the sink and started with a few slow splashes to the face that would have made me shiver if I wasn't already racked with violent spasms. As the water turned warm, I unwrapped a bar of soap and used it to wash, scrubbing every inch of my face with the pads of my fingers, trying to massage the pain out. I wobbled to the shower and started it running. The double bolt on the door did not seem formidable enough, so I pulled the dresser across the carpet to block myself in. It was so heavy it took me almost twenty minutes. By then, the whole room was humid from the shower. I went to the windows and checked those locks, then back to the bathroom, where I peeled off the little black dress, the same one I'd worn to visit the reverend, and disappeared into the steam. A long time later, I was on the floor of the tub, legs pulled up and gathered in by arms that couldn't hold them tight enough, rocking back and forth and trying to stop shaking.

chapter 23

HARVEY STOOD NEXT TO ME, LAYING THE crime-scene photos of Robin Sevitch on his desk one at a time, pausing after each one for emphasis. It was his subtle way of saying "I told you so."

They were hard to look at. In the wider angles, you could see the position of the body, the way it slumped against the wall of what the police described as a concrete drainage canal. Her left hand was caught behind her back, but the other lay on the concrete at her side, palm up, with fingers curled in. She looked as if she were beckoning for help. Or showing her nails—torn, split, and painted with the brownish tint of her own dried blood.

When he got to the close-ups of her face, I reached up and touched the bruises on my throat. Her nose was broken, and she had a gash that looked as if she'd bitten through her lower lip. One eye was pinched shut by the cauliflowered mass around it, but the other gazed out from behind dark and bruised tissue.

"Harvey . . ."

"She died of a broken neck." He continued with the parade of grotesque images.

That her spine had been snapped at its most vulnerable point was obvious from the awkward way her head hung from her shoulders. An unbroken arc of pale skin pressed against the smooth curve of muscles and tendons that ran from the base of her left ear to the hollow of her throat. Absent blood and bruises, it gleamed under the camera's flash, obscenely undamaged to be hiding such a catastrophic rupture beneath. My heart shuddered against its vulnerability, this last part of her that still looked like her, offered up by the exaggerated tilt of her head, undefended by arms that lay still at her sides.

I reached over and stopped him from putting any more down. "Harvey, enough."

He stared down at me, looking more vigorous than I had ever seen him. His strength was fueled by his anger. I had waited until I had flown back to Boston from Chicago to give him the news of my attack, thinking it might go better in person. I might have been wrong about that.

"How could you not tell me? How could you keep this from me? Why did you not call me right away?"

"I didn't want to upset you."

"A large man attacked you in your hotel room in a strange city and tried to kill you. Why would that upset me? I told you your plan was too risky."

I wanted to pull my feet up in the chair and curl myself around my legs. This day had already been difficult enough. I had worked my trip home as scheduled, moving through a world of strangers like a big, raw nerve, wondering which of them might, without warning, raise a hand or a weapon and try to hurt me. It had taken a lot of energy. I wasn't sure I had enough in reserve to properly defend my incautious and possibly stupid behavior.

"You told me the fake date was too risky. This was something different. Besides, he wasn't trying to kill me."

"Alex, please." He took a step back to lean against his desk. "Even you cannot be this obtuse."

"There was something odd about this whole thing. He left me on the bed, Harvey. After I passed out—"

"After he choked you to unconsciousness."

"—he put me on my bed with my head on a pillow, and he left a glass of water for me on the nightstand."

"How gracious. A turndown service to go with the strangling."

"He was there to deliver a message, one that made no sense to me. He said he wanted me to leave someone alone, a guy named Arthur Margolies, and to destroy the videos. I looked up Arthur Margolies. He's a big frequent flier on OrangeAir out of Chicago."

"So?"

"I think he was after Monica and not me."

"What? Why?"

"I think he's a client of the hooker ring—of Monica's, specifically—and I think she's trying to extort him using videos. Probably sex videos." I looked up at him. "That's the only thing that makes sense."

"None of this makes sense."

"Maybe not, but I have to try to make sense of it so I can continue to function. I don't think this guy was after me, which means I don't think he will come after me. That's important."

He crossed his arms and hunched his shoulders. He didn't look to be in the mood for new theories. He liked the one where we all stayed locked in our houses afraid for our lives, because that was more or less what he did every day anyway. "You believe the last-minute switch confused your attacker?"

"I believe he was set up on the trick, the man who was supposed to be hiring Monica for the evening. How, I don't know. Maybe he had inside information that Reverend Cole was her scheduled date. It would have been easy enough for someone to check his reservation and see what hotel he'd booked. The big guy saw me come out, followed me to my hotel, and attacked me—by mistake. I got a message that was supposed to be for Monica."

He reached down and began kneading the muscles in his thigh. "What does Monica say?"

"Good question. She was supposed to work the trip home with us, but suddenly she's on emergency leave. I'm pretty sure he was after her and not me, and she knows it."

"Do you think she switched dates on purpose?"

"I don't know. I plan to ask her."

I looked over and saw that his leg was beginning to shake. It started quietly but quickly turned into a jackhammer. He gripped his balky quadriceps with both hands. I jumped up and tried to give him the closest seat—mine—but he wanted to go around to his desk chair. I helped him around the desk and held his chair so it wouldn't swivel as he sat down in it.

"Are you all right?"

He nodded, pulled a handkerchief from his pocket, and mopped his forehead. I went back to my seat, and the two of us sat in silence. The only sound was the sharp ticking of the old mantel clock that kept perfect time because Harvey wound it religiously. His great-grandfather, a clockmaker, had brought it from Poland.

"This man," he said quietly, "he could have done worse to you."

"But he didn't. I'm fine."

"Alex." He folded his handkerchief, looking more bereft than angry. "Am I so little comfort to you?"

I sank back into my seat and closed my eyes. I was mentally, physically, emotionally, and every other possible way exhausted. Did he really want to talk about this now?

"Please," he insisted. "Say what you are thinking."

I had to work hard to figure out what I was thinking and how much of it I could say. "I care about you, Harvey, and I hate seeing you this way. I didn't call you because I didn't want you sitting here by yourself in the dark . . . worrying."

"You were afraid you would make me sick?" His eyes blinked rapidly, and I could tell by the way he tried to hold himself that his body was still in turmoil. "My disease causes my symptoms, not you. Let me make my small contribution, even if it is only to sit in my house by the phone and worry about you."

"That's not your only contribution." It was hard for me to look at him. He was trying in his clumsy way to talk about something important, to sort out our roles and what we were to each other and maybe what we should be. It made me want to be truthful. "I didn't call anyone, Harvey."

"You didn't?"

"No. I never do. When I'm in trouble, I deal with it myself. It's not you. It has nothing to do with you being sick. I'm just not someone who takes comfort easily from anyone. I've always been that way. I can give it, but I never learned how to take it." I wanted again to pull my feet up into the chair. This time I did it. "It's one reason I'm still alone."

He let out a sigh that seemed to calm him. "I suppose we have that in common, then."

I hadn't thought about it that way, but he was right.

Harvey bristled at the thought of accepting help from anyone. "You are important to this case," I said. "You are important to me. While I'm out there, I'm always asking myself, what would Harvey think? Mostly it's in the sense of 'Harvey will kill me if I do this.' " That elicited a hesitant grin. "I don't take direction well, and I always think I'm right about everything, but that doesn't mean I'm not listening."

He seemed all right with that. I waited a few moments to make sure. Sometimes it took him a few minutes to get his thoughts out. He was still; he wasn't shaking anymore, and his breathing was steady. The subject seemed to be closed. Thank goodness.

I pulled one of Robin's pictures back in front of me. "What's the story with this? I thought it was a homeless man."

"The official story was that Robin Sevitch went out for a long walk, roamed too close to a dangerous area, and was beaten to death by this homeless man. He was convicted." He took off his glasses and rubbed his eyes. "There are doubts in some quarters, however, that he was, indeed, the guilty party."

"Really?" I put my feet down on the floor and sat up straight. "What did you find out?"

"I told you I had a hard time getting anyone to talk to me."

"Right, right. Civic black eye and all that. How did you get the file?"

"The gentleman who was the lead detective on the case is now a private investigator. He kept his own file. He suspected Miss Sevitch was murdered by someone she knew. He thinks it was a trick, but he was pressured heavily to go with the homeless theory, and ultimately the man confessed."

"Who pressured him?"

"It was never clear to him where it came from. He went to great lengths to impress upon me that the Omaha PD is a conscientious and professional organization. This was not a case of incompetence."

"Was she robbed?"

"All of her money and identification was in her hotel room."

"Was she raped?"

"It did not appear so."

"This homeless man, what was supposed to be his motive?"

"He is a man with a low IQ, borderline schizophrenic. He had no motive, none that he could give, anyway."

I flipped through the pictures. It was certainly possible one person could beat a perfect stranger that savagely for no good reason. "Did this homeless man have a history of violence?"

"No."

"Okay, so that makes no sense at all. Let's try the trick theory. Was there any sign of struggle in her hotel room?"

"No."

"So maybe she went with this person voluntarily. Was she killed in the ditch?"

"Yes."

"These hookers are high-class. They don't typically have dates in drainage canals. She wasn't raped, but had she had sex?"

"She had had sex recently, but she was a prostitute. There was no semen. The former detective believes the man wore a condom."

"What about trace evidence and all that good stuff? Fibers and blood evidence."

"You need something to compare to. If it was a trick, he could have boarded a plane and flown away. If he had no police record and no connection to the victim, it would be very difficult ever to find him."

"This detective didn't buy the homeless theory, either?"

"His biggest concern was the lack of motive."

There was a motive. It just wasn't his. "Was Angel in the area?"

"Unclear. If she was, she was never questioned. There was not a broad investigation. The man confessed, and that was that."

"According to Tristan, Angel had reason to get rid of Robin Sevitch. Was it possible she could have hired this man?"

"No. There was no indication of anything like that."

"She could have hired some pros to kill her."

"Professionals," he said, quite reasonably, "do not linger at the crime scene to beat their victims."

"Is the homeless man in jail for this?"

He blew out a long and heavy sigh. "He is homeless no more. For life."

I collected all the pictures into one pile. As I looked at them, it was hard not to feel the beating Robin had taken in my own face, in the fragile bones that would break, in the soft tissue that would bruise and swell under the pounding. Beaten to death connoted suffering. It was a brutality far more intimate than could come from the cold disgorgement of a bullet from a gun, or even from the ripping of a knife through flesh. A knife still separated killer from victim, if only by the length of its blade. Whoever murdered Robin Sevitch had walked away with blood on his hands.

Or hers.

"Can I keep these, Harvey?"

"Certainly. The photos must be returned."

"So, where are we?" I asked. "We have less than a week before the review. We have one dead hooker, one live hooker who is possibly a blackmailer and possibly in hiding. We have a bunch of surveillance photos that prove very little. And we have Angel, who may or may not have gotten away with murder and may or may not call back, depending on whether I passed her test."

"That is not all." He gave me a tight little smile. "We have top swappers."

"We do?"

"Indeed, we do. Would you care to see them?"

"Indeed, I would."

He moved a large stack of files and reports from the corner of his desk to the middle of what was now his clean desk. He went through the stack like a blackjack dealer, laying exhibits and printouts and reports on the desk one by one. "This is a copy of the as-bid schedules for the Boston base over the past six months." That was a particularly fat document. "This is the as-flown schedule." Equally fat.

"You got those from Carl Wolff?"

"He had someone send them." He put down a third document that was slender compared with the others. "This is the list of all the trips that were traded over the past six months, and these"—he laid down a single page—"are your so-called top swappers."

"Cool." I reached for it. "So, these are our hookers?"

He pulled it back. "These are flight attendants who do a high level of swapping during the month on average. I would hesitate to label them all prostitutes, primarily because you are on the list."

"I am?" That was a surprise, although not really

when I thought it through. It stood to reason that if I were following swappers around, I would have to do a high level of swapping myself.

"Step two, as you will recall, was to overlay the swap list with anyone who appeared to have more assets in her name than could be reasonably supported by her reported income. I used their W-2 salaries, which include all premiums."

"That step would definitely eliminate me."

"As it did several." He pulled another single sheet from the file and dangled it in front of me. "This is the subset of names that resulted."

"Then *these* are our hookers." I snatched the page from him. There were thirty-five names on the list. Some of the names were surprises. Some weren't. Most surprising of all were the names that weren't there.

"Where's Angel? Where are Sally and Ava and Claudia and Charlotte? None of them is on this list."

"Yes."

"Yes, why?"

"Their names come up in the financial filter, but they do not qualify on the swapper criteria. They fly the schedule, for the most part, as they bid it."

"Why would that be?" I put the page back on the desk—it suddenly represented a major disappointment—and got up to stretch out stiff muscles and wander a bit. I ended up at Harvey's bookshelves, staring blankly at some of the titles. Mostly he read biographies, history, and business books, but he did have a weakness for good science fiction. I liked looking at those best, because it was a part of him that was unexpected. Also because of the cool titles.

"Maybe the top women have regulars," I said, trying the best explanation that came to me. That didn't mean it was a good one. "Maybe they can plan their liaisons further in advance. But they would still have to do some swapping. Where do they fall on your list?"

"Who am I looking for, exactly?"

"Just look for Angel and Sally. Velesco and Prentiss."

He took his glasses off and held his list of swappers at arm's length. Every once in a while, he'd put it flat on the table and check something from another pile. Eventually, he had his answer. "In the top one hundred."

"Out of six hundred fifty total at the base, right?"

"Yes, but only eight-five percent are women."

"Would it be possible that they could get their dates to come to them? Wouldn't that be amazing?"

I went back to my chair and settled in with my arms folded on the desk in front of me.

"You seem disappointed," he said.

"No, not at all. More like devastated. That report only gets the soldiers, not the generals. You have to cut off the head of this snake to kill it. Angel would just hire more women."

"You do not know that."

"There are so many things we don't know. If Angel and the others are hookers, why aren't they on that report? What's a pool girl? What was Monica up to, with this blackmail scheme, and is Angel part of that?" I glanced at the file at my elbow. "What happened to Robin Sevitch?"

Harvey leaned in and put both palms on the desktop. He looked as if he were making handprints in cement. "We have accomplished much. You have accomplished a great deal, and if we were to stop now, which I suggest we do, you can be happy with what you have done."

"I don't feel as if I've accomplished anything." I

picked up the file and climbed out of the chair. "I'm going home to bed."

It was after three when I walked into my apartment. It seemed as if it should be much later, but only because I had been up for almost two days. It was a brisk afternoon. Since my apartment basked in the morning sun, it chilled in the afternoon shadows, so it was cool inside. I dropped today's slug of mail on the counter, punched up the first of two phone messages, and went to open one of the radiator valves.

Za, got your message. I was thinking . . . I've been going running most mornings I've been up here along the river, and I was wondering . . . if you wanted to come . . . I mean, I would like for you to come with me if you can make it. If you want to.

There was a pause where he could have been thinking what I was, that it would be like old times for Jamie and me to go running together.

Anyway, if you want to meet me, I'll be at the Dartmouth footbridge at five-thirty tomorrow morning. If you can't, that's cool, too. I'll catch up with you later.

It was good to hear his voice. There was something about the case and being in Angel's world that made me feel lonely and hungry for some kind of deeper connection, one that Harvey and I couldn't give each other. In spite of all our ups and downs, Jamie was still the one person in the world who knew me best. When I called his cell phone, I got his voice mail. I left a message that I would meet him to go running.

I erased Jamie and punched up the next message.

Dear, where are *you? Have you fallen from the face of the earth? I cannot find you anywhere.*

The sound of Tristan's voice was instantly guilt-inducing. I had not answered his calls to my cell phone, once because I'd been with Angel and twice when I'd been with Harvey. If I'd answered, I would have had to make up some story about where I was. I had already lied to Tristan enough.

I want to know how things went with brother Jamie. You have called him, haven't you? Also, Barry and I are having a small dinner party tomorrow at eight. A couple of his real estate friends are coming. Irene is bringing Claire. We want you, of course, and anyone you might want to bring. Bring Jamie! It will be very extravagant. So RSVP me, dahling. Talk to you soon. There was a pause, but he didn't hang up. *I hope . . . is everything all right? Call me when you get this. I'm worried about you.*

I picked up the phone and dialed, but it wasn't to call Tristan. I dialed Felix in Miami.

"Hey, Miss Shanahan."

It never failed to throw me when someone answered the phone with my name instead of hello. As far as I was concerned, caller ID had disrupted the very fabric of the universe. "Um . . . Felix?"

"Hi. I'm glad you called. I was just working on your stuff."

"So, you got everything? No problem with the encryption?"

"Huh? Oh, no. Piece of cake. I've already figured it out."

"Figured what out?"

"The Web site you sent me. I know exactly what he's doing. It's pretty cool, too. I haven't seen this before. Not personally. I've read about it."

He sounded enthused, which caused me to feel a flutter of hope as I opened the refrigerator door and stared in. Could this actually be good news? "What's he doing?"

"Using time-limited reverse proxy servers. I think it started in Russia or Estonia or . . . I don't know, one of those Eastern Bloc countries."

"Time-limited what?"

"Oh, it's a new trick that hackers use to hide their identity."

"Hide their identity?" I felt less hopeful. I closed the refrigerator and opened the freezer and discovered that I'd already eaten all my four-minute microwave meals. I would have to settle for a protein shake. I got out the blender, the protein powder, and an ice tray. "How does it work, Felix?"

"What he does is download a rogue program over the Internet to some innocent person's PC, one with DSL, because with DSL the door is always open. He hijacks that machine and uses its high-speed connection to do his stuff, but he sets it up so that it looks like it's coming from a big server, a master Web server. Whoever's PC it is never even knows it's being used as a proxy. It makes it almost impossible to track."

"Hold on, Felix." I hit the puree button and let the blender run until dinner was ready. Then I took my milkshake and retired to the couch. "Can't you track back through the proxy to the server to the hacker?"

"Nuh-uh. That's the time-limited part. What makes it work is that he uses these proxy PCs only for a few minutes at a time before rotating. By the time I identify the first proxy, he's on to the next one. It's a constantly moving target. It's pretty smart. It's what makes him almost completely anonymous, which is why I haven't found him yet. Oh, I guess that's, like, bad news, huh?"

"You can't track him?"

"I can track him, but the quickest anyone has done it

is in seven or eight days." Which was too long. All I had was five days.

"So, this guy is good?"

"This guy is very good, Miss Shanahan. But," he hastened to add, "not better than me. No. No way he's better. I'll find a way to track him. I promise you."

Dueling hackers. This should be interesting. Showdown at the IT Corral.

"If you can do it in less than seven days, that would be very helpful, Felix. Did you actually get into the site?"

"I did, but there's not much in there. Just some input screens for name, address, and flight number. Do you want me to send you a password so you can look at it?"

"Please. Send it to my partner, too, if you don't mind."

"You have a partner?"

I gave him Harvey's e-mail address and an explanation. The last time Felix and I had worked together, I had been someone between jobs looking into a friend's death.

"Wow. So you'll be a real private investigator with a license and everything?"

"I'm working on it."

"You are so cool, Miss S. You'll be so good at this."

It was unexpectedly and deeply satisfying to feel his enthusiasm. It was exactly what I needed to hear after Harvey's grim and graphic scolding. "Is there anything I could get you, Felix, that might speed up the process?"

"Just send me anything you can get. You never know which piece is going to be the one, you know?"

I had another thought. I found my backpack, dragged it over, and dug out my notepad.

"Felix, I don't know what you can do with this, but take it down." I read him Arthur Margolies's e-mail address, which I'd pulled out of the OrangeAir reservations system, and spelled out his name.

"Who's this person?"

"I think he's the victim of an extortion scheme, probably perpetrated by a hooker named Monica. Monica Russeau. She might have been sending demands through e-mail. Do you think you could get into his computer through his e-mail program?"

"I'll check it out. If he has DSL, I might be able to get in and scope it out."

"Look for anything from, to, or related in any way to Monica Russeau."

"Okay. I might be able to track back to hers, too. Would that help?"

"Anything helps at this point, Felix."

After we hung up, it was quiet. There wasn't much going on in my building at three in the afternoon. I reached up and probed the tender areas of my throat. When I touched all the places Mr. Lemon Chiffon had squeezed so effectively, it took me back to the moments before I lost consciousness, the paralyzing fear, and the feeling of being completely overwhelmed and helpless.

Maybe Harvey was right. Maybe it wasn't worth it. Maybe this case was already as good as it needed to get. Maybe my deepest, darkest fear was not a fear at all but a fact: I was already in way over my head.

I sat back, drank my shake, and felt at least a partial rejuvenation from the infusion of protein. I thought about what Felix had said, and another interpretation occurred to me. If, indeed, I was already in over my head, perhaps the key phrase was that I was *already in,* and the only way to get to the other side was to keep swimming.

I went to my desk, dug out my base roster, and looked up Monica Russeau's home phone number. I didn't expect to get an answer, and I didn't. I hung up without leaving a message. I wasn't about to give her fair warning. She hadn't given any to me.

chapter 24

THE STONE STEPS ON THE BANK OF THE Charles River were dark and deserted. Jamie wasn't there yet. I had gotten a good night's sleep and rolled out of bed with a lot of energy. The fresh air felt good.

In the early-morning darkness, all the sounds were magnified. Early-fall leaves drifted across the stone steps, dead and dried, pointed tips brushing the ground like fingernails. Across the river down at the salt-and-pepper bridge, the sound of the red line blasted through deep quiet that seemed to rise up from the river like fog.

Stretching would have been a good idea. On a cool morning like this, my perennially tight hamstring had the feel of hardened chewing gum. But I hated stretching, so instead I watched the rowers out on the water. I loved to watch them on the river early in the morning, knifing through the black water in their thin slices of boat. The solo rowers seemed especially peaceful.

I glanced up and saw Jamie coming over the footbridge. It wasn't light enough to see his face, but I recognized the way he walked. When he got closer, I saw that he was elegantly disheveled, as if he'd reached into a dark closet and pulled out whatever was on top of a pile of really nice running gear.

"It's cold," he said. He bounced on the balls of his feet, hands squeezed into fists at his side, shoulders pulled forward. "Which way do you usually go?"

"West. This way." I pointed us in the right direction, and we were off. He ran faster than my normal pace; his legs were longer. I was huffing and puffing before we even got to the Mass Avenue Bridge, and even though I didn't want to, I had to give in.

"Jamie, we have three and a half miles to go. Can we ease off the pace?"

"Oh, sorry." He slowed, and I felt better as we crossed the river, running through the pools of light draped around the bottom of the streetlights. The wind, as usual, pushed hard against us on that stretch.

It felt strange being with Jamie. Or maybe it was the strangeness that felt strange. I wanted to try to make it go away, maybe by telling him what I was really doing, that I was starting a new career. I wanted to share my excitement with him. But I had to find just the right approach, just the right—

"Za, what's going on with you?"

I reached up and wiped the moisture from my cheek with the back of a dry hand. The cool air in the morning always made my right eye tear up. Never my left, only my right.

"What do you mean?"

"How's this flight attendant thing working out for you? Do you like it?"

"Yeah. Sure. It's okay."

"How long do you think you'll do it?"

"I don't know." We hit the other bank of the river. The second we made the turn east, the wind disappeared.

Jamie cleared his throat. "I don't mean to be patronizing. I really don't, but are you doing it because you couldn't find anything else?"

"No, I found a job. A management job earlier this year, but—"

"You did? That's great. What was it?" Something snapped into place for him as he went from uncomfortable uncertainty to relief. It was in his voice, as though we could now be friends again. We were back on the same page. My eye would not stop tearing.

"VP of operations with a start-up carrier."

"Impressive. I guess it depends on how big, though. Could be a big title with no responsibility. Stock options?"

"Yeah, but—"

"Salary increase?"

"It was, but—"

"Bonus?"

"Yes, but obviously I didn't take it."

"Why not?"

"For one thing, it was in Detroit, but that wasn't—"

"I can remember when you'd move anywhere for the right opportunity." We were passing the Harvard boathouse and the boats that were docked there. In another month or two, the plastic coverings would come out, and they would spend the coldest months of the winter shrink-wrapped. "But," he said, "I'm sure that gets old. I can see why you wouldn't want to live in Detroit, anyway."

He was quiet after that. All I heard was his steady breathing and his feet hitting the pavement.

"Look," I said, "I know it seems strange to be doing something so different, but isn't that okay? We don't have to keep doing the same thing just because we've always done it, right? That's what we said the other night about respecting each other's choices?"

I kept my eyes on the path in front of me. It was still dark, and I didn't want to trip and fall down.

"Are you gun-shy? Is it because of the Logan thing?"

"I am not gun-shy. This is my choice." I started to run faster. He caught up easily.

"Because that would be perfectly understandable if you needed a break."

We made the turn at the Museum of Science, and I was running full out, setting the pace the way I had when we were kids and I had been the one with the longer legs. Jamie wasn't even breathing hard, but I knew I was reaching my limit. I made it around the next corner and down to the boathouse before I gave out.

"I'm stopping." I bent over, breathing hard, and put my hands on my knees. Sweat clung to the underarms of my running suit and dripped from my face. The cool morning air gave me a chill.

Jamie walked in circles, hands on his hips. He seemed to be winding himself tighter with every revolution.

I took a few more deep breaths and stood up. "Why are you being this way?"

"What way?"

"Why can't you be excited for me, no matter what choice I make, and not make me feel ashamed for wanting something different from you? You're just like Walter." I paused to let that sink in. He didn't say anything, but he didn't have to. He crossed his arms, and his neck stiffened. "These past few years, Jamie, I feel around you exactly the way I used to feel around him. I expected it from him. I never expected it from you."

"How do I make you feel?"

"Disappointing."

With his arms still folded, he shifted his weight back

and stared across the river at the gorgeous canvas of lights that lined the Cambridge side. He came back and leaned over the way I was. "I'm sorry. I'm not saying any of this right. I'd like to see you do what you want to do and not what you have to do."

"That's exactly what I'm doing."

"Okay." He put his hand on my back. "Are you all right? Getting too old for this?"

"Hey . . ." I stood up straight. "I'm a little out of shape is all. Give me two minutes."

"Can I ask you one more thing?" He stared straight down the running path, even though there was nothing there to see. It was still too dark. "How can you afford to live in your neighborhood on what you make?"

That made me smile. It was probably the question he had been dying to ask all along. As with Walter, money and the things it could buy meant a lot to Jamie. "The owner of my unit is a trustee of the building. He hired me to do the condo association's books every quarter, and it partially offsets my rent. I don't have a lot of spare cash, but I'm doing fine."

"If you need money, Za, will you ask me? Will you promise me that?"

If in his mind money equaled love, then I could take the offer as a good thing, and I did. "If I need help, I promise to ask you. Thank you."

He stiffened his arms and clapped his hands together. "How far from here?"

"Half a mile back to the footbridge."

"Do you think you can make it?"

"Let's go."

We took off again. Maybe I would wait until next time to tell him about my new career.

* * *

The run felt good. It had been a while since I'd run that far. Later in the morning, after I had come back from the grocery store, I had reason to feel even more pleased that I had gotten it in, because I was about to become very busy. Angel had called.

So doll, I have good news, and I have good news. You passed your test. Good for you, and I hope it was *good for you. To celebrate, we're taking you out for a shindig. Be ready at nine o'clock tonight. We'll come and get you.*

chapter 25

I FELT SILLY STANDING IN THE LOBBY OF MY building in my party clothes, but I wanted to be ready to go when Angel rolled up. She had insisted on picking me up, and for some reason, I didn't want any chance that she would come up to my apartment. I didn't want her in my private space.

I'd been out that day shopping, looking for something appropriate to wear that I could afford. After several hours of fruitless searching, I gave up and went with expediency and my credit card. I bought a pair of low-rise black leather pants that felt as if they might slip down off my hipbones at any second and leave me mooning whoever was behind me. On top, I had a fuzzy little red boatneck sweater that looked good with a scarf but made me sneeze. The scarf was necessary to cover my still-healing bruises.

I was watching the cars go by on the street, trying to pick out Angel's vehicle, which was why I didn't notice Irene and Tristan sooner. They were up the steps and practically through the door before I realized it. They weren't supposed to be there. They were out of uniform and out of context, and I was annoyed that I was going to have to make up a lie.

I walked out to join them on the front steps.

"Alexandra, you look fabulous. Yet another surprise from your closet. It's racier than I would expect from you, but it's only a dinner party. Why are you here? Why aren't you—"

I blinked at them and offered a vague smile, trying hard to catch up to where they were. But I had no idea what he was talking about.

Tristan glanced at Irene. "Something tells me, Reenie, that she forgot all about my dinner party."

"What dinner—" When I looked at his face, I heard his voice on my machine, and I remembered his message. *Is everything all right? I'm worried about you.* He had invited me to a dinner party. I had never even bothered to call him and acknowledge the invitation. When did I become *such* an asshole?

"Tristan, I am so sorry."

"We were worried," Irene said. "We just walked down to check on you. I'm glad you're all right."

"We called." Tristan reached over to check out my scarf. "This is a new look for you. It's nice."

"I was in the shower." I had seen the messages when I got out, seen who they were from, and ignored them. While I was doing my makeup, the phone had rung again. I had let it roll to voice mail. The fist of guilt tightened around my conscience. "I'm sorry." I didn't know what else to say except *Please leave before Angel gets here.*

"Where are you going? Tell me you have a big date, and all is forgiven. You must, because you look amazing."

There was Tristan, filling in all the blanks for me. "Thank you. I am going out, and I feel terrible about not calling you. I . . . I screwed up my schedule. I just . . . I didn't . . ." I saw the limo out of the corner of my eye. It was cruising up Beacon slowly, going at checking-addresses speed. Angel hadn't said she would send a limo, but when I saw it, I had no doubt it was about to pull up in front of my building. The adrenaline gates opened. "I'm not firing on all cylinders right now."

"It's so hard to keep track of your schedule when you're flying," Irene said. "I forget things all the time." She was trying to make me feel better, but that was a fib. She was a single mom with a thirteen-year-old. She never forgot anything.

Now Tristan caught sight of the limo, probably because I couldn't tear my eyes from it. I felt the way you do when you see a traffic accident unfolding. He smiled with delight.

"Is that for you? Someone is taking you out in a limo? Why didn't you tell me? Of course you can blow me off for a date in a limo. Can we meet him? Why didn't you say something?"

The long black vehicle sailed up and anchored. The door opened, and the driver stepped out. If I were really lucky, he would be the only one to step out. "Miss Shanahan?"

"Yes, I'm coming."

I folded my arms tightly across my chest. I was afraid if I didn't, my friends would see my heart trying to beat its way out, right through my chest and that fuzzy red sweater. I sneezed.

"Are you all right?" Irene asked. "You look pale."

"I'm just tired. Please, please give my apologies to Barry. I'll make it up to you, Tristan." I gave him a quick kiss. "I'll call you tomorrow, I promise. Irene, I'm sorry."

Another fifteen seconds, and I would have made it. I would have been in and gone, and they never would have seen Angel, who was right then popping out through the limo's back door. She was dressed to party and walking straight toward us.

"Oh. My. God." Tristan lifted his nose in the air. "I wondered what that stench was. Greasy french fries and chicken gizzards. It could only be Miss Dairy Queen come to grace us with her skanky presence. What is she . . . what are you doing here?"

Angel smiled at him with supreme satisfaction. "Are you ready to go, doll?"

Tristan's and Irene's heads swung around so they could gape at me full on. I was humiliated down to my split ends. But then they sprang into action. Tristan swung around to my right side and Irene stood to my left, putting me right in the middle of a concern sandwich.

"This way, dear." Tristan dropped his arm across my shoulders. "We have a place all set at the table for you." He tried to guide me away, but my high-heeled boots were planted.

"Tristan, please. Angel and I—"

"No, Alexandra." His tone was fatherly, but insistent. "I don't know what's been going on with you, but it stops now. Consider this your intervention."

As gently as I could, I took his hand and removed it from my shoulder. It popped right back.

"He's right about this," Irene said, with palpable unease. "You should come with us."

Angel addressed herself to Tristan, as though Irene wasn't even there. "Why don't you back off and let her make up her own mind?"

"I hate the sound of my name coming from your mouth, Angela, dear, because there is no way of knowing just what has been *in* your mouth."

"That's funny, coming from a sky fag like you."

"Better a sky fag than a sky whore."

Angel took her excoriation in stride, but I found myself looking around, hoping no one from my building wandered by. Tristan turned me to face him and put a hand on each shoulder. "Alexandra, I'm trying to help you."

"I know." I could feel his will pressing in on me. Irene's, too, both trying to get me to walk away. I didn't look at Angel, but I could feel her eyes on me and I had no doubt that this was the tipping point. Regardless of whether or not I had passed the test in Chicago, I had one more thing to do. I had to declare my allegiance in front of my friends. My real friends.

I looked at Tristan. " 'They may be hookers, but they're our hookers.' Isn't that what you said?"

"Did you say that, *Trissy?*" I had never heard anyone else use Irene's nickname for Tristan. Angel wielded it like a scalpel.

I made myself look directly into Tristan's eyes. I wanted to signal somehow that I didn't mean it, that this wasn't me.

"If I get in trouble," I said, "I hope you will defend me."

But it was too late. A subtle shift in the currents had tilted the sidewalk from starboard to port, and I had let go of the railing and rolled across the deck.

Angel wasted no time moving in to claim her prize. "Let's go, doll." She looped her arm through mine. "We've got some serious celebrating to do tonight, and you're the guest of honor."

"Let's go, T." Irene was in full arbitration mode. "Alex, we'll go out another time. Just call one of us when you're feeling better. We'll be . . . well, you know where we are."

They were still on the curb staring when I settled into the limo with Angel and several of her crew. I took one last look at Tristan from behind the smoked glass. I could see him, but he couldn't see me.

As it ever was.

I woke up the next morning sitting on my couch, fully clothed, blinking into bright sunshine. The blinds were all open. My window was wide open, and Jamie's disembodied voice floated in from the kitchen, where the machine was recording his message. It must have been the phone that had finally pierced my thick skull and brought me back to life, such as it was. From the angle of the sun, I knew it was late. I knew something else, too. If I didn't finish this case fast, I would need a stint in rehab.

I dragged myself out to the kitchen for some much-craved liquid refreshment, grabbed a carton of orange juice, and punched up Jamie's message. The machine announced the time and date stamp for the call. That it was eleven-forty was alarming enough, but Jamie's message was what made me really feel the pain.

I had promised him another run this morning. I'd completely blown him off, and he was worried. I'd have to call him back when I was coherent and make up an excuse. Maybe I would tell him that I overslept. That wasn't a lie.

After threatening to fall down all night, the leather pants were ridiculously hard to peel off. They had molded to my body, which is apparently what happens when you leave them on too long. The red sweater was going right to Goodwill the second I had a free moment. It had made me sneeze all through dinner. After having promised me a party of my own, Angel had spent little time with me, leaving me to fend for myself with the exotic Sylvie. At twenty years old, she was the one I wished the most had never showed up on our radar screen. Last night, she had been the only one in the group with any time for me. She had wanted to know who had done my eyes, because I looked so good for my age. I considered that a compliment. I considered it sad and depressing that she was thinking of getting hers done.

I shuffled to the shower, wondering if the whole thing had been a clever ruse on Angel's part to weaken my defenses for our first real meeting this afternoon. If it had been, it worked. I was a wreck.

The second I got my hair soaped, the phone rang. I stepped out and padded into my bedroom, leaving a trail of soapy water across the hardwood. There were few people for whom I would interrupt a hot shower. Felix was one.

"Hello?"

"Miss Shanahan?"

"Hey, Felix. What's going on?"

"I got into Arthur Margolies's computer last night. Ohmygosh. Wait until you see this. I pulled it up, and I was, like, holy cow! You are not going to believe what I found."

chapter 26

THE WAY HARVEY FLUSHED WAS LIKE NO ONE I'd ever seen. The crimson started at points below each ear, then worked its way like twin flames up the sides of his face and joined at the bridge of his nose. He was in full bloom thirty seconds into Monica's video. The fact that his monitor was old and the picture wasn't as sharp as mine might have prevented a stroke.

What we were looking at was a man's penis. Actually, it was a man in naked repose on a bed of garish, fringed pillows, but all I saw was his penis, because it was the biggest one I'd ever seen. Granted, my sample universe was not vast, but this thing was a redwood. It towered majestically above his pubic briar patch, just one more of the mighty muscles this man had on casual display.

Harvey reached for his mouse and froze the image. "What are you showing me?"

I reached past him and restarted it. "That's Arthur Margolies, one of the hookers' clients, and you need to see this."

"I cannot imagine why."

Into the frame crawled Monica, also naked, with breasts so large and heavy I was concerned about rug burn as she moved across the floor on all fours toward her prey. I hadn't remembered them being that large—each bulbous mass was roughly the size of her head—but I had been concerned with other things at our last meeting.

"Is that Monica?" he asked.

"Yes."

"And this man is Arthur Margolies?"

"Yes."

"How do you know?"

"Felix confirmed it. He trolled around in the guy's computer and found photos of him, mostly with his kids."

"Your friend Felix? You showed this to him?"

"He sent it to me. I asked him to check out Margolies's computer, so he hacked in. The guy apparently tried to erase everything connected with Monica, e-mails included. Felix only found this because it was buried in some obscure download file. Margolies probably doesn't even know he has it."

With her head poised at the man's pelvis, Monica waited a teasing moment before moving in. The participants joined as promised—her lipstick around his redwood, his fingers in her hair—and commenced the dance. It was a slow, slippery rhythm at first, which built within seconds to a theatrical crescendo of bucking and flopping and twisting and grinding, all accompanied by a sound track of amazingly loud closed-mouth moaning (hers) and wild, spasmodic grunting (his). I had already seen it a couple of times . . . well, maybe more than a couple . . . so I didn't find it that titillating anymore. But Harvey's blood pressure seemed to be rising as he watched the display.

"Is there," he wanted to know, "a point to this?"

"It's coming up." When the image was right, I froze

the pair in sticky postfellatio glow. "There." I pointed to a tiny row of type at the bottom right-hand corner of the screen. "See this?"

He leaned in. "Barely."

"It's a series of numbers and letters that Felix thinks is some kind of filing tag or catalogue code. That's what it looks like."

"Implying there are more videos like this?"

"Of other men. It could be. The code has part of this man's last name in it."

"Meaning what?"

"I'm not sure. One thought is that this extortion gig is a cottage industry for Monica, and she does this to lots of clients. I really, really want to talk to her."

"Why?"

"If it's true, she's putting Angel's whole empire at risk. It's great leverage for us. Monica has been in this game for a while. I think there is a lot we can learn from her."

He blinked at the screen.

"I mean, in terms of Angel's operation. Felix is trying to track back and get into Monica's computer to see what he can learn. We might find a whole catalogue of these videos."

"Have you had any luck finding her?"

"No. She doesn't answer any phones. OrangeAir claims they don't know where she is. She's on leave is all they'll say. Tristan could probably find her using his union connections, but we don't seem to be speaking to each other at the moment. I'm still working on this one."

"And Angel?"

"I'm headed that way now. We're supposed to meet at four o'clock."

He inspected my outfit—T-shirt, sweatpants, and running shoes. "Where are you meeting?"

"Apparently, I've wandered into some kind of endurance test. Party all night and work all day. We're meeting at the LA Sports Club. She wants to work out."

chapter 27

I HAD NEVER BEEN IN THE LA SPORTS CLUB, the trendy workout facility that was part of the new Ritz-Carlton development. When I stepped off the elevator, I was confused. The club's reception area, with its muted colors, marble floors, and hushed ambience, was like the lobby of an expensive hotel. I thought maybe I'd come in at the wrong entrance. But then I looked beyond the front desk and saw the glassed-in weight room in the background. Same as any other weight room—except for the plush midnight-blue carpet.

I went to the desk to check in, then through to the locker room. Judging solely on the basis of locker rooms Angel frequented, I would have to say she led a pretty upscale life. I stowed my gear and went out. Angel was nowhere to be found, and I had plenty of nervous energy to burn, so I started without her. I was finishing my last reps on the leg lift when I felt two strong hands land on my shoulders and commence a brisk massage.

"Darlin', you have got some good tone going on there. I'm impressed. You're nice and hard. But so tense." Angel had arrived.

I shrugged out of her grasp and climbed off the machine. She handed me the towel that I'd hung on one of the spars. "What's got you so tied up in knots? Do I make you nervous?"

"Tied up in knots is my normal state of being." I used the towel to dry my face, found my bottle of water, and took a long swig.

She laughed. "If that's true, doll, then you need to get yourself laid. Again."

Angel was decked out in black tights and a hot-pink top that guaranteed maximum cleavage and made her look like a World Wrestling babe. She took my seat at the leg lift.

"Add ten more pounds for me, would you?"

I added the weight, and she started lifting, setting a rapid pace. I hated doing leg lifts, but she had a sturdy set of quads that rippled under her tights as she worked them. When she was finished, she asked for another ten pounds, which I added.

"Tell me," she said, "exactly how this little arrangement between us would work. Did you bring me some more names? I liked that last batch you gave me."

"Three sessions to start. You get one-third every time you pay me. I get a check, and you get a disk."

"Paid how much?"

"Three thousand dollars a day."

The chest press had been in use my first time through. I saw that it was free, moved to it, and set my weight at the usual level. I was halfway through my first set of reps when she pulled up next to me.

"I don't know too many gals," she said, "worth that kind of money. I am, of course, but you seem a little . . . inexperienced."

"That's chump change to you, Angel. You make that much in a few hours' work, and we're both experienced, just at different things."

I finished my first set, and she motioned me off, stopping first to add more weight. She did an elaborate chest press with lots of squeezing that caused her cleavage to expand and contract accordingly.

"What if I don't like your terms?"

"You can call up McKinsey and Company, and I'll go out to LA. Start-ups are generally less risk-averse and more aggressive than going concerns."

She finished her set, and I rotated in. I knew I should reduce the weight, but I went with what she had lifted, which was a mistake that I appreciated the second I started. I struggled mightily to get through three reps. I had to rest after the fifth. When she smiled broadly at me, I thought it was because I had failed to match her little strength test.

"What?"

"Start-ups? Risk-averse? I'm starting to get you now, doll. You're scared. You don't think you can do it."

"Do what?" I started on the sixth press, but my arms shook badly. She moved in and spotted me, pushing on the machine's arms to help me complete the motion.

"All this high-and-mighty bullshit about not wanting to turn tricks, you think men wouldn't be attracted to you."

I let go of the press. The weight dropped, the arms snapped back, and she barely got her hands out of the way in time. Oops.

"That's what all this steely professionalism is about." She walked around in front of me as if to take in the whole view. "It's all over you. It's in how you dress, how you do your hair." She could have been referring to my dowdy running shorts and raggedy Bruce Springsteen T-shirt from a concert ten years ago. "The way you move. You don't know how to use your body. You have no idea what it's like to walk into a room and have every man in the place want to throw you down and have his way with you."

"Sounds romantic."

"Sex is never about romance, darlin'. Don't you know that? It's about power. It's about one person getting over on another." She shooed me off the seat and added yet another ten pounds. This time, when she pressed, it was all about showing off her strength and not her cleavage. She had to work it. The effort raised the muscles in her neck and throat and distorted her face into an angry grimace. "Make them your victim before they do it to you." She dropped the weights, finishing the last press with a loud clang, a fitting exclamation point.

I stood to the side and watched her catch her breath. "I'm not looking to make any victims," I said. "I'm looking to make some money and stay out of trouble."

"Well, they do say this is a victimless crime, so maybe we can do some business."

"Good."

"All you have to do is tell me about the last man you fucked."

"What?"

She gave me a breathy smile and a wink. "If you want me to show you mine, you have to show me yours. Come on, sugar, a few little details just so I know we can be friends. If you can't do that, or maybe you don't want to, we're done talking. Besides, I want to know that you can get your nose out of the air long enough to put it someplace useful."

She moved off the press and over to a corner where the large exercise balls were stored on a rack. She took one down, sat on it, lay back, and started doing situps with her hands behind her neck.

"The last man I was with was the trick in Chicago. Is that what you want to know about?"

"Oh, God, no. Tricks don't count. The last man you cared about."

So, this was how it was to be. She liked making people strip with their clothes on, which was not that surprising when I thought about it. She was an exhibitionist herself. She wouldn't trust anyone who wasn't. I could make up a story, but I had the sense her bullshit detector was pretty sensitive. Or I could take something that really did happen and spin it into something she might like. I went over and took down a ball for myself.

"The last man I was with held a powerful position in the company where I worked."

"At Majestic? Ooooh. This sounds good. Tell me everything, because you know you want to. Give me all the sweaty details. Was he worth it? Was he good? Did he have a big dick?"

"It ended badly, at least for me. I lost my job."

"Was the sex good?"

"Yeah."

"How did he like to do it?"

"Why do you need to know this stuff?"

"I like to hear you say it, because I know you don't want to. Why did you do it? What was it about this man?"

"He liked to take what he wanted, and he lived his life as if there were nothing he couldn't have. He could be a real bad boy, which could be very appealing. He was smart and sexy and charming. And I liked his power."

"There it is. That's what did it for you right there."

"Maybe. Until he used it to threaten and humiliate me. Eventually, he fired me. When I told him I'd sue him for sexual harassment, he told me he would have his lawyers turn me into a public joke. I knew he could do it. I knew him well enough to know he would. I backed down. I lost my career and everything I had invested in that company."

"You made a mistake."

"Obviously."

"I mean, in how you came at him." She rolled her ball closer, until our knees almost touched. "You can't threaten a man like that with a lawsuit. It wouldn't scare him."

"There wasn't much that scared him."

"Everybody has something to hide, and everybody has something to lose. You have to find what it is, those deep, dark desires that a man—or a woman—has no choice but to give in to. For some men, it's young girls. For others, it's boys. Some get off on getting beaten or dressing in women's lingerie. When you know those things, that's when you truly have control. You find what it is that can hurt them, and then you squeeze until you get what you want." She curled her fingers into a fist to demonstrate. I looked at her face, and I knew there was nothing in this world she would not wrap those fingers around and squeeze to get what she wanted.

"I'm guessing you're not a big fan of romantic love."

She laughed. "Love is for losers, darlin'. It's nothing but another form of payment, when it comes down to it."

"Payment for what?"

"Sex. 'I'll let you screw me if you love me.' How is that different from 'I'll let you screw me if you pay me'?"

"Because love is more than sex. It gives you things you can't get from a purely physical relationship."

"Like what you got from that big dick boyfriend of yours at Majestic? You loved him, right?"

She smiled at my awkward hesitation. She had a way of creeping up on you one slow, silent step at a time, until she was upon you and it was too late.

"Everyone has their own way of looking at things." I said it, even knowing how feeble it sounded.

"This is my way of looking at things. We all have our price. For some, it's love. For others, it's less. It's always good to know what it is for you. Now . . ." She reached toward me, and I flinched. But all she was after was a dry corner of my gym towel. Without taking it from around my neck, she used it to dry her forehead.

"Let's go do some business."

chapter 28

ANGEL SLAMMED HER CELL PHONE CLOSED and flung it into her gym bag. Then she picked up the bag and flung it into the corner, nearly knocking the smoothie right out of its tall, soda-shop glass.

"What's the matter?"

"I just lost another one," she snapped.

"Another what?"

"One of my gals just got her transfer to LA. They're like cattle thieves, picking them off one by one. Picking me clean is what they're doing. I should brand their butts."

We had settled in the Sports Club juice bar at a table isolated in one of the corners. It was called a juice bar, and it did serve juice. It also served baked cod with pineapple salsa—not your usual juice bar fare.

"That's where we need to start. What do you call the women who work for you?"

"Grubbing, griping, greedy bitches."

I looked at her. She looked right back. She was steaming.

"Why don't we call them your assets?"

"Asses?"

"Assets. In your business more than most, your people are your assets. When they walk, they take their clients with them, and the clients take their revenue stream."

"I can replace both. It's just a goddamn pain in the ass, is what it is."

"It's more than that. You might be able to replace the business, but you can't do anything about what it does for your competitor. That's business they don't have to develop on their own. You might as well stuff a bunch of bags with hundred-dollar bills and send them over."

She put her elbow on the table and leaned her head against her palm. It mussed her hair, which was loose around her face. It made her look like a young girl. "I hate this already."

"Tell me why they're leaving."

"Because they're stupid. They think they're going to be instant zillionaires with merchandising deals and their own Web sites and starring in their own videos. 'Sell your lace panties, and make a million bucks.' It all sounds really sexy, and it's all *very* LA, but it won't work."

"Why wouldn't it?"

"Our thing works for one reason and one reason only. It's low-profile. You cannot have your face or your tits or anything else plastered all over the Internet. Someone will find out; then the airline will find out; then you will lose your job."

"If I'm making enough on the side, why would I care about my low-paying flight attendant wages?"

"The job is the key to the whole deal. We have built-in access to customers who sit in first class, the ones who think a little tail on the road is part of their executive privilege and have the expense accounts to make it happen. My clients don't troll porno sites on the

Internet. They want exclusive and discreet, and they're willing to pay for it. That's my thing, and it works. Plus, it helps to be able to fly around for free."

She sat back and sipped her smoothie through a straw. She was still dressed in a way that displayed her own best assets. But when she talked about her business, the extracurricular posing and flaunting fell away, leaving a calmer, more focused version. She sounded like the head of any small business, which was a place where we could relate to each other in some way besides predator and prey.

"You have to find a way to make them care about your business in the same way you do."

"They don't care about anything except collecting their fees. The ones making the most want more. The ones making the least want more. The gals in the pool are jealous of the ones who aren't. The ones who aren't in the pool don't like having to change their schedules at all, and why are you smiling?"

"Was I?" I knew I was smiling inside. "What's the pool?"

"When they first start out and don't have any clients, I put them in the pool. All that means is they have to be on call and go where I tell them and be with whoever I tell them to be with. For the clients, mostly the new ones, it's like a well drink in a bar. They get whoever I send them."

Which meant Tony the Actor had not been referring to a cabana girl, after all. His "just a pool girl" was a woman drawn from Angel's hooker pool. He hadn't bothered to learn her name. Mystery solved.

"What about the other clients? Who do they get?"

"Regular clients get to know who they want to see, and I try to give them who they ask for, or at least something close. When a gal gets enough regulars requesting her, she climbs out of the pool and has more say in things."

"Does that mean the new girls would end up doing most of the schedule swapping?"

"Hell, yes, it does. Part of the privilege of being in this game a while is being able to plan your schedule more. I can pick and choose. So can some of my top gals."

Another big reason to smile. This explained the results of Harvey's analysis. He had picked up the pool girls in his top swapper net. More senior hookers didn't have to swap so much. I couldn't wait to tell him.

"How do you keep track of all this? Who's in the pool and who's not, who earns what? This sounds complicated. Not to mention all the scheduling requirements and constraints."

"You don't have to worry about any of that. I've got all that under control."

"It must be a hell of a system. Do you have a guy?"

"I have it under control. Next question?"

At least I got two out of three. "What about fees? Do girls make more money once they've advanced outside the pool?"

"Usually. It depends on what I think they're worth."

"Do the women in the pool ever get any feedback on how they're doing? How close they are to climbing out?"

"Doll baby, all they need to know is where to go and who to fuck. The less they know, the better for me."

No wonder her women were griping. She had a classic human resources problem. I dug a pen out of my bag and used a napkin to make some notes. If I was going to be her consultant, I might as well give her her money's worth.

"You need a performance measurement system that gives people an idea of where they are in the organization, how they're doing, and where they're going. You need to lay out performance objectives. Then you need a hierarchy with different levels the women can achieve by meeting those objectives."

She finished off her smoothie with a loud pull on her straw. "You mean, like, if you recruit ten new clients in a month, you can climb out of the pool? Like that?"

"Exactly. It's a career path. Employees want to know they have a future and that you care about whether they achieve it, which leads to the most important part." I pointed my pen at her for extra emphasis, because this was the most important part for me. "Once we build the system, we have to communicate it."

"Communicate it? What should I do, sugar, call a town meeting? Maybe we can have us a conference call. I know. We'll invite everyone over for a potluck supper. We'll fire up the grill and tap a keg."

"How do you communicate with them now?"

"By e-mail."

"Well, there you are." I put my pen down and waved the problem away. "We'll come up with a plan and communicate it via e-mail. I can write that stuff for you. Your Web master can send it out."

She tipped her head back and went all cagey. "My what?"

"Your Web master. Your guy. You have a Web site, so I assume you have someone who keeps track of all that for you. If your guy is any good, he'll know ways of sending messages so they can't be traced back to you. Either that, or give me an address list, and I'll do it."

"Let's not get too far ahead of ourselves here."

"All right." She wasn't going to make this easy for me. "We can stop there for now."

"That's it? That's all you've got for me? Communicate more? What about that program you were touting? When do I get to hear about that?"

"Next time. I wanted to get a sense of your business so I could customize it for you." I took my napkin notes and pushed them down into my backpack. "What I have in mind will make your providers want to stay. You might even get some of them to come back."

"Don't want them back."

"Why not?"

"They're dead to me." Interesting choice of words. "Do you want to hear my idea for keeping the gals from leaving home?"

I didn't need to ask. She couldn't wait to tell me.

"I was thinking I would send some people I know to find one of those little sluts, take her out behind the woodshed, and slash her face. The message will get out real loud and real clear that they best not be leaving a good thing."

That was about ten miles beyond what we could tolerate as an undercover investigation. If she were intent on assaulting someone, we would have to shut her down. It was possible we should do that anyway based on the threat. But I had serious doubts about whether we had enough to shut her down.

"Back to Pimping 101," I said, hoping she wouldn't reach over and clock me.

"I told you—"

"What could possibly draw more attention to what you're doing than a brutal attack like that?"

"It would never get back to me. I'm covered on that front. You don't have to worry about it."

"Covered how? You can't get arrested? You can't get prosecuted? What?"

"You don't need to know." She leaned back and looked at me with luscious satisfaction. She was very pleased with herself.

"If that's true, you don't need me. Use your secret mojo to take out the LA crowd. Save yourself some money and me the trouble."

She dismissed that notion with a toss of her hair. "They're not worth it. What I have is like a nuclear bomb"—only she pronounced it "nucular," like any good Texan—"and I don't want to have to go and use it unless there is no other way. But I will use it to save my business. I will do anything to save my business."

I looked around to make sure no one had edged close enough to overhear. Not to worry. There wasn't a person in this trendiest of hangouts who wasn't more interested in him- or herself than anyone else in the room.

"If you want to do something short of slashing faces and detonating nuclear bombs, I'm with you. But I'm not up for hurting anyone."

She turned and found something interesting to look at on one of the three big-screen TVs.

"What's it going to be, Angel?"

The quickest way to walk home from Angel's neighborhood was across the Common and through the Public Garden. The second I was out of her range, I called Harvey.

"I saw Angel," I told him when he picked up. "I just left her."

"You just left? It's almost eight o'clock."

"She insisted that we go to dinner."

"What did you learn?"

"I learned why your top swapper list excludes the senior women."

I explained Angel's organization and the concept of pool girls to him, occasionally checking around to see if anyone nearby was listening to me. My side of the conversation would have made for some bizarre eavesdropping. Harvey liked the explanation because it made perfect sense. I was more interested in how to fill the gap in our investigation.

"We definitely have to get to the Web master," I said. "If Felix can't get in through the back door, then I need to get to him through Angel."

"How would you do that?"

"I tried to get her to talk about him, but she wouldn't bite. She gets how important he is. We've set up another meeting tomorrow to talk about the frequent fucker program."

"Another workout?"

"No. She wants me to come up to her house in New Hampshire."

As I passed the tennis courts, I was delighted to hear that my favorite busker was out, even at this hour. The accordion player was on his customary stoop under a big oak, spinning sweet songs in minor keys and making a crosswalk in the middle of a Boston park feel like an outdoor café in Paris. He smiled and nodded as I dug out a dollar and dropped it in his case. I sat on a nearby bench to listen while I finished my conversation with Harvey.

"There's something else," I said. "Angel has no fear at all of getting caught and going to jail. None. She acts as if she has some kind of get-out-of-jail-for-free card."

"What could that be?"

"I don't know. Maybe a rabbi. Someone to watch out

for her. From the sound of it, it would have to be someone pretty powerful. She calls it her nuclear bomb. Whatever it is, it gives me some concern."

"How so?"

"Let's say we build a case against Angel. Will she be able to pull out this hole card and use it to beat us? Would it be something that keeps the airline from firing her?"

"It is not our job to guarantee her termination. Only to give the client what he has asked for." Harvey was veering into lecture territory, which meant it was time to change the subject.

"I finally got Monica's address. I'm heading over to her apartment as soon as I change. I want to try to get over there before it gets too late."

"Do you think she will be there?"

"Not a chance. But I would feel pretty stupid if she's there watching Oprah and not answering the phone and I never even went by and knocked on her door."

The accordion player finished "La Vie En Rose" and put down his instrument to take a break.

"Alex, are you there?"

"I'm here." I had been thinking abut Angel's threat to have someone slashed. I was thinking mostly about how perfectly capable she was of doing it.

"There's one more thing, Harvey. Have you had any more conversation with the retired detective in Omaha?"

"No. Should I?"

"I think so. We need to look more closely at this Robin Sevitch murder."

chapter 29

I CALLED FELIX FROM THE CAR ON THE WAY TO Monica's. With the reintroduction of Felix to my life, I'd had to rearrange the turbo-dialing buttons on my cell phone. Felix's number replaced the Majestic Airlines reservations line. The last electronic vestige of my association with my old airline got bumped down to regular speed dial.

"Hey, Miss Shanahan."

"Hi, Felix. I'm just checking in. How are things?"

"I had an emergency at the airport. The bag belt broke down, and I had to go in and fix it."

"We agreed that your airport job takes priority."

"I know, but it shouldn't be so much trouble, you know? The problem is, it's such a lame program. It breaks down all the time. I'm working with the manufacturer to get some of the bugs out. It wasn't designed to handle variable workload, which is really kind of useless when you think about the fact that it was built for an airline, an operation with variable schedule *and* variable workload. It needs to be run against dynamic—"

"Felix."

"Yes, ma'am?"

"Have you had any progress on the case?"

"I've been looking around Mr. Margolies's hard drive, and I found a couple of other bits and pieces related to that video. The one with—well, you know. Ohmygosh, Miss Shanahan. That was really something. Do you know that lady?"

I had to pause for a smile. Felix's outsized competence made him seem so mature, it was hard to remember how young he was. He had hormones that raged like any kid barely out of high school.

"She had her clothes on when I met her."

The red taillights were lined up for blocks down Commonwealth. "Hold on a second, Felix." I put the phone down and cut across two lanes so I could turn, take Storrow, and miss the lights. That put me in a long line of left-turners but gave me plenty of time to listen.

"Go ahead, Felix. Did the bits and pieces tell you anything?"

"Just that he uses a lot of layers and misdirection. But I already knew that."

"You said 'he.' You don't think Monica could have sent it?"

"Well, I'm not saying she couldn't have. I mean, she could be a hacker, too, that lady in the video. The hacker could be a she, is what I'm saying. Just because she looks the way she looks doesn't mean . . . that would be sexist, right? To think that way would—"

"Felix."

"Whoever he is, he's the same person who set up that other site you sent me. The one using the reverse proxy server."

"Wait a second. The guy who set up the scheduling site for Angel?"

"Him, yeah. I call him Web Boy because he's like a super-hacker. Only he's a dark force."

"How do you know it's the same person?"

"Because he left a fingerprint."

"A fingerprint?"

"In the code. Hackers are like that. They like to sign their work, you know? For other hackers who know what to look for."

"I'll be damned. That means Angel's Web master is in on this blackmail scheme."

"Same fingerprints on both the Web site and Mr. Margolies's stuff, basically. Only I don't think he was as careful with the video program as he was with the site. If we could find the e-mails that came with it, I could probably tell you who it is."

"Or"—this was starting to feel significant—"if we could find Monica, then we might be able to get to the Web guy through her. What did you call him?"

"Web Boy, the Dark Hacker."

As distinct from Felix, the Boy Genius. I liked that. "Maybe Web Boy is the one who catalogues all of Monica's videos." Which meant both of them would have something to hide from Angel.

"He could be."

My light had been green for a while, but the traffic wasn't moving. When it finally loosened up, it was just enough to get me all the way up to the front of the line, where I was hitting the gas as the yellow light turned red again. I slammed on the brakes and sat back to wait through another cycle.

"Anything else, Felix?"

"Not so far."

"Good job. Keep working on finding Web Boy. I'll work on finding Monica."

* * *

It had taken me longer than it should have to find Monica's address. To its credit, the airline wasn't too forthcoming with personal details about employees, even to other employees. If Tristan had been speaking to me, it would have been a snap to get it, but instead I had to go through Dan, who knew a Majestic flight attendant who was dating an OrangeAir flight attendant who sneaked it out of the system for me. I had tried to call Tristan several times since the disastrous dustup at the limo. He wouldn't return my calls. Irene said to give him time. I knew her mainly through Tristan, so I had really lost them both. I missed them. I pictured the two of them on an overnight, sitting on a patio somewhere, perhaps in the Caribbean, having dinner alfresco under a softly swaying palm tree. That sounded a lot better than what I was doing.

No one had answered Monica's buzzer in her North End building. None of the neighbors knew where she was, so I was climbing the fire escape to her third-floor unit, hoping she was in the habit, as I was, of leaving a window open. It was the right time of year for it. I didn't think she was hiding in there, but I thought there might be something that would point me in her direction.

The fire escape was tucked into a vertical culvert behind one building and between two others. That and the fact that I had a flashlight were the only reasons I had the guts to climb up there. I crept past the window of the first-floor unit. The guy on the second floor was watching a baseball game. Was it a playoff game or the Series? I couldn't believe I had lost track. When he got up and left the room, I tiptoed past his window and continued my climb.

When I got to Monica's window, I found that she was

not in the habit of leaving hers open. Or unlocked. That was inconvenient, as was the fact that she had not left on a single light in the place. It was pitch-black in there, worse still because of the outdoor floodlight shining from the building across the alley. Holding my flashlight up to the glass, I blocked off the space around my eyes and peered in. I could just barely make out the silhouettes of a couch and a television and a chair and—

My head snapped back, I lost my balance, and careened back against the railing. The base of my flashlight hit an iron strut and flipped over the side.

A man's face had materialized directly in the beam of my flashlight, our noses separated by little more than the thickness of the glass. At least I thought it had. It was gone, and now so was my flashlight. It hit the pavement below with a heavy, muted pop. I looked down. I heard tapping. I looked back. The face was there, back in the window, looking even more ghostly in the reflected light from the neighboring building. A cadaverous smile formed and I knew what he was tapping with even before my eyes could register the image. I knew it was a gun. I knew he was tapping the glass with the barrel of his gun.

I lurched toward the stairs and stumbled down. I tried to yell, but anything that took energy away from getting down the stairs was taking too much. Halfway down, I heard the ghoul's footsteps on the landing. I felt the structure shake. He had climbed through the window. He was coming down the fire escape behind me.

Holding tight to the railing, I took the last set of stairs in two giant leaps. When I hit the ground, I wanted to go right, to head for my car, but he was too close. I could never get to the Durango, get it unlocked, get in, start it . . . *try something else.*

I turned left. All I knew of the North End was a few Italian restaurants, the Old North Church, and endless narrow, winding streets and alleys. It would be easy to get lost, or maybe lose him. When I emerged from the alley, I turned toward the sound of cars moving, toward where I thought there would be restaurants and liquor stores and people on the sidewalks.

I heard the scratchy sound of a walkie-talkie. It was in front of me . . . no, behind. I looked back. The ghoul had made the corner. He was still coming, holding a device, shouting into it. But his voice was coming out . . . somewhere else. I twisted back around, searched the street, and spotted him. A second man stepped out of a doorway half a block down and looked around until he caught sight of me. He wore a suit, a pinstriped blue suit with a vest, which struck me in that moment of absolute adrenaline overload as weird. He was also squeezing a walkie-talkie, and I realized he'd been standing in front of Monica's building. I had made a loop back to her front door.

Now he was coming, too, and I took off. He had turned me around, away from the lights, and I was going the other way along a dark and narrow sidewalk, up and down on the curb, around parked cars and parking meters until I came to an opening. It was a yard, a way to get off the street and out of their sight. Then I was through it and into an open field, and I was running flat out again. It was a relief to have the space to move, and at the same time I was thinking if I could see ahead, they could see me. I thought I was going toward the harbor, toward the water, because of the vast stretch of darkness ahead. But a chain-link fence with orange reflector signs came up fast and I knew I was completely off course. It wasn't the water I had run to. It was a construction zone, a massive construction zone. I had stumbled upon the Big Dig, the world's biggest road project. With no one around, it looked a lot like the far side of the moon. Only instead of craters and mountains, there were backhoes and wheelbarrows, cement pillars and exposed cables and large mud basins where rainwater had collected.

I didn't want to go in there, but they were coming. The ghoul, tall and bony, was out front. The other one lagged behind, his suit coat flapping behind him.

I looked for any sign of life. Security guard. Police cruiser. Someone armed would be good, because now they were shooting at me. A round pinged against a metal container a few feet away. I resisted the urge to drop to the ground and roll into a fetal position and went instead up and over the fence. I couldn't tell where the second round hit, but it got me moving. I crawled on my belly around a thicket of Do Not Enter signs, got to my feet, and lurched down a ramp and into a tunnel.

At first there was enough light for me to make my way. I could see to move easily among the piles of wood and the bags of cement. But very quickly, it got dark, and soon I was tripping over coils of cable and stumbling into bags of cement. I had to move more and more slowly until I was stopped.

". . . dark . . . motherfucker . . . crazy bitch . . ."

"Keep . . . down here . . . spread out . . ."

They were in the tunnel with me.

I couldn't find the direction of their voices. They seemed to be coming from all around. I reached out with both arms and shuffled along until my fingers connected with . . . machinery . . . a machine. Cold steel. Solid. I grabbed onto it and felt my way along until I found one of its tires. Okay, a tire I could visualize. I crouched beside it and listened. They were closer. How would they approach? One on each side? Both up the middle? If I could figure that out, I could go the other way . . . but what if I . . . what if they . . . *wait.* Where was the middle?

I no longer knew where the walls were. I had turned to listen to them and lost my bearings, and now I didn't know which way to go, and my heart was flapping around my chest, and I seemed to be taking in more air than I could let out. My lungs were about to burst, and it had been a terrible mistake to come down here, because now I was trapped, and they had at least one gun, and I had to calm down.

I turned away and closed my eyes and made myself breathe. Listening to them was causing the panic. I had to make my own plan and that plan had to get me out. I was too scared in the dark. I leaned over with my hands on my knees and eyes closed and listened closely. I pointed myself to where I thought the voices were coming from. When I figured out where that was, I decided they were still behind me, which meant I had to find a way to get behind them.

I got down on my knees and felt along the ground. Nails? Too light. Gravel. Too small. Something hard. Heavy. A brick. A stack of bricks. Too heavy for what I needed.

A crash not far away. "Son of a *bitch.*"

"Shut up. I can't hear."

"Like we're going to find her in here."

I crawled along the ground, using their noise for cover, feeling with my hands. There was something cold . . . aluminum or metal . . . cylindrical with a label. It was a can. Maybe a paint can. Two cans, each with a handle. Perfect.

I grabbed one, but when I reached for the other, I tipped it over and made it clatter. When I tried to catch it, I only managed to make it roll farther. They shouted to each other, and one of them began to drift in my direction. His footfall sounded like leather soles on pavement and I thought it might be the one in the suit. I stabbed at the darkness around me, trying to touch something, to find something to flatten against. I was out in the open, exposed. For all I knew, he would walk right into me.

He stopped. I had to stop. My muscles cramped. The paint can smelled of chemicals—solvent, maybe—and I wished I were a smoker with a lighter. I listened, but there was nothing, which meant that he was listening, too. I began to shake.

Then I heard him wheezing. Even though he was very close by, I felt a small relief that he was the one closer to me. He was struggling to breathe the heavy air and I knew, of the two, he was the one I could outrun, if only I could see where to run.

He stood for a long time. When he finally moved past, my whole body unclenched, and I nearly fell over. I waited for a good long time, until I couldn't hear him anymore. When I straightened up, I hoped that my bones wouldn't audibly creak. I took a deep breath and counted to myself. *One* . . . I wrapped my hand around the handle of the paint can . . . *two* . . . whirled around, which was not easy in total darkness, and . . . *three* . . . let it fly.

It seemed to take forever to come down. When it did, it hit dead solid on something hard and heavy. The noise boomed like an explosion from deep within a cave.

They yelled to each other. I started to feel my way along, going in the direction I had picked. I put one foot lightly in front of the other, slowly at first, but then it was hard to hold back, hard not to shut down my brain, let my instincts take over, and go crashing out of there as fast as I could. I held back until I saw the light spilling down the ramp. I began to jog toward the entrance, and then a fire kicked in, and I was running full out, and I couldn't have stopped for any reason. If they were behind me, I didn't know, because the only thing I could hear was the drumbeat of my own feet pounding the ground, my own heart pushing me forward.

I was flying.

The opening was ahead, the light washing into the dark tunnel like the tide rising onto the shore. I wanted to feel that light on me. The ramp was steeper than I had realized. I was breathing in a rhythm—in-in, out-out—every two steps, but the air seemed to hold less and less oxygen. At the moment when I felt I had to slow down, I heard the shots, loud and sharp, like the crack of an old tree branch snapped off in a windstorm. One of the rounds ricocheted off the ground in front of me. I knew they could see me against the light. I ran left and right in a jagged zigzag, aiming for the top of the ramp. I started to feel that something was pulling me forward, pulling me to safety. The opening was in front of me. I would make it. Fifty feet. Thirty. Twenty.

I didn't even see him.

The collision was monumental, at least from my end. There was no time to stop, to turn, to do anything but plow right into him, which was like running headfirst into a Sequoia. I slammed into his chest. My head snapped back, and I was crumpling to the ground when he caught me. He had me by both arms. If I hadn't been dazed from the crash, I would have been too spent to do anything anyway, so all I could do was stare at him.

He was big, especially across the shoulders. His head

was square. His sport coat looked, in the dim light, to be a dusty rose over a black turtleneck. With a dizzying, disorienting rush of recognition, I realized I knew this man, and if I hadn't been nearly unconscious I would have been scared, because the last time I had seen him was in Chicago, where his jacket had been lemon yellow. I expected any second for one of his big hands to release my arm and grab me by the throat.

It didn't.

He turned his thick shoulders and looked down into the tunnel, probably seeing down there what I could hear—my two pursuers coming up the ramp.

"Go," he said. He let go of my arms and turned me around. "Run."

I wanted to drop to my knees. I wanted to let my head hang down until I could breathe again, but I could hear the other two coming. I put one hand on my aching side and started moving again, limping back toward the fence. When I turned to look back, he was gone.

I couldn't get the dust out of my nasal passages. I kept blowing, sniffing, snorting, and mashing my nose against my face. Whether it was in my snout or in my mind, I couldn't say, but I had an itch there that I couldn't scratch, and it kept me on the razor's edge of a sneeze. I smelled as if I'd just come in from a long run, only terror sweat is more pungent and rancid than exercise sweat. Both of my shoulders throbbed, the right one more than the left. I hoped I hadn't torn something important.

I had found my way to the Fleet Center complex, which led directly to North Station, where there were plenty of people hanging out waiting for commuter trains to the suburbs. I sat on a bench along one wall and watched them. It had been more than an hour since

I had crawled out of the tunnel, and I was trying to figure out if it made sense to go back to my car in the North End. It was either that or call Harvey, which seemed almost harder than any other option I could think of.

I was pretty sure the two men at Monica's had been waiting for her, not me, probably for the same reason as the big guy had been after me . . . her in Chicago. Blackmail schemes gone awry. This was a dangerous game Monica was playing. Why did I keep paying the price? The big guy must have figured out his mistake, which was why he'd had no use for me tonight.

I did not want to deal with Harvey, so I went outside and hailed a cab that took me to the North End. I gave the cabbie five dollars extra to wait until I got safely into my car.

When I reached up to grab my seat belt, I noticed the business card in the visor. Printed on the front was the name Djuro Bulatovic. Below it was an 800 number. On the back was a handwritten note.

My sincerest apologies. Please call.

They say first impressions are the ones that last. I wasn't sure I would ever be able to think of Djuro Bulatovic as anyone but the man in the lemon chiffon jacket who choked me until I passed out.

chapter 30

EVEN WITHOUT THE ROBIN'S-EGG-BLUE JACKET, he wouldn't have been hard to spot. He was twice the width of any two people sitting on the benches around him, and he wore a smartly coordinated tam. Based on the data points I had collected so far, I imagined the Djuro Bulatovic closet to be a tidy repository of pastel, home to a disciplined row of ecru, dusty rose, mint green, and lavender sport jackets, all with muted silk linings, each as big as a sleeping bag.

He read his newspaper and never looked up. He seemed content to wait for my approach. The only problem was, I was having a hard time putting myself within the radius of his lightning-fast reach.

But there were plenty of people around on the street, many of them late-season tourists moving in the direction of the Prudential Center, embarkation point for the ubiquitous duck tours. It was the perfect low-humidity, light jacket day for such an outing.

The first step out to the sidewalk was the hardest. Then I put my head down, jaywalked across the street, and inched up to the man who had terrorized me . . . and saved me. When I was close enough to read his newspaper, he folded it and put it on his lap.

"Thank you for coming," he said. "I brought you soup for lunch. Goulash. It's good. Thick." He pointed to the two cardboard cartons next to him on the bench. Steam curled up from the holes in the lids.

"You brought me soup?"

"Goulash. Did you want for us to take the tour? I wasn't sure when you said to meet here. I bought tickets in case that was your intention."

Goulash and a duck tour. He wasn't exactly making me cower. The moon-shaped face, thick eyebrows, and sledgehammer forehead—they were all there, but now arranged in an expression that was deferential, almost gentle.

"I'll skip the duck ride." In spite of everything that had happened the night before, I had finally gotten a good night's sleep. I'd spent the morning taking a long hot bath to soothe my aching muscles. I had no desire to go on an open-air, amphibious crawl through the crowded city streets of Boston and up the Charles River. "I don't know where Monica is."

"That is not," he said, "why I wanted to see you."

"Then what do you want?"

"Only to talk."

"Why would I talk to you? You almost killed me."

"No." He was greatly offended. "I did not. I was asked to send a message in a forceful way. Did you get the message?"

"In the most forceful way. Except you gave it to the wrong person."

"Yes." His hands were on his knees and his large head tilted at an attitude of true contrition. "I'm sorry I hurt you. I hope I helped you last night."

"You did." I shoved my hands into my pockets. "Thank you for that."

"Please, sit."

I did, although it took a few seconds. I was still pretty creaky. "I assume you haven't found Monica and that's why you were there last night. You're still looking for her."

"Yes. I was watching for her when those two men came." He dismissed them with a snort. "Amateurs."

"Are these amateurs still breathing?"

"Of course. We had a discussion."

"You didn't happen to get who they worked for?"

"This is not what we discussed. We spoke about what would happen if they bothered you or Monica again. That is how a professional approaches work. Not with a gun."

I tried to peek under his jacket. I couldn't see it, but I had to believe he had a weapon of his very own. "This is what you do, then? You—"

"I make sure that debts are paid and agreements are honored."

"For Arthur Margolies?"

"For many clients. He is one."

He seemed pretty forthcoming, so I pressed on. "Is Monica blackmailing him with sex tapes? Is that why you're after her?"

"Yes. She made them with a secret camera and she is trying to sell them back to him. I was asked to intervene."

I knew it. This had to be Monica's bright idea. Angel was too smart to cannibalize her own business. "But you don't know what she looks like? I mean, how could you mix us up?"

He seemed pained to be reminded of his gaffe. "I have never seen the videos. My client deleted them."

Or so he thought. "Then how were you supposed to find her?"

"I was told to follow a man, that he would lead me to her."

"Told by your client?"

"Yes."

"Any idea how he knew which man?"

"No."

That was curious. Why wouldn't he have his guy set up on Monica's hotel? Why the trick's hotel? Maybe he didn't know where she would be staying, but somehow did know who her date would be. How would he know that? I was pretty sure the reverend wasn't in league with Arthur Margolies. Maybe he had inside information. Maybe he got Monica to tell him herself. Maybe she was senior enough to know in advance who her guy was. And maybe there was no way I could answer any of these questions myself.

"I don't suppose you would hook me up so I could talk to Arthur Margolies?"

"Why?"

"I have questions for him."

"I cannot let you speak to Mr. Margolies."

Figured. "Who is he, anyway?"

He shook his head. "It was not his fault. It was a sloppy error on my part, for which you paid the price. Once again, I offer my sincerest apologies." He picked up one of the cartons. "And soup."

When he offered it to me, I remembered the glass of water on the night table in Chicago and the neatly made bed in which I had found myself. I accepted his steaming offering of peace.

The carton had some weight to it and felt warm in my hands. I lifted the lid. It smelled absolutely rejuvenating and made me realize how famished I was. When he offered a plastic spoon from his pocket, I snagged it and dug in, proving just how easy it is to win me over.

"Are you from Bosnia?"

He had the kind of face that transformed completely with a smile. "How did you know?"

"You're reading a paper from Sarajevo, and I can't pronounce your name."

"I am from Dubrovnik. You can call me Bo."

"How do you say your name?"

What he said sounded like "Juro Boolahtovitch." He seemed pleased that I'd asked. When I finished, he nudged the second carton into my space without even looking at me.

"You've paid your debt," I said.

"It is yours. Please, what else can I do for you?"

This was an opportunity I didn't want to waste. Not the soup, but the offer of support. "I need to find Monica. I need to talk to her."

"She is not at work," he said. "She is not at home, and no one knows where to find her."

"Do you think . . . I mean, would your client have done something to her? Or had someone else do something to her?"

"No. He left it to me to handle. He does not want her hurt. Only to understand that what she was doing was not acceptable."

I watched one of the duck boats, a dark purple one named *Beantown Bettie,* chug out of the parking lot and merge into the heavy flow on Boylston. It was fully loaded in October, which spoke to the inexplicable popularity of these cheesy tours.

"Bo?"

"Yes."

"When did you figure out that I wasn't Monica?"

"In Chicago. I looked at your driver's license."

"After I passed out."

"Yes."

"So if your client had wanted me dead, I would be dead?"

He let his gaze drift up to the clouds. "I do not see any point in making hypotheticals. He did not, and you are not." He looked at my face and then my throat. "I remain in your debt."

He was clearly a man of high standards—attacking the wrong victim being a definite violation—and proud of his adherence to them. There was something in there worth trusting.

"Does that mean you would be willing to do me a favor?"

"I would need to know one thing," he said. "Why did you not call the police in Chicago?"

"It was not in my best interest to get the authorities involved."

"Is it because you do what Monica does?"

"Am I a prostitute?"

"No," he asked. "Are you a blackmailer? Is that why you want to see Mr. Margolies?"

"No. I'm not a blackmailer, and I'm not a prostitute. I'm looking for Monica because I need to find people she's working with. I'm trying to break up the prostitution ring."

"Tell me what you need."

"Can you get me the e-mails that delivered Monica's video to your client?"

"I have them. He sent them all to me."

"Good. Here's what I'd like for you to do."

I called Harvey on my way up to New Hampshire. He had left four messages for me. There was only so long I could avoid him, and, given our new spirit of sharing and cooperation, I had to brief him on my night in the North End. He took it remarkably well.

"This man," he asked, "this Bosnian, he helped you?"

"I told you he wasn't after me. He's looking for Monica, one of many people looking for Monica. He's going to help me find her."

"Who were the other two men?"

"No idea. My best guess would be that they worked for some other client of hers that she's trying to extort."

"My word. Where are you off to now?"

"I'm going up to New Hampshire to meet Angel. She has a cabin up there."

"You are aware, are you not, that we are almost out of time. This will no doubt be your last chance to see her before the review."

"I know. I'm going to really push to meet her programmer. If I can't get her to agree, I've got something working with Felix. Beyond that, I'm out of ideas."

"Be careful," he said. "Please keep me posted. Let me know you are safe."

"I will."

"And thank you for telling me about last night."

"Sure. Thanks for not yelling at me." I hung up.

He hadn't said a word about her, so how come all I could think about was Robin Sevitch?

chapter 31

ANGEL FLIPPED HER HAIR OFF HER SHOULDER. Her long blond mane looked particularly untamed today, as if she'd swept her fingers through it when she got up and let it fall where it wanted. It added to her relaxed appearance, which came, no doubt, from her stay in "the country," as she called it.

The two of us had settled in the den of her cabin, yet another of her many properties. It was lovely, exactly what you would expect in the woods of New England. It had a deep front porch with split log railing and a pitched roof with a stone chimney. The sound of a running stream came from the back of the property, but otherwise there was a blessed absence of sirens and car alarms and garbage trucks and grocery carts filled with aluminum cans rattling down alleys. It was peaceful. The air smelled clean. It was like being in a sacred place, which made our discussion feel all the more inappropriate.

"I need a what, doll?"

"A frequent fucker program," I said. "That's the answer."

"What was the question?"

"How do you make both your women and your

clients want to stay with you? You build a loyalty program and lock them in."

Her first reaction was a tweak around the corners of the mouth that could have been the beginning of a smile, but then she sank back into the couch's downy cushions and continued to file her nails. "That won't work."

I was only a fake consultant and she was only a fake client, and a criminal at that, but I had enough pride of ownership to want her to appreciate the subtlety and the creativity of the idea, and the absolutely pitch-perfect solution it represented.

"Why not?"

"Because I would have to give away free pussy and I don't want to do that. Especially since I don't have to."

I scooted out a little farther on my end of the L-shaped couch. The inside of the cabin had the same rough-hewn quality as the outside only softened in a very un-Angel-like way with lots of pillows and cushions and quilts. The couch was so soft I had a hard time sitting comfortably. If I wasn't careful, I would sink down and disappear into its cushy folds.

"You're looking only at the cost. Let's talk about the benefits first."

"I'm all ears."

"A good, well-designed loyalty program would keep your current clients in the fold, it would be powerful enough to pull back the ones who have left, it would give your providers a reason to stay, and the best part is . . ." I paused for dramatic effect. "You can do it, and the women in LA can't."

A slightly different tilt of her head signaled a subtle shift in the way she was listening. I had her attention.

"How would it work?"

"Just like the airline programs. It will have different tiers, or status levels, which clients qualify for based on the number of points they have. They earn points by buying services."

"My services. Dates."

"Right. The more they buy, the more points they earn. The more points they earn, the more hooked in they are to the provider of those services—you. You know how people are about their frequent flier miles. They're insane."

"Which brings us to the awards, right? The free dates?"

"You can't think about them as being free. These guys will probably increase their activity to earn more points. More dates mean more revenue for you and your women. You also charge an annual subscription fee, right?"

"I do."

"Every time a member qualifies for a higher tier, you raise his subscription fee. That will make it seem more valuable to him. You can name the tiers to reflect the status. Bronze, silver, and gold, or—"

"Emerald, ruby, and diamond. I like that better. It's not so common."

I made a note, although it was hard to see. When it had gotten dark outside, Angel had lit the fire in the fireplace with a flip of a wall switch. It was apparently a gas unit, now our only illumination. "The idea is to hook your customers and to dangle some free stuff out there to encourage them to spend more. It also gives you a way to reward the women who are the top earners."

"How does it do that?"

"Right now you have a pool of beginners, women

just starting out. You stop referring to them as the pool and start calling them emeralds. The other—"

"I could even give the gals a little something, a kind of emerald pin or ring or doodad showing that they're one of mine. 'Emerald class.' I like the sound of that."

I had her. She had put her fingermail file down, she was sitting up straight, and she was starting to think of the idea as her own, which meant it would work, at least for what I needed. "A little recognition never hurts. You use the emeralds just as you use your pool now—to service your lowest-tier clients. But once the woman develops enough of a list, she's earned her right to move to the next level. What did you call them?"

"Rubies."

"So, then she services your ruby-level clients, who have earned the right to be more selective because they've earned the points. They pay a higher subscription fee. At the same time, you raise the per-session fees so the women can make more money, too. That gives them incentive to climb the ladder and a reason to stay with you."

"What does a diamond get?"

"Whatever you want to give him. You make this the ultra-elite tier and make it really hard to attain. They'll love that. Once they get there, though, you have to give them something good. Maybe you put only your most expensive, experienced, and in-demand women in there. People like you."

"I'm a double black diamond, doll baby. There is no one else in my tier." In spite of herself, a note of edgy excitement had worked its way into her tone. "What's to keep the LA bitches from copying it like they do everything else?"

"You have something they don't have. You have history."

She nodded, which meant it was true, which meant I was one step closer to Web Boy.

"So what? That's all in the past."

"If you have records of all your clients' activity to date, you can award points and status retroactively based on prior transactions. You'll lock in the current customers, and you might get back some who have left you. Throw out a limited-time offer. Tell them they can come back within the month and get credit for all their prior activity."

"The LA group can make up history."

"It's not the same. You know how much guys love those loyalty programs. They covet the status, they love earning those points or miles and getting free stuff, and they love to play the game. They love to *game* the game. This will work, Angel."

"This is like a real marketing strategy."

"It is a real strategy, and it solves both of your big problems."

She eased back and put both feet on the coffee table. In her loose-fitting jeans, bulky sweater, and thick woolen socks, she looked as if she'd just come in from a day of skiing. The dim light of the fire softened the rougher edges that usually showed in her face. Without all her makeup, she looked almost vulnerable. It was time to move in and try to wrap it up.

"Ultimately," I said, "the group in LA will figure it out and catch up. Competitors always do, so we should get started right away."

"We? You figure on sticking around, do you?"

"Someone has to design the program."

"That's why I have Sluggo."

"Sluggo?"

"He's my programmer. He looks like a slug."

The nape of my neck tingled. Finally, she acknowledged his existence, and he even had a name . . . sort of.

"You just write it all out, and I'll give it to him."

"To design a good program that fits your setup, I need to know how your data are stored and tagged. No offense, but using you as a go-between, it would take forever to go back and forth on this stuff."

"Sorry, sugar. No one meets Sluggo but me."

"If you don't trust me, we can meet him together." Not ideal but . . .

"Bits and bytes make my eyes glaze over. Besides, every time I get around that boy, he drools all over me. I don't believe he's ever had sex. I should initiate him someday. That might be fun. His head would probably fly off." She glanced over at me, looking for a reaction. I gave her nothing. "Cheer up, doll. I like your idea. It's fun. I'm going to use it."

This was a problem. If she used my idea and didn't give me what I needed to get her busted, I was in danger of actually making her business stronger. Not what the client had in mind. "You would put the future of your business into the hands of a programmer? A guy?"

"My business already is in his hands. Besides, why would I put my business in your hands? I barely know you."

I set my notes on the coffee table. Shadows from the fire danced on the rug beneath it, clearly visible through the glass top. It was hard not to show my frustration. I'd already spent the entire afternoon with her, I had a long drive back to Boston, and I was bumping up on a deadline. Harvey was right. This was my last shot at her. If I were ever going to get what I needed, it would have to be now. I ran through my options. Offer up the rest of the names I had stolen in LA? It wouldn't be enough. She understood that her programmer was her biggest vulnerability. Threaten to take the idea to her competitors? That was an empty threat. The only way to get what I needed was to play her game.

"What would I have to do to get you to trust me, Angel?"

"Do you really want to know?"

"The rent is due, my credit cards are maxed out, and I'm out of money. I need to know what it will take. Whatever it takes, I'll do it."

She looked at me with a satisfied smile as she stretched out and rubbed her feet together, feline style. She understood what I was doing, and she liked it.

"There might just be something you could do for me." She grabbed a strand of her hair and looked at it, as if inspecting for split ends. "Tell me, Alexandra, have you ever fucked a boy on the first date?"

"A boy?"

She shrugged. "A man. Have you ever put out on the first date, just because you couldn't keep your hands off him?"

"No."

"Have you ever been in a threesome?"

"I'm not as adventurous as you."

"Have you ever had sex with another woman?"

"I like men."

"Men are pigs." She said it dismissively, as if it were a scientific fact. "Cocks with wallets is all they are. Or wallets with cocks if you like that better."

"Your sample is skewed. The men you do business with might all be pigs, but—"

"What type is that?"

"Those willing to pay for sex."

That brought one of her whoops of delight. "Oh, doll baby. You really do need to learn the ways of the world. There isn't a man alive who isn't about one cocktail away from blowing everything he has in his life for a secret poke." She winked. "Especially if it's with me. I don't care who or what he is, I'll lead him to the trough, and I guarantee you, he'll be snout deep in all that forbidden fruit before you know it. Men are easy. It's women that are hard. Do you know why?"

"Why?"

"Because they're so much smarter. Like you for instance." She pulled her legs up underneath her and went up on all fours. Then she started toward me, doing a slow, seductive tiger crawl across the couch. Her hands and her knees sank down into the soft cushions so that when she was right next to me, it was hard not to tumble into her.

Angel up close was such a vivid presence, she was almost too much to take. Her size. Her scent. The way her eyes shone. Tristan had said it best. She was always hungry, and I was just figuring out how famished she seemed tonight. She was almost purring. "You never answered my question."

"What was—"

"Have you ever been naked with another woman?"

"I've never had sex with another woman."

"But you've thought about it, haven't you?"

I was trying to stay a step ahead of her, trying to figure out what answers she would want to hear. But in the back of my mind, I couldn't help thinking that I had started something I wouldn't be able to stop, something that wouldn't go well for either one of us. "Maybe."

"That's what I thought." She curled her legs beneath

her and sat back, which had the advantage of moving her half an arm's length away. "When you close your eyes alone at night in your bed, you think about it, don't you? About the way a woman's lips would feel touching your skin or a tongue that knows what it's doing, all warm and wet and exactly where you want it." She started moving her hands over her own body, caressing herself. "Does this get you hot? Because I'm all hot now, sugar. I think you should stay here with me tonight."

She pushed closer and put her hand on my thigh. I watched her do it. I didn't flinch. I didn't pull away. I felt her fingers through the fabric of my jeans. It didn't turn me on. It didn't feel erotic. It felt like business.

"If I stayed with you tonight, you would introduce me to your programmer?"

The heat was coming off her in waves. I imagined I could hear the blood racing beneath her skin. She was revving. "Put your tongue in my mouth right now," she said, "and I will give you whatever you want." She tried to kiss me. I turned my head. When her hand began to creep into forbidden territory, I put mine over it.

"You know, Angel, I keep trying to treat you with respect. I keep trying to maintain a professional relationship with you, because you say that's what you're about. But the truth is, you're a whore, plain and simple."

She pulled away. I turned to find her staring at me. Then she pulled her hand off my thigh. "What did you just say?"

"I've come to you with a good marketing strategy. I've provided you with important proprietary information from your most aggressive competitor. I've even screwed a man for money because you said to. I've done everything you asked and more. What's your response?

You will only trust me if I have sex with you. I'm beginning to think you have trust issues."

"Did you . . . did you just call me a whore?"

"You think like one, you act like one, you make decisions like one. You hate yourself like one. That's why you can't trust me. You can't understand anyone who would give you something and not expect sex in return."

She was still kneeling on the couch next to me, holding perfectly still. The only sound in the room was the hissing of the gas fueling the fire. She didn't seem horny anymore. She seemed speechless.

"So what happened to you? Were you molested by your father? Raped by your brother? What was it that turned you into such a cliché? Or do you even know?"

"You'd better stop right there."

"Am I hitting close to home? You like poking around in other people's psyches and you're good at it. It's probably what makes you good at your job. But when the game turns around, you run. You're scared."

"I've got nothing to hide."

"All you do is hide. Behind your big tits and your makeup and your fancy clothes and your money. You've had fun dissecting me and making me strip for you. Come on out here into the light and show me what you've got."

"Ooh. Are we going to play doctor now? Should I stretch out on the couch for this part? I'd much rather stretch you out. I could make you forget all about men." She tried to sound sultry, but she was off her rhythm.

"That's not going to work with me. I want to know about you, but I don't want to have sex with you. Can you grasp that?"

"Why?"

"Because I want to do business with you. You know better than anyone how important it is to understand your client. I'm trying to understand you."

She stared for a long time before letting her shoulders relax. She put her elbow up against the back of the couch and rested her head against her hand.

"Nothing," she said.

"Nothing what?"

"Nothing happened to me. I saw the way the world worked and I made a choice. That's all."

"How does the world work?"

"When I was fifteen years old, I had to take a job in a department store after school, because my daddy was such a dumb bastard that he couldn't support his own family."

I recoiled slightly, the way I always did when I heard one person call another one dumb, and especially someone they were supposed to love. But I also thought that maybe, just maybe, this could go in the direction I wanted it to.

"There was a dress in stock that I wanted to wear to the freshman dance. It was a teal green with a sweetheart neckline. I thought it was the most beautiful thing I'd ever seen, and there was no way on God's green earth I could pay for it. I was going to steal it, but then one day the store manager saw me pawing it. He was this dickhead who wore short-sleeved shirts where the sweat stains under his arms never quite came out. His oldest daughter was in school with me. He told me I could have the dress if I went to the back room and sat on his lap. I remember he had this pocket watch he used to wear. It was a gold watch and he wore it on the end of this cheap old chain. I never did understand that. The chain got caught under my thigh, that's what made me think of it. He came in thirty seconds." She smiled. "I came home with my dress, and I wore it to that dance, and I had a blast. After that, I could get anything I wanted if I went with him to the stockroom. Easy as pie."

"That's your life-altering moment? You fucked a man for a dress, and that set your life on the course it's on?"

"Not really. I fucked a priest. That's probably what did it."

"You . . ." I looked at her more closely. She stared into the fire.

"You're a Catholic, aren't you?"

"I was raised Catholic," I said.

"I knew it. I can always tell." Her voice had gone all dreamy. "Dried-up old men in collars and nuns in burkas, they teach you that sex is dirty and anyone who engages in the sins of the flesh is a filthy heathen who will rot for eternity in hell. What do they know? They've never gotten any in their lives. The only priest that ever taught me anything worth knowing was the one who stuck his dick in my mouth." She gave me a half smile. "He taught me everything."

"What happened?"

She shrugged as though revealing this much had left her with a chill. "I went down on him, up on him, inside and out with him. It's the ones who know they're doing wrong that make me the hottest."

"Did you ever tell anyone?"

"Tell them what?"

"That you were molested?"

"Doll, if there was any molesting going on, it was me doing it to him. I was what you'd call an early developer. He couldn't resist me. No man ever could and I needed it, too."

Right. "How old were you?"

She offered a gentle smile. Her face softened. She rested her hands on her thighs. She looked as tranquil as I'd ever seen her. She dropped her head and looked as though she were in some kind of meditative pose. I almost wanted to reach out to her. Then she raised her head and I saw into her eyes. Something had gone off inside, some kind of light had been extinguished. She stared right through me. When she spoke, her voice was scarily dull, completely devoid of emotion.

"So tell me, Alexandra, does any of this get you hot?"

"Molestation? Not generally."

"Because you won't let it." She started to come at me again, moving slowly. She reached over and started to play with my hair, running her hands through it and pushing it behind my ear. "You know what your problem is? You're all about control. You need to lose control, or have it taken away from you. Then you could just lie back and enjoy."

"That would be rape, wouldn't it?"

"Yes, that would be rape. Don't you ever fantasize about being raped? Taken against your will with all choice removed. No choice means no games, no angst, or confusion, or questions. Just giving in. Letting go . . . and enjoying. It makes it so easy."

"That's not one of my fantasies."

"Taken by someone more powerful and more experienced than you are. Someone who would know what you wanted before you did and would do it to you even when you said no. Someone who would make you do . . . things . . . to her . . . that you've never done before."

The smile was still there, but tighter, crueler, and deeply unsettling. She moved her hand to my face. This time when she touched me, it set off an adrenaline surge that ripped through my bloodstream with one clear message: *run.*

I tried to get up. She put her knee and all her weight on my thigh and locked me down. At the same time, she grabbed my wrist, wrenched my arm around, and held it up between us like half a turkey wishbone. The come-on was over. The pretense was gone. Now we were down to the pure, unvarnished conflict that had been there between us all along.

"You've been trying to get close to me, sugar." Her smooth-as-maple-syrup voice was back. So was her attitude. "Is this close enough?"

"Angel, all I was doing was—"

"You bitch." She twisted my arm half a turn in the wrong direction. It hurt like hell. "You think you're so smart. Did you find out what you wanted to know? Do you understand your client now?"

I did understand some things. First, that there wasn't much point in engaging in discussion. I could look into her eyes and see what I hadn't seen before. Second was that it wasn't the sex that turned her on. It was the manipulation. She got off on making people do what they didn't want to do. She liked making them uncomfortable and ashamed, how she might have felt giving a blow job to a priest. Sadly, I understood too late that making her feel that again would result in this kind of reaction.

"You're nothing but a whore like me. What's your price? What will make you do what you don't want to do?"

She was now stroking my forehead with her free hand. I tried to figure out if I could push her off. Probably not. If I could twist out from under her.

Doubtful. If I had any advantage at all. Not really. Not physically.

"I could force you," she said.

She looked crazed, like an animal. It reminded me of something I had read about wolves, about how the weaker wolf in a fight can save itself by offering its throat, giving the stronger animal the choice to rip it out. Or not. All I had left was to offer her my throat.

I let the wave of pain in my arm subside and tried to talk slowly, with some semblance of confidence. "I know you could force me. I know you could hurt me, and I believe you would. If that's your plan, then do it. Otherwise, let me go."

She stared into my face and twisted my arm again, this time approaching the limit of what my normal skeletal structure could endure. My fingers went completely numb. Tears sprang to my eyes. It was as if her shell had fallen away, leaving something truly scary to look at. It was raw physical desire and a bottomless pit of loathing, for herself and everyone else. I wasn't sure which was fuel for the other, or even if one could be separated from the other.

"I could force you," she whispered again, "if I wanted."

She twisted until we were both shaking. When I finally cried out, she let go of my arm and backed off of my thigh.

I was on my feet instantly. When I dropped my hand to my side, the blood rushed back in, making my fingers hurt as if they were throbbing against a thousand needles. I grabbed my things and started backing out the front door.

"Twelve," she said, without looking at me.

"Twelve what?"

"I was twelve years old."

I left her sitting alone in the dark, staring into the fire.

I could barely keep my car on the road on the way back to Boston. After I had blown out of Angel's place and buckled in, a wave of delayed adrenaline had washed through me. I had started shaking and sweating and hadn't stopped. Felix heard it in my voice when I called him.

"What's the matter, Miss S? You sound freaked out."

That was the perfect description. "I just had a disturbing experience." At least I was out of the cabin, but I was out without the contact information for Sluggo. "Did you get e-mails and attachments from a guy named Bo or Bulatovic?"

"They just came in. What are they?"

"They're the original blackmail correspondence to Arthur Margolies. I was hoping you could use them to track back to Web Boy. I need to get to him fast. You're my only option now."

"Maybe," he said. I heard his keys tapping. "I'm looking at it, and it won't be that straightforward. Let me get to work, and I'll get back to you."

I didn't want to hang up, but I wasn't sure what else to say. "Felix, can you stay on with me for a little while?"

"Yeah, yeah. Absolutely. Sure thing. Did I tell you about the boarding pass printer problem I've been working on?"

chapter 32

HARVEY LEFT ON THE THREE-FIFTEEN P.M. DEparture to Orange County the next day. I stood in one of the windows and watched him take off. We had decided it was best for him to go on without me. He could do the briefing on his own. Felix had worked through the night trying to find Web Boy. He thought he was close, so I stayed behind to try one last-ditch effort to get what we knew was out there. Harvey had set midnight in California as the absolute deadline for adding new information to the presentation. If I couldn't come up with anything new by then, he would go with the case we had.

I watched the aircraft rumble down the long concrete launch pad and lift into the afternoon sky. I had to force myself not to try Felix again. I knew he was working as hard as he could. Every time I stopped at a light all the way home, I had to resist all over again. There was no way I could stay in my apartment and not call him, so I went for a run. The phone was ringing when I got back.

"Hello?"

"I've got him, Miss Shanahan."

"Felix, you're my hero." I know he was dying to tell me how he'd figured it out, but I didn't have the time. I found a pen and my notepad. "What have you got?"

He gave me the address of Stewart Belkamp, a.k.a. Sluggo, a.k.a. Web Boy, the Dark Hacker. Without Angel to introduce me, I'd had to come up with another way to get in to see him. I had one. I just hoped it would work.

"Felix, can you send an e-mail that looks as if it came from Monica?"

"Sure. Piece of cake."

"Remember, you have to fool Web Boy. He'll probably check to make sure it came from her account."

"No problem. What do you want Monica to tell him?"

"The Dark Hacker is about to get an offer he can't refuse."

Angel had said she didn't like being with Stewart Belkamp because he had a tendency to drool all over her. The second he opened his apartment door, I knew what she was talking about. With a tuber-shaped body, frizzy red hair, and a starchy complexion, he was physically unattractive. He was probably in his mid-twenties, but he stared with the slackjawed lust and overblown impudence of a sixteen-year-old boy who had learned everything he wanted to know about women from *Maxim* magazine.

"You're Stewart?"

He talked around the wad of bagel in his mouth. "Who are you?"

"Jane Doe."

I stepped past him and into his standard, no-frills, new-construction apartment, which was located near the heart of the Cambridge tech and biotech centers. He wasn't well fixed for things to sit on, but he had lots of toys to play with—a big-screen TV sat flanked by two high-end speakers and a bookcase full of video games and DVDs.

"Where's your computer?"

He couldn't maintain eye contact but couldn't keep his eyes off various other body parts. Of course, he did think I was a hooker, so maybe I was fair game. "It's in the back. Where's Monica?"

"She decided not to come. Let's get to work. We have a lot to do."

He shoved in front of me. "How do I know you won't tell Angel I've been talking to you?"

"Because I work for the women in LA, and our goal is to put Angel out of business. Why would I want her to know we're courting you?"

"Courting me?"

"Monica told you, didn't she? I'm here to look over your system so we can decide if we want to hire you. According to everything we hear, we want you working for us."

He stuck his thumbs into the front pockets of his jeans but didn't move out of the way.

"Stewart, have you ever considered living in California? Maybe a little bungalow on the beach? It's warm out there all year round. I think you'd like it."

"You're a . . . you're one of the hookers?" From the way he was checking me out again, it wasn't hard to figure out what he was considering.

I tried to look sultry. "You can make all sorts of demands, Stewart, and have every reason to believe they will be fulfilled, beyond your wildest imagination."

He shifted from one foot to the other and wiped the crumbs from his upper lip. He didn't seem completely comfortable with the situation, but he was intrigued enough to go to the next step. "My stuff is back here."

He led me down the hall to a depressingly dim room with a low ceiling and wood-grain blinds. There was an unmade twin bed shoved into a corner. One full wall was taken up by a glass étagère that displayed an octopus of a stereo system, a vast array of CDs, fancy camera and video equipment, more DVDs, and a vast and colorful collection of comic book heroes. There were statues large and small of Batman, the Green Lantern, Superman, the Incredible Hulk, and a bunch I couldn't identify, certainly more than I ever knew existed.

Stewart's work area included two large monitors, multiple CRTs and printers, and lots of modems and switches and drives. There was enough cable to wrap around the apartment complex twice, a sprinkling of crumbs on the desktop, and a trash can that smelled vaguely of fried rice. He had the space set up like a cockpit, with room for only one chair.

I looked at him. "Where do I sit?"

"Over there." With a tight little smile meant to look wicked, I presumed, he nodded to the messy bed.

I didn't want to sit on his bed, partly because it was his bed but mostly because it wasn't close enough to see anything. "I need to watch what you're doing."

He snickered. "As if you'd even understand."

"You want me to understand, Stewart, so I can appreciate the sophistication of your work and be duly impressed."

With a blubbery sigh of acceptance, he left the room and came back dragging a stiff-backed chair behind him. He placed it well behind his own comfy swiveler, but I grabbed it and wedged it forward before he had a chance to plop down and completely freeze me out. That put our knees bumping together beneath his keyboard tray, something that I wasn't crazy about but didn't seem to bother him.

"So, you people are running hookers out of LA? That explains what's been going on with the numbers."

"Has her revenue declined?"

"Angel's revenue never declines. It just hasn't been going up as fast as before."

Prostitution. An unlimited market driven by infinite demand. No wonder it was the oldest profession. Angel's business was under heavy attack by a direct competitor, and she was still growing, only at a slower rate. I wondered what the depressed growth rate might be. Twenty percent? Fifty?

"We've heard about you in LA, Stewart."

"You have?" He puffed up a little.

"We've heard that you're the key to Angel's success."

He let out the long and lonely sigh of the unappreciated. "She couldn't do anything without me. Until she found me, she was so small-time."

"My only question is why put up with her?"

"What do you mean?"

"She takes all the credit for your work. She talks about you as if you're some kind of trained monkey. You know what she calls you, right? Sluggo?"

His face clouded over, and his jaw jutted out. Stewart didn't have much of a poker face. "Sometimes she pays me with sex." He pouted. "That's the only reason I stay with her is . . . is because she's a great piece of ass."

"Uh-huh." I pulled back so that less of me touched less of him. He was lying about Angel, and I didn't want him getting any ideas about me. At least none beyond the ones I wanted to give him.

His fingers hovered over the keys for half a second before he started pounding. His keyboard was dirty and his mouse stained dark from what must have been thousands of touches from his right palm, but the second he started typing, he became a different person. It was as if his hands on the keys completed a circuit, and the power that ran through the computer animated him as well. The slouch fell out of his shoulders, his breathing steadied, and everything about him was more grounded and confident.

"What do you want to see?"

"I want to see how your data are stored and organized, how you keep track of customers, activity, payments, schedules—"

"I'll show you the tables and whatnot, but I'm blocking out all the data."

"Without the data, I can't get a good sense of how your system works."

"There is no way I'm showing you anything about clients or hookers. No way. I don't work for you, and I'm not giving up the goods until I see some green."

Perhaps the whinier version of Stewart would have been preferable. I knew one thing: he was my last option, and I wasn't leaving without that list of hookers.

I sat back in my chair and checked out my thumbnail. "You probably don't have what we need, anyway. We have pretty advanced ideas of what we want to do."

"Advanced?" He snorted. "What is it you think you need?"

"History. We'd like to keep a database of all of our clients' activity to use for a loyalty program. Does Angel have that?"

"She doesn't. I do. I know everything every one of her clients has done, where, when, and who with."

"That's sensitive information. We would want to make sure it's totally inaccessible, for obvious reasons."

"No one can get into my system. No one can hack me."

"Why not?"

"Because"—big sigh, total exasperation—"I have firewalls on top of firewalls on top of firewalls. I designed and built them myself. If I ran Microsoft, they would never have any of those dumb security failures they have."

"Can I see how you store the data?"

"Like I said—"

"I know, no names. Just the structure of the tables."

He came into the program through a back door. There were no input boxes or other customer interface screens. Instead, he showed me a lot of tables and templates with rows and columns that had labels but no data. No names.

Stewart might have had the social skill of a sixteen-year-old, but he was clever about system design. I told him some of my ideas for the frequent fucker program, and he knew exactly how to implement them and, in some cases, improve on them.

"All we have to do," he said, "is to assign an ID number to each customer, see? Some kind of a tag so that we can trace all their activity. Then we add a column to the customer tables."

"Like the airlines' frequent flier IDs."

"The airlines' programs are retarded. Mine would be a whole lot better."

We worked our way into an uneasy truce based on his desire to strut his stuff and, I noticed, just how much contact our knees made. It was like flipping a switch. The more I rubbed up against him, the more forthcoming he was.

"We're thinking of setting up a performance management system."

"What's that?"

"A way to evaluate the performance of the providers."

"You mean the hookers? Like how many different ways they can do it?" He giggled and rubbed his shoulder against my upper arm. I got even closer, going with him on every subtle shift his body made.

"Sort of. Like how much revenue they generate and how many new customers they bring in. Some of the girls are really energetic. They work hard, generate lots of revenue, and bring in new customers. I would want to know who they are so I could reward them properly. Any ideas?"

"That's easy. I'll show you." He stroked a few keys. "I can show you without giving you the names."

He built a table with a column for standard rate, one for what he called average revenue per hooker, one for dates per hooker, and one for revenue earned to date for the year. Instead of names, he used numbered rows, from one to thirty-two.

"I can sort it any way you want. How do you want it?"

"Highest to lowest by rate." I figured that way, the elites would be grouped right at the top, and they were. Only one woman made $2,500 per date. It had to be Angel. Several were just below her at $1,500 to $2,000, and on down the list in descending order.

"Now, can you put in a column that shows the date of each woman's activity? And the city?"

"What for?"

"I want a way to tell who works how often and who travels the farthest."

"Um . . . okay." He whipped up a comment column that included the information. I checked for the date when I had taken the pictures of Angel and Sally. When I saw that the two hookers at the top had been in Pittsburgh on that night, I could barely contain my delight. This was exactly what I needed, data that could be matched to flight schedules and the surveillance photos we'd taken to tell a story that was compelling, traceable, and incriminating.

But only if it included the names of the women.

The clock in the lower right-hand corner of his screen read twelve forty-five A.M. I'd been there for two hours already, and I had taken him as far as he would go on the promise of a bungalow on the beach and a couple of cheap feels. To get the good stuff, I knew I would have to offer him something he really wanted, something for which he had no good defense.

I leaned over the arm of my chair to look at the screen and put myself well into his personal space. He took a deep breath, his face inches from my hair.

"Would you print all those out for me? I want to take them back to my people to show them what you can do."

As the pages began to roll off the printer, I pulled one off and set it on his lap. "You know what would be really helpful for us? To see the names of these women, so we know who to recruit to our side."

"I can't do that."

I pressed on the rows at the top with my finger. That was about mid-thigh for him. "We would be interested in these women." I ran my finger down the page, which happened to be up his thigh. "But not these."

He sucked in a breath that caught in his throat. I turned my upper body toward him. "Come on, Stewart. Let me see our competition. Angel doesn't have to know."

"I can't."

"Can't . . ." I put my hand full on his thigh, and he jumped. "Or won't?" He held perfectly still. He didn't even look as if he were breathing.

"You said she sometimes paid you with sex. I know that's not true, Stewart. She won't let you near her women."

"So?"

"So, maybe we can work out a side deal. An exchange of services, so to speak." I let my fingers begin that slow climb again, up the inside of his thigh, moving steadily until I was close enough to feel his response. I'd never done anything like this with someone to whom I didn't have at least a passing attraction. I had to be careful not to push too far too fast. He was pretty excitable. "You're the one with all the power, Stewart. She needs you"—I gave him a little tweak—"as much as you need this."

As his desire surged, so did my own sense of confidence, and for the first time, I started to understand what Angel knew. Sex was power, but power was the aphrodisiac. There was nothing about Stewart to get hot about, but making Stewart do what he didn't want to do, that was hot, and when he reached for the keyboard and started typing, I felt almost as flushed as he looked.

I tried to get hold of myself by mentally mapping out the exhibits I would spin for Harvey out of this solid gold information. Angel was about to get slam-dunked, another thought that was nearly orgasmic, yet another indication that I had to get off this case, and fast.

Stewart finished and leaned back. I looked at the screen, and they were all there. Angel's name was right at the top. Below were Sally's and Charlotte's and Ava's and the rest. I slipped my hand off his leg, and he gasped again. I moved it up and laid it on his soft chest, a touch that elicited a low, ragged groan from him. "Print those out for me, baby, and make me a diskette."

He couldn't move fast enough. He typed in the commands, copied the files, and handed me the diskette. Then he got up and left, which made more room for me. As the pages rolled from the printer, I pulled them off one by one and tried to think if I dared ask for anything more. It was too late. I had to get going.

Where was . . . I turned around to find where Stewart had gone. He was on the edge of his bed peeling his clothes off. Uh-oh.

"Stewart, stop."

"Why?"

I slipped the printouts into a file folder, dropped the disk into my pocket, and gathered everything together. I stood up and faced him, faced the result of my deception. He was already naked from the waist up, which was highly distracting, considering the way he was shaped.

"I misled you, and I'm sorry."

"What?"

"I'm leaving now."

"You're—" He reached up and scratched his left shoulder with his right hand. "Aren't we going to fuck?"

"Not tonight. I need to get this stuff to my clients. The faster they see it, the faster you get your offer. Think of it that way, and . . ." I inched toward the door. "Thanks for your help. You'll be hearing from us soon."

chapter 33

THE LAST EXHIBIT SHOT OFF TO HARVEY VIA e-mail around three in the morning, East Coast time. He was so nervous I decided to stay up in case he called with more questions. I did, in fact, stay up, but not awake, and when I heard the neighbor's door slam and opened my eyes, it was six-thirty. The last time I remembered checking the clock was at three twenty-five.

I went into my room and fell onto my bed without bothering to change. The next time I was conscious was after eleven. When I sat up, my neck was stiff. I couldn't turn it to the left without sending shooting pains down my back, and I wondered if I would have to make only right turns all day. I also wondered about the nagging feeling that kept tapping me on the shoulder, telling me I was supposed to be somewhere. It was as if I could feel it, but when I whipped around to see it, it was gone. I chalked it up to oversleeping.

It was eight o'clock on the West Coast, which meant that Harvey's presentation was in progress. I probably should have felt nervous in sympathy with him, but I didn't feel much of anything. There was no more that I could do. I thought I should have felt more satisfaction. We were going to nail Angel. But all I felt was spent—

physically, emotionally, and mentally. I felt like one of those climbers standing on the summit of Mount Everest. To me, they always looked as if they were dying. They had spent so much of themselves to get there, there was no way to enjoy it. They didn't always get back all that they had spent, either.

By the time I dragged myself out, it was eleven-twenty. I was headed for the shower when I thought to wake up my computer and check my calendar for whatever important thing I was supposed to be doing. When I clicked up the activities for the day and saw what it was, I froze, then grabbed my backpack and flew out the door, wearing the clothes I had slept in and an expression of sheer panic.

Four people were already lined up at the Boston Police Department shooting range when I stumbled in. They had their weapons ready and their headgear in place. The officer conducting the test patrolled the platform, arms folded over the clipboard trapped against his chest.

He barely acknowledged me when I approached him, which made for an awkward pause as I tried to catch my breath. "I'm . . ." *Breath* . . . "Alex . . ." *Breath* . . . "Shanahan."

"You're late."

"Yes, I am, and I'm . . ." *Breath* . . . "Sorry."

He didn't say anything. Didn't have to. Every cell in his pressed-uniform body said it for him. What kind of an idiot shows up for her range test late, smelling like a locker room, and looking as if she'd slept in her clothes? I had done exactly what Tristan had told me not to do—screeched into the Moon Island parking lot late, rattled, and unprepared. If we had still been friends, he never would have let me do this.

The large-boned, dour-faced officer waited. I figured

the fewer words, the better. "I'm a flight attendant, and I had a difficult time setting up this test around my flight schedule. I'm sorry to disrupt things. Will you allow me to take it even though I'm late?"

Either he appreciated the direct approach, he felt sorry for me, or he wanted to see if a flight attendant could shoot. I wasn't sure which it was, but he pulled out his clipboard and made a notation. "Take the last target. You've got two minutes to set up."

"Thank you. Thank you so much."

It took the whole two minutes to get settled and two seconds to realize what a mistake I had made. As soon as my hand closed around the .38, I knew I should have rescheduled. My shoulders ached, my hands felt weak, the gun felt heavy, and I could not picture any set of circumstances under which I would pass this test today. I hadn't fired a shot, and I'd already failed, and I knew it.

When I got the signal, I squeezed the trigger, the gun kicked, and the round was on its way. It missed. I let out a long, slow breath and tried to adjust. Squeezed off another round. Missed. The weapon was like some alien object with a foreign mass and shape that I'd never touched before. I wanted to stop, to tell them right then and there that I could shoot. I really could shoot. I had worked and practiced and refined my skills, but this was a bad day, and I had made a bad decision by racing over here, and could I go away and try another day?

Round three, and it was getting worse. I was starting to shake badly. The cumulative effect of the exhaustion and the missed shots was adding up to a weight I couldn't bear. *Grow up,* I told myself. *Pull yourself together. If you're this intimidated by the cops, how will you fare with the bad guys who are not just laughing at you but trying to kill you, to boot?*

I aimed the fourth round for the bull's-eye and squeezed off four, five, and six in quick concession. I was perfect. Not a single one had hit the target. If I could have run out of there, I would have, but I managed to remove my gear, gather my things, and not look at a single soul as I walked out the door. I had failed the test. I didn't need anyone to tell me.

Harvey called in the early afternoon when I was unpacking from my last trip so I could use the suitcase for my next one. I had dumped the contents on the floor, right onto the pile of dirty clothes that had overwhelmed my laundry basket. I was sorting the lights from the darks and the dry cleaning from everything else, when the phone rang.

"Alex, we did it. We nailed it. We knocked it out of the park." Harvey was so filled with enthusiasm and clichés I almost didn't recognize him.

"They were so impressed with us. You were absolutely right about those last exhibits. They made the case so effectively that even I could not mess it up. I wish you could have been here, too."

"I think it worked out the way it was supposed to."

"Is everything all right? You sound down."

"I'm okay." I thought about telling him about the test, but he sounded too happy. He wouldn't get it, anyway. "I had a disappointment this morning. I'll get over it."

When it occurred to me I couldn't tell the light clothes from the dark, I got up to turn on a lamp and realized the blinds hadn't been opened for weeks. I pulled the cord and welcomed the sun and the world back into my bedroom.

"Carl has promised me a check for the balance of what they owe us before I leave here tomorrow."

"You're on a first-name basis with Mr. Wolff?"

"He wants to take me to dinner tonight. I think he might want to talk about more work for us."

"Are you serious? The same people who wanted to fire us two weeks ago are not only paying us but offering more work?"

"I told him we would be happy to entertain any proposals."

"We'll have to see if we can squeeze him in. That's . . . astoundingly good news, Harvey." I didn't have the luxury of wallowing in success. I had someplace to be. "Not to spoil the mood, but when do they plan to take Angel out of service?"

"The issue is being discussed, but I think immediately, if not sooner."

"Good. They should move fast before the word gets out and Angel has a chance to mount a counterattack, which you know she will. The rumors are probably already flying. Not to mention the sooner she's gone, the sooner I can quit being a flight attendant."

"They know what they are dealing with."

"I'm not sure they do. I won't be here when you get back. I'm going down to visit my brother and his family in New York. I might stay a few days, so if you need me, call me on my cell phone."

"Alex."

"What?"

"I was the last one to think we could get to this point, and yet somehow here we are. You made this case, and I will be forever grateful."

"We made it together, Harvey. Have a safe trip home."

chapter 34

JAMIE'S NEW HOUSE IN WESTCHESTER WAS impressive. It was not exactly a castle, but with its stone façade, arched windows, multiple chimneys, and massive front door, it wasn't far from it. It stood, as did all of the dwellings on the street, on a large lot clustered with big, sheltering trees that had been there for generations. There were pumpkins on porches and swing sets in yards and a fading afternoon light that bathed everything in early-autumn gold.

I went down the walkway, climbed the steps, and stood on the porch. I had a bunch of flowers in one hand and champagne in the other. The flowers were for Gina, because I wasn't exactly sure how else to approach the woman who was married to my brother to whom I had not spoken in almost a year. The champagne I had hoped to break out when I announced my new career, the successful completion of our first case, and the possibility of a long-term contract. But that whole idea of celebrating a prostitution case seemed grossly out of sync in this bucolic setting. This was a place for families.

Before I had a chance to ring the bell, the knob turned, and the massive door swung open. Gina reached out. "Come here, you." She pulled me into a warm embrace, hammering home the realization that any worries about getting a cold shoulder from Gina were more about my head than her heart.

"It is so good to see you," she said, stepping back to let me in. She looked the way she always did, as if she could feed Cheerios to the kids with one hand, review a corporate contract with the other, and run straight up Mount Rainier and back before lunch. "You're staying with us tonight, aren't you? Maybe tomorrow, too?"

"Yeah." I realized I had left my overnight bag in the trunk. I handed her the flowers. "These are for your new house. It's good to see you, too."

"They're gorgeous. What kind are they?"

"I don't know. I picked them because I liked the way they smell."

She closed her eyes and breathed in their sweet fragrance. "They smell so fresh. Look at these, Maddy."

Peeking out from behind her was a big-eyed girl whose head came to the back of Gina's knee, and I realized what a difference there was between a two-year-old and a three-year-old. Madeline looked like a person now, albeit a very small one. I squeezed myself down to her height. She had fine blond hair that recalled her mother's Swedish heritage, two perfect curves for eyebrows, and deeply mischievous eyes that hinted at my own mother's sense of rowdy fun. She also had no idea who I was.

"I brought flowers for you, too, Madeline." I fished around in my backpack until I found the tiny pink T-shirt with a bright bouquet of daisies embroidered on the front. It had looked like a doll's shirt when I bought it, but when I held it up to her, it seemed that I had guessed right, and I took satisfaction in that. Her entire face smiled when she saw it.

"Is it for me?"

"You're the only one around here who will fit it."

She touched the shirt as if it were made of the finest silk; then she filled both fists with wads of it and held it up. "Mommy, look. *Look,* Mommy."

"It's beautiful, and so very you. Did you say thank you?"

"Thank you, um . . . um . . . do you want to see my new dress?"

"Yes," I said, honored to be asked. "I do want to see your dress."

She peeled off and started up a grand staircase in the middle of the foyer. Even at three years old, she moved with the solid confidence of the athletes both her parents were. Even so, judging from the number of stairs she had to negotiate, she would be gone for a while.

"She's amazing, Gina."

"Isn't she?" Gina absentmindedly reached to close the door but misjudged its width by half and laughed at her own confusion. "Have you ever seen such a big door? It's embarrassing. I feel as if I live in a barn. Let's go to the kitchen, where I can get my bearings. Bring the champagne."

Given the design of the house, I half expected to find an open hearth in the kitchen with a rabbit on a spit turning above it. Nope. It was a cook's kitchen with black marble countertops, a powerful gas stove, and all the sleek, obligatory Sub-Zero accoutrements. It looked and smelled as if Gina had cooked there for years. Whatever we were having for dinner smelled great.

"Jamie should be home any minute," she said. "He called from the airport."

"Was he traveling?"

"He had another overnight trip to LA."

"Your house is beautiful. I like the way it feels."

"Do you? I'm beginning to like it. Jamie wanted it the minute he saw it. Men are so impressed by size. But I had to be convinced." She spoke slowly and thoughtfully, as many people do from the Northwest, without the verbal flourishes and smug self-assuredness one might expect of a corporate lawyer. "We don't have enough furniture, and half the time I don't know where my children are. You can sit if you want." She pointed me toward the kitchen table. It was covered with cookie sheets, Ritz crackers, small boxes of raisins, a jar of peanut butter, and pretzel sticks. "You can help me make spiders."

"Spiders?"

She brought a fully assembled arachnid over, a peanut butter Ritz cracker sandwich with pretzel legs and raisin eyes. "The kids got bored, but I'm still stuck making thirty more for Sean to take to school tomorrow. Couple of smart gals like us . . . we should be able to knock them out in no time. Don't you think?"

"I'm ready."

"Oh, wait. Let me find something for these." She started a search of her lower cabinets while I rolled up my sleeves and got into assembly mode.

"What are you doing, Mommy?" Sean had materialized at his mother's side. He put his arm around her neck and leaned against her the way kids do. She pulled him into a quick Mommy squeeze and gave him a big smooch on the cheek. "I'm looking for something to put these flowers in."

Gina reached up and pulled down the bunch so he could see. "Those are beautiful, Mommy. Where did you get them?"

"Your aunt Alex. Go say hello."

He turned and looked at me for the first time. He was as I remembered him, only more so—a handsome boy with the kind of openly expressive face that draws the eye of even the other parents at the Christmas pageant. He was blond, like his mother, but his steady dark blue eyes were all Jamie—curious and serious and soulful.

"Hi, Sean."

"Hi." He sidled over, flopped an arm onto the kitchen table, and pigeontoed one foot on top of the other.

"Do you remember me?"

"You're Aunt Alex, only my daddy calls you Za." He looked everywhere but at me, then searched out his mother, who had found a vase and was now trimming the stems. She wasn't watching, but she was listening.

"Tell her what grade you're in, sweetie."

"I'm in kindergarten." He stared at his feet until a thought came to him, one of his very own, and then looked up with great excitement. "I'm in a new school, but I don't have a new best friend yet."

"New schools can be tough," I said. "I went to a lot of new schools growing up. So did your daddy.

"Why did he?"

"We moved around a lot."

"I went to Hartsfield Day School before, and . . . and . . . I had . . ." His eyebrows drew together, and I could almost see the complex process that turns thought into language at work in his head. "I had eight friends there."

"That's a lot of friends. Who was your best friend?"

"Zachary Zalinsky."

"Wow. What a long name he has. Did you call him Zach for short?"

"No." He said it with absolute conviction. "His name is Zachary."

"I see. What did you like about Zachary?"

His face brightened even more. "He was funny."

"Did he make you laugh?"

"Yeah." The giggles that rolled out seemed to lift him up. They lightened the space around me, too.

"Hey, Sean, do you like Spider-Man?"

"Spider-Man was bitten by a spider, and it was this *magic* spider, and it had *thirteen legs,* and it had *special powers,* and it made him *sick* until Peter Parker became Spider-Man. That's why he's Spider-Man."

I reached into my bag of tricks and pulled out the blue and red Spider-Man T-shirt I'd found at the mall. The gum-snapping saleswoman with the heart tattooed on her wrist had assured me it was all the rage for five-year-old boys. I was relieved to see Sean's eyes lock onto it when I shook it open for him to see.

"Is it mine?"

"It's yours."

He snatched it and raced to show Gina his prize. "Mommy, can I put it on?"

"Did you say thank you?"

He scooted back over—"Thank you for the new Spider-Man shirt"—then bounced back to his mother. "Can I put it on?"

She slipped his soccer jersey over his head and dropped the T-shirt on, seemingly all in one motion. The shirt came down to his knees. "Can I watch my Spider-Man DVD? Can I, please?"

Gina pondered that. "You can watch until Daddy comes home. Then we're having dinner, and you and Daddy are doing your homework."

Before she had even finished the sentence, he was gone. I watched him whip past and wondered what it was I had been doing that was so much more important than being part of this, even if it was a small part.

Gina brought the flowers to the table and set them in the one spot not scattered with spider parts. "I love hanging out with them," she said.

"Jamie told me you'd left your job," I said. "How long ago?"

"Six months." She settled in and handed me a couple of crackers and a handful of pretzels.

"Why did you leave?"

"Because kids change everything. I wanted to be with them."

One of the things I had always liked about Gina was her ability to take a complicated issue and make it accessible and understandable. It's what had made her a good lawyer. It also made her good for Jamie. He and I both had perfected the opposite trait, which is to take something that should be simple and complicate it to the point where it makes your head explode.

"What about you?" she asked. "Jamie says you've made some career choices of your own." She tucked her hand under her chin and settled in, ready to be absorbed. "I want to hear all about it."

"There's not that much to tell."

"Are you kidding? You're talking to someone whose longest trip of the day is down to the Grand Union in the minivan. Where was your last flight?"

"Chicago." I automatically reached up to touch my throat. The bruises had faded, but it was still my conditioned response to thinking about the trip from hell.

She shook her head and smiled as she graced one of the spiders with its two raisin eyes.

"What?"

"I just . . . I admire you."

"You do?"

"I always have. What I did, making the choice to leave my job, I never would have had the guts to do it without the kids. But you did it for yourself. How cool is that?"

As I worked on my spider assemblage, I had the strongest urge to tell Gina about the case. For the first time in a long time, I felt that I had made the right choices, that things would work out for me. I wanted to share that, but not with Gina and without Jamie. I could tell them together later.

The sound of the front door closing floated through the house.

"Where is everyone?" Jamie's voice echoed ahead of him.

A smaller voice chirped down the front stairs. *"Daddy, Daaaaaaddy."*

Jamie came through the kitchen door with Madeline in his arms, her face close to his. In the briefest of glances, I could see in his eyes that something was wrong. He reminded me of the baby titan on my flight to Chicago, the phone flipper who had been almost in tears. "Za, you made it. Any problems with directions?"

"No. I came right here."

I wanted to ask what was wrong but wasn't sure it was my place. He crossed the kitchen to give his wife a light kiss on the lips. She smiled at him. He didn't smile back. He turned abruptly and grabbed a cracker.

Gina was also picking up a strange vibe. I could see it in her face. "How was your trip?" She reached up to straighten the tiny tiara Madeline wore on her head. It went with the miniature pink chiffon prom gown.

"I have to go in early tomorrow." Jamie looked at Madeline. "Where's your brother, Princess Magpie?"

"Watching Spider-Man."

Jamie walked over and looked down at the table. "What are you doing?"

I proudly displayed one of my completed units. "Making spiders."

"There's a spider theme around here tonight." He scooped up a handful of pretzel sticks and headed for the door. "Let's go find your brother, Magpie."

She thought that was a good idea, but not so the eating of spider legs, a fact that she commented on all the way up the stairs.

"Mr. Grumpy Guy." Gina found a big mitt and opened the oven door to check on whatever was in there. It smelled like pot roast. "Jamie's really missed you this past year," she said. "In case he doesn't remember to tell you."

I wasn't sure what to say. "Yeah, I'm sorry . . . about all that. About—"

"I hope," she said, gently interrupting, "that we see more of you. I really want my kids to know their aunt Alex."

chapter 35

IT WAS A SWEET AND POWERFUL BONDING EXperience to be standing at the sink, handing dripping plates to Jamie again. Many a night when we were growing up, we had stood side by side washing dishes in the kitchen of the old house on Rivalin Road. It was always after my father had shuffled off without comment to his well-worn spot in front of the TV.

My place, since I was older, was always at the sink, washing, rinsing, and directing the operation. Jamie cleared, stacked, and dried, never fast enough to match my pace. He would stack each piece of silverware in the dishwasher one by one, asking me things I didn't know. Who was faster, the Flash or the Green Hornet? What would happen if the earth started spinning the opposite way? What caused emphysema? Why was everyone smarter than he was? Sometimes I got frustrated with him and just did the job myself. Later we found out his disability made it hard for him to focus on specific tasks.

"You can let that soak," he said, standing next to me in the kitchen of his brand-new mansion. He had worked ahead and was waiting for me to finish scrubbing the pot roast pan. It was the last, the biggest, and the most obstinate.

I used the nonsudsy back of my hand to push the hair off my forehead. The humidity from the hot water and the exertion of trying to scour the pan had moistened everything above the collar of my shirt.

"I will not be defeated by a crusty pan. Never." With one last furious effort, I scraped the last of the crust, rinsed, and handed it off in triumph.

Jamie dried it quickly and began searching his new kitchen to find the place where it lived, opening and closing cabinet doors high and low and mumbling to himself. He gave up and set it across two of the six gas burners. Then he turned and searched the countertops. "Where's my cup?"

"I washed it."

"I wasn't finished."

"It was on the counter. Fair game."

He dried his hands with the dishtowel. "Still as obsessive-compulsive as ever." He was kidding, but there was an edge to his tone.

He opened a cabinet, took down another mug, and filled it with what was left of the coffee Gina had brewed.

A scattering of crumbs still littered the surface when we went back to the table to sit, mostly where Sean had been sitting. I brushed the offending specks into one of the napkins. Oh, for one of those nifty crumb sweepers possessed by waiters at fine restaurants everywhere.

Jamie looked almost prayerful as he sat with his arms extended in front of him. He could be praying. Jamie still went to church. I could feel sadness in him, something pressing hard. It made me anxious.

"Are you all right?" I asked him.

"Yeah. Sure."

He wasn't. He knew I knew, and the silence that followed was awkward. In the quiet, I could hear Maddie and Sean's sweet voices floating down from upstairs, where they were getting ready for bed.

"Maddie looks like Mom," I said. "She does that thing with her mouth, where it pulls down at the corners as if she's about to tell you a secret or a joke or . . ." I rummaged around for the words to capture my mother's face, but I didn't need the words. He already knew.

"You're the only other person who could see that."

"I saw it at dinner," I said. It had reminded me of her voice. My mother's voice that used to tease me for being so serious.

Gina came down the stairs and scoped out the clean kitchen. "You two are awesome. You can wash dishes in my house anytime."

"Just don't let Jamie near the gravy boat," I said.

"Gravy boat?" She gave her husband a cunning glance, and I sensed an opportunity.

"Jamie, you never told her about the gravy boat?"

"No." His voice was dull, and he didn't look as if he wanted to tell her now, but Gina hustled over and settled in with us, pulling one foot up on the chair with her.

"Tell me," she said. "I never get to hear the family stories."

I leaned in. "It was Christmas night after we'd had this big dinner. Jamie and I were helping Mom wash the dishes," I said. "How old were you?"

"Five."

"He was five, so I was ten. We'd had people over for this big extravaganza. They were members of my father's family whom we didn't really know. Now, my mother was wonderful, but she wasn't the greatest cook. She could never get organized, and she was really nervous about this dinner. She wanted so much to make a good impression, so she pulled out the one and only gravy boat from her set of good china. It was a wedding gift."

"From someone at the dinner," Jamie said.

"Is that true?" I hadn't remembered that.

"Aunt Bobbie. She was married to the guy who wore the sweater vest and smelled like cigars, so I guess she was technically a cousin, or cousin-in-law, but she wanted us to call her Aunt Bobbie."

"Right, right." I thought back on the evening, trying to see the house in my mind. It was one that we didn't live in for long, so I had to reach for the details. "So, everyone is lolling around in the living room, gorged and half in the bag from drinking wine all afternoon. Everything is quiet, until Jamie reaches up to put something on the counter and bumps the gravy boat. I was across the kitchen," I said, "but I saw the whole thing. It teetered on the brink just for a second, before it went over. Everything switched into slow motion. It was like a John Woo film. There should have been doves flying."

Gina was delighted. "And long coats flapping."

"Exactly. It's important to appreciate that the floor in that kitchen was tile. It was like a gravy bomb had gone off. There was gravy on the cabinets, on the walls, on my mother's dress, on my new shoes." I felt an ancient twinge of regret, remembering how I'd had to throw those gravy-drenched shoes away. "We were finding gravy boat pieces well after Easter dinner, at which, of course, we couldn't have any gravy, because, well . . ."

Gina laid her head against her knee and peeked around it at Jamie. "Someone broke the gravy boat."

He shook his head. "Everyone came running in. Dad was yelling and screaming about why was I in there to begin with. I'm standing in the middle of all this mess, crying, thinking . . . I ruined everything." He looked down into his coffee cup. He reached up and rubbed his thumb across his eyebrow. "Mommy got down on the floor with me, right down in the gravy, and gave me that look like . . ." He nodded to me. "Like the one you were talking about on Maddie. She told me to take five deep breaths, and she would tell me a secret."

He paused, and I remembered him standing there when he was five years old, trying so hard to stop crying when he felt so bad, and my mother with her hands on his shoulders.

"Then she whispered so I would have to stop crying to hear. She said she never liked that gravy boat anyway and that my help was worth more to her than a hundred gravy boats."

Gina reached over and grabbed hold of his thumb. "I wish I'd known your mom," she said. "She sounds cool."

I stared down at the tablecloth, where a renegade crumb had managed to remain on the loose. "She was," I said. "Our mom was very cool."

Gina kissed Jamie on the forehead. She came around the table and gave me a hug. "I'm so glad you're here." Then she went back upstairs to the kids, leaving Jamie and me alone again.

"Are you sure you're—"

"I'm fine." He wiped his eyes with the back of his hand and checked his watch, which prompted me to check mine. It was only seven forty-five, but it seemed later because it was already dark outside. I was thinking of going out to the car to get my overnight bag, when I heard the muted call of my cell phone. It was in my backpack, which was in the other room at the bottom of the stairs. I got to it before it rolled to voice mail.

The spy window said it was from an out-of-area caller.

"Hello."

"What did you tell her?" There was panic in the voice and a solid infusion of cold, hard anger but nothing at all that was familiar.

"Who is this?"

"Monica Russeau. What did you tell Angel?"

The elusive one emerges. Of all the people I might have expected to hear from, she might have been the last. "What do you want, Monica?"

"*What* did you *tell* her, you goddamned bitch? I need to know now."

I checked the hallway and the top of the stairs. There was no one around to listen, but I still felt vaguely dirty taking this call in Jamie's house while his kids were upstairs listening to bedtime stories. I wandered into an unfurnished room, where the only light came from a streetlamp shining through a bay window.

"I didn't tell her anything about you, although I guess there is a lot to tell."

"Then why is she trying to kill me? Huh? Why is she trying to kill me?" I could just see her pacing wherever she was, going back and forth with her palm to her forehead. That's how she sounded, anyway.

"The last I checked, a lot of people were after you. I met some of them personally."

"Artie doesn't want me dead. Besides, he told me that was taken care of."

Taken care of by me, thank you very much, and what was she doing talking to the man she'd been trying to blackmail? "That's nice for Artie, but what about all the other men?"

"What other men? Did you tell her there were others?

Goddamn you. What did I ever do to you? Is that what you told her?"

"Where are you, Monica?"

"Quit . . . will you *quit* answering my questions with questions and just tell me what she knows so I can decide what to do? She's coming to kill me. Do you get that, you stupid, fucking, lying bitch?"

This was getting old fast. When I had needed Monica, she was nowhere to be found. I didn't much feel like taking her abuse. "Monica, if Angel found out what you were doing, it wasn't from me. If she is after you, you need to go to the police and get help."

"She told me."

"Told you what?"

"She sent me a message saying she was going to kill me, and it was because of you."

More Angel games, no doubt. "It's not because of me, and if you have a message like that, print it off, and take it to the police. If you tell me where you are, I'll send someone over to help you."

She was silent for a few seconds. All I could hear was the static, and I thought she might accept my offer. "I hope you die of cancer," she hissed. Nope. Not accepting. "I hope you get AIDS. I hope someone cuts off your—"

"It's for you, Za." I spun around to find Jamie lurking behind me, cordless phone in hand. "It sounds like a party going on somewhere. Do you want to call her back?"

I took the cordless from him, held it to my other ear, and listened. He was right. There was some kind of an organized ruckus going on at the other end.

She must have heard me breathing.

"Is that you, sugar?" Angel's voice was like an ice cube dropped in my ear. "Did you hear the news?"

"Hold on." I turned to see if Jamie was still there. He wasn't. I put the cordless under my arm, covering the mouthpiece, and got back to Monica. "Are you still there?"

"Who is that? Is that her? You're tracing this call, aren't you?"

"Monica, I'll try to find out what's going on, but you have to tell me how to get in touch with you."

She hung up.

I dropped the cell on the floor and grabbed the cordless. "What do you want, Angel?"

"That's no way to greet a friend. Especially since I'm calling with news. I was taken out of service. But you already knew that. You knew it before it happened, didn't you?"

She had called my brother's home phone, hoping, I was sure, to rattle me. She had. I went to the window and stared out at the street. Even in the dark, the neighborhood looked cozy and peaceful.

"What are you talking about?"

"It wasn't too hard to realize who the fox was in my henhouse. But don't you worry. We're having a little party to celebrate our reinstatement."

"Reinstatement?"

"We were back before we were even gone. I told you before I'd be ready, didn't I?"

She paused for a response, but if what she was saying were true, there weren't any words that came close to what I was feeling.

"Are you there? I know you're there."

"What do you want with Monica?"

"You'll know soon enough. Was that your brother who answered? I'll bet he's a cutie. Cute little brother with a cute little family and a—"

"Angel, why are you calling me?"

"I wanted to tell you myself that we have not finished our business just yet. Not by a long shot. Keep a close eye on your e-mail. You'll be hearing from me in case you haven't already."

"We have nothing left to say to each other."

"There are still a few things I can teach you. Here's a good lesson to always keep in mind. When you poke at a hornet's nest, you're not the only one who's likely to get stung. Buzz, buzz, doll."

chapter 36

JAMIE'S OFFICE WAS YET ANOTHER SPACIOUS room in the mansion, this one tucked toward the back of the house. It had warm cherry paneling, abundant overhead lighting, and wall outlets of all varieties. So far, there was only a desk in the middle of the hardwood floor. Temporary, he'd said, until he could find the one he really wanted. The framed picture of his family with Mickey Mouse down in Orlando was one I also had at home. The heavy clay paperweight that looked to be some kind of hedgehog was from Sean. It said so right on the bottom. "To Daddy from Sean." Only the *n* was really tiny because he'd run out of space.

I had checked it all out while my laptop made its scratchy way to the Internet. I was in now and checking the unread messages in my box. It was mostly spam. One had a blank space where the address should have been, which usually meant spam, but it also had a subject heading that could be from only one person.

all men are pigs

When I saw that a video file was attached, my mouth went dry. I clicked on the download icon, and my jaw started to quiver, but nothing else happened. My clicker finger, stiff and jerky with adrenaline, would not work right. I concentrated, tried again, and got it started.

It was a big file, so I had plenty of time to sit and wonder what Angel would send me and why. She had a reason for everything she did, and as the seconds ticked away and the file loaded, I found that I couldn't stay in my seat. It was taking a long time, but there was no speeding it up. I watched the progress monitor as the file built. Ten percent. Twenty-five. It seemed to stick for a while around forty percent. When it got to ninety-eight percent loaded, I took my seat. When it was all finally there, I scanned for viruses, pulled up the media player, and waited again. I could barely stand all the waiting. But then I started to dread what was coming, and by the time the image hit the screen, I was almost afraid to watch.

Something bad was coming.

The picture was high-resolution and in color. There was no doubt about what was on the screen: a man and a woman, naked on a bed, having sex. The woman was on top doing all the work. I didn't have to see her face to know it was Angel. Besides her bleach job and her wide, muscular shoulders, I could have recognized her from the way she devoured her partner.

Angel was a hooker. This was what she did, which meant she was showing me the man. But all I could see of him were his fingers splayed across her butt. His gold wedding band gleamed against the pale pillows of flesh, and a sick, shaky premonition wormed up through my gut and tried to find a place to break through.

The two of them ground out the familiar rhythm, complete with a guttural sound track of maximum sexual exertion. He tilted his knees slightly, the better to thrust. She leaned forward and braced her hands, palms down, on either side of him, and they started chugging, faster and faster, muscle on muscle, flesh slapping flesh—as they climbed toward the pinnacle of mutual carnal satisfaction. I couldn't turn away for any reason, and I couldn't bear to watch, because I knew it was coming, this thing that was bad.

They burst together upon the summit of completion with a throaty chorus of groans and cries that could spring only from the thing they were doing. They rolled across the pinnacle and down the other side, losing momentum slowly until they were finally still, the man clearly exhausted, Angel still draped across him like a tablecloth.

She was the first to move. Rolling back up to a sitting position, she dropped her head back. The way her hair swept across the bare skin of her back reminded me of the backless evening gown she had worn that first night when I had taken her picture in Pittsburgh, when she had turned in my direction, and I had seen in her face that look of a predator's pure bloodlust.

On the screen, she reached one of her long arms down to the side of the bed and pulled a pillow from the floor to tuck under her partner's head. She dismounted, turned full on toward the camera and, with her partner's face revealed, smiled at me.

His favorite pie was custard. He liked green apples but not red. He was allergic to cats. The large bone in his right forearm was softly curved from the time he pitched off his skateboard and broke it.

These were some of the things I knew about my brother. I knew in the way we always know things about our families. Some of them are hardwired into our genes. Some are absorbed over the years of living under the same roof, folding each other's underwear, and eating from the same ice cream carton. There were enough details to let me believe I knew him, when in fact what I knew about him, the things I remembered, made up an infinitesimal slice of whatever it was that made him who he was.

One of the things that fell squarely on the side of stuff I didn't know about my brother was how he could be in bed with a prostitute.

chapter 37

JAMIE HAD GONE INTO THE DEN TO WATCH TV, only he'd never turned it on. He sat stiffly on the couch, staring at a blank screen. When he noticed me in the doorway, it must have been in my face, because he knew. His face looked the same as it had the day I'd showed up at his school unexpectedly.

He had known that day, too.

"She passed." That's what the counselors and teachers had whispered to each other about my mother that day, as if she'd been a car in the next lane or a horse coming up on the backstretch. Passed what? Passed go? Passed counterfeit bills? To this day, I hated that gutless euphemism. She died. She'd been dying for a long time, her breath rattling around in her chest, sounding as if she were trying to breathe underwater. Sometimes lucid, sometimes not, but always dying. Jamie was eight, but he knew that, and he knew there was only one reason I would show up at his school in the middle of the morning, and when he walked into the room and took in the scene, he immediately erupted, crying hard and heavy just from the sheer terror of what I might say. He cried so hard it scared me. The counselor tried to move in, but I shoved her aside and put my arms around him.

We sank into a pile on the floor, and it smelled like bananas in that room, because some kid had left one in his desk, and the rain outside poured as it often does in Seattle in March, as if it were falling from tipped buckets, and I said it in his ear so they wouldn't all hear.

"I'msorryI'msorryI'msorry."

Bananas and rain and Jamie crying with so much anguish I would have done anything to make the thing that was hurting him stop.

But we weren't in a classroom. We were in his house in Westchester, and it seemed to me he knew now, just as he had known then, that his world was about to crash down, and I was the one wielding the ax.

"I need you to see something."

I could barely make myself move, but I turned and went back down to his office. When he showed up, I closed the door. I walked over and clicked the start button, and the show began. Jamie watched, blinking a lot, looking as if he'd awakened from a deep sleep and opened his eyes into the glare of a bright light.

His face turned ashen. His lips parted just enough to let all the air exit his body. When he tried to grab the mouse, he knocked it off the desk. It swung by its cord until he captured it with both hands and returned it to its pad. By then, his motor control was so far off he couldn't manipulate the cursor. He tried and tried, but he couldn't get it, and his fumbling failure was like a key that opened a door inside me. My eyes filled, and I tried to stop the tears with the heels of my hands, but they slipped out anyway and ran down my face. I took the mouse away from him and stopped the video.

He lowered himself into his desk chair as a man recovering from malaria might do it. There was another chair in the room, but the wheels on it scared me. I stood. I waited. Eventually, Jamie, staring at the frozen image, squeezed out a thought. "She taped it. Why would she tape it?" That thought led him to his next. His perspective seemed to widen from the screen to include the computer, the room, and ultimately me. "How did you get this?"

"Can we get the larger issues out of the way first, like since when did you start patronizing hookers?"

"Hookers?"

"Yes."

He gestured weakly at the screen with his palm up. "Alex, why do you have this?"

"Angel sent it to me. Will you answer my question?" I needed to know. I really needed to know if he was one of those cocks with wallets Angel had talked about or if this was a onetime thing. Please let it be that.

"Who is Angel?" He answered my question with his own, and I felt what Monica must have felt in her moment of crisis: boiling rage.

"She's the woman you are screwing in this video for all the world to see, and if we don't get our shit together right now, all the world will see it."

He went from stunned to bewildered to defeated in record time, all of it showing right on his face. Then he closed his eyes. His shoulders gave up. With wrists together, his hands dropped into his lap. Then he did the last thing I expected.

He laughed.

"Is this funny?" I was stunned, and I was angry. "I'm thinking of Gina and Sean and Maddie, and I'm thinking this is not quite so hilarious as you seem to find it."

He slouched down into the seat, let his head roll back, covered his eyes with his hands, and laughed some more. He sounded almost loony. "This *is* hilarious. Fucking hysterical. Don't you find it hysterical?" He looked at me from under the visor of his hand. "You're right. It's not funny. It's . . . ironic. That's a better word. *Ironic.*"

"What is ironic about this?"

He looked at me as if I were a simpleton. "I haven't seen you or talked to you in almost a year. I run into you completely by chance. Then I do something so goddamned stupid I want to kill myself, and before I can even turn around, you're on it. You are *on* it. I mean . . . what . . . how—"

"You're upset that I found out your secret? That's what is bothering you?"

"Don't play high and mighty with me." He got up from his chair but once on his feet didn't seem to know where to put himself. That seemed to get him more and more wound up, and when he got near a wall, he punched it with his fist. Then he turned on me with his jaw tight and his finger jabbing the air in front of my face. "This is my house. What gives you the right to come into *my house,* drag me in here, and start making accusations about things that are not even close to being any of your business?"

"So, you're telling me there is some innocent explanation for this?" I pointed to the monitor. "That somehow I got the wrong impression from watching you screw this woman? Why don't you set me straight, Jamie? Let's hear it."

"What do you want to hear? That I fucked up? I did. I fucked up. Does that make you happy?"

"No, it doesn't, and what I need to hear is whether this is a one-time fuckup or if you are a regular customer of this hooker ring."

"Hooker ring? Is that what you think of me?"

"I don't know what to think of you."

His hand dropped to his side. Now he looked stunned. "I make one stupid mistake with one woman, so that means I frequent prostitutes?" He went off on another flight of sour amusement. "She's a marketing consultant."

"She is? How many marketing consultants do you know who make secret sex videos and use them for blackmail?"

"Blackmail?" That stumped him but only briefly. "If this is blackmail, why did she send it to you?"

"Because she wants—" Oh, man. This was getting too complicated. We had to step back and look at this thing piece by piece, and Jamie needed to know the truth if he was going to tell me the truth.

"Jamie, sit down."

Not only did he ignore me, he raised his foot to the chair on wheels and gave it a wicked shove across the floor. It went skittering into the wall and tipped over on its side. I knew that rolling chair was a bad idea. He stared after it, with dull eyes. "I'm fucked. It's hard to believe how fucked I am."

"Jamie, would you please sit down before Gina hears us and comes in here."

That idea seemed to break through. He dragged himself back to his desk and sank into the chair that was still upright. I picked up the other one and pulled it over so we could look at each other face-to-face.

"Listen to me," I said. "That woman you were with is not a marketing consultant. She's a prostitute. Her name is Angel Velesco. She works with me as a flight attendant, and she's a hooker."

He wanted to argue, but deep down, he knew I wouldn't lie to him that way, and even though he shook his head no, he said nothing. He looked scared.

"We will fix this," I said, not at all sure that we could. "I promise. But I need to know some things. Are you saying you didn't know this woman was a hooker and you didn't approach her for sex?"

"No."

"How did you meet her?"

"She was on the flight yesterday morning to LA."

"Yesterday? This happened . . . last night?" I tried to put the pieces together, fit the events to the timeline I understood. The night before, I had been with Stewart, Harvey had been on his way to Orange County, and nothing had happened yet.

"Was she working the trip?"

"I told you she's not—"

"Would you please just answer my questions?"

"She was in the seat next to mine. We started talking, and she asked me if I would be her guinea pig for a survey she was putting together. She wanted to see if I . . . if her questions made sense. She told me her name was Marilyn."

Guinea pig. Marketing survey. The seat next to his. She'd sought him out. Why? How had she known? She must have heard rumblings. She must have been tipped off somehow. But how did she know about Jamie? Did I ever . . . I had never mentioned him to Angel, had I? *Had I?* A palpable feeling of dread began to take over the function of my heart, because even though I didn't know how, I knew I was responsible.

"She asked you personal questions?"

"Demographic stuff," he said. "Age. Zip code. Family. Occupation. The product she was flacking was some kind of a combination cell phone–PDA. She had questions about how I kept track of my life."

"About your family?"

"Yes."

"Place of business?"

"All of that."

Business . . . business . . . *business* card. I stood up. I walked to the back wall of the office, which was the point in the room farthest from him. Jamie's business card, the card he had given me on the flight to LA. I had lost it. I thought I had, but I hadn't. I remembered where I put it. At the hotel before leaving for the party, I took it out of the pocket of my uniform. For reasons I didn't understand then or now, I slipped it into the pocket of my sweater, the one I had worn to the party, the one Angel had returned to me at the spa. Jamie's business card with his home phone number on the back.

He said something. I turned to look at him. "What?"

"She was nice. She was easy to talk to, so I talked to her. It turned out she was . . ." He was starting to get it. "She was staying at my hotel."

Of course she was. Easy enough. She could have checked his reservation record and found out in advance where he was booked. I didn't want to hear the rest, but the more he told, the more he seemed to want to tell. His chance to unburden had calmed him down considerably.

"She asked me to meet her for drinks that night. I said no, but I came in late from a client dinner, and I stopped by the bar, and . . . and I looked in. I don't even know why I did it. If I'd gone straight up to my room . . ." He sat there, quietly staring down the road not taken.

I could see her sitting in the bar waiting for him, dressed up to look like a professional woman, being whatever woman she needed to be to lure him into her trap. "I can make any pig come to the trough," she'd said. She must have had a good time doing it to Jamie, knowing he was my brother.

"We had a couple of cocktails. We showed each other pictures of our kids."

It seemed hot in the office. "She said she had kids?"

"One. A boy Sean's age."

I thought maybe my blood had turned to kerosene and I would burst into flame at any moment. "What else?"

"She asked me to her room. I told her no, but . . ."

"But then you went with her anyway."

"No." He was firm, the way Sean had been firm in his insistence that Zachary Zalinsky's name was not Zach. "I went up to my own room. I brushed my teeth. I got in bed. I called Gina. Then here comes the knock on the door." He might have been sweating, too. He wiped the back of his hand across his forehead. "She had a bottle of champagne and a couple of glasses. I stood there with my hand on the knob looking through the peephole. She had this sheer blouse thing on." He did an awkward, incomplete demonstration with his hands. "I could see right through it, and this tight little skirt. I knew when I turned that knob I was dead. I knew it, and I did it." His voice got very small. "I did it."

"Why?"

"She was there. I was there. I didn't think about how it would feel afterward. I wasn't thinking about Gina. She came in. She poured the champagne. We had a couple of glasses, and . . . we did it, and she left." He rubbed his hands on his knees. "Now it's like I have her fingerprints all over me. I can't even look at Gina. I think she knows somehow."

"I don't think so, Jamie."

"I keep thinking . . . I keep thinking I can't fix this one."

"Fix what?"

"This mistake. I'm always making mistakes. I go too fast . . . I do things, but I can always go back and slow down and figure out how to fix them. But this one, I think this one can't ever be fixed."

And gravy boats can't be put back together. "Angel is masterful at this stuff. She knows what she's doing, and she does it all the time."

"How much does she want?"

"What?"

He swallowed hard and looked right at me. "You said this was blackmail. How much does she want?"

Everything felt in a knot in my sternum, and I couldn't think, and it was possible I was having a heart attack. Chest tight. Pulse racing. Breath short. I had to make this right. I had to fix this thing. But first I had to tell him.

"She doesn't want money. She doesn't want anything from you."

"Then what does—" He glanced at the computer, my computer, and the light went on. He seemed almost excited that something finally made sense. "She wants something from you."

"Yes."

"What?"

"I don't know yet."

"You don't know?" I was not doing this right, and he was sensing that he was not the only guilty one in the room. "What's going on?"

"Angel runs a prostitution ring at OrangeAir. I was hired by the airline to investigate her. That's why I'm working as a flight attendant. I'm undercover."

He blinked. Then he blinked again. "You're not really a flight attendant?"

"It's my cover job. I've been investigating Angel for months."

"Are you kidding?"

"No."

He got up and wandered away from the desk. "You're *not* a flight attendant. But she *is* a flight attendant, *and* she's a hooker."

"Yes."

"She's not married?"

"No."

"No kid?"

I shook my head.

He didn't know which revelation to deal with first, but it didn't take him long to get to the heart of the matter. "She used me to get to you. That's what this is?"

"Yes."

He found his chair again and sat. He put his elbows on his knees and covered his face. This time, when he emerged, it was with a sense of bitter acceptance. "Could I be any stupider?"

"I told you, she's a pro. She does this a lot."

"What does she want you to do?"

"I don't know. I got her fired, but she apparently didn't stay fired. I don't know what she wants. She might just be screwing with me." I looked at him. He didn't appreciate the choice of words. "Jamie, I'm sorry. I'm sorry about this whole thing."

"What will happen if you don't do what she wants?"

I didn't want to tell him that I thought she would do what Monica had tried to do to Arthur Margolies, but he deserved to know. "Probably send it out to everyone in your e-mail address book. Your office, your church, the kids' schools. Gina."

As he listened, he banged his head with the heel of his

hand as if it were a vending machine and the thoughts he needed had gotten stuck on the way down the chute. It's what he used to do when he was a kid and he got confused and couldn't think straight. When he was trying really hard and getting nowhere. I couldn't stand to see him do that.

"Mother of God. Mother of *God*. What did I do?" His muttering was mostly to himself.

"Jamie, please calm down. I'll take care of this. I promise."

"Will you do . . . what she's asking?"

"I don't think it will matter. She won't give it back no matter what I do. I have to find another way to get it back, and I will."

"Jesus Christ." He got up and started swerving around the room, looking as if he wanted to cry but grinning instead. "This must feel pretty good to you, huh?"

I stared at him.

"Jamie fucked up again. Time to pull poor, dumb Jamie's ass out of the fire *again.*"

"That is not what is going on here. I never meant for this to happen."

"And yet somehow here we are, you rescuing me again, so all is right with the world."

"That's crap." I could feel the conversation tipping, teetering on the edge of the slippery slope. "Stop talking like this. You're upset."

"Upset? I am beyond upset. Private *investigator*? Did you just wake up one morning and decide you wanted to be Magnum, PI?"

"Stop it. Just stop."

"Do you have any idea what you're doing, or have you completely lost your mind? What am I supposed to do now? Should I . . . should I call the police? Should I tell Gina?" He slammed the wall again, this time with his open hand. "Tell me, Magnum, what should I do?"

"Hey, I might be the one who put her in your life, and I am sorry about that. But if you hadn't opened the door and let her into your room, we wouldn't be having this conversation."

"You get off on this." There was that jabbing finger again. "You always have. All this bullshit all these years about protecting poor Jamie from mean old Daddy. Big hero, you are. You wouldn't have had it any other way."

Now I was up, and we were facing each other across the desk, and I could not stop the words that were coming out of my mouth, and I didn't know where they were coming from. "Is that what Walter said? Is that what the two of you talked about at Christmas? How what he did to you is *my fault?*"

He shifted his weight back and chewed the inside of his lip. "That's what's really bothering you, isn't it? That I have a relationship with him and you don't."

"Horseshit."

"The one thing he never did was treat me like a baby or someone who couldn't take care of myself or make my own decisions."

I waved a flailing hand at the computer. "Look what happens when you make your own decisions." He looked as if I had slapped him, but I didn't care. I couldn't stop. "No, he didn't treat you like a baby. He treated you like crap. He treated you as if you embarrassed him and he wished you were never born. He made you cry. Have you forgotten all that? Because I can't." I also couldn't breathe. "All I ever tried to do was make it easier for you."

"Maybe it's the other way around." His voice was quiet, like the iceberg that sank the *Titanic* was quiet.

"What?"

"Maybe you kept him from me. You stood in between us so we couldn't have a relationship, and now that I'm trying to have one, you can't stand that."

"That is crap. That is so much crap, I don't even . . . I can't . . . I cannot believe you just said that."

"Come to think of it, Mom dying worked out pretty good for you, didn't it?"

I took a step back from the desk. I had never struck Jamie for any reason, but I had never felt such a compulsion to do it as I did right then. My fists clenched until my fingernails dug into my palms. My eyes hurt. My face hurt. My heart was about to explode. I couldn't take this. I couldn't stand feeling this way. I wanted it to end. I wanted to stop this now, so I said the one thing I knew would stop it, would stop everything.

"Jamie, if you believe that, then you are stupid. You're just as stupid as he said you were."

The minute I said it, I regretted it. Before it was even all out. I thought maybe . . . if I could just throw my hand up and knock those words down, remove them from the one space in the universe where they never should have been—between us. I could grab them and wrap them in my palm and hold them until they stopped burning, turned to ash, and fell to the floor.

His expression never changed, but something underneath gave way. I could tell. Some critical, load-bearing beam cracked and collapsed inside him, and I was the one who had wielded the ax.

Saying good-bye to Gina and the kids had been the hardest. I'd had to wash my face and put drops in my eyes and drops in my nose and wait until I looked normal again. Gina had been so disappointed that I had to leave, but more because she knew we'd had a fight.

"You have to go tonight?"

"It's a scheduling thing. I'll come back."

Sean gave me a kiss good-bye and thanked me again for his new shirt. He wanted to know if I would ever come back. When I bent down to kiss Maddie, she wrapped her small arms around my neck. They felt like two feathers lying there. She didn't seem to want to let go. I knew I didn't want her to. Jamie was nowhere to be found. I had nothing to say to him, anyway.

The first number I dialed when I got to my car was the one that started with 800 on Djuro Bulatovic's business card. He answered promptly.

"Bo, are you after Monica again?"

"No. I told you I would leave her to you."

"Do you know where she is?"

"No."

That was disappointing. I had no good way to find her on my own. "Will you call me if you hear anything?" I gave him my cell phone number. "Where are you? Are you still in Boston?"

"I'm close."

"Can you stay close? I might need you tonight."

He said that he would. I checked my watch. Eight-thirty. If I was really lucky and really reckless and irresponsible behind the wheel, I could still make the ten o'clock shuttle back to Boston.

I tried Harvey next. Maybe I could catch him before he left to meet Carl for dinner. He didn't answer his cell phone, which was not surprising. When I called his hotel, they said that he had checked out, which was more than surprising. It was disturbing. When he didn't answer his home phone in Boston, I was more than disturbed. I was worried. Harvey rarely deviated from his planned schedule.

I was still trying to find him, leaving urgent messages at both his numbers, when I had to board the ten o'clock flight home.

Back in Boston, the hunt for a parking space was the usual nightmare. The cars double-parked up and down Beacon Street with their parking lights flashing signaled another bad night for anyone in the Back Bay without an assigned parking space. I circled the block several times before giving up and making my way to the mammoth parking garage under the Boston Common, where there was always space for those willing to pay. I hated paying for parking in my own neighborhood.

The idea came to me as I rode the elevator up to the surface. Without giving myself a chance to overthink it, I turned on Charles instead of crossing and walked the short distance to the familiar dwelling on Chestnut Street. I stood for what seemed like a long time on the front steps with my finger poised over the buzzer. I collected myself, pushed the button, and waited. When the answer came, I talked fast.

"It's me. It's Alex. Please don't hang up. I need to talk to you." What came back was a ringing silence that managed somehow to be cold and angry.

"Tristan, please."

The buzz that released the building's front door lock was the most welcome sound I'd heard in a while. I pushed through and headed up the stairs.

chapter 38

TRISTAN WAS DRESSED COMFORTABLY AND smashingly in midnight-blue sweatpants and a celery-colored pullover. There was just no way to catch him looking sloppy and unkempt. He stood in the middle of the living room of the two-bedroom condo he shared with Barry. With its fresh-cut autumn flowers and large cathedral windows, the place was as serene as a church, a jarring juxtaposition to what was going on between us.

I stood close to the front door, leaving it to him to determine the distance between us. As a union officer, he knew everything that was going on, including my part in it. He was not taking it well. "Tristan, please don't look at me that way."

"How should I look at you? Tell me, Alexandra. Shall I look at you as a friend, because it's hard for me to see you as a friend just now. Is Alexandra Shanahan your real name? Or do you have a code name? Something like Double-O Lying Bitch."

Some people sputtered when they were angry and searched for words. Tristan wasn't one of them.

"All this time, I've been looking out for you and trying to protect you, and now it turns out . . ."

"Turns out how?"

"It turns out that you're not my friend at all. You've been using me for my contacts and abusing my trust, and you humiliated me in front of Irene. I was so hurt by what you did." He drifted to the window and ran a finger along the edge of one of the slats in the blinds, along a line that was long and straight and predictable. It wouldn't throw him any unexpected curves.

I moved in enough that I could lean against a chair. I wasn't sure I could make this right, but I had to try. "This was supposed to be a simple job," I said. "I would collect evidence on a few hookers, the airline would confront them, they would quit, and I would be out of there and on to the next assignment. But things got complicated. I never meant to involve you, or hurt you. Meeting you was the only bright spot in this whole mess."

"No, dear." He shook his head. "That will not play."

"What?"

"You cannot simply say you're sorry, and can't we be pals anyway, and that will be that. You had lots of chances to tell me the truth and trust me, and you never thought fit to do so."

"I'm telling you now."

"Now that cats are flying out of bags everywhere?"

He wouldn't look at me. "Look, you're angry, and you have every right to be. But I was hired to do a job, and as part of doing that job, I had to pretend to be someone I'm not. If that offends you, so be it. I can't change what I did. I would do it over again, and it's not over yet. There is a lot going on tonight."

He turned and looked at me as if I'd just declared the sky blue. "Ya think?"

"What have you heard?"

"Only that Angela is circulating a rumor that I helped

you get her fired." He moved to the mantel to adjust the spacing of the high-end trinkets arranged there. Most of them were souvenirs from his around-the-world travels. "I think she's planning on hurting someone."

"Why do you think that?"

"Because she says she is. It feels like it, too. Everyone is edgy."

"What is she saying?"

"She's saying she will find the people who did this to her, and she will get them. Are you happy with what you've done to us? It's absolute chaos around here."

"If you want to blame someone, Tristan, blame Angel. She's the one who did it to you, and she's been doing it for years." What I didn't say was that he had allowed it to go on, but his sixteen-foot ceilings were too low for that high horse. "Do you think you're in danger?"

"I don't know. I sent Barry up to the house in Maine."

Which meant he was worried, which really worried me. I moved farther into the room, from leaning on a chair to leaning against the arm of the couch. "If you think she's coming after you, you should leave. You should pick up a trip and leave town."

His laugh was bitter. "As if that would save me. Angela is everywhere, dear. Besides, I think she's more interested in you."

"So she said. Is it true she's coming back to work?"

"She never left. She was back before the ink was dry on the notification letters."

It was one thing to hear this news from Angel. She could have been lying. But hearing it from Tristan, union officer, meant it was official. I felt like crying from sheer frustration, but I was pretty much cried out for the evening. Maybe tomorrow. "What kind of deal did she cut?"

"I don't know. Whatever she did, it had nothing to do with the union. She doesn't need us. She has friends in high places."

"What does that mean? Friends at the company?"

"Way higher. The rumor is, it was some U.S. senator who got involved behind the scenes."

"A U.S. senator?" The surprising news just kept coming. I was starting to feel numb. Since it didn't seem that Tristan was about to throw me out, I went ahead and sat down on the couch.

"He sits on a subcommittee that has something to do with the bailout loans to the airline industry. One phone call from him was all it took."

"One of her clients," I said.

"Undoubtedly."

"Angel told me she had some kind of secret weapon. She called it her nuclear bomb. This guy must be her weapon. Still, I'm surprised a U.S. senator would get involved in something like this."

"It's all hush-hush."

"You know about it."

"I know everything. Everyone talks to me."

"The same could be said for Matt Drudge. How did the airline react?"

"Are you kidding? Only too happy to oblige."

"They were?" I wondered if Harvey knew.

"Of course. Do you think they'd want the press that goes with firing a bunch of flight attendant hookers? I think the good senator gave them exactly what they wanted: a reason to wash their hands of the whole affair."

"But why would he do it? It seems like high-risk behavior for someone so high-profile."

"Well, either she's the best piece of ass that ever walked, or Angela has dirty pictures of him."

I remembered the moment when I had seen Jamie's face in that video for the first time. There would be few things more powerful than a video of a naked senator doing it with a hooker, especially with the high-quality digital equipment these women were using. That had to be it. Why would he risk his job unless it was to save his job? "She does."

"Does what?"

"Angel has a sex video of this senator. That's how she got him to do what he did."

"How do you know?"

"Look, I know you're still pissed at me, but I'm going to tell you some things that I hope you will keep in confidence."

He waved an exasperated hand. "*Now* you want to trust me?"

"I always trusted you. I just couldn't tell you everything."

He considered that. "Answer one question honestly. If you weren't in trouble and needing my help, would you have ever rung my buzzer again?"

"Yes."

"That was quick." He put a finger to his chin. "I wonder, do I believe you?"

"You asked me to tell the truth." I stared down at my shoelaces. "I felt like a shitheel every time I lied to you. I tried not to, but you're a good man, Tristan. I couldn't help but confide in you, even when I knew it was unfair to do it. So, when it comes down to it, and this part cannot be denied, the fact that I had to lie to you was your fault."

When I looked up, he was clearly trying to figure out if I was serious. I smiled. I really did miss him. "I'm sorry, Tristan. I don't know what else to say."

His jaw seemed to unclench slightly. "Let me get

some refreshments, and you can tell me your secret-agent stories."

I sank back into the leather couch and thanked whoever was watching over me that Tristan was a big enough person to forgive. He came back with an ice bucket and a tray with several bottles of sparkling water. He set the tray down and handed me one of those techno cold packs that you keep in the freezer. "This is Barry's. It's for his sinus headaches, but he won't mind if you use it."

"For what?"

"Have you seen your eyes lately?"

His dedication to flawless service ran deep. "Thank you."

I didn't want to talk to him without looking at him, so I put the cold pack on my forehead as I told him everything. I told him about Monica and Arthur Margolies and the possibility that she was blackmailing several of her clients.

"Busy, busy girl," was his comment.

I told him about Monica's call to me in New York and Angel's mysterious threat to her. Then I told him about Jamie and what Angel had done with him, and he with her. Tristan might not have had sympathy for me, but he did for Jamie.

"How is he?"

"Shattered. We had a monumental fight. Really hurtful to each other."

"I'm sorry."

"Me, too. She called me at his house. I don't know how she knew I was there."

"She didn't have to know. All she had to do was try it and get lucky. I told you from the beginning, she's an evil, evil bitch. You should have included me. I could have helped you."

"You also said that you would defend her, no matter what."

He thought about that. "Part of that was me spewing rhetoric, and part of it was true. I have no love for management, especially since I worked in it. But she has gone beyond the pale."

"How would you have helped?"

"I would have told you not to trust the airline. They do not have the backbone to take on Angela and win. I would have told you the only real way to get rid of her would be to go to the police. If she goes to jail, she gets fired for sure. It's in the contract. There is no deal they could make to bring her back."

An intriguing idea. Whatever Angel was up to, I had no doubt we'd all be better off with her in jail. That wasn't even considering the personal satisfaction I would get from seeing her incarcerated. But . . . "It's too late now."

"Why?"

"She knows we're on to her. She'll have switched everything up. We would have to rebuild the entire case from scratch, and if it's true the airline is bailing, I would have to do it without their resources or the access I had undercover. My partner is already squirrelly. Can't be done."

"Unless," he said, "you can get an insider to come forward and testify."

I looked at him. I liked where he was going. "An insider like Monica?"

"If it's true Angela is after her for this blackmail scheme, you might be her best alternative at this point."

"She didn't sound very cooperative last time we spoke. Besides, I can't go to the police until I get Jamie's video back."

"Could she help you with that?"

"I believe she can. She knows Web Boy."

"Who?"

"Stewart Belkamp, Angel's Web master. He's involved in both the blackmail scheme and Angel's business. If I threaten to tell Angel he's working against her, it might be enough to get him working for us. The question is, can we get Monica working for us. You know her better than I do. Will she talk?"

"I'll get her to talk." With a nonchalant wave, he dismissed any thought that she could resist him.

"We have to find her first."

"I'll find her, but not tonight."

I checked my watch. It was three-thirty A.M. "Oh, man."

"I know. You sleep here. I'll get you a blanket."

He got no argument from me. I put the cold pack over my eyes and was fast asleep before he had even left the room.

My cold pack was no longer cold when I woke up. I put my bare feet on the floor and rubbed the sleep from my eyes. It was cloudy outside, so the room was dim with the blinds closed, which might have been the reason I had slept until ten. On my way back from the bathroom, I found Tristan's note on the dining-room table. True to his word, he was out looking for Monica.

I dug out my cell phone and checked messages at home. No word from Harvey. No word from Jamie, although I hadn't expected any. No word from anyone. I was poised with my thumb over Felix's turbo button when another call came in. I looked at the spy window and punched it up.

"Harvey, where are you?"

chapter 39

HARVEY EMERGED FROM THE POOL, CLIMBING one shallow step at a time and gripping the silver bar with his thick, square fingers. His disease had not diminished his bulk above the hips—his torso was thick, and his spongy belly hung down over the waist of his bathing suit. Yet he seemed fragile. If the waist of his suit was too small, the leg openings were too big. As he climbed the steps, the wet fabric bunched around his shrunken thighs.

He found his glasses by the side of the pool and put them on. When he caught sight of me watching him, he reached across his body to grab the rail with his other hand. The effect was to turn his belly away and show me his back.

"You're early," he said. "You weren't supposed to come back here."

"They told me out front it was all right."

He held himself perfectly still. All that moved were rivulets of water that dripped from the ends of his hair. He turned cautiously to look at me. His heavy glasses had slipped down to the end of his nose. I knew he wanted to push them back up but couldn't let go of the rail. Instead, he peered over the tops, as if this were how corrective lenses were supposed to be worn.

"I'll leave," I said. "I'm going now. I'll meet—"

"No. Stay here. I want to talk to you. Just . . . give me a minute."

He managed to negotiate the last steps and climb onto the deck but then froze in the face of the several-foot-wide expanse that separated him from a rack of thick towels. He seemed torn between two bad options: standing in front of me with his pale body mostly exposed or lurching ungracefully toward the rack and risking a fall. I couldn't stand it. I went to the rack, grabbed a towel, and draped it around his shoulders.

"I can wait for you out front."

"No." He pulled the corners of the towel together under his chin and pushed his glasses up. "Thank you, but that will not be necessary. It takes me a long time to get dressed." He motioned to a grouping of deck chairs. "Let us sit here and talk."

I pulled two of the chairs closer, sat in one, and waited for him to make his way to the other. To keep from staring at him, I scanned the swimming space. It had that echoing quality of all indoor aquatic facilities and that sharp aromatic cocktail of chemicals and the fungus it was supposed to kill. Two people worked in the water at the other end, an older woman wearing a rubber swim cap, possibly a stroke survivor from the way she moved, and her therapist, a black man with a slight build but strong arms and a soothing way about him.

"The exercise . . ." Harvey had settled in next to me, breathing hard. "It takes a lot out of me. I was never a good swimmer, but it is the only suitable exercise. Overheating exacerbates my symptoms. Do you swim?"

"I don't like the water."

"You?" His surprise was too exaggerated to be genuine. "I would have guessed that nothing scared you."

"Plenty of things scare me, but the idea of drowning most of all. Harvey—"

"Can't you swim?"

"I can swim. It's not water. It's drowning I'm afraid of. Not being able to breathe. I don't know where it comes from. We need to—"

"Phobias by their definition are irrational. It is a terrible thing to be afraid."

I watched him use the towel to tumble-dry his hair. Then he took off his glasses and carefully wiped both lenses. When he was finished, his hair stood on end, but his glasses were firmly in place, and he seemed connected to the world again. He also seemed more vulnerable than I had ever seen him.

"Harvey, what are you doing back here? You weren't supposed to be back until later."

"I took the red-eye last night. I could not wait to come back to tell you our news."

"Do you know that Angel is back?"

"Yes."

"What happened?"

"I did not ask."

I blinked at him. "You didn't ask?"

"It was the client's decision. Do you wish to hear my news?"

This was not feeling right to me. The Harvey who had left two days before was not the one who was sitting in front of me. "How could you not ask? Don't you want to know?"

"We have more important issues at hand."

"We do?"

He turned his body slightly, enough to imply an attitude of confidentiality. "OrangeAir has offered us a contract. We are still working out the details, but I can give you the broad outlines, and I must say it is most exciting."

I started to feel more uncomfortable. The thick green turtleneck I'd thrown on at home was perfect for the cool, dry weather outside but too heavy for the steamy air of an indoor swimming facility. "What kind of contract?"

"A guaranteed engagement of two years. We would act as outside security consultants working on projects as assigned by Carl Wolff."

"Security consultants? Harvey, do you . . ." I had to pull that turtleneck off. I couldn't have it on for one more second. I whipped it over my head, leaving the T-shirt underneath. "Do you know what's going on here? Angel is on the rampage. She's making threats. She's after Monica. She's after me."

He dismissed it all with a wave of his hand. "We can make it part of her reinstatement deal that she stays away from you."

"You just told me you didn't know anything about her reinstatement." I sat back and stared at him. "Are you lying to me?"

"Ticket fraud, theft and pilferage, smuggling. You said you wanted to specialize in crimes against airlines. What better launch could you have? This is the best part. The fees are guaranteed, whether we work or not. It is a retainer."

The more excited he got, the more crushed I felt. I wanted to stop this conversation before we got to the truly hurtful part, but I couldn't. I was having lots of hurtful conversations. "How did you get this deal, Harvey? It wouldn't be because the client has returned a criminal to its payroll and doesn't want us to tell anyone, would it?"

"Of course not. Miss Velesco has made certain guarantees as part of her reinstatement agreement. Whatever she was before, she is a criminal no longer."

"In other words, they asked her to stop being a criminal, and she agreed. Why didn't we think of that?"

"Your sarcasm is not appreciated."

"Here's something I don't appreciate." It was my turn to twist around to face him. "You suddenly turning into a company toady because they dangled a few bucks under your nose."

If I had pulled his chair out from under him and let him tumble to the ground, he wouldn't have looked any more surprised. I didn't care. If I'd had any propulsion left, I would have been up and moving around. But I didn't, so all my angry energy came right out of my mouth.

He finally found his voice again. "I negotiated a good deal for us. Guaranteed income for the next two years, a check that arrives in the mail every month whether you work or not. Can you not call that success?"

"I call that a bribe."

"Do you want to know what I call it?" He pulled the towel tighter around his shoulders. "Health benefits. A way to pay my medical bills and premiums without having to worry about the next job and where it is coming from. That is what I call it."

"What did you promise them?"

"I beg your pardon?"

"Did you sign a nondisclosure form? Did you promise not to go to the police or tell anyone anything about this case?"

He sat uncomfortably in his chair. He looked as if he wanted to stand up and walk around but had nothing to hold on to. "I did what was standard."

"If that's what you had to promise, there is no way I can take that deal."

"Those women are back at work. That was the client's choice, and nothing will change it. Taking or not taking the deal will not change it. So tell me, what do you accomplish by turning it down?"

"We're not just talking about her job anymore. The stakes are higher now, and she's the one who raised them."

"What does that mean?"

"She made a video of my brother having sex with her. I can't leave this alone, because she has the ability to ruin his life. I will do whatever it takes to get that video back. Do you understand?"

"No, I do not. Why did your brother have sex with her?"

"It's a long story and not relevant right now."

"But it is. He made a choice. If he is in trouble for the bad choices he made, then I am sorry. But I did not make this choice to be ill."

"Don't put this on me. Do not put this on me."

"I am not—"

"Yes, you are. You said it yourself the other day. I am not the one who makes you sick. It is the disease that makes you sick, and it is not my responsibility to make you feel secure."

"Please do not ruin this for me. Do not take my one last chance at security."

A noise drifted over from across the pool. Not a groan so much as a cry of physical exertion. The woman in the bathing cap was struggling with her left side. She was working hard, the way Harvey probably did when he was doing his therapy. His burden was a heavy one. From watching him, I knew that MS was a cruel and capricious disease. It toyed with him, came and went at will, changed symptoms without warning, and doomed him to a continually diminishing quality of life and an early death. I felt for him. I really did.

"Harvey, your life sucks. You got a raw deal, and everything in me wants to help you and try to fix it for you and make it easier. I want to see things get better for you. But this woman is dangerous. She's angry with me, she knows where my family lives, and I don't believe the answer is to take the money and hope she goes away."

"Because you do not need the money."

"There is no amount of money that would make me trade my family's future and my own peace of mind. But I understand if you need it. Take it without me."

"Do you actually believe they would retain me while you are actively working at cross-purposes? That is your plan, is it not? To approach the authorities?"

"Yes."

"What makes you think the authorities will be any more responsive?"

"If they're not, I'm pretty sure I can find a newspaper that will listen. It's a juicy story."

"Then you are not above employing your own leverage."

"That's what it's all about. If I learned anything from this case, that's it."

He stared at me for a long moment. Maybe we were both disappointed in each other. He finally flinched first, letting his gaze drop to the deck and the rust-colored, nonslip rubber tiles with the shamrock cutouts. His feet were crossed at the ankles in a bow-legged attitude that exposed the thick calluses on his heels.

"Is there nothing I can do to change your mind?"

"No. I'm sorry."

"I will inform the client." He stood up, wrapped his towel close around his shoulders, and started to move off toward the entryway to a locker room.

"Harvey . . ." He stopped but didn't turn around. "Harvey, I need to know. You won't work against me, will you?"

Then he did turn on me, as quickly as his feeble state would allow, which wasn't fast. In some ways, that made it even more devastating when he said it.

"Shame on you, Alex. Shame on you."

Out on the curb, I sat in my parked car for a long time. More than once, someone pulled up next to me, hoping to grab the space when I pulled out. A vacant stare and an anemic shake of the head sent them off in a huff, but I wasn't leaving until I had someplace to go. I was having a hard time catching up to what had just happened. But why should I be surprised? Harvey was motivated by a very real fear that he would run out of money and be too sick to earn any more. Carl Wolff had understood that and used it against him. Against me. Bastard.

I sat there a long time before my phone rang. I checked the spy window and answered. "Tristan?"

"I found Monica. You need to get back here, Alexandra."

I felt for the keys and started the engine. "Is she with you? Will she talk?"

"Oh, she already is."

"Anything good so far?"

"How about who killed Robin Sevitch?"

chapter 40

It was strange to see Monica sitting on Tristan's couch, looking, if not scared, at least less self-possessed than the last two times I had seen her. The first time, she had been the one with the razor-blade smile swiping my date in Chicago. The last time, she had been the one with her clothes off and her sense of self-confidence firmly in place.

"Hello, Monica."

"I'm only here because Tristan asked me. I trust him."

Tristan stood behind the couch at her left shoulder. Over his left shoulder, resting on the mantel in the middle of his international trinkets, was the deadliest trinket of all, his .44 Special. I hadn't expected Tristan to be Monica's private bodyguard, although, as I thought about it, there was no way he would bring her out of hiding unless he intended to protect her as best he could. I thought that would be pretty well.

I sat down next to Monica. She looked good for someone in hiding, better than I felt. Tristan had given me the story on Monica in our long, overnight chat. She was from Paterson, New Jersey, and had tried for a career as a singer and dancer on Broadway. She'd given up almost immediately, because she didn't like that part about being poor. She'd bought some breast implants and shifted her act to prostitution, where every night she could be someone new. With her lively brown eyes, long legs, and thick, dark hair, it was not hard to see her as an entertainer.

At this point, I didn't have the mental capacity to do much besides ask her to start talking and see if I could follow along.

"Tell me," I said, "everything that is going on. Start with Robin Sevitch."

"Angel killed Robin. Tristan, can I smoke in here?"

"No, dear."

He said it calmly, which led me to believe he had heard this already. I hadn't, and I was appropriately unsettled, despite Monica's blunt nonchalance. "Are you saying Angel had her killed?"

"No. She did it herself." Monica shook out her arm to loosen her bracelets, a whole wristful that jangled like a bag of coins. "She told Robin she wanted to meet her to negotiate, because, you know, Robin wasn't too cool with Angel taking over her business. She flew out there. They went for a walk. She picked up a brick somewhere along the way and beat her head with it until she was dead."

My lips kept sticking together. They were pasty because my mouth was dry. My mouth was dry because I kept picturing Robin's savaged face and thinking about how much time I had spent alone with her murderer.

"Were you there? Did you see this happen?"

"No. She told me."

She ran her fingers through her long hair and crossed her legs. She seemed calm on the outside, but I also sensed that she could really use a smoke. "Then how do you know it's not just a story?"

"Because she has the brick. Angel brought it back with her." She glanced from me to Tristan and back. "It has her blood on it. That's what she said, anyway."

I looked at her closely. Could this be her own bit of performance art? What would be her reasons to lie? "You've seen this brick?"

"She showed it to me. It was last year sometime, not long after she did it. It was sometime in the summer, because that's when we had our thing."

"You and Angel had a relationship?"

She nodded. "I was at her cabin one night. We were having a bottle of wine, or maybe a few. She pulled it out and showed it to me. She told me what it was. It kind of scared me. I didn't go up there after that, not alone, anyway."

"Did you see where she keeps it?"

"In a desk drawer."

What she was saying was horrifying on so many levels. I had been alone in that cabin with Angel and her murder brick, which Monica talked about as if it were some kind of gruesome paperweight. My brother had also been alone with her. I wrapped both arms around myself and squeezed. "Why would she keep a murder weapon in her house?"

"That's just Angel. It's like a souvenir. Also, I don't think she wanted to leave it in Omaha. She watches *CSI* like everyone else."

I looked at Tristan. "I need a drink," was all he said, and headed for the kitchen.

"Angel was never mentioned in the Omaha investigation."

"Of course not. She was covered."

"Covered how?"

"She had a trick out there, someone to keep her

name out of it. I don't know who it was, but that's why she picked Omaha to begin with."

I thought about the senator. I thought about Jamie's video. I thought about Monica's blackmail scheme and some of the pieces started to float together. "Meaning what?"

"Meaning whoever it was, she had him in a dirty movie. All she had to do was send it to him along with a list of his private e-mail addresses, and he took care of it. That's how she gets everything she wants. She uses her archive."

I leaned forward on the couch, poised to absorb every word, but then Tristan came back with his serving tray of ice, glasses, and bottled sparkling water and stepped between us.

"Tristan, baby, do you have something stronger than fizzy water?"

"What would you like?"

"Do you have any beer?"

He disappeared again but came back quickly with an open longneck and handed it to his guest.

I took up my listening post again. "Monica, what is Angel's archive?"

I had to wait as she took a long pull from the bottle and swallowed. "Her dirty movies."

"Mov-*ies*, like more than one?"

"Like hundreds of them. She has a whole catalogue with an index to keep them straight. There are politicians and lawyers and cops and sports stars and entertainers and CEOs. She has something for everything she needs."

I glanced again at Tristan. His eyes were wide. Each thing this woman said was more hair-raising than the last, although it would be hard to top the brick. "Where does she get these movies?"

"We make them for her. Everyone who goes to work for her gets a little digital camera and a laptop and a lesson on how to set up so you're sure to get the trick's face. If you screw it up, you just have to do it again, and you have to keep doing it until you get it right."

"It's all done in secret?"

"What do you think?"

"Do you record every date?"

"We record the first date with every trick."

"What do you do with them?"

"Send them to Angel. That's what the PCs are for." And that was what the catalogue numbers were for in the lower right-hand corner of the video. I sat back to let it all settle in. It was Angel's archive, not Monica's, and it was a vast and powerful thing.

Tristan leaned over and dropped a few more cubes into his glass. "You were right about the senator," he said.

"And so many others. It's a blackmail factory. That's her secret weapon. It's not one guy; it's all guys. Everyone in her archive is vulnerable to her. No wonder she's so damn confident." I looked at Monica. "But you were the one extorting Arthur Margolies, right?"

She snorted and rolled her eyes. "Trying to."

"Who is he to you?"

"He's one of my clients, a gambler in Chicago. I should have just asked him for the money. He would have given it to me."

"Did you swap dates with me in Chicago because you knew he was after you?"

"No. I didn't know about that. I knew your date. Curt the Chiropractor, we call him. He pays off like a slot machine. The more you beat him, the more he pays, and I really need money right now."

"Why do you need money?"

"Are you a moron or what? She's afraid of what I know, and she wants to kill me, and I'm trying to leave the country."

"Why now?"

"Uh, because I don't want to die?"

"You said it was last summer when she showed you the brick. Why is she suddenly concerned that you'll talk now?"

She drank down the last of her beer and fixed me in a withering gaze. "Because you've been sniffing around Robin's murder. She told me that you told her that I told you about Robin."

Tristan laughed. "What did you just say?"

Monica was focused on me. "Did you tell her that I told you she killed Robin?"

I reached out to put my glass on the coffee table, almost missed, then set it there solidly. This was starting to make sense in a twisted, Angel sort of way.

"So, it's true." Monica crossed her arms to match her crossed legs. "You did tell her. I can't believe it. I asked you point blank on the phone, and you lied to me."

"I did not lie to you. I had no idea what you were asking me. We've been looking into the Omaha murder because we knew Angel had a motive to kill Robin, and the investigation they did stinks. Now you're telling me why. You're saying someone in Omaha helped Angel stay out of it."

"That's true. Someone with a lot of juice."

"Well, think about it. Whoever it was must have tipped her off about recent inquiries. I didn't tell Angel anything about you. How could I? I didn't know you knew all this."

"Why have you been looking for me?"

"I wanted to find her Web guy, and I thought, since you were working with him on these blackmail schemes, you could lead me to him."

"What schemes? Just the one with Arthur, and Sluggo and me, we weren't exactly working together. Please . . ." She dismissed the idea as too distasteful to ponder.

"Then you do know Stewart Belkamp."

"Sure. He came out to the cabin once. Thank God I didn't have to fuck him. That's the only good thing about this whole mess."

"Why would you have to?"

"I needed a copy of my Artie video, and he didn't want to give it to me. I had to promise him a freebie if it worked out and I got some money for it."

Poor Stewart. He'd been left at the altar not once but twice. "I thought his identity was a big secret."

"It is. I only knew because we had our thing. Angel let down her guard a little with me. I wish to hell she hadn't. I am going to be so murdered."

"Not if you go to the police."

"Why would I do that? As long as she has her dirty movies, there's no one who can touch her."

I climbed off the couch to walk around. The couch had not made a good bed. It had been too soft to sleep on, and my back was sore. I ended up by the window. The sky was still overcast, looking a lot more like winter's approach than it had the past few days. "Monica, what do these archives look like?"

"What do you mean?"

"Are they electronic files? Are they on tape? Are they CD-Roms?"

"I don't know. You'd have to ask Stewart."

"I plan to." I turned to Tristan. "I need a gun."

"Did you pass your test?"

"I failed it."

"Then the answer is absolutely not."

"Tristan—"

He moved instinctively to the .44 on his mantel, as if to protect it from me. Or me from it. "Are you planning on shooting Sluggo?"

"Of course not. But I want a way to threaten him."

"Never take a gun where you don't intend to use it. I won't give you one. I'm sorry. Besides, what happens to me if you shoot someone with my gun? I'll be in deep yogurt, and you'll be in jail. If you want me to come with you, I'll bring it. But I'm not giving you one."

"You can't come. You have to stay here with Monica."

"While you do what?"

"Get the archive. The second I have it, I want her sitting in the police station telling her story. I don't want Angel getting out of this." I looked at Monica and thought about the two "amateurs with guns," as Bo had called them. I was pretty sure Angel had sent them, which meant Monica needed protection. "In fact, I'm sending someone else over to stay here with you." I went to the table, where Tristan's note from that morning still sat. I used the pen he'd used, wrote out "Djuro Bulatovic," and gave it to him. "This man will come and stay with you. Call him Bo."

"How will I know it's him?"

Monica chuckled. "Do what we do. Give him a code word."

Tristan looked at me, and I shrugged at him. "Might as well go with what works."

A mischievous spark showed in his eyes. "I know exactly what to use."

chapter 41

I WAS ON FOOT, HEADED THROUGH THE NEIGHborhood and back to my car, when my cell phone rang. I was expecting Felix, hoping for Tristan, and would have taken almost anyone except the person whose name showed up on caller ID.

"Hello, Angel."

"Well, doll, what did you think of the show?"

"I think you're sick and in need of professional help. But mostly, I think you need to go to jail."

"Your little brother is so the stud. Girl, he wore me out. We did it standing up, sitting down, in the shower, on the carpet, on the tile. We even did it in the bathroom sink."

"I already know everything that happened. Don't waste your time embellishing." Still, having seen the one image of the two of them, it was hard not to conjure the others she described.

"Really? Why don't you tell me sweet Jamie's version, because we know he would never tell a lie."

"You pursued him, you lied to him, you came into his hotel room, and the two of you fucked. One time."

"One time or ten times, it makes no never mind when you're cheating on your wife."

"He also didn't know you were a hooker."

"Tell me why that matters, doll."

"We both know he never would have touched you if he knew what you really are."

"You're hurting my feelings."

The sound of a car horn made it hard to hear, mostly because it was loud and getting louder, not to mention unrelenting, which was when I realized it was attached to the Audi that was bearing down on me. I had wandered into the middle of Arlington Street at Beacon, one of the more treacherous pedestrian intersections in the city, which was saying a lot in Boston. I made a dash for the other side. If I were to be run over, it might as well be going forward.

"This is between you and me, Angel. My family has nothing to do with it."

"Are you under the impression we are playing by some set of rules? He talked about you, by the way. Do you want to know what he said?"

"If I do, I'll ask him. Tell me specifically what it is you want, so we don't have any unfortunate misunderstandings."

"I want to fuck as many men as will pay me, make more money than God, and retire to my very own cattle ranch in Texas. But right now, I'll settle for Monica. You tell me where I can catch up with her, and I'll send you back Jamie's dirty movie. Did I tell you how much he likes to—"

"Why do you want Monica? So you can beat her to death with a brick?"

There was the slightest pause, which I enjoyed. Angel speechless was a thing to behold. "I see you two have hooked up. Do you like how I did that? Sending her to you so I would know where to find her?"

"Yeah, you're a real mastermind."

"I know what's bothering you deep down, sis. Little brother's got a few more moves than you knew about. Here you've been thinking all along he's sweet and innocent. But come to find out he's just as twisted and screwed up as the rest of us. As you and me, sweet pea."

"Jamie is not like you."

"Oh, my. Listen to you. Still protecting little brother from the big, bad world. That was him in that bed with me, wasn't it? Between my thighs, pumping away like a house afire. Must be he doesn't get everything he needs at home, or else why would he be rolling around in the mud with the likes of me?"

"You don't live in the mud. You live in the sewer, and you can't get the stink off, no matter what you do. Isn't that right?"

"Only you can't protect him from this. You're the one who caused it to happen to him in the first place."

"Is that all? Are we done?"

"I'll give you until midnight to decide. If I don't hear from you, I will send out copies of our little fun time to Mrs. Jamie and the little Jamiettes, to the partners at the firm, to the friends, the kids' private schools, and anybody else in his address book who looks interesting. I'll tell you something else, too, darlin'. I'll find Monica, anyway."

I was close to the playground, and it was afternoon, prime time for screaming and squealing tots. It was hard to hear, but there wasn't much more to talk about, anyway. I knew the game. I knew the stakes. I knew what I had to do. "I'm about to go underground and lose my signal," I said. "But remember one thing. No matter what you try to do to Jamie, no matter what you do to me, you will always be what you are."

"What's that, doll?"

"The girl who fucked the parish priest back in West Texas."

I snapped the phone shut and found a bench in the Public Garden to sit on. Judging by the disapproving scowl, the white-haired woman walking her Scottish terrier must have heard that last part. I ignored her and smiled at the dog, the less judgmental of the two.

I felt terrible. My whole body was stiff and brittle, and I was still trying to recover from my meeting with Harvey. I wasn't sure what would cure my ills, short of putting my fist into Angel's face, but I did have a thought about something that might help.

I flipped open the phone and turbo-dialed Jamie. I didn't know what I would say, although, when it came down to it, I had only one thing to say. His voice mail picked up.

"Jamie, I'm sorry. I wish I could say these things to you live, but I can't wait. The things I said . . . they were terrible. You didn't deserve it, and I'm so sorry I got you into this situation. I'm trying hard to fix it. That's all I wanted to say, that I'm sorry and I hope we can talk soon." I started to punch off, but I'd forgotten the one thing I had called to tell him. "Jamie . . . I love you."

I punched off, pulled out Bo's card, and dialed his number. The way things were going, I would have to program him into speed dial. When he answered, I got straight to the point.

"Will you do me another favor?"

He said he would, and I told him where he could find Tristan and Monica. He didn't ask a lot of questions, but, given his earlier experience of mistaken identity, he had the same one Tristan had had. How would they recognize each other?

"When you ring the buzzer," I said, "tell him who you are. Your part of the code is *Rob.* He'll answer with *Lowe. Rob Lowe.*"

"Okay. Is there anything else you need?"

I looked across the garden at the lush but fragile carpet of leaves that covered the ground. More were falling—spinning, dipping, and floating on the leading edge of a cold front that was barreling down from Canada, they said. I checked around to make sure that no one was close enough to hear.

"There is one more thing I need."

chapter 42

STEWART'S DOOR WAS LOCKED WHEN I TRIED the knob, but I knew he was in there. I heard his stereo pounding. I thought about crashing through the window but decided to go with a knock. I didn't need the element of surprise, not with Bo's Glock in my waistband.

Alarmingly, Stewart wasn't surprised at all to see me. He stepped aside without comment and let me in, then headed for the back room. "What you want is back here."

I stood for a moment, trying to decide if the fact that he had expected me was a bad thing. Angel had obviously filled him in. Ultimately, I decided it didn't matter. I wasn't leaving.

Back in the bedroom, Stewart was watching Jamie's video. He'd turned his stereo off, so the sound track was clearly audible. He froze the picture when he saw me, hit a button on his keyboard, and brought up a list of ten or twelve e-mail addresses.

"This is the distribution list Angel gave me for this little art house film." His voice had a sharp edge of confidence, as if he had total control. It showed in his eyes, too. "Take a look."

My e-mail address was on the list. So was Gina's. I saw the address for Jamie's new company and what looked like Sean's private school. There was an address for St. Anthony's Parish and—my stomach turned to stone—my father. I imagined Walter pulling up a copy and feeling vindicated for every nasty thing he'd ever said about Jamie.

"Where did you get these?"

"I hacked into his e-mail account. Watch this." Stewart used his mouse to move the cursor over the send box . . . and clicked it. He *clicked* it. *He sent the messages.*

"Did you . . . what did you do? What did you just *do?*"

"Relax. They're not quite gone yet. They're locked away in a safe place on the server for now." Which meant there was nothing I could do from his computer. "I can stop them any time in the next ten minutes. But after that, they're gone, and nothing can stop them, and no one can get them back. Think of it as a ticking time bomb, and only you can defuse it."

I felt Bo's gun against my back. I heard Tristan's words floating in my head. "Don't bring a gun unless you intend to use it." I had to leave it as my last resort.

"What do you want?"

"You still owe me a fuck, you cockteasing bitch."

I took a step back—recoiled was more like it. "If you were the last asshole on earth, I would not let you lay a finger on me."

"Is that your final answer?" He reached for the mouse. "I can always send them early."

"Stop. Wait."

"The clock is ticking." He clicked on something else, and the horrid video began again, with all the attendant noise, and I could hear Jamie moaning, and I could hear

Angel, gasping and wailing like the porn queen she was.

"Turn that off." He killed the volume but left the image playing. "I said to turn it off, you . . ." I couldn't even think of what to call him. My vocabulary was a little light for this situation. "Child."

He clicked it off and looked at me. He kept wiping his hands on his pants.

"Ask me for something else," I said. "Money. I'll buy it from you."

"No. All I want is you naked. For an hour."

"An hour? What would we do for the fifty-eight minutes after you were done?" *Ass*hole. "I'll get what I need some other way."

"You won't, and besides"—he tapped the monitor—"I thought what you wanted was to stop this mailing. It's your brother, right? Is that what you said?"

"I didn't say."

"She must have told me. Anyway, it doesn't matter. It's someone you're trying to protect. That's what I know." He reached for his mouse and clicked around the screen quickly. "Have you seen the whole thing? This one is triple-X-rated. Whoo-hoo."

"I saw it."

"I know what you saw. I'm the one who clipped it out for her. There's more. There is so much more. Believe me, the stuff they did, you don't want this thing getting out. You sure don't want his wife looking at it."

It was hard to keep from imploding, from simply caving in under the weight of a problem that just grew heavier and heavier with each passing second. I looked at his clock. Five minutes, thirty seconds . . . twenty-nine . . . twenty-eight. Had we been debating for five minutes? I had to do something. I should walk out is what I should do. I should either pull the gun or walk out. Information. I needed to know more.

"What about Angel's copy?"

"She doesn't have one."

"You're lying."

"Okay, I am. But all you need to know right now is that this thing is going out in"—he checked the countdown clock—"five minutes if you don't get your clothes off right now."

That was it. I reached around, pulled the gun, and pointed it at his head. It felt kind of good . . . until he started laughing. "You can shoot me if you want, but this thing will still go out. Or you can give me the gun and let me ball you and make it stop. What's it going to be?"

He was so repulsive, and he wasn't as cool as he was pretending to be. There was a thin line of sweat on his upper lip under his downy patch of light red facial hair. I put the gun right against his forehead. "Do you want to die, Stewart? Would it be worth it to die for Angel?"

"No, but I also want to get laid, and I don't think you have the guts to shoot me."

He couldn't turn his head, but his eyes slipped sideways to the screen. I was trying to think fast. An idea was trying to pull itself together in my brain. It must have been somewhere in my subconscious, because the conscious side was pretty panicked at the moment.

"I'll do it." I pointed the gun down and stepped back. "Turn it off."

"Give me the gun."

I hit the release, popped out the clip, and handed it to him. "I keep the gun, and you keep the clip. That's the only way it works."

He took the clip, put it in a desk drawer, pulled a key from somewhere, and locked it. When he turned and found the barrel of the gun up in his eyes again, his head snapped back.

"There's one round chambered," I said. "I'll put it right through your head if you don't turn that off right now."

He held perfectly still. He was no longer smiling. "It won't fire without the clip. It has a disconnector."

I opened my mouth to answer and closed it again. How the hell did he know about disconnectors?

"This is a Glock, Stewart. It doesn't have a disconnector." Thank God for Tristan and his firearms lessons.

"It does," he said, "if it was purchased in Massachusetts after the regulation went into effect." Without moving his head, he rolled his eyes up to look at me. "Do you know how old that gun is?"

A geek who knew his firearms. Besides the obvious and immediate drawback, it made me wonder if he had some of his own stashed around. I didn't know how old the gun was, which meant I didn't know if I was bluffing or not. Not exactly a strong position to be in.

"Do you want to find out, Stewart?"

He took a deep breath and swallowed hard and reached his hand out. For one precious moment, I thought it was to stop the clock, but it found my thigh instead. "Let's find out together. Fire off a test round, and we'll see." He gave me a squeeze through my blue jeans. When I pulled away, he smiled. I didn't much like being the canary that had gotten caught, especially given the consequences.

"Two-minute warning."

I watched him get up and walk toward the bed. With a quick flourish, he pulled off both his buttoned shirt and his T-shirt and dropped them on the floor. He had breasts. He unbuttoned the top button on his pants, then sat down to remove his ratty running shoes and socks.

"What's it going to be?"

"Shut up."

Under his showy bravado, I could see the sweaty little social outcast he must have always been, lumbering down the soccer field with his bright red frizzy locks and his hairless, pillowy body under an extra-large jersey made for boys twice his age. A rejection magnet is what he was, and he was so afraid I would walk out the door and leave him there with his hard-on I could almost smell the desperation coming off him. I hated him. How could I let him touch me?

"One minute and counting."

I reached up to push a strand of hair out of my face and caught a glimpse of myself in the mirror over his dresser. I still couldn't get used to my blond hair. It made me feel like a stranger to myself. I remembered how my mother used to push the hair out of my eyes so she could "see my pretty face." What would she think of me now? I hadn't done anything yet, and I could already feel the abscess forming on my soul.

It wasn't worth it. I knew that. It was dangerous. It could change me. It could change the way I thought about sex or how I could be with a man I wanted to be with or how I thought about myself. It could launch a chain of events that couldn't be stopped and could never be reversed. It could . . . it was . . . it wasn't worth it.

But it was time.

I looked at Stewart looking at me. "Do you have condoms?"

He took in a quiet breath and licked his lips as he reached over to show me the box. He had not come into this unprepared.

"Pop out that round," he said, nodding at the gun I forgot I even had, "and I'll turn it off."

I dropped my hands and pointed the gun at the floor. "Turn it off."

"Clear the chamber first, and you'd better hurry up."

I did. The round dropped to the carpet at my feet.

He reached out for the gun. "Let me have it."

"Fuck you, Stewart. You keep the clip, and I keep the gun, and that's the only way this works."

He thought about that. Then he reached over and picked up a remote control next to his bed. I turned around to look at the screen. He'd stopped the clock with twelve seconds remaining.

I went over to my backpack and dropped the Glock in. When I walked back and stood in front of him, I thought he would faint. He couldn't get his pants off fast enough. I pulled my sweater over my head and started to unbutton my jeans.

He stopped me. "I get an hour. Not a minute less." I watched him put his hands on me. The sweat glistened around the edges of his palms. I watched him move them over me. I let him touch me wherever he wanted.

"No kissing," I said. "Don't touch my face."

"Your face," he said, moving me closer, "is not what I'm interested in."

The large muscles of my back and shoulders, the muscles of resistance, had twisted into a massive knot of dull, aching pain. When I tried to swivel the tension out of my neck, it cracked and popped. But where it hurt most was in my gut. All the terrible thoughts in my head and all the memories of what Stewart had done—of what I had let him do—had slipped down into the boiling, spitting, churning pit of my stomach and hurt so much I was doubled over with my forehead on the steering wheel.

I was still in the parking lot of Stewart's building. I had dressed as quickly as I could, pulled each article of clothing on with the clear conviction that I would burn it before wearing it again. They all smelled of him, and of me with him, and I wanted nothing more than to find a shower somewhere and wash myself clean. But what I understood, what was making my stomach hurt so much, was knowing that I couldn't get clean with soap and water.

Jamie's CD was on the seat next to me. I'd watched Stewart burn the loathsome file onto it. I'd watched as he'd gone through and deleted the same file from several directories. There was no guarantee that he didn't have copies stashed somewhere, but I had done everything I could think of to erase at least his copies of Jamie's bad deed. I had done more than I thought I ever could, and I still hadn't gotten to Angel's copy.

A wave of dead air came over me, then a disorienting pressure in my face. I closed my eyes, and all I could see was Stewart's face floating over me and my own looking back at me in his mirror. I saw Robin Sevitch's battered head and Harvey's eyes when he'd said, "Shame on you." I saw Jamie shattered, and I saw Tristan betrayed, and I started to think there wasn't anything I had done so far that was right. Then I saw Angel. I heard her laughing at me. I squeezed my eyes shut and ground my teeth until my ears rang. I waited for the pressure to ease. When it did, I reached into my glove box and pulled out the extra clip Bo had pressed on me. I took the gun from my bag and popped it in. I knew exactly what I had to do. Seldom in my life had I been as clear about anything.

chapter 43

STEWART HAD THE STEREO CRANKED UP AGAIN, so when I hoisted the nearby bag of potting soil through his front window, he didn't hear. He didn't hear me when I climbed through or came down the hall to find him lounging at his desk. Just the sight of him, bloated and satisfied, set off a storming rage inside, some for what he had done, a lot for what I had done, and all of it directed at him.

The first thing I needed was to make the music stop. I switched the gun to my left hand, reached over with the other, and tried to push the shelf unit over, the one with the stereo, the CDs, and the statues of comic book characters. It was heavy, so I had to slip my knee in for more leverage. I rocked it until I could feel it poised on the brink. A group of statues from one of the higher shelves slipped off and took headers straight into the hardwood floor. I pushed, and the music stopped. In its place was the sound of very expensive electronic equipment crashing about with magnificent force. It went on for a while.

Stewart bolted from his chair and ran for his life. He ended up in the corner with palms pressed against the sides of his head. By the time the last of the CDs had skated across the floor, he had his hands lifted to the heavens as if to plead for intervention. I raised the gun and pointed it at him. He wasn't getting any.

As I lined him up in my sight, I didn't feel anything. He could have been a paper target. He might have sensed that, because he stood frozen, staring at me in the silence, which was resounding after my cacophonous entrance.

"I had another clip, Stewart. Why don't you come back and sit down?"

"You won't kill me."

I walked toward him, stepping around the pieces of equipment but directly on top of as many CD cases as I could. Some of them had sprung open, which left their discs vulnerable to the bottom of my boot. I liked the way they crunched underfoot.

I put the barrel against his right temple. "Look into my eyes, Stewart."

He looked into mine, and I bored into his with every ounce of fury and hatred I could summon. He looked for a long time. I knew what he was staring at. It was ugly. I could feel it. Finally, he moved back to his chair and sat.

"Put your hands on the armrests."

He did. But the armrests were too short, which meant he had to pull his elbows in close to his mushy body, which pushed his shoulders up around his ears.

"Don't hurt me," he pleaded in a small voice. "It was her idea. Please, don't hurt me."

I didn't want him looking at me. I never wanted his eyes on me again. I turned the chair so he faced away, found his keys, and opened his desk drawer. I pulled out the clip he'd taken and stuck it in my pocket.

"What was her idea?"

"She told me you would do anything to get the video of your brother back. She told me what she wanted, and she said I would get a bonus."

"If what?"

"If I could get you to have sex with me."

I looked around at the equipment on the floor. "Did you make a video?"

"She said she didn't need one."

This was where I was supposed to fly into a rage, but I was already beyond rage. "Pull up the index of Angel's archive. Use one hand."

He had a hard time keeping his hand steady enough to maneuver, but eventually, he got to what I wanted to see. He clicked on the file, and a list came up. It looked like a directory list. Politicians—federal, state, and local. Law enforcement—federal, state, and local. Lawyers—civil and criminal. Judges and district attorneys. Media, sports, education, financial—brokers, investment bankers. He clicked on the file labeled "Lawyers," and a list of names fell out. Next to each name was a code.

"What are the codes?"

"It's how the videos are filed. There are no names on the files. Just the codes." Like the ones I had seen on the Margolies video. "You have to have the key to know who everyone is."

"Send the index to this address." I read out Felix's e-mail address to him, and he set it up and sent it.

"What kind of files did you make for Angel?"

"W-w-w-hat do you . . ."

"What *format?*"

"CD-Rom."

"Tell me where Angel keeps her copies."

He paused just long enough for a moment of calculation. "I don't know."

I spun him around so I could see his face. He was pale, his skin was clammy and damp, and his jaw was trembling. But he was lying, and I wasn't leaving without the information I needed. I had nowhere else to get it.

"Get out of the chair."

"What?"

"Kneel on the floor, and put your hands on the back of your head." I wasn't sure who was talking. It sounded like me. The words were coming out of my mouth.

"Why?" I thought he'd been panicky before, but now I saw the true state of Stewart's desperation. As he lowered himself, his entire body vibrated. The frizzy ends of his hair sparkled with perspiration. "Why do you want me to get down on the floor?"

"I'm not getting played by you again. I'd rather have you dead."

"At the cabin." The words squeaked out. "They're at her place in New Hampshire in a . . . in a hole under the floor."

"What room?"

"In front of the fireplace. It's under the rug."

"Is it locked?"

"I don't think so."

"Where are your copies?"

"I don't have copies."

"You're full of shit. There is no way you didn't keep copies for yourself."

"She told me she'd have me buried alive if she ever found out I'd taken anything from her. She knows people . . . people who are in those archives. They're bad. She knows people like that. I believed her."

"I'm sure you believed her, Stewart. You just didn't think she'd ever catch you, because you're so goddamned smart. How would she ever know that you kept your own copies to get off on because you can't get a date to save your life, and you have to force yourself on a girl to ever get any?"

"I'm sorry. I didn't mean—"

"Yes, you did. You knew exactly what you were doing, and you enjoyed it." I nudged him with the gun. He squeezed his shoulders together and punched his head forward and away from contact with the barrel.

"I kept electronic files. No hard copies. I didn't want her to ever find anything. My copies are all on the C drive. There aren't any more. Please." His head was still forward, his neck distended. He started to cry. "Please don't kill me."

I made him wait a few more seconds before relieving the pressure.

"Move over to the CPU very slowly, and take out the hard drive."

He slipped over, barely raising his head, and went to work. He had become impressively docile, which was why I let him stand up when he was finished and hand the drive to me.

"Get me the other one, too."

He put his hands lightly on his hips and shifted his weight, which gave him a slightly less-docile profile. "I don't have another one."

"You have a D drive. I saw it in your directory when I was here with you last time."

"All my personal stuff is on the D drive—my taxes and my address book and my—"

I raised the gun and smashed the butt down on his keyboard. The tray it was on sheared off its mooring under the desk with a loud crack. Everything tumbled to the ground. Then I shoved one of his monitors over the edge of the desk. It teetered and finally crashed down onto the pile.

"Okay. *Okay. Stop!*" His arms flailed at nothing. "I'm doing it. Stop it."

He fell to his knees next to the CPU and made all the appropriate disconnections. He handed me the second drive, but when he tried to wobble to his feet, I reached down with the barrel of the Glock and tapped his shoulder.

"Stay down, and put your hands behind your head."

His raised his arms slowly. I couldn't see his face, but his shoulders started pistoning in time with his loud sobs. "I did everything you wanted. Please, don't kill me. I'm sorry for what I did. Please."

I stared at him kneeling in the ruins of his audio equipment, gasping for breath. I hadn't come intending to hurt him. I certainly hadn't planned on killing him. But my focus began to drift as I stared at him trembling and begging on his knees and thought back to the way he'd enjoyed taking his pleasure from me when none had been offered. It didn't help that Stewart scared for his life and Stewart having sex released approximately the same odor. Smelling him again made me think about the way he'd hovered over me, searching my face for reactions I had refused to give him. He had gotten off on the dominance. Now he was completely vulnerable to me, and I thought of all the things I could do to pay him back, right up to and including putting a bullet in his brain, and I wondered if I could do it.

I put my finger on the trigger and lifted the gun to his head to see . . . just to see what that might feel like.

"Don't." More whimpering. "Please, don't. You lied to me. You said we would fuck, and then you walked out."

It didn't feel real. It felt like TV or the movies. Bo had warned me that it was a light trigger, so I touched it gently, caressing it with my finger. In my mind, I felt the gun kick. I felt his blood and brains blow back on me. I breathed in the smell of cordite and felt it burn my nasal passages. But then the smoke cleared, and it was quiet, and all I felt was the big void that would open up in that room if he were dead and I was the one who had made him that way. If his soul departed, leaving me standing alone with a smoking gun in my hand, there would be too much space around me, probably forever.

I dropped the C drive on the floor, the one with all the dirty movies, and stomped it hard. That felt so good, I stomped it again. And again. I stomped it until Jamie's mistake was pulverized and my mistakes were demolished, until what I had done with Stewart was ground into powder and grit and tiny metal shards embedded in the hardwood floor. I kept stomping until I could barely raise my leg, while Stewart cowered next to me in a classic duck and cover. Then I dropped into the swivel chair to figure out what to do next.

I reached down under the desk, grabbed a handful of the wires and cables, and gave them a vicious yank. All the electronic toys they were supplying jumped and flinched and popped and eventually went dark.

"Put your hands behind your back."

He did so promptly. I put the gun down, wrapped one of the cables around Stewart's left wrist, and tied it off. As I tied his left hand to his right, I gave him his instructions.

"I'm going to call Angel now. When she answers, I'm

going to put the phone to your head and you're going to give her a message from me."

"What about my D drive?"

"I'm holding on to it. I don't want you calling her back after I leave. That's how you keep me from stomping it, too. Do you understand?"

"What do you want me to tell her?"

chapter 44

ANGEL'S CABIN WAS COMPLETELY DARK. I looked through the window, and it reminded me of looking through Monica's apartment window. For a moment, I expected a face, maybe Angel's face, looking ghoulish instead of gorgeous, to pop in front of me.

I listened to the stream flowing nearby and tried to calm down. My heart was barely keeping up with me. I had left Stewart tied up on his floor, then gone out to my car and pointed it toward this place. On the way, I had called and checked on various quarters. Bo and Tristan and Monica were fine. They were playing Trivial Pursuit, guns at the ready. When I told Tristan where I was going, all he said was to be careful. If Stewart had kept his word and not called her back, Angel would be looking for me at the Ritz-Carlton, but we both knew there was no guarantee that Angel had believed him.

I went back to the window, took a deep breath, and rammed my elbow through the glass. It wasn't easy. I had to hit it a few times. Fortunately, the window cracked before my elbow did. I pushed the glass into the house. It fell onto an un-Angel-like yellow quilt that was lying neatly over a single bed below the window. I reached in, found the lock, unhitched it, and scrambled through, careful to crawl around the glass on the bed.

No one was around, but still, I winced when I put my feet to the floor and heard the floorboards creak. Using my flashlight, I found my way to the bedroom door and out into a hallway. With one hand glued to the wall and the other holding the flashlight on the floor in front of me, I made my way to the den.

I probably could have turned on a light but felt more comfortable down on my hands and knees with the flashlight. Every piece of furniture had a rug underneath it. I found one that looked as if it had been moved recently. It had a minor speed bump in it. The chair that sat on it was heavy, but once I got the right leverage, it tipped right over. I grabbed a corner of the rug, flung it completely out of the way, and found what I was looking for. Cut into one of the wide planks of the floor was a small, neatly milled, rectangular trapdoor. I stared at it, breathing hard. I hadn't realized how winded I was. I mopped the sweat from my forehead with the back of my sleeve, but it didn't do any good. I was damp again immediately.

The opening was the width of my shoulders. It had two half-moon crescents carved out of the sides so you could put your fingers in and lift it out. I got down on my knees and tried to pry it out, but it was heavy and wedged tightly into its opening. I got up and framed the opening with one foot on either side. I wormed my fingers in, gave it a quick tug straight up, and it came out.

The hole it covered was about six inches deep and lined with metal. Inside were stacks and stacks of jewel cases. I pulled up the first stack and flipped through it. Using my flashlight, I saw the codes that labeled them. There were about forty per disc. Each code represented a man, each man a life. He had a wife or kids or a girlfriend. A career to be lost. A reputation to be tarnished. Maybe Angel would say that's what they deserved. Any man who had made the choice to cheat on his loved ones deserved to have that choice used against him. I didn't know. I couldn't figure all that out. All I knew was that one of them was Jamie's, and Angel shouldn't have them. I reached down to take them away from her, and the fireplace roared to life.

It was like a grenade going off in the dark room, and I couldn't keep from turning to look at it. When I did, I knew she was behind me. I felt her there. I dropped the boxes and reached for the gun, but it was too late. As I turned back, her arms were already on the way around, driven toward my head, it seemed, by the accelerating force of her guttural scream. I dropped to my knees with both hands to the floor. A vicious tear opened in the space above my head. I could tell by the sound that she was swinging a fireplace poker, an iron sword that was flying toward me again from her backhand side, this time with lower trajectory and better aim. I tried to flatten and roll away, but she caught my elbow with the downward hack, and the gun went flying. The pain from my elbow shot straight up my arm, across both shoulders, and down to my stomach, where it lurched around and threatened to blow straight up the back of my throat. Jesus, it hurt. I cradled it to my side. My body wanted to wrap itself around the injured limb, but she was coming, moving through the field of furniture with the poker over her head.

I scrambled into the nearest cover, a crawl space between the couch and the coffee table. She hacked off the corner of the glass tabletop. It was a clean break and a deafening pop right next to my ear. Her second try was a direct, shattering blow to the heart of the thick glass plane. I turned away. Shards flew. Large sections of glass dropped like heavy rocks straight to the floor. I kept moving. She kept coming, tripping around the furniture, chopping and hacking at me, strangling on her screams. I pulled pillows and cushions from the couch to cover my head as I went. Anything I could put my good hand on—ashtray, statue, magazine, potted plant—I tossed back at her, trying to slow her down. Something finally did. The poker tangled in the table's low legs. I grabbed for it, wrapping my good hand around the tip, the only part I could get to, but she had all the leverage and ripped it away, nearly taking the skin off my palm in the process. I crawled over the field of broken glass and skirted around the end of the couch.

She was loud and noisy and clumsy with rage, wild to get to me. Every frenzied whack came with a roar that started in her throat and ended with the sound of splintering wood or shattering glass or the thudding of objects raining down around me. My only hope was that all the flailing and swinging might be wearing her out.

I had to get to my feet. There was no shot on my hands and knees. My elbow was hot and throbbing and swollen massively, but it seemed to still work as a hinge. When I tried to straighten it, the pain was dizzying, but it responded. I crawled on my belly under a side table. She whacked the Stiffel lamp that was sitting on it, pulverizing the lightbulb and sending the shade flying across the room. The heavy base of the lamp crashed to the floor in front of me, then twitched as it reached the end of its electric cord. I reached out for it, grabbed hold, and tried to reel it in, but she had come around. When she saw what I was trying to do, she stepped on the cord. I barely pulled my hand back in time before the sharp end of the poker came down, spearing the hardwood floor. This time, when I grabbed the tip, I pulled it up and toward me, yanking it with my entire body. She didn't let go. The side table, my shield, tipped back as her countertug yanked me out into the open.

Goddammit, she was strong.

I strangled that poker, knowing what would happen if I let go. I tried to climb the ladder, hand over hand, but she kicked at my head and tried to stomp me. When she hit my elbow, I screamed. She screamed back. I rolled over to protect the arm, still holding onto the poker, still connected to her. She stomped on my back, maybe a kidney, and a bright white light exploded behind my eyes. I couldn't breathe, and it was the hardest thing I ever had to do to keep from closing my eyes and going to sleep.

She would kill me if I did. She would beat me with that poker until I looked the way Robin Sevitch had. I kept my eyes open . . . and saw my chance. The lamp. It was right there, the base of it staring me in the face. To grab it, I had to let go of the poker. I had to let go with one hand, grab the lamp, and swing it all at once, because she would use the chance to raise the weapon over her head, and bring it down hard enough to crack my skull open.

My brain was telling me to move, to move *fast* and *move now,* but my body wouldn't respond. I felt drugged. She made the choice for me when she twisted the poker hard and jerked it away. I grabbed for the lamp. It rolled away. I lurched after it. The poker came down, hit the arm of a chair and then my shoulder. I couldn't feel anything now. I couldn't hear anything. All I could see was the brass lamp. She saw it, too, and tried to kick it away. I grabbed at it again and got it this time.

I swung it at the most vulnerable part of her I could reach—her knees. Nothing ever felt so good as the sickening collision of brass against bone when I made contact. She teetered but didn't fall. I got to my knees and swung again with more leverage. Her shriek punched through the cotton that filled my head, and I could hear again.

She dropped like a bag of stones and rolled over on her side, one hand resting lightly on her devastated knee. Just for good measure, I hit it again and heard it crack. When she saw me moving toward the poker, she made a disturbingly strong grab for it. I got to it first and pulled it away. She didn't go after it.

I tried to get up, staggered against the couch, and didn't make it. I tried again and this time my legs engaged, and I was upright, standing over her with the poker swinging from my good hand.

She was on her side with her upper body twisted facedown on the floor. Her hair had spilled across her face, so I couldn't see whether her eyes were open. Even with one leg cracked and bent beneath her, she looked lethal. I wasn't sure about getting so near, but I wanted to see if she was conscious. I inched close enough to nudge her damaged knee with my foot.

She jerked violently and let loose with a long, loud scream that was raw and disorganized but powerful enough to make me feel that this wasn't over.

"Stop *pushing* at me, you wicked bitch. It's not enough for you to break my goddamned knee?" She rolled over and stared up at me. "Now you've got to stand over me and poke at me like I'm some kind of a dead dog in a ditch." She tried to leg-whip me with her good leg. I was slow, but she was slower and clearly in agony. I shuffled out of her range and left her lying on her back, face twisted and eyes squeezed tight. She tried to control the pain through her breathing—long, deep breaths sucked through her nose and exhaled steadily through her mouth.

"Surprised to see me, weren't you, doll?" She had to stop for a few breaths. "Old Sluggo, he's not much of a liar."

I stared down at her. I couldn't think. I didn't know what to do. I knew I couldn't get close to her. The gun. *Turn on the light, and find the gun.* But then I started to feel sick.

"You should see yourself, sugar." She let her head roll from side to side as if she were enjoying the feel of a feather pillow beneath her. She could barely talk, but she could still smile. "The way you're looking at me."

The poker felt slick in my hand. I looked down and saw the blood running down my arm and dripping into a pool at my feet. I didn't know where I was bleeding from or why. I could feel myself getting lighter, as if I were pumped full of helium, ready to take off. My face burned. The room began to spiral. I thought I might just let go and flow with it. It would be easier than fighting it to stand up. I felt so hot.

"You want to kill me. I know you do."

Her voice was hypnotic, the only thing that made sense. The sound of it, the tone and the texture were familiar. The way she said certain words. She had been the center of my world, the first thing I'd thought of in the morning and the last before I closed my eyes to sleep. Now her voice was the only thing I recognized, the only thing to hold on to as I started to disappear.

"You'd better kill me, too, because I swear to almighty God, after you pass out, you will pass from this world, because I will take that poker from you and run it straight through your heart. Then I'll sit down and smoke a cigarette over your body."

I backed away from her. I felt as if I were backing up a mountain. Why was it so hot? I had to sit down. Couldn't sit down. She was coming. Why was I so . . . heavy? She'd rolled over and started to pull herself across the floor on her belly. A sick, twisted cry pushed out every time she moved. She was looking up at me, saying something. She was reaching toward me . . . she had it. She had the poker in her hand. Had I left it . . . it was supposed to be . . . it had been in my hand.

I staggered back and fell into the couch. I sank into . . . glass. There was glass on the couch. Huge, heavy chunks of it. It was under my feet. It was under her. I heard her moving over it. Everything was slowing down.

I had to get up. She couldn't walk. If I could get up, all I had to do was get far enough away from her and . . . and what? Lie down and wait for someone to find me and save me? My feet wouldn't move. She was in front of me now, using a chair to pull herself up. I heard the effort. I saw the way her body shook, every muscle engaged, every shred of her will lasered in on getting in position to kill me. I knew she would do it.

When she was up, she was towering again, her head swimming high above me. She tried to set her feet but could barely stay upright. She held the chair with one hand and raised the poker with the other. She held it like a dagger, aimed at my chest.

"Wait."

"For what, darlin'?"

"Kiss me."

Her right hand, the one that held the poker, dropped slightly. I looked at her face.

"Kiss me once. Please, Angel." Every word felt like a lead weight that I had to lift, one at a time, to form into a sentence. "You said . . ." *Breath.* "You said . . . you wanted to. I wanted it, too. Please."

"Oh, baby. You're telling me a lie now, aren't you?"

"No. What difference . . . anyway?" I reached out to her. "I don't want to die alone."

It seemed like forever we stayed that way. My arm reaching out, Angel staring in. She took a long, deep breath and held it. As she breathed out, she tipped her head back and looked down at me with half-closed eyes. She let the tip of her tongue glide across her upper lip. Her face contorted with pain as she inched slowly toward me, shortening the grip on her poker so she could keep it aimed at my throat. But her eyes were wild, as if she were on fire, burning from the inside. She could love me or kill me. To her it was the same.

I thought I would smell her perfume as she came closer, but all I could smell was blood, hers and mine. When she was close enough, I lifted my damaged arm and reached behind her head to pull her closer. Her hair was stiff and brittle, not soft the way it looked. My arm began to quiver when I touched her hair. It shook up to my shoulder as I twisted my fingers in it and pulled it taut. Her head slammed back, presenting her throat to me. I flashed on the image of Robin and that pale stretch of undamaged skin, the only part of her that still looked like her. The difference was the artery. Angel's was pumping as hard as it could, especially after I kicked her in the knee.

She screeched, thrust the poker at my chest, and missed. She tried to twist out of my grip but had no leverage on a broken leg and fell instead into my chest. I held her head all the way back, took the heavy glass shard from the couch, and, with my strong hand, shoved it into that throbbing vein.

Someone floated over me. I heard a voice. I tried to open my eyes, but my lids were too heavy, and it just didn't seem worth it. I was moving, or being moved. I didn't have the strength to do anything. I was in a car. Something tight around my arm. It hurt. It was too tight. I tried to pull away, but he wouldn't let go. I managed to get my eyes barely open and saw the big face under the car's dome light. This time, he was wearing a mint green sport coat, and my blood was all over it. I put my head back down and went to sleep.

chapter 45

I CLOSED MY EYES AND TRIED TO FEEL THE STILLness in the early-morning air, to pull it inside of me and hold it there. Each time I breathed out, I tried to let go of a little more tension in my shoulders and my neck and my back. I let my arms hang at my sides. And then I tried to do the same with my mind, to let it relax and open up to whatever impulse I wanted to send its way. I wanted to empty it of all the events of the past few weeks, all the emotions save one. I held on to the anger. I let my mind go blank except for a bright, burning red stain that drew my complete focus. I took that stain and projected it out, across the distance from me to the target, and onto the bull's-eye. The rest of the target fell away.

I picked up the gun. It felt comfortable in my hand. My fingers found their place around the grip, my index finger extended to the trigger. Everything felt right, and all I could see was the bright red target in front of me. As I raised my arm, the target grew larger. They say athletes who get in a zone see the basket or the cup or the baseball grow so big they can't miss it. That's how I felt. I was locked in on a target that looked to me as big as the entire wall. I knew I couldn't miss it. I knew I wouldn't.

I went through the checklist in my mind, the one Tristan and I had worked on. Arms raised, elbows slightly bent. Feet shoulder-width apart. Headgear and protective glasses in place. I adjusted my sleeve so that it didn't make the stitches on my arm so uncomfortable. My wounds were almost completely healed.

The legal issues would take longer to sort out, but it looked as though self-defense would hold up. The cops had found enough in the cabin to support my story. What they hadn't found was the archive. Bo had taken it. He had replaced it in the floorboard hideout with the brick that had killed Robin Sevitch. He had pulled it from the desk, exactly where Monica had told him it would be. The police had considered that a most interesting discovery.

Jamie was working through his issues. When he asked me if I thought he should tell Gina, I remembered the way I had felt the first moment I had seen his face on the screen. I told him I didn't think she should pay the price for something he had done. We had done. I would keep his secret. I knew he would keep my secrets, too, if ever I had the courage to tell them to him. To anyone. I needed someone to tell my secrets to.

Harvey had come to visit in the hospital, and I had been glad to see him. We had decided to leave things on hold for a while. He was not, I was happy to hear, working for OrangeAir. With the exception of Monica, who had cut a nice deal for herself, neither were thirty hookers from Angel's ring.

"Fire whenever you're ready."

I squeezed off the first round, and the target flinched. I didn't even need to look to see where the bullet had passed through it. I fired again and again until the .38 was empty. I felt steady. I felt sure. I felt that I was in the